THE B
COLLECTION

Betty Neels's novels are loved by millions of readers around the world, and this very special *2-in-1 collection* offers a unique opportunity to relive the magic of some of her most popular stories.

We are proud to present these classic romances by the woman who could weave an irresistible tale of love like no other.

So sit back in your comfiest chair with your favorite cup of tea and enjoy these best of Betty Neels stories!

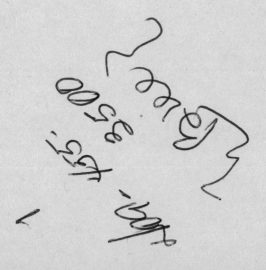

Romance readers around the world were sad to note the passing of **Betty Neels** in June 2001. Her career spanned thirty years, and she continued to write into her ninetieth year. To her millions of fans, Betty epitomized the romance writer, and yet she began writing almost by accident. She had retired from nursing, but her inquiring mind still sought stimulation. Her new career was born when she heard a lady in her local library bemoaning the lack of good romance novels. Betty's first book, *Sister Peters in Amsterdam,* was published in 1969, and she eventually completed 134 books. Her novels offer a reassuring warmth that was very much a part of her own personality, and her spirit and genuine talent live on in all her stories.

BETTY NEELS

The Awakened Heart

and

The Moon for Lavinia

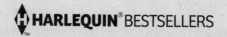

HARLEQUIN® BESTSELLERS

ISBN-13: 978-0-373-60594-1

This edition published by arrangement with Harlequin Books S.A.

For questions and comments about the quality of this book, please contact us at CustomerService@Harlequin.com.

HARLEQUIN®
www.Harlequin.com

Printed in U.S.A.

CONTENTS

The Awakened Heart

CHAPTER ONE

THE DULL OCTOBER afternoon was fast becoming a damp evening, its drizzling rain soaking those hurrying home from work. The pavements were crowded; the wholesale dress shops, the shabby second-hand-furniture emporiums, the small businesses carried on behind dirty shop windows were all closing for the day. There were still one or two street barrows doing a desultory trade, but the street, overshadowed by the great bulk of St Agnes's hospital, in an hour or so's time would be almost empty. Just at the moment it was alive with those intent on getting home, with the exception of one person: a tall girl, standing still, a look of deep concentration on her face, oblivious of the impatient jostling her splendid person was receiving from passers-by.

Unnoticed by those jostling her, she was none the less attracting the attention of a man standing at the window of the committee-room of the hospital overlooking the street. He watched her for several minutes, at first idly and then with a faint frown, and presently, since he had nothing better to do for the moment, he made his way out of the hospital across the forecourt and into the street.

The girl was on the opposite pavement and he crossed the road without haste, a giant of a man with wide shoulders, making light of the crowds around him. His 'Can I be of help?' was asked in a quiet, deep voice, and the girl looked at him with relief.

'So silly,' she said in a matter-of-fact voice. 'The heel of my shoe is wedged in a gutter and my hands are full. If you would be so kind as to hold these...'

She handed him two plastic shopping-bags. 'They're lace-ups,' she explained. 'I can't get my foot out.'

The size of him had caused passers-by to make a little detour around them. He handed back the bags. 'Allow me?' he begged her and crouched down, unlaced her shoe, and when she had got her foot out of it carefully worked the heel free, held it while she put her foot back in, and tied the laces tidily.

She thanked him then, smiling up into his handsome face, to be taken aback by the frosty blue of his eyes and his air of cool detachment, rather as though he had been called upon to do something which he had found tiresome. Well, perhaps it had been tiresome, but surely he didn't have to look at her like that? He was smiling now too, a small smile which just touched his firm mouth and gave her the nasty feeling that he knew just what she was thinking. She removed the smile, flashed him a look from beautiful dark eyes, wished him goodbye, and joined the hurrying crowd around her. He had ruffled her feelings, although she wasn't sure why. She dismissed him from her mind and turned into a side-street lined with old-fashioned houses with basements guarded by iron railings badly in need of paint; the houses were slightly down at heel too and the variety of curtains at their windows bore testimony to the fact that subletting was the norm.

Halfway down the street she mounted the steps of a house rather better kept than its neighbours and unlocked the door. The hall was narrow and rather dark and redolent of several kinds of cooking. The girl wrinkled her beautiful nose and started up the stairs, to be stopped by a voice from a nearby room.

'Is that you, Sister Blount? There was a phone call for you…'

A middle-aged face, crowned by a youthful blonde wig, appeared round the door. 'Your dear mother, wishing to speak to you. I was so bold as to tell her that you would be home at six o'clock.'

The girl paused on the stairs. 'Thank you, Miss Phipps. I'll phone as soon as I've been to my room.'

Miss Phipps frowned and then decided to be playfully rebuking. 'Your flatlet, Sister, dear. I flatter myself that my tenants are worthy of something better than bed-sitting-rooms.'

The girl murmured and smiled and went up two flights of stairs to the top floor and unlocked the only door on the small landing. It was an attic room with the advantage of a window overlooking the street as well as a smaller one which gave a depressing view of back yards and strings of washing, but there was a tree by it where sparrows sat, waiting for the crumbs on the window sill. It had a wash-basin in one corner and a small gas stove in an alcove by the blocked-up fireplace. There was a small gas fire too, and these, according to Miss Phipps, added up to mod cons and a flatlet. The bathroom was shared too by the two flatlets on the floor below, but since she was on night duty and everyone else worked during the day that was no problem. She dumped her shopping on the small table under the window, took off her coat, kicked off her shoes, stuck her feet into slippers and bent to pick up the small tabby cat which had uncurled itself from the end of the divan bed against one wall.

'Mabel, hello. I'll be back in a moment to get your supper…'

The phone was in the hall and to hold a private conversation on it was impossible, for Miss Phipps rarely shut her door. She fed the machine some ten-pence pieces and dialled her home.

'Sophie?' her mother's voice answered at once. 'Darling, it isn't anything important; I just wanted to know how you were and when you're coming home for a day or two.'

'I was coming at the end of the week, but Sister Symonds is ill again. She should be back by the end of next week, though, and I'll take two lots of nights off at once—almost a week…'

'Oh, good. Let us know which train and someone will pick you up at the station. You're busy?'

'Yes, off and on—not too bad.' Sophie always said that. She was always busy; Casualty and the accident room took no account of time of day or night. She knew that her mother thought of her as sitting for a great part of the night at the tidy desk, giving advice and from time to time checking on a more serious case, and Sophie hadn't enlightened her. On really busy nights she hardly saw her desk at all, but, sleeves rolled up and plastic apron tied around her slim waist, she worked wherever she was most needed.

'Is that Miss Phipps listening?'

'Of course…'

'What would happen if you brought a man back for supper?' Her mother chuckled.

'When do I ever get the time?' asked Sophie and allowed her thoughts to dwell just for a moment on the man with the cold blue eyes. The sight of her flatlet would trigger off the little smile; she had no doubt of that. Probably he had never seen anything like it in his life.

They didn't talk for long; conversation wasn't easy with Miss Phipps's wig just visible in the crack of her door. Sophie hung up and went upstairs, fed Mabel and opened the window which gave on to a railed-off ledge so that the little beast could air herself, and put away her shopping. What with one thing and another, there was barely time for her to get a meal before she went on duty. She made a pot of tea, opened a tin of beans, poached an egg, and did her face and hair again. Her face, she reflected, staring at it in the old-fashioned looking-glass on the wall above the basin, looked tired. 'I shall have wrinkles and lines before I know where I am,' said Sophie to Mabel, watching her from the bed.

Nonsense, of course; she was blessed with a lovely face: wide dark eyes, a delightful nose above a gentle, generous mouth, and long, curling lashes as dark as her hair, long and thick and worn in a complicated arrangement which took quite a time to do but which stayed tidy however busy she was.

She stooped to drop a kiss on the cat's head, picked up her roomy shoulder-bag, and let herself out of the room, a tall girl with a splendid figure and beautiful legs.

Her flatlet might lack the refinements of home, but it was only five minutes' walk from the hospital. She crossed the courtyard with five minutes to spare, watched, if she did but know, by the man who had retrieved her shoe for her—in the committee-room again, exchanging a desultory conversation with those of his colleagues who were lingering after their meeting. Tomorrow would be a busy day, for he had come over to England especially to operate on a cerebral tumour; brain surgery was something on which he was an acknowledged expert, so that a good deal of his work was international. Already famous in his own country, he was fast attaining the highest rung of the ladder.

He stood now, looking from the window, studying Sophie's splendid person as she crossed the forecourt.

'Who is that?' he asked Dr Wells, the anaesthetist who would be working with him in the morning and an old friend.

'That's our Sophie, Night Sister in Casualty and the accident room, worth her not inconsiderable weight in gold too. Pretty girl…'

They parted company presently and Professor Rijk van Taak ter Wijsma made his way without haste down to the entrance. He was stopped before he reached it by the surgical registrar who was to assist him in the morning, so that they were both deep in talk when the first of the ambulances flashed past on its way to the accident room entrance.

They were still discussing the morning's work when the registrar's bleep interrupted them.

He listened for a minute and said, 'There's a head injury in, Professor—contusion and laceration with evidence of coning. Mr Bellamy had planned a weekend off…'

His companion took his phone from him and dialled a number. 'Hello, John? Rijk here. Peter Small is here with me; they want him in the accident room—there's a head injury just in. As I'm here, shall I take a look? I know you're not on call…' He listened for a moment. 'Good, we'll go along and have a look.'

He gave the phone back. 'You wouldn't mind if I took a look? There might be something I could suggest…'

'That's very good of you, sir; you don't mind?'

'Not in the least.'

The accident room was busy, but then it almost always was. Sophie, with a practised glance at the patient, sent the junior sister to deal with the less urgent cases with the aid of two student nurses, taking the third nurse with her as the paramedics wheeled the patient into an empty cubicle. The casualty officer was already there; while he phoned the registrar they began connecting up the various monitoring tubes and checked the oxygen flow, working methodically and with the sure speed of long practice. All the same, she could see that the man on the stretcher was in a bad way.

She was trying to count an almost imperceptible pulse when she became conscious of someone standing just behind her and then edging her gently to one side while a large, well kept hand gently lifted the dressing on the battered head.

'Tut, tut,' said the professor. 'What do we know, Sister?'

'A fall from a sixth-floor window on to a concrete

pavement. Thready pulse, irregular and slow, cerebrospinal fluid from left ear, epistaxis…'

Her taxing training was standing her in good stead; she answered him promptly and with few words, while a small part of her mind registered the fact that the man beside her had tied her shoelaces for her not two hours since.

What a small world, she reflected, and allowed herself a second's pleasure at seeing him again. But only a second; she was already busy adjusting tubes and knobs at the registrar's low-voiced instructions.

The two men bent over the unconscious patient while she took a frighteningly high blood-pressure and the casualty officer looked for other injuries and broken bones.

Presently the professor straightened up. 'Anterior fossa—depressed fracture. Let's have an X-ray and get him up to Theatre.' He took a look at Peter Small. 'You agree? There's a good chance…' He glanced at Sophie. 'If you would warn Theatre, Sister? Thank you.'

He gave her a brief look; he didn't recognise her, thought Sophie, but then why should he? She was in uniform now, the old-fashioned dark blue dress and frilly cap which St Agnes's management committee refused to exchange for nylon and paper.

The men went away, leaving her to organise the patient's removal to the theatre block, warn Night Theatre Sister, Intensive Care and the men's surgical ward, and, that done, there was the business of his identity, his address, his family… It was going to be a busy night, Sophie decided, writing and telephoning, dealing with everything and the police, and at the same time keeping an eye on the incoming patients. Nothing too serious from a medical point of view, although bad enough for the owners of sprained ankles, cut heads, fractured arms and legs, but they all needed attention—X-rays, cleaning and stitching and bandaging, and sometimes admitting to a ward.

It was two o'clock in the morning, and she had just wolfed down a sandwich and drunk a reviving mug of tea since there had been no chance of getting down to the canteen, when a girl was brought in, a small toddler screaming her head off in her mother's arms, who thrust her at Sophie. ''Ere, take a look at 'er, will yer? Fell down the stairs, been bawling 'er 'ead off ever since.'

Sophie laid the grubby scrap gently on to one of the couches. 'How long ago was this?'

The woman shrugged. 'Dunno. Me neighbour told me when I got 'ome—nine o'clock, I suppose.'

Sophie was examining the little girl gently. 'She had got out of her bed?'

'Bed? She don't go ter bed till I'm 'ome.'

Sophie sent a nurse to see if she could fetch the casualty officer and, when she found him and he arrived, left the nurse with him and ushered the mother into her office.

'I shall want your name and address and the little girl's name. How was she able to get to the stairs? Is it a high-rise block of flats?' She glanced at the address again. 'At the end of Montrose Street, isn't it?'

'S'right, fifth floor. I leave the door, see, so's me neighbour can take a look at Tracey...'

'She is left alone during the day?'

'Well, off and on, you might say, and sometimes of an evening—just when I go to the pub evenings.'

'Well, shall we see what the doctor says? Perhaps it may be necessary to keep Tracey in the hospital for a day or two.'

'Suits me—driving me mad with that howling, she is.'

Tracey had stopped crying; only an occasional snivel betrayed her misery. Sophie said briskly, 'You'd like her admitted for observation, Dr Wright?' and at the same time bestowed a warning frown on him; Jeff Wright and she had been friends for ages, and he understood the frown.

'Oh, definitely, Sister, if you would arrange it. This is the mother?' He bent an earnest gaze upon the woman, who said at once,

'It ain't my fault. I've got ter 'ave a bit of fun, 'aven't I? Me 'usband left me, see?'

Sophie thought that he might have good reason. The woman was dirty, and although she was wearing make-up and cheap fashionable clothes the child was in a smelly dress and vest and no nappy. 'You may visit when you like,' she told her. 'Would you like to stay until she is settled in?'

'No, thanks. I gotta get some sleep, haven't I?'

She nodded to the child. 'Bye for now, night all.'

'Be an angel and right away get the children's ward,' said Sophie. 'I'll wrap this scrap up in a blanket and take her up—a pity we can't clean her up first, but I can't spare the nurses.'

All the same, she wiped the small grubby face and peeled off the outer layer of garments before cuddling

Tracey into a blanket and picking her up carefully. There were no bones broken, luckily, but a great deal of bruising, and in the morning the paediatrician would go over the small body and make sure that no great harm had been done.

She took the lift and got out at the third floor and walked straight into the professor's vast person. He was alone and still in his theatre gear.

'Having a busy night, Sister?' he asked, in a far too cheerful voice for the small hours.

Her 'Yes, sir' was terse, and he smiled.

'Hardly the best of times in which to renew an acquaintance, is it?' He stood on one side so that she might pass. 'We must hope for a more fortunate meeting.'

Sophie hoisted the sleeping toddler a little higher against her shoulder. She was tired and wanted a cup of tea and a chance to sit down for ten minutes; she was certainly not in a mood for polite conversation.

'Unlikely,' she observed crossly. She had gone several steps when she paused and turned to look at him.

'That man—you've operated?'

'Yes; given a modicum of luck and some good nursing, he should recover.'

'Oh, I'm so glad.' She nodded and went on her way, her busy night somehow worth while at the news.

The senior sister, when she came on duty in the morning, was full of complaints. She was on the wrong side of forty and an habitual grumbler; Sophie, listening with inward impatience to peevish criticisms about the weather, breakfast, the rudeness of student nurses and the impossibility of finding the shoes she wanted, choked back a yawn and presently took herself thankfully off duty.

Breakfast was always a cheerful meal, despite the fact that they were all tired; Sophie poured herself a cup of tea, collected a substantial plateful of food, and sat down with the other night sisters. There was quite a tableful, and despite the fact that they were all weary the conversation was lively.

Theatre Sister held the attention of the whole table almost at once. 'We scrubbed at nine o'clock and didn't finish until after two in the morning. There was this super man operating—Professor something or other. He's from Holland—a pal of Mr Bellamy's—and over here to demonstrate some new technique. He made a marvellous job of this poor chap too.'

She beamed round the table, a small waif of a girl with big blue eyes and fair hair. 'He's a smasher—my dears, you should just see him. Enormous and very tall, blue eyes and very fair hair, nicely grey at the sides. He's operating again at ten o'clock and when Sister Tucker heard about him she said she'd scrub…'

There was a ripple of laughter; Sister Tucker was getting on a bit and as theatre superintendent very seldom took a case. 'Bet you wish you were on duty, Gill,' said someone and then, 'What about you, Sophie? Did you see this marvellous man?'

Sophie bit into her toast. 'Yes, he came into the accident room with Peter Small—I believe he's just arrived here.' She took another bite and her companions asked impatiently,

'Well, what's he like? Did you take a good look…?'

'Not really; he's tall and large…' She glanced round her. 'There wasn't much chance…'

'Oh, hard luck, and you're not likely to see him again—Gill's the lucky one.'

'Who's got nights off?' someone asked.

The lucky ones were quick to say, and someone said, 'And you, Sophie? Aren't you due this weekend?'

'Yes, but Ida Symonds is ill again, so I'll have to do her weekend. Never mind, I shall take a whole week when she comes back.' She put up a shapely hand to cover a yawn. 'I'm for bed.'

They left the table in twos and threes and went along to the changing-room and presently went their various ways. The professor, on the point of getting out of the silver-grey Bentley he had parked in the forecourt, watched Sophie come out of the entrance, reach the street and cross over before he got out of the car and made his unhurried way to the theatre, where Sister Tucker awaited him.

Sophie, in her flatlet, making a cup of tea and seeing to Mabel's breakfast, found herself thinking about the professor; she was unwilling to admit it, but she would like to meet him again. Perhaps, she thought guiltily, she had been a bit rude when they had met on her way to the children's ward. And why had he said that he hoped for a more fortunate meeting?

She wasn't a conceited girl, but she knew that she was nice-looking—she was too big to be called pretty and, though she was, she had never thought of herself as beautiful. She never lacked invitations to go out with the house doctors, something she occasionally did, but she was heart-whole and content to stay as she was until the right man came along. Only just lately she had had one or two uneasy twinges about that; she had had several proposals and refused them in the nicest possible way, waiting for the vague and unknown dream man who would sweep her off her feet and leave no room for doubts…

Presently she went to bed with Mabel for company and slept at once, ignoring the good advice offered by her landlady, who considered that a brisk walk before bed was the correct thing to do for those who were on night duty. That she had never been on night duty in her life and had no idea what that entailed was beside the point. Besides, the East End of London was hardly conducive to a walk, especially when there was still a faint drizzle left over from the day before.

Sophie wakened refreshed, took a bath, attended to Mabel, and, still in her dressing-gown, made a pot of tea and sat down by the gas fire to enjoy it. She had taken the first delicious sip when someone knocked at the door.

Sophie put down her cup and muttered crossly at Mabel, who muttered back. Miss Phipps, a deeply suspicious person, collected her rent weekly, and it was Friday. Sophie picked up her purse and opened the door.

Only it wasn't Miss Phipps; it was Professor van Taak ter Wijsma.

She opened her mouth, but before she could utter a squeak he laid a finger upon it.

'Your good landlady,' said the professor in a voice strong enough to be heard by that lady lurking at the bottom of the stairs, 'has kindly allowed me to visit you on a matter of some importance.' As he spoke he pushed her gently back into the room and closed the door behind them both…

'Well,' said Sophie with a good deal of heat, 'what in heaven's name are you doing here? Go away at once.' She remembered that she was still in her dressing-gown, a rather fetching affair in quilted rose-pink satin. 'I'm not dressed…'

'I had noticed, but let me assure you that since I have five sisters girls in dressing-gowns hold no surprises for me.' He added thoughtfully, 'Although I must admit that this one becomes you very well.'

'What's so important?' snapped Sophie. 'I can't imagine what it can be.'

'No, no, how could you?' He spoke soothingly. 'I am going to Liverpool tomorrow and I shall be back on Wednesday. I thought that a drive into the country when you come off duty might do you good—fresh air, you know… I'll have to have you back here by one o'clock and you can go straight to bed.'

He was strolling around the room, looking at everything. 'Why do you live in this terrible room with that even more terrible woman who is your landlady?'

'Because it's close to the hospital and I can't afford anything better.' She added, 'Oh, do go away. I can't think why you came.'

'Why, to tell you that I will pick you up on Wednesday morning—from here?—and take you for an airing. Your temper will be improved by a peaceful drive.'

She stood in front of him, trying to find the right words, so that she could tell him just what she thought of him, but she couldn't think of them. He said gently, 'I'll be here at half-past nine.' He had picked up Mabel, who had settled her small furry head against his shoulder, purring with pleasure.

Sophie had the outrageous thought that the shoulder would be very nice to lean against; she had the feeling that she was standing in a strong wind and being blown somewhere. She heard herself saying, 'Oh, all right, but I can't think why. And do go; I'm on duty in half an hour…'

'I'll be downstairs waiting for you; we can walk back together. Don't be long, for I think that I shall find Miss Phipps a trying conversationalist.'

He let himself out, leaving her to dress rapidly, do her hair and face, and make suitable arrangements for Mabel's comfort during the night, and while she did that she thought about the professor. An arrogant type, she told herself, used to having influence and his own way and doubtless having his every whim pandered to. Just because he had happened to be there when she'd needed help with that wretched shoe didn't mean that he could scrape acquaintance with her. 'I shall tell him that I have changed my mind,' she told Mabel. 'There is absolutely no reason why I should go out with him.'

She put the little cat in her basket, picked up her shoulder-bag, and went downstairs.

Miss Phipps, pink-cheeked and wig slightly askew, was talking animatedly to the professor, describing with a wealth of detail just how painful were her bunions. The professor, who had had nothing to do with bunions for years, listened courteously, and gravely advised a visit to her own doctor. Then he bade her an equally courteous goodnight and swept Sophie out into the damp darkness.

'I dislike this road,' he observed, taking her arm.

For some reason his arm worried her. She said, knowing that she was being rude, 'Well, you don't have to live in it, do you?'

His answer brought her up short. 'My poor girl, you should be living in the country—open fields and hedgerows...'

'Well, I do,' she said waspishly. 'My home is in the country.'

'You do not wish to work near your home?' The question was put so casually that she answered without thinking.

'Well, that would be splendid, but it's miles from anywhere. Besides, I can get there easily enough from here.'

He didn't comment on her unconscious contradiction, and since they were already in the forecourt of St Agnes's he made some remark about the hospital and, once inside its doors, bade her a civil goodnight and went away in the direction of the consultant's room.

In the changing-room, full of night sisters getting into their uniforms, she heard Gill's voice from the further end. 'He's been operating for most of the day,' she was saying. 'I dare say he'll have a look at his patients this evening—men's surgical. I shall make an excuse to go down there to borrow something. Kitty—' Kitty was the night sister there '—give me a ring when he does. He's going away tomorrow, did you know?' She addressed her companions at large. 'But he'll be back.'

'How do you know?' someone asked.

'Oh, I phoned Theatre Sister earlier this evening—had a little gossip...'

They all laughed, and although Sophie laughed too she felt a bit guilty, but somehow she couldn't bring herself to tell them about her unexpected visitor that evening, nor the conversation she had had with him. She didn't think anyone would believe her anyway. She wasn't sure if she believed it herself.

Several busy nights brought her to Wednesday morning and the realisation that since she hadn't seen the professor she hadn't been able to refuse to go out with him. 'I shall do so if and when he comes,' she told Mabel, who went on cleaning her whiskers, quite unconcerned.

Sophie had had far too busy a night and she pottered rather grumpily around her room, not sure whether to have her bath first or a soothing cup of tea. She had neither. Miss Phipps, possibly scenting romance, climbed the stairs to tell her that she was wanted on the phone. 'That nice gentleman,' she giggled, 'said I was to get you out of the bath if necessary.' She caught Sophie's fulminating eye and added hastily, 'Just his little joke; gentlemen do like their little jokes…'

Sophie choked back a rude answer and went downstairs, closely followed by her landlady, who, although she went into her room, took care to leave the door slightly open.

'Hello,' said Sophie in her haughtiest voice.

'As cross as two sticks,' answered the professor's placid voice. 'I shall be with you in exactly ten minutes.'

He hung up before she could utter a word. She put the receiver back and the phone rang again and when she picked it up he said, 'If you aren't at the door I shall come up for you. Don't worry, I'll bring Miss Phipps with me as a chaperon.'

Sophie thumped down the receiver once more, ignored Miss Phipps's inquisitive face peering round her door, and took herself back to her room. 'I don't want to go out,' she told Mabel. 'It's the very last thing I want to do.'

All the same, she did things to her face and hair and put on her coat, assured Mabel that she wouldn't be away for long, and went downstairs again with a minute to spare.

The professor was already there, exchanging small talk with Miss Phipps, who gave Sophie an awfully sickening roguish look and said something rather muddled about pretty girls not needing beauty sleep if there was something better to do. Sophie cast her a look of outrage and bade the professor a frosty good morning, leaving him to make his polite goodbyes to her landlady, before she was swept out into the chilly morning and into the Bentley's welcoming warmth.

It was disconcerting when he remained silent, driving the car out of London on the A12 and, once clear of the straggling suburbs, turning off on to a side-road into the Essex countryside, presently turning off again on to an even smaller road, apparently leading to nowhere.

'Feeling better?' he asked her.

'Yes,' said Sophie, and added, 'Thank you.'

'Do you know this part of the world?' His voice was quiet.

'No, at least not the side-roads; it's not as quick…' She stopped just in time.

'I suppose it's quicker for you to turn off at Romford and go through Chipping Ongar?'

She turned to look at him, but he was gazing ahead, his profile calm.

'How did you know where I live?' She had been comfortably somnolent, but now she was wide awake.

'I asked Peter Small; do you mind?'

'Mind? I don't know; I can't think why you should want to know. Were you just being curious?'

'No, no, I never give way to idle curiosity. Now if I'm right there's a nice little pub in the next village—we might get coffee there.'

The pub was charming, clean and rather bare, with not a fruit machine in sight. There was a log fire smouldering in the vast stone fireplace, with an elderly dog stretched out before it, and the landlord, pleased to have custom before the noonday locals arrived, offered a plate of hot buttered toast to devour with the coffee.

Biting into her third slice, Sophie asked, 'Why did you want to know?' Mellowed by the toast and the coffee, she felt strangely friendly towards her companion.

'I'm not sure if you would believe me if I told you. Shall I say that, despite a rather unsettled start, I feel that we might become friends?'

'What would be the point? I mean, we don't move in the same circles, do we? You live in Holland—don't you?—and I live here. Besides, we don't know anything about each other.'

'Exactly. It behoves us to remedy that, does it not? You have nights off at the weekend? I'll drive you home.'

'Drive me home,' repeated Sophie, parrot-fashion. 'But what am I to say to Mother…?'

'My dear girl, don't tell me that you haven't been taken home by any number of young men...'

'Well, yes, but you're different.'

'Older?' He smiled suddenly and she discovered that she liked him more than she had thought. 'Confess that you feel better, Sophie; you need some male companionship—nothing serious, just a few pleasant hours from time to time. After all, as you said, I live in Holland.'

'Are you married?'

He laughed gently. 'No, Sophie—and you?'

She shook her head and smiled dazzlingly. 'It would be nice to have a casual friend... I'm not sure how I feel. Do we know each other well enough for me to go to sleep on the way back?'

CHAPTER TWO

So Sophie slept, her mouth slightly open, her head lolling on the professor's shoulder, to be gently roused at Miss Phipps's door, eased out of the car, still not wholly awake, and ushered into the house.

'Thank you very much,' said Sophie. 'That was a very nice ride.' She stared up at him, her eyes huge in her tired face.

'Is ten o'clock too early for you on Saturday?'

'No. Mabel has to come too…'

'Of course. Sleep well, Sophie.'

He propelled her gently to the stairs and watched her climb them and was in turn watched by Miss Phipps through her half-open door. When he heard Sophie's door shut he wished a slightly flustered Miss Phipps good morning and took himself off.

Sophie told herself that it was a change of scene which had made her feel so pleased with life. She woke up with the pleasant feeling that something nice had happened. True, the professor had made some rather strange remarks, and perhaps she had said rather more than she had intended, but her memory was a little hazy, for she had been very tired, and there was no use worrying about that now. It would be delightful to be driven home on Saturday…

Casualty was busy when she went on duty that evening, but there was nothing very serious and nothing at all in the accident room; she went to her midnight meal so punctually that various of her friends commented upon it.

'What's happened to you, Sophie?' asked Gill. 'You look as though you've won the pools.'

'Or fallen in love,' said someone from the other side of the table. 'Who is it, Sophie?'

'Neither—I had a good sleep, and it's a quiet night, thank heaven.'

'If you say so,' said Gill. 'I haven't won the pools—something much more exciting. That lovely man is operating at eight o'clock tomorrow morning. I have offered to lay up for Sister Tucker—' there was a burst of laughter '—just so that everything would be ready for him, and I shan't mind if I'm a few minutes late off duty.' She smiled widely. 'Especially if I should happen to bump into him.'

Joan Middleton, in charge of men's medical, the only one of them who was married and therefore not particularly interested, observed in her matter-of-fact way, 'Probably he's married with half a dozen children—he's not all that young, is he?'

'He's not even middle-aged,' said Gill sharply. 'Sophie, you've seen him. He's still quite young—in his thirties, wouldn't you think?'

Sophie looked vague. 'Probably.' She took another piece of toast and reached for the marmalade.

Gill said happily, 'Well, I dare say he falls for little wistful women, like me…' And although Sophie laughed with the rest of them, she didn't feel too sure about that. No, that wouldn't do at all, she reflected. Just because he had taken her for a drive didn't mean that he had any interest in her; indeed, it might be a cunning way of covering his real interest in Gill, who, after all, was exactly the type of girl a man would fall for. Never mind that she was the soul of efficiency in Theatre; once out of uniform, she became helpless, wistful and someone to be cherished. Helplessness and wistfulness didn't sit happily on Sophie.

Sophie saw nothing of the professor for the few nights left before she was due for nights off. She heard a good deal about him, though, for Gill had contrived to waylay him in Theatre before she went off duty and was full of his good looks and charm; moreover, when she went on duty the following night there had been an emergency operation and he was still in Theatre, giving her yet another chance to exchange a few words with him.

'I wonder where he goes for his weekends?' said Gill, looking round the breakfast-table.

Sophie, who could have told her, remained silent; instead she observed that she was off home just as soon as she could get changed, bade everyone goodbye, and took herself off.

She showered and changed into a rather nice multicheck jacket in a dark red with its matching skirt, tucked a cream silk scarf in the neck, stuck her feet into low-heeled black shoes, and, with her face carefully made-up and her hair in its complicated coil, took herself to the long mirror inside the old-fashioned wardrobe and had an appraising look.

'Not too bad,' she remarked to Mabel as she popped

her into her travel basket, slung her simple weekend bag over her shoulder, and went down to the front door. It was ten o'clock, and she didn't allow herself to think what she would do if he wasn't there…

He was, sitting in his magnificent car, reading a newspaper. He got out as she opened the door, rather hampered by Miss Phipps, who was quite unnecessarily holding it open for her, bade her good morning, took Mabel, who was grumbling to herself in her basket, wished Miss Phipps good day, and stowed both Sophie and Mabel into his car without further ado. He achieved this with a courteous speed which rather took Sophie's breath, but as he drove away she said severely, 'Good morning, Professor.'

'I suspect that you are put out at my businesslike greeting. That can be improved upon later. I felt it necessary to get away quickly before that tiresome woman began a conversation; I find her exhausting.'

An honest girl, Sophie said at once, 'I'm not put out; at least, I wasn't quite sure that you would be here. As for Miss Phipps, I expect she's lonely.'

'That I find hard to believe; what I find even harder to believe is that you doubted my word.' He glanced sideways at her. 'I told you that I would be outside your lodgings at ten o'clock.'

'I don't think I doubted you,' she said slowly. 'I think I wasn't quite sure why you were giving me a lift—I mean it's out of your way, isn't it?'

'I make a point of seeing as much of the English countryside as possible when I am over here.'

She wasn't sure whether that was a gentle snub or not; in any case she wasn't sure how to answer it, so she made a remark about the weather and he replied suitably and they lapsed into a silence broken only by Mabel's gentle grumbling from the back seat.

Sophie, left to her thoughts, wondered what would be the best thing to do when they arrived at her home. Should she ask him in for coffee or merely thank him for the lift and allow him to go to wherever he was going? She had phoned her mother on the previous evening and told her that she was getting a lift home, but she hadn't said much else…

'Would you like to stop for coffee or do you suppose your mother would be kind enough to have it ready for us?'

It was as though he had known just what she had been thinking. 'I'm sure she will expect us in time for coffee—that is, if you would like to stop…'

'I should like to meet your parents.' He sounded friendly, and she was emboldened to ask, 'How long will you be in England?'

'I shall go back to Holland in a couple of weeks.'

A remark which left her feeling strangely forlorn.

They were clear of the eastern suburbs by now and he turned off on to the road to Chipping Ongar. The countryside was surprisingly rural once they left the main road and when he took a small side-road before they reached that town she said in surprise, 'Oh, you know this part of the country?'

'Only from my map. I find it delightful that one can leave the main roads so easily and get comfortably lost in country lanes.'

'Can't you do that in Holland?'

'Not easily. The country is flat, so that there is always a town or a village on the horizon.' He added to surprise her, 'What do you intend to do with your life, Sophie?'

'Me?' The question was so unexpected that she hadn't a ready answer. 'Well, I've a good job at St Agnes's...'

'No boyfriend, no thought of marriage?'

'No.'

'And it's none of my business...' he laughed. 'Tell me, is it quicker to go through Cooksmill Green or take the road on the left at the next crossroads?'

'If you were on your own it would be best to go through Cooksmill Green, but since I'm here to show you the way go left; there aren't any villages until we get to Shellow Roding.'

It really was rural now, with wide fields on either side of the road bordered by trees and thick hedges, and presently the spire of the village church came into view and the first of the cottages, their ochre or white walls crowned by thatch, thickening into clusters on either side of the green with the church at one side of it, the village pub opposite and a row of small neat shops.

'Charming,' observed the professor and, obedient to Sophie's instruction, turned the car down a narrow lane beside the church.

Her home was a few hundred yards beyond. The house was old and bore the mark of several periods, its colour-washed walls pierced by a variety of windows. A stone wall, crumbling in places, surrounded the garden, and an open gate to the short drive led them to the front door.

The professor brought the car to a silent halt, and

got out to open Sophie's door and reach on to the back seat for Mabel's basket, and at the same time the door opened and Sophie's mother came out to meet them. She was a tall woman, as splendidly built as her daughter, her dark hair streaked with grey, her face still beautiful. Two dogs followed her, a Jack Russell and a whippet, both barking and cruising round Sophie.

'Darling,' said Mrs Blount, 'how lovely to see you.' She gave Sophie a kiss and turned to the professor, smiling.

'Mother, this is Professor van Taak ter Wijsma, who has kindly given me a lift. My mother, Professor.'

'A professor,' observed Mrs Blount. 'I dare say you're frightfully clever?' She smiled at him, liking what she saw. Really, thought Sophie, he had only to smile like that and everyone fell for him. But not me, she added, silently careless of grammar; we're just friends…

Mrs Blount led the way indoors. 'A pity the boys aren't at home; they'd have loved your big motor car.'

'Perhaps another time,' murmured the professor. He somehow conveyed the impression that he knew the entire family well—was an old friend, in fact. Sophie let Mabel out of her basket, feeling put out, although she had no idea why. There was no time to dwell on that, however. The dogs, Montgomery and Mercury, recognising Mabel as a well established visitor, were intent on a game, and by the time Sophie had quietened them down everyone had settled down in the kitchen, a large, cosy room, warm from the Aga, the vast dresser loaded with a variety of dishes and plates, the large table in its centre ringed by old-fashioned wooden chairs. There was a bowl of apples on it and a plate of scones, and a coffee-pot, equally old-fashioned, sat on the Aga.

'So much warmer in the kitchen,' observed Mrs Blount breezily, 'though if I had known who you were I would have had the best china out in the drawing-room.'

'Professors are ten a penny,' he assured her, 'and this is a delightful room.'

Sophie had taken off her coat and come to sit at the table. 'Do you work together at St Agnes's?' asked her mother.

'Our paths cross from time to time, do they not, Sophie?'

'I'm on night duty,' said Sophie quite unnecessarily. She passed him the scones, and since they were both looking at her she added, 'If there's a case—Professor van Taak ter Wijsma is a brain surgeon.'

'You don't live here, do you?' asked Mrs Blount as she refilled his coffee-mug.

'No, no, my home is normally in Holland, but I travel around a good deal.'

'A pity your father isn't at home, Sophie; he would have enjoyed meeting Professor van Taak…' She paused. 'I've forgotten the rest of it; I am sorry.'

'Please call me Rijk; it is so much easier. Perhaps I shall have the pleasure of meeting your husband at some time, Mrs Blount.'

'Oh, I do hope so. He's a vet, you know; he has a surgery here in the village and is senior partner at the veterinary centre in Chipping Ongar. He's always busy…'

Sophie drank her coffee, not saying much. The professor had wormed his way into her family with ease, she reflected crossly. It was all very well, all his talk about being friends, but she wasn't going to be rushed into anything, not even the casual friendship he had spoken of.

He got up to go presently, shook Mrs Blount's hand, dropped a casual kiss on Sophie's cheek with the remark that he would call for her on Sunday next week about eight o'clock, and got into his car and drove away. He left Sophie red in the face and speechless and her mother thoughtful.

'What a nice young man,' she remarked artlessly.

'He's not all that young, Mother…'

'Young for a professor, surely. Don't you like him, darling?'

'I hardly know him; he offered me a lift. I believe he's a very good surgeon in his own field.'

Mrs Blount studied her daughter's heightened colour. 'Tom will be home for half-term in a couple of weeks' time; I suppose you won't be able to come while he's here. George and Paul will be here too.'

'I'll do my best—Ida's just back from sick leave; she might not mind doing my weekend if I do hers on the following week. I'll see what she says and phone you.'

It was lovely being home; she helped her father with the small animals, drove him around to farms needing his help, and helped her mother around the house, catching up on the village gossip with Mrs Broom, who came twice a week to oblige. She was a small round woman who knew everyone's business and passed it on to anyone who would listen, but, since she wasn't malicious, no one minded. It didn't surprise Sophie in the least to hear that the professor had been seen, looked at closely and approved, although she had to squash Mrs Broom's assumption that she and he had a romantic attachment.

'Oh, well,' said Mrs Broom, 'it's early days—you never know.' She added severely, 'Time you was married, Miss Sophie.'

The week passed quickly; the days weren't long enough and now that the evenings were closing in there were delightful hours to spend round the drawing-room fire, reading and talking and just sitting doing nothing at all. She missed the professor, not only his company but the fact that he was close by even though she might not see him for days on end. His suggestion of friendship, which she hadn't taken seriously, became something to be considered. But perhaps he hadn't been serious—hadn't he said 'Nothing serious'? She would, she decided, be a little cool when next they met.

He came just before eight o'clock on Sunday evening and all her plans to be cool were instantly wrecked. He got out of the car and when she opened the door and went to meet him, he flung a great arm around her shoulders and kissed her cheek, and that in full view of her mother and father. She had no chance to express her feelings about that, for his cheerful greeting override the indignant words she would have uttered. He was behaving like a family friend of long standing and at the same time combining it with beautiful manners; she could see that her parents were delighted with him.

This is the last time, reflected Sophie, going indoors again. All that nonsense about casual friends and needing male companionship; he's no better than a steamroller.

Anything less like that cumbersome machine would

have been hard to imagine. The professor's manners were impeccable and after his unexpected embrace of her person he became the man she imagined him to be: rather quiet, making no attempt to draw attention to himself, and presently, over the coffee Mrs Blount offered, becoming engrossed in a conversation concerning the rearing of farm animals with his host. Sophie drank her coffee too hot and burnt her tongue and pretended to herself that she wasn't listening to his voice, deep and unhurried and somehow soothing. She didn't want to be soothed; she was annoyed.

It was the best part of an hour before the professor asked her if she was ready to leave; she bit back the tart reply that she had been ready ever since he had arrived and, with a murmur about putting Mabel into her basket, took herself out of the room. Five minutes later she reappeared, the imprisoned Mabel in one hand, her shoulder-bag swinging, kissed her parents, and, accompanied by the professor, now bearing the cat basket, went out to the car.

The professor wasn't a man to prolong goodbyes; she had time to wave to her mother and father standing in the porch before the Bentley slipped out of the drive and into the lane.

'Do I detect a coolness? What have I done? I could feel you seething for the last hour.'

'Kissing me like that,' said Sophie peevishly. 'Whatever next?' Before she could elaborate he said smoothly,

'But we are friends, are we not, Sophie? Besides, you looked pleased to see me.'

A truthful girl, she had to admit to that.

'There you are, then,' said the professor and eased

a large well shod foot down so that the Bentley sped through the lanes and presently on to the main road.

'When do you have nights off?' he wanted to know.

'Oh, not until Tuesday and Wednesday of next week...'

'I'll take you out some time.'

'That would be very nice,' said Sophie cautiously, 'but don't you have to go back to Holland?'

'Not until the middle of next week. Let us make hay while the sun shines.'

'Your English is very good.'

'So it should be. I had—we all had—an English dragon for a nanny.'

'You have brothers and sisters?'

'Two brothers, five sisters.' He sent the Bentley smoothly round a slow-moving Ford driven by a man in a cloth cap. 'I am the eldest.'

'Like me,' said Sophie. 'What I mean is, like I.'

'We have much in common,' observed the professor. 'What a pity that I have to operate in the morning; we might have had lunch together.'

Sophie felt regret but she said nothing. The professor, she felt, was taking over far too rapidly; they hardly knew each other. She almost jumped out of her seat when he said placidly, 'We have got to get to know each other as quickly as possible.'

She said faintly, 'Oh, do we? Why?'

He didn't answer that but made some trivial remark about their surroundings. He was sometimes a tiresome man, reflected Sophie.

When they arrived at her lodgings he carried Mabel's basket up to her room under the interested eye of Miss

Phipps, but he didn't go into it. His goodbye was casually friendly and he said nothing about seeing her again. She worried about that as she got ready for bed, but in the chilly light of morning common sense prevailed. He was just being polite, uttering one of those meaningless remarks which weren't supposed to be taken seriously.

She spent the morning cleaning her room, washing her smalls and buying her household necessities from the corner shop at the end of the street. In the afternoon she washed her hair and did her nails, turned up the gas fire until the room was really warm, made a pot of tea, and sat with Mabel on her lap, reading a novel one of her friends had lent her; but after the first few pages she decided that it was boring her and turned to her own thoughts instead. They didn't bore her at all, for they were of the professor, only brought to an end when she dozed off for a while. Then it was time to get ready to go on duty, give Mabel a final hug and walk the short distance to St Agnes's. It was a horrid evening, damp, dark and chilly, and she hoped as she entered the hospital doors that it would be a quiet night.

It was a busy one; the day sister handed over thankfully, leaving two patients to be admitted and a short line of damp and depressed people with septic fingers, sprained ankles and minor cuts to be dealt with. Sophie saw with satisfaction that she had Staff Nurse Pitt to support her and three students, two of them quite senior, the third a rather timid-looking girl. She'll faint if we get anything really nasty in, thought Sophie, and handed her over to the care of Jean Pitt, who was a motherly soul with a vast patience. She did a swift round of the patients then, making sure that there was nothing that the casualty officer couldn't handle without the need of X-rays or further help. And, the row of small injuries dealt with and Tim Bailey, on duty for the first time, soothed with coffee and left in the office to write up his notes, she sent the nurses in turn to the little kitchen beside the office to have their own coffee. It was early yet and for the moment the place was empty.

Not for long, though; the real work of the night began then with the first of the ambulances; a street accident, a car crash, a small child fallen from an open window—they followed each other in quick succession. It was after two o'clock in the morning when Sophie paused long enough to gobble a sandwich and swallow a mug of coffee. Going to the midnight meal had been out of the question; she had been right about the most junior of the students, who had fainted as they cut the clothes off an elderly woman who had been mugged; she had been beaten and kicked and slashed with a knife, and Sophie, even though she saw such sights frequently, was full of sympathy for the girl; she had been put in one of the empty cubicles with a mug of tea and told to stay there until she felt better, but it had made one pair of hands less…

She went off duty in a blur of tiredness, ate her breakfast without knowing what she was eating, and took herself off to her flatlet, and even Miss Phipps refrained from gossiping, but allowed her to mount the stairs in peace. Once there, it took no time at all to see to Mabel, have her bath and fall into bed.

That night set the pattern for her week. Usually there was a comparatively quiet night from time to time, but each night seemed busier than the last, and at the weekend, always worse than the weekdays, there was no respite, and even with the addition of a young male nurse to take over when one of the student nurses had nights off it was still back-breaking work. On Monday night, after a long session with a cardiac failure, Tim Bailey observed tiredly, 'I don't know how you stick it, Sophie, night after night…'

'I do sometimes wonder myself. But I've nights off—only two, though, because Ida isn't well again.'

'You'll go home?'

She nodded tiredly. 'It will be heaven, sleep and eat and then sleep and eat. What about you?'

'Two more nights, a couple of days off and back to day duty.' He put down his mug. 'And there's the ambulance again…'

Sophie ate her breakfast in a dream, but a happy one; she would go home just as soon as she could throw a few things into a bag and get Mabel into her basket. Lunch—eaten in the warmth of the kitchen—and then bed until suppertime and then bed again. She went out to the entrance in a happy daze, straight into the professor's waistcoat.

'You're still here?' she asked him owlishly. 'I thought you'd gone.'

'No, no.' He urged her into the Bentley. 'I'll drive you home, but first to your room.'

She was too tired to argue; ten minutes later she was in her flatlet, bundling things into her overnight bag, showering and dressing, not bothering with her face or hair, and then hurrying down to the door again in case he had changed his mind and gone. Her beautiful, anxious face, bereft of make-up, had never looked lovelier. The professor schooled his handsome features into placid friendliness, stowed her into the car, settled Mabel on the back seat, and drove away, not forgetting to wave in a civil manner to Miss Phipps.

Sophie tossed her mane of hair, tied with a bit of ribbon, over her shoulder. 'You're very kind,' she muttered. 'I hope I'm not taking you out of your way.' She closed her eyes and slept peacefully for half an hour and woke refreshed to find that they were well on the way to her home.

She said belatedly, 'I told Mother I'd be home about one o'clock.'

'I phoned. Don't fuss, Sophie.'

'Fuss? Fuss? I'm not—anyway, you come along and change all my plans without so much as a by your leave… I'm sorry, I'm truly sorry, I didn't mean a word of that; I'm tired and so I say silly things. I'm so grateful.'

When he didn't answer she said, 'Really I am—don't be annoyed…'

'When you know me better, Sophie, you will know that I seldom get annoyed—angry, impatient…certainly, but I think never any of these with you.' He gave her a brief smile. 'Why have you only two nights off after such a gruelling eight nights?'

'The other night sister—Ida Symonds—is ill again.'

'There is no one to take her place?'

'Not for the moment. The junior night sister on the surgical wards is taking over while I'm away.'

They were almost there when he said casually, 'I'm going back to Holland tomorrow.'

'Not for good?'

Her voice was sharp, and he asked lightly, 'Will you miss me? I hope so.'

She stared out at the wintry countryside. 'Yes.'

'We haven't had that lunch yet, have we? Perhaps we can arrange that when I come again.'

'Will you be back soon?'

'Oh, yes. I have to go to Birmingham and then Leeds and then on to Edinburgh.'

'But not here, in London?'

'Probably.' He sounded vague and she decided that he was just being civil again.

'I expect you'll be glad to be home again?'

'Yes.' He didn't add anything to that, and a few moments later they had reached her home and were greeted by her mother at the door before the car had even stopped, smiling a warm welcome. Not a very satisfactory conversation, reflected Sophie, in fact hardly a conversation at all. She swiftly returned her mother's hug and went indoors with the professor and Mabel's basket hard on her heels. He put the basket down, unbuttoned her coat, took it off, tossed it on to a chair and followed it with his own, and then gave her a gentle shove towards the warmth of the kitchen. Montgomery and Mercury had come to meet them and he let Mabel out of her basket to join them as Mrs Blount set the coffee on the table.

'Will you stay for lunch?' she asked hopefully.

'I would have liked that, but I've still some work to clear up before I return to Holland.'

'You'll be back?' He hid a smile at the look of disappointment on her face.

'Oh, yes, quite soon, I hope.' He glanced at Sophie.

'Sophie is tired out. I won't stay for long, for I'm sure she is longing for her bed.'

He was as good as his word, saying all the right things to his hostess, with the hope that he would see her again before very long, and then bidding Sophie goodbye with the advice that she should sleep the clock round if possible and then get out in the fresh air. 'We are sure to meet when I get back to England,' he observed, and she murmured politely. He hadn't said how long that would be, she thought peevishly, and he need not think that she was at his beck and call every time he felt like her company. She was, of course, overlooking the fact that her company had been a poor thing that morning and if he had expected anything different he must have been very disappointed. All the same, she saw him go with regret.

The two days went in a flash, a comforting medley of eating, sleeping and pottering in the large, rather untidy garden, tying things up, digging things out of the ground before it became hard with frost, and cutting back the roses. By the time she had to return to the hospital she was her old self again, and her mother, looking at her lovely face, wished that the professor had been there to see her daughter. She comforted herself with the thought that he had said that he would be back and it seemed to her that he was a man whose word could be relied on. He and Sophie were only friends at the moment, but given time and opportunity… She sighed. She didn't want her Sophie to be hurt as she had been hurt all those years ago.

It was November now, casting a gloom over the shabby streets around the hospital. Even on a bright summer's day they weren't much to look at; now they were depressing, littered with empty cans of Coca Cola, fish and chip papers and the more lurid pages of the tabloid Press. Sophie, picking her way towards her own front door a few hours before she was due on duty again, thought of the street cleaners who so patiently swept and tidied only to have the same rubbish waiting for them next time they came around. Rather like us, I suppose, she reflected. We get rid of one lot of patients and there's the next lot waiting.

Miss Phipps was hovering as she started up the stairs. 'Had a nice little holiday?' she wanted to know. 'Came back by train, did you?'

Sophie said that yes, she had, and if she didn't hurry she would be late for work, which wasn't quite true, but got her safely up the rest of the stairs and to her room, where she released Mabel, fed her, made herself a cup of tea, and loaded her shoulder-bag with everything she might need during the night. She seldom had the chance to open it, but it was nice to think that everything was there.

The accident room was quiet when she went on duty, but Casualty was still teeming with patients. She took over from the day sister, ran her eye down the list of patients already seen, checked with her Staff and phoned for Tim Bailey to come as soon as possible and cast his eye over what she suspected was a Pott's fracture, and began on the task of applying dressings to the patients who needed them.

Tim arrived five minutes later. 'I've seen this lot,' he said snappily. 'They only need dressings and injections; surely you—?'

'Yes, I know and of course we'll see to those… This man's just come in—I think he's a Pott's, and if you say so I'll get him to X-Ray if you'd like to sign the form.'

She gave him a charming smile and she had sounded almost motherly, so that he laughed. 'Sorry—I didn't mean to snap. Let's look at this chap.'

She had been right; he signed the form and told her, 'Give me a ring and I'll put on a plaster, but give me time to eat my dinner, will you?'

'You'll have time for two dinners by the time I've got hold of X-Ray; it's Miss Short and she is always as cross as two sticks.'

The man with the Pott's fracture was followed by more broken bones, a stab wound and a crushed hand; a normal night, reflected Sophie, going sleepily to her bed, and so were the ensuing nights, including the usual Saturday night's spate of street fights and road accidents. The following week bid fair to be the same, so that by the time she was due for nights off again she was more than a little tired. All the same, she thought as she coaxed Mabel into her basket and started on her journey home, it would have been nice to find the professor waiting for her outside the door.

Wishful thinking; there was no sign of him.

CHAPTER THREE

HOME FOR SOPHIE was bliss after the cold greyness of the East End. The quiet countryside, bare now that it was almost winter, was a much needed change from the crowded streets around the hospital. She spent her days visiting the surrounding farms with her father and pottering around the house, and her nights in undisturbed sleep. She was happy—though perhaps not perfectly happy, for the professor had a bothersome way of intruding into her thoughts, and none of the sensible reasons for forgetting him seemed adequate. If she had been given an opportunity she would have talked about him to her mother, but that lady never mentioned him.

She went back to the hospital half hoping that she would see him—not that she wished to particularly, she reminded herself, but he had said that he would return…

There was no news of him, although there was plenty of gossip around the breakfast-table after her first night's duty, most of it wild guessing and Gill's half-serious plans as to what she would do and say when she next saw him. 'For I'll be the lucky one, won't I?' She grinned round the table. 'If he's operating I can always think up a good reason for being in Theatre during the day…' There was a burst of laughter at this and she added, 'You may well laugh, but I'll be the first one to see him.'

As it turned out, she was wrong.

Sophie, bent on keeping a young man with terrible head injuries alive, working desperately at it, obeying Tim's quick instructions with all the skill she could muster, stood a little on one side to allow the surgical registrar to reach the patient, and at the same time realised that there was someone with him. She knew who it was even before she saw him, and although her heart gave a joyful little leap she didn't let it interfere with her work. He came from behind and bent his height to examine the poor crushed head, echoing Peter Small's cheerful 'Hello, Sophie' with a staid 'Good evening, Sister'.

She muttered a reply, intent on what she was doing, and for the next half an hour was far too busy to give him a thought, listening to the two men and doing as she was bid, taking blood for cross-matching, summoning X-ray and the portable machine, and warning Theatre that the professor would be operating within the hour. She heard Gill's delighted chuckle when she told her.

At breakfast Gill gave everyone a blow-by-blow account of the professor's activities. He had done a marvellous bit of surgery, she assured them, and afterwards he had had a mug of tea in her office. 'He was rather quiet,' she explained, 'but he had only been here for a couple of hours, discussing some cases with Peter; he must have been tired...' She brightened. 'There are sure to be some more cases during the night,' she added pensively. 'I've got nights off in two days' time. He's on the theatre list to do two brain tumours tomorrow; probably he'll be free after that.'

She called across the table, 'Hey, Sophie, didn't he go to the accident room? Did he say anything to you?'

'He said, "Good evening, Sister", and asked me where the man came from.'

Gill said happily, not meaning to be unkind, 'I dare say he likes small, fragile-looking girls like me.'

They got up to go then and Sophie changed out of her uniform and made for the entrance. It was raining again, which was probably why she felt depressed.

The professor was lounging against a wall, studying the notice-board. He straightened up when he saw her and walked towards her. When he was near enough he said, 'Hello, Sophie,' and smiled. It was a smile to warm her, and she smiled back from a tired unmade-up face.

'I'm glad you were there,' she said. 'Will he do?'

'I believe so—it's early days yet, but he's got a chance.' He fell in beside her, walking to the door. 'Are you glad because I was there to deal with the patient or were you glad to see me, Sophie?'

She stopped to look at him. 'Both.'

He tucked a hand under her elbow. 'Good, still friends? I'm not operating until this afternoon and we both need some fresh air. Come along.'

She was whizzed through the door, by no means willingly. 'I have no wish for fresh air,' she told him, peevish after a long night's work. 'I'm going to bed.'

'Well, of course you are, but not just yet. We'll go to Epping Forest, have a brisk walk and a cup of coffee, and be back here by midday.'

'Mabel,' said Sophie feebly.

'We'll go there first. I shall come up with you, otherwise you might forget me and go to sleep.'

'No, no. You mustn't come up. I won't be more than five minutes or so.'

He stuffed her into the car and got in beside her and a few minutes later got out to open her door and usher her across the pavement and in through the shabby front door. 'Five minutes,' he reminded her and turned to engage in conversation with Miss Phipps, who had darted out, her wig askew, intent on a chat.

Mabel's wants attended to, her face made up after a fashion and her hair tidied, Sophie went back downstairs and was forced to admire the way in which the professor drew his conversation with her landlady to its conclusion in such a way that the lady was under the impression that it was she who had brought it to a close.

'Anyone would think that you liked her,' said Sophie waspishly. She wished suddenly that she hadn't come; thinking about it, she couldn't remember saying that she would in the first place.

'No, no, nothing of the sort, but if she should take a dislike to me she might show me the door, and then we would have to meet in the street or a park—all very well in the summer, but this is no weather for dallying around the East End.'

Sophie drew a deep breath. 'What do you mean—"have to meet"? We don't have to do anything of the sort.'

'My dear girl, use your tired wits. How are we to get to know each other unless we spend time in each other's company?'

'Why do we have to get to know each other? You don't even live here.'

She realised what a silly remark that was as soon as it was uttered.

'A powerful argument for our frequent meetings when I am,' he told her placidly. 'You have been home since I saw you last?'

His gentle conversation soothed her. She was tired but no longer edgy and by the time they reached the comparative quiet of the forest she was ready enough to walk its paths with him. Indeed, when presently he suggested that they should go in search of coffee she felt reluctant to leave, not sure whether it was the peace and quiet around them or his company which she was loath to give up.

They had been in the car five minutes or so when she pointed out that he had left the road back.

He reassured her. 'I thought we might have our coffee at Ingatestone; there's rather a nice place on the Roman Road.'

The nice place was a fifteenth-century hotel, quite beautifully restored. It would be busy in the evenings, she judged, but now there were few people there. They sat in a lovely room by a pleasant fire and drank their coffee, but Sophie wasn't allowed to stay for long. 'If we sit here much longer,' observed the professor, 'you'll fall asleep and I shall be forced to carry you upstairs to that room of yours, and all my efforts to keep Miss Phipps sweet would be useless.'

Sophie, warm and content, laughed at that.

Back once more, he saw her very correctly to the front door, bade her a brief goodbye, and drove away, leaving Sophie to fend off Miss Phipps's curiosity with the observation that she was almost too sleepy to get to her room…

She didn't see him during the next night. For once it was fairly quiet and all the night sisters were in the canteen at the same time for their midnight meal. It was Gill who mentioned him first. 'He operated at one o'clock,' she grumbled. 'I simply couldn't get up in the middle of the day, and besides, I couldn't think of a good excuse to turn up in Theatre. But luck is on my side, girls; he's operating at half-past eight this morning, so I shall forget something and go back to Theatre and chat him up.'

'I must say, you're keen,' said someone. 'Don't any of us get a look-in?'

Gill beamed round the table. 'Let's face it, I'm just his type; big men like little women.'

Sophie, her mouth full of scrambled egg, said nothing.

She saw the Bentley parked in the consultant's parking space as she left the hospital. He would be operating by now and doubtless Gill had found an excuse to go back to Theatre on some pretext or other. It was probably true, reflected Sophie, walking back to her flatlet in the teeth of a nasty little wind, that big men liked small girls. If so, why did he bother to see her? To go to the trouble of meeting her mother and father, take her for brisk walks for her health's sake? She pondered the problem and she couldn't find an answer. A conceited girl might have concluded that it was her strikingly pretty person which attracted him, but she wasn't conceited; three brothers had seen to that. She bade Miss

Phipps an absent-minded good morning and gained the solitude of her room to find Mabel waiting for her with impatience. She fed her, had a bath, made herself a mug of cocoa, and went to bed trying not to think how pleasant a brisk walk in Epping Forest would have been. Tomorrow, she told herself sleepily, she would take a bus and tramp round Hyde Park even if it poured with rain. She closed her eyes and, lulled by Mabel's gentle purr, she slept.

A disgruntled Gill told her as they sat at their midnight meal that although she had gone back to the theatre with some excuse the professor had already started to operate and hadn't finished until the early afternoon. 'And on top of that,' she went on, 'he's gone to France—a last-chance op on a little girl with a brain tumour. There are several more cases lined up for him here, so he's bound to come back.' Her blue eyes were screwed up with annoyance. 'I wish I were on day duty. On the other hand, I'd see more of him at night.'

'Only if some poor unfortunate came in with severe head injuries, and who would want that?' Sophie had spoken tartly, and Gill gave her a searching look.

'Well, no, of course not. Sophie, I do believe that you haven't a spark of romance in you. If you weren't so large yourself you'd have the men falling about to get at you.'

There was a burst of laughter; 'large' hardly described Sophie's magnificent shape, and several voices pointed this out, while she, unperturbed, spooned her milk pudding, aware that a gratifying number of men had proposed to her and professed themselves in love with her. She had liked them all, but not enough to marry them—the only one she had felt differently about was a dim memory now, and she wasn't sure if she believed in love any more… Her thoughts were interrupted by her bleep and she sped away to deal with a very drunk man who had fallen through a glass door. His injuries weren't serious but needed a good deal of stitching, and it took some time to get his address and get his wife to come and fetch him home. It was the worst hour of the long night by now—almost four o'clock, when the desire to sleep was strong, to be countered by cups of tea and the hopeful tidying-up of the accident room and Casualty, although Sophie couldn't remember a morning when there hadn't been at least two patients arriving just as everything was pristine and ready for the day staff.

True to the promise she had made herself, she spent an hour in Hyde Park that morning, walking at a good pace and actually rather enjoying it. The weather had improved too and the air there was fresh, and the Serpentine gave an illusion of the country. She took a bus back to her lodgings, made her cocoa, had a bath, and fell into bed to sleep at once and not wake until Mabel, impatient for her food, roused her with an urgent paw.

Three more days, thought Sophie, diving into her clothes while the kettle boiled, and it's nights off again.

The night ahead of her, did she but know it, was going to be a very busy one, and at the end of it she was too tired to eat her breakfast; she pushed cornflakes round her plate, drank several cups of tea, and got up from the table.

'You've had a busy night,' observed the men's medical ward sister, who hadn't. 'You must be dying for your bed.'

'It was rather much—luckily it isn't like that every night. There was this rally about something or other, and they always end up in a fight…'

'Nights off soon?' asked someone.

'Three more nights, and I've been promised a male student nurse; as long as Ida doesn't go off sick again, the future looks rosy. Bye for now.'

She went along to change, flinging her clothes on anyhow, something she would never dream of doing normally, but now all she wanted was her bed.

The professor was just outside the door as she went through it. He took her arm and marched her across the forecourt, opened the Bentley's door, and urged her inside. Only when they were sitting side by side did he say, 'Good morning, Sophie, only I see that it isn't for you. You've had a bad night?'

She found her voice, indignant but squeaky with tiredness. 'Yes, and if you don't mind I want to go home and go to bed—now.' She added as an afterthought, 'Good morning, Professor.'

'So you shall. Did you eat your breakfast?'

'I'm not hungry.' As she spoke she was aware that if she went to bed without a meal she would wake after an hour or two and not sleep again, but that, she considered, was her business.

The professor edged the car out into the street. 'First we will see to Mabel, then we will go together and have breakfast, and then you shall go to bed.'

'I don't want—' began Sophie.

'No, of course you don't, but just be a good girl and

do as I say.' He had stopped before her door and was already helping her out. 'I'm coming up with you.'

She stood where she was. 'Indeed you're not. Miss Phipps—'

'Sophie, I beg you to stop fussing; just leave everything to me.'

He opened the street door and pushed her ahead of him. 'Go on up,' he told her and turned to Miss Phipps, already with her head round the door.

Sophie did as she was told, vaguely listening to his deep voice. He sounded serious and she could hear Miss Phipps making sympathetic noises. She wondered what he had said to earn that lady's concern as she unlocked her own door, flung her bag on the divan, and went to get Mabel's breakfast. She was spooning the cat food into a saucer when the professor knocked and came in. The room was cold and he lit the gas fire, took the tin from her to finish the job, and told her to wash her face and comb her hair. 'And no hanging about, I beg you; I'm famished.'

She paused with a towel over her arm on the way to the bathroom. 'Don't they give you breakfast at St Agnes's?'

'Oh, yes, if I asked for it. I came over on a night ferry and came straight to the hospital.'

'An emergency?'

'If you are an emergency, then yes. Go and wash your face, Sophie.'

She went through the door and then poked her head back round it. 'Haven't you been to bed?'

'No, I drove down to Calais.'

Her dark eyes, huge with a lack of sleep, stared

across the room at him. 'But why...?' she began, only to be told at once to do something to her face. 'For I refuse to take you out looking "like patience on a monument".'

'"Smiling at grief",' muttered Sophie, hurrying down the stairs.

She returned five minutes later, her face washed and made-up after a fashion. She had brushed her hair too, so that it was tidy in front, although the coil at the back was in need of attention.

'Take the pins out and tie it back,' sighed the professor, which she did, finding a bit of ribbon in her work basket and making a neat bow.

He settled Mabel in her basket, switched off the fire, and opened the door. 'You shouldn't hide your hair,' he said as she went past him.

She looked at him in astonishment. 'I couldn't possibly go on duty with it hanging down my back.'

He only smiled down at her, and, for some reason feeling awkward, she added, 'I don't always bother to put it up when I'm at home.'

'Oh, good,' said the professor, pressing his vast person against the wall so that she might pass him.

He whisked her past Miss Phipps with a brief, 'We shall be back presently, Miss Phipps,' before that lady could so much as open her mouth, and gently bundled Sophie into the car.

Catching her breath as he drove away, she asked, 'Where are we going?'

'To my house to eat breakfast; it should be ready and waiting for us.'

'Your house? I thought you lived in Holland...'

'I do.' He didn't offer any more information and

somehow she didn't like to ask and sat silent while he drove across the city, but as he threaded his way through the one-way streets in the West End she ventured, 'You live in London?'

He turned the car into one of the narrow fashionable streets of Belgravia. 'Oh, yes.' He slowed the car and stopped before a terrace of Regency houses. 'Here we are.'

The houses were tall and narrow with bay windows and important doors gleaming with paint and highly polished doorknockers. He urged her across the narrow pavement, fished out a bunch of keys, and opened his door.

The hall was long and narrow, and as they went in a man came to meet them.

'Mornin', guv,' he said cheerfully. 'There's a nice bit of breakfast all ready for you and the lady.'

He was youngish, with nondescript hair and a round face in which a pair of small blue eyes twinkled, and he was most decidedly a Cockney.

The professor returned his greeting affably. 'This is Percy, who runs the place for me together with Mrs Wiffen. This is Miss Blount, as famished as I am.'

'Okey-doke, guv, leave it to me. Pleased to meet you, miss, I'm sure.'

His little eyes surveyed her and he smiled. 'You go right to the table and I'll bring in the food.'

He took Sophie's coat and opened a door. 'Gotta lotta post, guv,' he observed. 'It's in yer study.'

The professor thanked him. 'Later, Percy—let me know if there are any phone calls.'

The room they entered was at the front of the house,

not over-large but furnished with great taste, its mulberry-red walls contrasting with the maple-wood furniture. The table was circular, decked with a white damask cloth, with shining silver and blue and white china, and the coffee-pot Percy was setting on the table was silver, very plain save for a coat of arms on one side. Sophie took the seat offered by the professor and cast a quick look round her. She came from a family in comfortable circumstances, but this was more than comfort, it was luxury, albeit understated. There was a bracket clock on the mantelpiece which she was sure was eighteenth-century, perhaps earlier; it suited the room exactly, so did the draped brocade curtains at the bow window and the fine carpet, almost threadbare with age, on the floor. The professor interrupted her inspection.

'Pour the coffee, will you, Sophie? Do you want to talk about your night or shall we lay plans for our next meeting?'

A remark which rather took her breath. She had it back by the time Percy had served them with a splendid breakfast and then gone away again. 'Are we going to meet again?'

He handed her the toast rack. 'Of course we are; what a silly remark. When do you have your nights off?'

'I have three more nights to work.'

'Good. I'll drive you home, but shall we see if we can spend a little time together first? Could you manage to spend the afternoon with me before we go? Go to bed for a few hours and I'll fetch you about one o'clock; we can have lunch somewhere and walk for a while.'

She speared a mushroom and ate it thoughtfully. She

was feeling quite wide awake now and eyed him uncertainly. 'Well, yes, I could, but why?'

'Because some exercise will do you good and Epping Forest is on our way to your home.' Which didn't really answer her question.

She crunched a morsel of perfectly cooked bacon. 'Well, all right. It's very kind of you. I'd like to be home by suppertime, though.' She paused, looking at him. 'Perhaps you would like to have supper with us before you drive back here?'

'That,' said the professor gravely, 'would be most kind if your mother has no objection.'

'No. She'll be delighted. She likes you,' said Sophie matter-of-factly, not seeing the gleam in her companion's eyes. She applied herself to her breakfast with unselfconscious pleasure while they talked about nothing much, undemanding chat which was very soothing. It was a lovely house, she thought, welcoming and warm—one could live very happily in it…

She could have lingered there, uncaring of sleep, but the silvery chimes of the clock reminded her of her bed and she glanced at the professor, who nodded his handsome head just as though she had spoken.

'I'm going to take you back now,' he told her. 'Go to bed and sleep, Sophie, ready for another night.'

Percy came then to help her with her coat, and she thanked him for her breakfast. 'I hope it didn't give you too much extra work.'

'Lor' no, miss. Nice ter 'ave a bit of company. Me and Mrs Wiffen and the cat get lonely when the guv's away.'

In the car she asked, 'Why does Percy call you guv?

I mean, it's a bit unusual, isn't it? He's the houseman or valet or something, isn't he?'

'Ah, but Percy is unusual. I removed a tumour from his brain some five years ago and at the time he said that he would look after my interests until either he or I should die. I took him at his word and he is splendid at his job and always cheerful. As far as I'm concerned, he may call me what he likes. Did you like him?'

'Yes—I imagine you could trust him completely.'

'Indeed I do. There isn't much he can't do or arrange even at a moment's notice. I can go to and from Holland knowing that he will look after things for me.'

He had stopped the car outside Miss Phipps's house, and for a moment Sophie compared it with the house they had just left. A foolish thing to do, she reminded herself bracingly, and got out as the professor opened the door for her. Nothing could have been brisker than his manner as he saw her to the door and bade her goodbye.

'I suppose that was his good deed for the day,' said Sophie to an inattentive Mabel.

During the next three nights she heard a good deal about the professor. He was operating each day and Gill reported faithfully what he did and said to her and what she had said to him and thought about later; none of it amounted to much. There was no sign of him, though, and she went home to the flat at the end of her last night's duty feeling uncertain. True, he had said that he would drive her home, true also that he was calling for her at one o'clock and taking her out to lunch, but supposing he had forgotten or, worse, had issued a vague invitation, not meaning a word of it?

Common sense told her that that was unlikely; she went to bed as soon as she got to her room, with rather a nice tweed skirt and needlecord jacket with a washed-silk blouse to go under it lying ready to get into when she got up.

She set her alarm for half-past twelve, got up rather reluctantly, dressed, and, with her face nicely made-up and her hair in its smooth, intricate coils, urged Mabel into her basket, swung her shoulder-bag over her arm, and went downstairs.

The Bentley was outside with the professor at the wheel, reading a newspaper. He got out as she opened the door, dealt with the bag and Mabel, and settled her beside him.

'Lunch first?' he asked. 'I've booked a table at that place at Ingatestone.'

They talked in a desultory fashion as he drove, pleasant talk which required no effort on her part, and over their lunch he kept their conversation easygoing and rambling, not touching on any topic that was personal. Sophie, refreshed by her short sleep, agreed readily to a dish of hors-d'oeuvres, grilled Dover sole and sherry trifle and enjoyed them with an appetite somewhat sharpened by a week or more of solid hospital cooking and snatched sandwiches.

'That was delicious,' she observed, pouring their coffee.

'Splendid. We have time for an hour's walk before we need drive on to your home.'

A short drive brought them to Epping Forest. He parked the car and they started along one of the well marked paths running between the trees and dense shrubbery, almost leafless now, quiet and sheltered, winding away out of sight. Presently they came to a small clearing with an old crumbling wall overlooking a stretch of open country, and by common consent paused to lean against it and admire the view. The professor said quietly, 'May I take it that we are now good, firm friends, Sophie?'

She had had a sleep and a delicious lunch and the quiet trees around her were soothing. She smiled up at him; he was safe and solid and a good companion. 'Oh, yes.'

'Then perhaps you know what I am going to say next. Will you marry me, Sophie?'

Her smile melted into a look of utter surprise. 'Marry you? Why? Whatever for?'

He smiled at that. 'We are good friends; have we not just agreed about that? We enjoy doing the same things, laughing at the same things… I want someone to share my life, Sophie, a companion, someone to make my house a home, someone to be friends with my friends.'

She met his intent look honestly, although her cheeks were pink. 'But we don't—that is, shouldn't there be love as well?'

'Have you ever been in love, Sophie?' He wasn't looking at her now, but at the view before them.

She took a long time to answer, but he showed no impatience. Presently she said, 'Yes, I have. Oh, it was years ago; I was nineteen and I loved him so much. He threw me over for an older woman, a young widow. She was small and pretty and beautifully dressed and had money; I felt like a clumsy beanpole beside her. I would have given anything to have been five feet tall and slim… It's funny, but I can't remember what he looked like any more, but I'll never forget how I felt. I never want to feel like that again—it was like the end of the world.'

He still didn't look at her, but he flung a great arm across her shoulders and she felt comforted by it.

'You never think of him?'

'No. No, not for a long time now. It wasn't love—the kind of love that swallows up everything else—was it?'

'One is very vulnerable at nineteen, and had you thought that, if you had married this man on a flood of infatuation, by now, eight years later, you would be bitterly regretting it? One changes, you know.'

She turned to look at him. It wasn't just his good looks; he was so sure about things, so dependable and, underneath his rather austere manner, very kind.

'You haven't answered my question.'

'You answered it yourself, didn't you? You were hurt badly once; for that to happen a second time is something you will never allow. My dear, marriage isn't all a matter of falling in love and living happily ever after. Liking is as important as loving in its way; feeling comfortable with each other is important too—and friendship. Add these things up and you have the kind of love which makes a happy marriage.'

'What about Romeo and Juliet, or Abelard and Héloïse? They loved—'

'Ah—that is something which only a few people are fortunate enough to share.'

His arm was still around her, but he made no attempt to draw her closer. 'I think that we may be happy together, Sophie. We do not know each other very well yet, but we have so little opportunity to meet. Would you consider marrying me and getting to know me after? I am quite sure that we can be happy; but let us take our time learning about each other, gaining each other's affection. We will live as friends if you like until we are used to the idea of being man and wife; I'll not hurry you…'

'I don't know where you live—do you have parents?'

'Oh, yes. My father's a retired surgeon; he and my mother live in Friesland. I live there too; so do two of my sisters. The other three live in den Haag.'

'All in one house?' The idea appalled her.

He laughed. 'No, no. We all have homes of our own. Have you any leave due, Sophie?'

'A week, that's all.'

'Long enough. Can you manage to get free by the end of next week? I've nothing over here after that; I'll take you to Holland and you can make up your mind then.'

'I'm not sure, but I think this is a very funny kind of proposal,' said Sophie.

'Is it? I've not proposed marriage before, so I'm not qualified to give an opinion. Shall I start again and you tell me what to say?'

She laughed then and said, 'Don't be ridiculous,' and saw that he was smiling too, but she didn't see the gleam in his eye.

'I don't think that I can get a week off at such short notice,' Sophie said regretfully.

'Perhaps if I had a word… Apply to whoever it is who deals with such things when you get back on duty and see what happens.'

'All right, but I'm not certain…'

He said in a soothing voice, 'No, no, of course you're not. You would prefer to say nothing, I expect, for the time being.'

'Perhaps not at all,' said Sophie soberly.

'That seems to be a splendid idea.' He was all of a sudden brisk. 'Shall we go back to the car? Your mother doesn't expect us before the early evening, does she? Then let us find somewhere where we can have tea.'

It was obvious after a while that he wasn't going to refer to the matter again; she would dearly have liked to question him about his home in Holland, but she wasn't sure how to set about it. She liked him—there was no question about that—but she sensed that penetrating his reserve was something best left until she knew more about him. Sitting beside him as he drove away from the woods, she reflected that the idea of marrying him was beginning to take firm root in her head, which, considering she had never addressed him as other than professor or sir, seemed absurd.

CHAPTER FOUR

SOPHIE AND THE professor stopped at the Post House in Epping for their tea and, over buttered muffins and several cups of that reviving beverage, discussed everything under the sun but themselves. Sophie, ever hopeful, made several efforts to talk about her companion's life, but it was of no use; he gave her no encouragement at all. She gave up presently, feeling annoyed and trying not to show it, suspecting that he knew that and was secretly amused.

Her mother and father welcomed them with carefully restrained curiosity; the professor was becoming a fairly frequent visitor and, naturally enough, they were beginning to wonder why. It was after a leisurely supper, sitting in the comfortable drawing-room round the log fire, that he enlightened them.

'I am going back to Holland tomorrow for two days,' he told them in his calm, unhurried way, 'but I hope that I will see you again shortly.' He looked at Sophie. 'You won't mind, my dear, if I tell your parents that I have asked you to marry me?'

It was too late to say that yes, she did mind, anyway. Not that she did; she had been wondering all the evening what exactly she should say to her mother and father. Before they could say anything he went on, 'I shall be here for a week or so, which will give her time to decide if she will marry me or not. If she agrees, then I hope to take her to Holland with me so that she may meet my family and see my home. If she should refuse me I hope that she and I will remain friends and that I shall see you from time to time.'

Sophie found three pairs of eyes looking at her. 'I thought I'd like to think about it,' she said a little breathlessly. 'Just to be sure, you know.'

Her father said, 'Sensible girl,' and her mother observed,

'I would be delighted to see the pair of you married, but Sophie's quite right to think it over; love is for a lifetime.' She nodded her head in satisfaction. 'You're well suited,' she added.

They were content to leave it at that; the talk was of his journey the next day, Sophie's busy week and the various countries he visited from time to time, and presently he took his leave, and Sophie, feeling that it was expected of her, went with him to the door.

'When will you be back in England?' asked Sophie, once they were in the hall.

'In three days' time. I have to give a series of lectures.' He was standing close to her, but not touching her. 'Will you give me your answer then?'

She looked up into his face. He was smiling a little, friendly and relaxed and most reassuringly calm. 'I shall miss you.'

'And I you—that augurs well for our future, does it not?'

She said hesitantly, 'Well, yes, I suppose it does. I'll—I'll tell you when I see you.'

He bent his head and kissed her, a brief, comforting kiss, before he opened the door and got into his car, and drove away without looking back.

Tom, home from school while Sophie had nights off, declared himself delighted with the idea of her getting married. 'Splendid,' he crowed. 'Now I'll have somewhere to go for my holidays—'

'Don't count your chickens,' said Sophie severely. 'I haven't said I want to marry yet; we're not even engaged.'

'He's a prime fellow, Sophie, and he's got a Bentley.'

'Which is no reason for marrying anyone,' said Sophie firmly.

What would the reasons be if she did marry him? she wondered. He had been quite right; they got on well together and they liked each other. Liking someone that you were going to live with for the rest of your life was important. She would be a suitable wife to him too, since, being a nurse, she understood the kind of life he led and would make allowances for it. She wasn't a young girl either; she would be prepared to take over the duties of his household and cope with any special social life that he might have. She could see that from his point of view she was eminently suitable.

The thought depressed her, while at the same time she acknowledged his good sense in seeking a wife to suit his lifestyle. As for herself, she had no wish to fall in love again, with the chance of breaking her heart for the second time. On second thoughts, she acknowledged to herself that her heart couldn't have been broken, otherwise she wouldn't be considering the idea of marrying the professor. Rijk—she must remember to call him that.

Her parents had made no attempt to advise her, although they made it plain that they liked the professor; they also made it plain that she was old enough to make up her own mind, and George and Paul, when appraised of the situation, had given their opinions over the phone that he sounded a decent chap, and wasn't it about time she married anyway?

Sophie went back to St Agnes's with her mind very nearly, but not quite, made up, which was a good thing, because several busy nights in a row made it difficult for her to think of anything but her work and her bed.

Three days went by and there was no sign of the professor. There was no reason, she thought peevishly, why he couldn't have sent her a note at least, and surely he could have phoned her? She flounced out of the hospital with a cross, tired face, although she still managed to look beautiful.

The Bentley came smoothly into the forecourt as she crossed over, and the professor parked neatly and got out and strolled towards her.

His 'Good morning, Sophie' was cheerful, but she saw that he was tired.

She asked suspiciously, 'Have you just got here?' and then, remembering her manners, she said, 'Good morning, Rijk.'

'That is a most convenient ferry from Calais; even with delays on the motorway it still allows me time to reach you before you go to bed.'

He had a hand on her shoulder, urging her back to

the car. 'We will go and attend to Mabel and then we will breakfast together.'

'Yes, well—all right.' She got into the car with the pleasant feeling that she wouldn't need to bother about anything any more. Common sense warned her that this was a piece of nonsense, but she was too tired to argue with herself. She asked, 'Have you been to bed?'

'No.' He smiled suddenly at her, and all the tired lines vanished. 'I had too much to think about.'

He stopped outside Miss Phipps's house and got out to open her door. 'Ten minutes? I don't feel up to your landlady; I'll wait here.'

'I'll be quick…'

It was a chilly morning and Mabel most obligingly wasted no time on the tiny balcony but nipped back smartly to eat her breakfast.

'I'll be back quite soon,' Sophie promised. Without bothering to do anything to her face or hair, she hurried back to the car.

The professor was asleep, his face as calm and placid as a child's, and she went round the bonnet and stealthily opened her door. Without opening his eyes he said, 'You have been quick,' and was all at once alert and wide awake.

'I didn't mean to wake you,' said Sophie. 'Are you sure you wouldn't like to go to your house and go straight to bed?'

'We are going straight to my house. As for bed, that will come later. Breakfast first.'

Percy flung the door wide as they got out of the car and greeted them with a cheerful, 'Morning, guv, morning, miss. Mrs Wiffen's got a smashing breakfast laid on. 'Ad a good trip, 'ave you?'

The professor replied that indeed he had and took Sophie's coat and tossed it to Percy, who caught it and hung it tidily away in the hall closet.

'There's a pile of letters in the study, but you'll eat first, eh?'

'Yes, thank you, Percy. As soon as you can get the breakfast on the table.'

'Watch me,' said Percy, and whizzed away as the professor urged Sophie into the dining-room.

There was a bright fire burning and the table was laid invitingly with patterned china, gleaming silver and a blue bowl of oranges as its centre-piece. As they sat down Percy came in with a tray, coffee and tea and covered silver dishes which he arranged on the sideboard, and then made a second journey with the toast rack.

'Thank you, Percy,' said the professor. 'We'll ring if we want anything.' He got up to serve Sophie. 'Bacon? Eggs? A mushroom or two? A grilled tomato?'

Sophie, her mouth watering, said yes to everything, and, feeling that she should do her share, asked, 'Coffee or tea?'

'Coffee, please…'

She poured tea for herself and they sat in companionable silence, eating the good food, but when Percy appeared to take away their plates and bring fresh toast the professor said, 'Not too tired to talk?'

Sophie piled butter and marmalade on to a corner of toast. 'No, that was a lovely breakfast, thank you very much.'

He sat back in his chair, his eyes on her face. 'And

are we to share our breakfasts together, Sophie? You have had several days in which to decide. Bear in mind that I am impatient and like my own way, bad-tempered at times, too, although I have learnt to control it…'

'Are you trying to put me off?' asked Sophie. 'If you are it's too late, because I think I'd like to marry you.' She added diffidently, 'That's if you haven't changed your mind?'

He smiled at her across the table. 'No, Sophie, I made up my mind to marry you when I first saw you standing there in the middle of the pavement…'

She opened her eyes at that. 'You did? How could you possibly decide something like that so quickly?'

'I realised that I had at last found a girl who matched me in height and so I decided to snap you up.'

She looked at him uncertainly. 'You're joking, aren't you?'

He didn't answer, but got up and went and pulled her gently from her chair. 'I believe that we shall have a most satisfactory marriage,' he told her, and bent to kiss her—a quick, gentle kiss, so that she really didn't have time to enjoy it.

'I'll take you back now. I'm operating in the morning tomorrow; could you get up in time for tea? We can have it together; we have a great deal to talk about. When do you get nights off?'

'In four nights' time.'

'I may be in Bristol, but I'll come and see you at your home if your mother does not mind.' He thought for a moment. 'I shall be able to drive you home before I go.'

'There's no need,' began Sophie, and stopped when he said quietly,

'But I should like to, Sophie.'

He saw her to her door, remarking that he was unlikely to see her until her nights off, and drove away, leaving her to parry Miss Phipps's avid questions before she escaped upstairs to her room and Mabel's undemanding company.

Curled up in bed presently, nicely drowsy after her splendid breakfast, she admitted that she had been glad to see Rijk again. She thought it very likely that they might not see eye to eye about a number of things, but they weren't things which mattered. She looked forward to a well ordered and contented future, free from the anguish of falling in love and being rejected. She and Rijk were sensible, level-headed people prepared to make a success of a marriage based on friendship and a high regard for each other.

Upon which lofty and erroneous thoughts she went happily to sleep.

Two mornings later, when she was on her way to breakfast, she was asked to go to the office. She might leave, Matron told her graciously. Professor van Taak ter Wijsma had asked that the usual formalities of leaving might be overlooked, since he had to return to Holland shortly and was desirous of taking Sophie with him. Matron's features relaxed into a rare smile. 'I hope you will be very happy, Sister. The professor is a splendid man and very well liked here. He comes here frequently, as you know, so I hope that we shall see something of you from time to time.'

Sophie murmured suitably and got herself out of the room and started on the rambling passages which would take her to the canteen and breakfast. She didn't hurry; she had too much to think about, strolling along, contemplating her shoes while she viewed the future. Which meant that she didn't see Rijk until he stopped in front of her.

'Good morning, Sophie.' He appeared to be in no hurry. 'Have you been to the office yet?'

She nodded. 'Yes, just this minute. Matron was very nice; she said that I might leave whenever it was convenient for you…'

'And you,' he pointed out gravely. 'I shall be going back in five days' time; will you come with me and see what you think of Holland and my home? And if you feel you want to change your mind, no hard feelings, Sophie.'

He smiled then. 'You're on your way to breakfast, aren't you? And I'm expected in Theatre. I'll be outside on the day you leave. *Tot ziens*.'

She watched his vast back disappear down the corridor and hoped that *tot ziens* meant something nice like 'lovely to see you'. He had been rather businesslike, but probably he had his mind on his work…

She sat down at the breakfast-table, her mind full of all the things she had to do before she left, and the first one was to tell everyone at the table…

'I'm leaving in four days' time,' she announced during a pause in the talk, and, when they all looked at her in astonishment, hurried on, 'I didn't know until just now—it's been arranged specially. I'm going to marry Professor van Taak ter Wijsma and I'm going over to Holland to meet his family.'

The chorus of ohs and aahs was very gratifying; she was well liked, and only Gill looked disappointed, although she brightened presently. 'When you're married you can invite me to stay; there must be lots of people like him out there.'

Everyone laughed and then fell to congratulating Sophie and asking questions. She had to say that she didn't know to most of them. She wasn't even sure where Rijk was, only that he would be waiting for her when he had said.

There was so much to arrange; Mabel would have to be taken home while she was away, and she supposed that she would go home herself when they came back from visiting Rijk's home in Holland, and that would mean telling Miss Phipps. Unable to face that lady's curiosity, she stopped at a phone box on the way back to her flatlet and rang her mother.

Her parent's voice sounded pleased. 'I—your father too—think that you will be very happy; is there anything that you want me to do? It's rather short notice.'

'My passport—and would you just be a dear and look after Mabel? I've no idea where Rijk is, only that he said he'd see me on the day I leave. I'm leaving in four days' time. It's all a bit sudden, but he seems to have arranged things.'

'You're happy, love?'

'Yes, Mother. I'm a bit scared of meeting his family—all those sisters… Supposing they don't like me?'

'You're marrying Rijk, love, not his sisters. I'm sure it will be all right.'

Her mother's voice was reassuring.

She had very little time to make plans; the junior night sister was to take over from her and Staff Nurse Pitt was to be made junior night sister in her place. The three of them had been working together for a year or two, so there was little need to explain things to them. Sophie rushed through an inventory with one of the office sisters, staying behind after breakfast and going back to her room long after she should have been in bed, to find an indignant Mabel waiting for her and an inquisitive Miss Phipps, still unaware of her impending departure. Sophie, falling into bed, stayed awake long enough to decide that since Rijk was arranging everything with such speed he could deal with her landlady too.

He was waiting for her after her last night on duty. She had been and paid a last visit to Matron's office, said goodbye to her friends and also to Peter Small and Tim and the porters, and now, burdened by various farewell gifts, she went through the hospital doors for the last time.

The professor got out of his car and came to meet her. He took her packages and put them in the car and asked, 'What do you want to do first? We will be going over on the night ferry tomorrow; would it be a good idea if we go to your room and, while you collect Mabel and whatever you need, I'll see to Miss Phipps? I'll keep your room for a week or so so that when we get back you can come and pack up the rest of your things. That will give you the rest of today to sleep and put a few things in a case. I'll come for you tomorrow about six o'clock; we're going from Harwich…'

'You've thought of everything… How long will we be in Holland?'

'A week—I have to go to Leeds for a couple of days and then Athens. I'll bring you back here first; you'll want to be home for Christmas. I'm not sure how long I shall be there, but I'll come as soon as I can…'

'You'll be there for Christmas?'

'I rather think so.' He popped her into the car. 'But let us get you settled first before we discuss that.'

He was as good as his word and so Sophie, coming downstairs half an hour later with a hastily packed case and Mabel in her basket, found Miss Phipps waiting in the hall. The professor took her case from her and went out to the car and Miss Phipps said excitedly, 'Oh, my goodness, Sister, dear, what a romantic surprise—whoever would have thought it? Though I must say I did wonder… And don't worry about your flatlet; I'll keep it locked until you come back to get the rest of your things.' Her wig slipped a little to one side in her excitement. 'I don't know when I've had such a thrill.'

Sophie murmured suitably, assured her landlady that she would be back within a week or so, and bade her goodbye.

'You'll make a lovely bride,' breathed Miss Phipps as Sophie went out to the car.

The professor was leaning against the gate, looking relaxed. He was a man, Sophie reflected, who seemed to make himself comfortable wherever he was. He looked as though he hadn't an anxiety in the world. The thought reminded her that she hadn't either. She got into the car and he shut the door and got in beside her, glancing at his watch. 'Your mother said she would have coffee ready at eleven o'clock.' He turned to smile at her then and she thought how pleasant it was to feel so at ease with someone. At the same time it struck her that she was being swept along by his well laid plans even though never once had they caused her inconvenience or given her reason to grumble.

'Have you been up all night again?' she asked him sharply.

He slowed the Bentley at the traffic lights and glanced at her, smiling a little. 'You sound very wifely. I slept on the ferry.'

'I didn't mean to nag…'

'If that is nagging I rather liked it.'

Her mother was waiting for them, with coffee on the table and a large newly baked cake, and ten minutes later with Mabel sitting between the dogs, Mercury and Montgomery, before the Aga, they were sitting around the kitchen table.

'You'll stay for lunch?' asked Mrs Blount.

'I've one or two things to see to, Mrs Blount. I'll be here tomorrow evening to fetch Sophie—we're going over on the Harwich ferry and that will give me all day…'

'You couldn't spend Christmas with us?'

'I would have liked that. I shall be in Greece, although I shall do my best to get back to my home even if only for a day.'

'You poor man,' said Mrs Blount, and meant it.

He went presently, saying all the right things to her and giving Sophie a quick, almost brotherly kiss as he went.

'You are happy about marrying Rijk?' asked her mother as they went back indoors.

'We're not in love or anything like that, Mother. It's just that we… He wants a wife and we get on very well together and I do like him very much.' Sophie gave her mother a worried look. 'Rijk says that a good marriage depends on friendship and liking and that just falling in love isn't enough.' She filled their coffee-mugs again and sat down at the table. 'I've been afraid of falling in love ever since...'

'Yes, dear, I understand. As long as you aren't still in love—it is a long time ago.'

'I told Rijk I can't remember his face or anything about him, but I remember how I felt. I've been so careful to avoid getting too friendly with any of the men I've met. Somehow Rijk is different... I'm not explaining very well, am I?'

'No need, Sophie, dear. It seems to me that you are ideally suited to each other. Rijk is old and wise enough to know what he wants and so are you. I am quite sure that you will be happy together.'

Mrs Blount gave her daughter a loving look. The dear girl had no idea; it was a good thing that the professor was a man of patience and determination and that he had the ability to hide his feelings so successfully. Once they were married he would doubtless set about the task of making Sophie fall in love with him. She nodded her head and smiled, and Sophie, looking up, asked what was amusing her.

'I was thinking about a really splendid hat for your wedding, dear,' said her mother guilelessly. 'And, talking of hats, if you are not too tired, shall we go upstairs and look through your wardrobe? Pick out what you want to take with you and I'll get it pressed.'

A good deal of the rest of the day was taken up with the knotty problem of what to wear. Her Jaeger suit, Sophie decided; she could travel in it and it would look right during the day with a handful of blouses. A short dress for the evening—a rich mulberry silk, very plain with long sleeves and a straight skirt. And upon due reflection she added a midnight-blue velvet dress with a long skirt, very full, tiny sleeves and a low neckline.

'Take that jersey dress as well,' suggested her mother, so she added still another garment, dark green this time with a cowl neckline and a pleated skirt.

'It's bound to rain or snow or something,' said Sophie, and folded a quilted jacket with a hood, adding sensible shoes, thick gloves and a woolly cap, with the vague idea that Friesland sounded as though it might be cold in winter.

'I'll pack tomorrow,' she told her mother. 'Will Father be home for lunch?'

'Yes, dear, and this afternoon shouldn't you have a nap?'

She wasn't at all sleepy, Sophie decided, obediently curling up on her bed that afternoon; there was so much to think about. The next thing she knew was her mother's hand on her shoulder.

'A cup of tea, love, and supper will be about half an hour.'

She went to bed rather early, her hair washed, her face anointed with a cream guaranteed to erase all lines and wrinkles, determined to look her best for Rijk's family. It was to be hoped, she thought sleepily, that not all the five sisters would be there. And his brothers—would they be there too?

She fell asleep uneasily, suddenly beset by doubts.

There was no time for doubts the next day; there was the packing to do, the dogs to take for a walk, a last-minute anxious inspection of her handbag, and her father to drive to a nearby farm to attend a cow calving with difficulty. They got back home in time for tea and then it was time for her to go upstairs and dress for the journey. Rijk had said that he would come in the early evening, and she knew that the ferry sailed before midnight. The drive to Harwich wouldn't take much more than an hour, and her mother had supper ready.

He arrived while she was still in her room, studying her lovely face in the looking-glass, anxious that she should look her best, and, hearing the car and the murmur of voices in the hall, she hurried downstairs to find him, his overcoat off, sitting with her father. He got up as she went into the room and came to take her hand and give her a light kiss.

'I see that you are ready,' he observed. 'Your mother has kindly invited me to share your supper—we don't need to leave for an hour or so.'

'I'll go and help her,' said Sophie, suddenly anxious to be gone when only a few moments earlier she had been equally anxious to see him again. It was silly to feel shy with him; she supposed it was because she was excited about going to Holland. She joined her mother in the kitchen and carried plates of hot sausage rolls, jacket potatoes, mince pies and toasted sandwiches into the dining-room. There was coffee too and beer for the men, although the professor shook his head regretfully over that, at the same time embarking on a discussion with Mr Blount concerning the merits of various beers. Sophie, while glad that her father and Rijk got on so well together, couldn't help feeling a faint resentment at the professor's matter-of-fact manner towards her. After all, they were going to be married, weren't they? Surely he could show a little more interest in his future wife? Upon reflection, she had to admit that their marriage wasn't quite the romantic affair everyone, even Matron, had envisaged, and Rijk wasn't a man to pretend…

They left after a leisurely meal and the promise on Sophie's part that she would let her mother know that they had arrived safely.

'You can phone,' said the professor, 'during the morning.' He smiled at Mrs Blount. 'I'll take good care of her, Mrs Blount.'

Her mother leaned through the car window and kissed his cheek. 'I know that. Have a good trip and a happy week together.'

The ferry was half empty; they had more coffee and then parted for the night. 'I've told the stewardess to bring you tea and toast at six o'clock,' said Rijk. 'Sleep well, Sophie.'

It was rough on the crossing and, although she didn't feel seasick, she lay and worried, wishing that she had never agreed to meet his family, never agreed to marry him, for that matter, never allowed him to foster their friendship in the first place…

She drank her tea and ate the toast and dressed, somewhat restored in her spirits in the light of a grey overcast morning. She was looking out of the porthole when there was a knock on the door and the professor came in. He took a look at her face and flung an arm round her shoulders. 'You've been awake all night wishing you had never met me, never said that probably you will marry me, never agreed to come home with me.'

He gave her a sudden kiss, not at all like the swift

kisses he had given her, but hard and warm, and her spirits rose with it. 'Haven't you any doubts at all?' she asked him.

'Not one. We're about to dock. Come along, you'll feel better once we're on dry land.'

Strangely enough she did, relieved that her vague disquiet had melted away; she felt comfortable with him again, asking questions about the country that they were passing through.

'We'll stop for coffee,' he told her. 'It's about a hundred and forty miles to my home; we should be there soon after eleven o'clock. We shall be on the motorway for most of the time—not very interesting, I'm afraid, but quick.'

The road ahead was straight with no hills in sight, bypassing the towns and villages. Holland was exactly as she had pictured it: flat and green with a wide sky and far more built-up than she had expected.

'This is the busiest corner of the country,' Rijk explained. 'The further north we go, the fewer towns and factories. I think that you will like Friesland.'

They stopped for their coffee before they crossed the Afsluitdijk and by now, although it wasn't raining, there was a strong wind blowing, so that the water looked grey and cold.

The country had changed. They were across the *dijk* now and Rijk had taken a right-hand fork on to a motorway, passing Bolsward and circumventing Sneek before turning on to a country road. Villages were few and far between in the rolling countryside, but there were a few farmhouses, backed by huge barns, standing well apart from each other. In the distance a glimpse of water was visible.

'The sea?' asked Sophie, vague as to their direction.

'The lakes; Friesland is riddled with them. In the summer they're crowded with boats. That's Sneeker Meer you can see now. Presently we will go through a small town called Grouw, past more lakes. I live in a village well away from everywhere. We're going there first. Later we will go to my parents' home in Leeuwarden; that's only twelve miles or so.'

She was thankful to hear that. 'Will they be there? All your family?'

He gave her clasped hands on her lap a brief comforting squeeze.

'They will like you and you will like them.'

'Oh, I do so hope so. Is this Grouw?'

It was really a very large village on the edge of a small lake and with a small harbour. In the summer it would be delightful, she thought; even now on this grey day it was picturesque and the small houses looked cosy. There were a few shops too and a hotel by the harbour. She craned her neck to see as much as possible before the professor drove into a narrow road with another lake on one side and a canal on the other, to cross a narrow spit of land and turn north and presently back towards the shore of a much larger lake.

'This is the Prinsenhof lake—the village is called Eernewoude; I live just the other side of it. Very quiet in winter, but watersports in summer.'

'There aren't any hospitals near—doesn't it take you a long time to reach them?'

'We're still only twelve miles from Leeuwarden,

where I have beds, and Groningen is less than thirty miles—I have beds there too. I can reach the motorway to the south easily—Amsterdam is only a hundred miles and the Belgian-Dutch border another sixty miles or so.'

'Do you go abroad a lot? Other than England?'

'Fairly frequently.' They were driving slowly through the village—a handful of houses, a church, a small shop, and then a narrow brick road, the water on one side, a brick wall on the other, with great wrought-iron gates halfway along its length. They were open and a drive curved away, bordered by dense bushes and bare trees. The house was at the end of the curve and when Sophie saw it she took a sharp breath at the sight of it. She hadn't known what to expect, certainly not this imposing house of red brick and sandstone with its steep tiled roof, tall chimneys and square central tower surmounted by more tiles and an onion dome. It sheltered the vast door. The windows were long and narrow with painted shutters and to one side of the house there was what she took to be a moat.

The professor had stopped before his door and got out, opened her door and taken her arm.

He said in a comforting kind of voice, 'It's quite cosy inside.'

Sophie looked up at him. 'It's beautiful—I had no idea. I am longing to go in; I can't wait—and there's a dog barking…'

He smiled down at her excited face. 'Come inside and meet Matt.'

CHAPTER FIVE

SOPHIE AND RIJK climbed the shallow steps to the door together and it was opened as they reached it to allow a large shaggy dog to launch itself at the professor. Sophie prudently took a step back, for the animal was large and looked ferocious as well. The professor bore the onslaught with equanimity, bade the beast calm down, and drew Sophie forward.

'This is Matt. A bouvier. He'll be your companion, your devoted friend, and die for you if he has to.'

Sophie took off her glove and offered a balled fist and the beast sniffed at it and then rasped it with a great tongue. He had small yellow eyes and enormous teeth, but she had the impression that he was smiling at her. Indeed, he offered his head for a friendly scratch.

The man who had opened the door was as unlike Percy as it was possible to be, a powerfully built man with a slight stoop, grey hair and a round, weather-beaten face. The professor shook hands with him and clapped him on the shoulder and introduced him.

'This is Rauke, who looks after the house. His wife, Tyske, housekeeps and cooks; here she comes.'

Sophie shook hands with Rauke and then with the elderly woman who had joined them in the porch. She was as tall as Sophie, with a long face and grey hair and clear blue eyes. Her handshake was firm and she said something with a smile which Sophie hoped was a welcome.

The porch opened into a vestibule which in turn opened into the hall, square and white-walled, with a staircase facing the door, lighted by a long window on its half-landing. The ceiling was lofty and from it hung a brass chandelier, simple in design and, thought Sophie, very old. There was an elaborately carved side-table too and two great chairs arranged on either side of it. It was exactly like a Dutch interior, even to the black and white marble floor. Still gazing around her, she was led away by Tyske to a cloakroom under the staircase, equipped with every modern comfort. She had time to think while she did her face and tidied her hair, and back in the hall she said at once, 'You might have told me, Rijk.'

'What should I have told you?' He looked amused.

'Why, that you had such a grand house. I don't know what I expected, but it wasn't this.'

'It is my home,' he said simply, 'and it isn't grand—on the large side, perhaps, but I use all the rooms—not all the time, of course, but I live here, Sophie. Come and have a cup of coffee and presently we will go over it together.'

He ushered her through a double door into a room with windows overlooking the grounds at the back of the house. It was light by reason of the lofty ceiling and was furnished with sofas and easy-chairs arranged around the hooded fireplace, in which a fire burned briskly. The walls were panelled and hung with faded red silk and there were a great many paintings on them, mostly portraits. There were glass-fronted cabinets against the walls, filled with porcelain and silver, and a handsome Stoel clock hanging above the fireplace, and scattered around, with a nice regard for the convenience of the room's occupants, were small tables with elegant table lamps.

Matt came to meet them as they crossed to the fire and once they were seated facing each other he stretched out between them, breathing gusty sighs of content, one eye on the coffee-tray and the plate of biscuits beside it.

They drank their coffee in companionable silence broken only by the crunching of the biscuits the professor offered to Matt.

'He must miss you,' said Sophie.

'Oh, yes. He goes with me to Leeuwarden and Groningen, though. He will be delighted to have your company while I'm away.'

'You don't have to go away?'

The dismay on her face made him say at once, 'No, no. I was talking of when we are married.' He put down his coffee-cup and sat back at his ease. 'We have a whole week to be together, Sophie.'

And at the uncertain look on her face, 'My mother and father will come back here and stay with us for a week. They have many friends living around here; they will be out every day.' He grinned suddenly. 'You see how careful I am to observe the proprieties—unnecessary in this day and age, but we're a strait-laced lot in Friesland.'

Sophie, with a slightly heightened colour, looked him in the eye. 'I'm strait-laced too.'

'Which strengthens my argument that we are very well suited.'

He got up and Matt got up with him. 'Would you like to see the house?'

They crossed the hall with Matt keeping pace with them, and the professor opened a door on its opposite side. 'The dining-room,' he told her, 'but when I'm on my own I use a smaller room at the back of the house. I have asked Rauke to set lunch there for us.'

It was a splendid room; she could imagine a dinner party sitting around the rectangular table, decked no doubt with silver and crystal, and with the wall sconces sending a flattering glow on the women guests. There was a sideboard along one wall with flanking pedestal cupboards surmounted by urns and several large oil-paintings hung on the walls; a second door led to a smaller room—a kind of ante-room, she supposed. In turn it opened into a room at the back of the house with doors opening on to the terrace from which steps led to wide lawns and flowerbeds. It was a charming room, furnished with easy-chairs and a circular table; there was a television set in one corner and bookshelves and a dear little writing-table in another corner. There was a bright fire burning here and the professor declared, 'This is one of my favourite rooms—we shall lunch here, just the two of us.'

He opened a door beside the windows. 'This is the library.' It was a splendid room with enormous desks at each end of it, leather chairs arranged around small tables, and shelves of books.

'One more room,' he observed and led her through a

door into the hall again and opened a door close to the staircase. 'My study.'

It was austerely furnished with a partners' desk, a vast leather chair behind it, a couple of smaller chairs facing it and again shelves of books. There was a computer, too, an electric typewriter and an answering machine all arranged on a smaller table under the two long windows.

'I have a secretary who comes three or four times a week and sees to my letters.' He flipped over the pile of correspondence on his desk. 'Let us go upstairs.'

The staircase was of oak with a wrought-iron balustrade with a half-landing from where it branched to the gallery above. It was quiet there, their footsteps deadened by the thick carpet as he led her to the front of the house. There were a pair of rather grand double doors here and he opened them on to a beautiful room, the vast bed and furniture of satin wood, the curtains and bedspread of ivory and rose brocade. Sophie rotated slowly, looking her fill.

'What a beautiful room. You have a lovely home, Rijk—it's a bit big, but it's so—lived-in.'

'I'm glad you like it. Come this way.' He opened a door to a bathroom which led in turn to a smaller bedroom and then into the corridor.

There were passages leading to the back of the house and he led her down each one in turn, opening doors so that she might look at each room before going up a smaller flight of stairs to the floor above.

The rooms were smaller here but just as comfortably furnished, and right at the end of one passage there was a large, airy room with bars at the windows and a high fireguard before the big stove. There was a rocking-horse under the windows and a doll's house on one of the numerous shelves. Sophie wondered what toys the closed cupboards held.

'Your nanny must have had a busy time,' she observed. 'You and your brothers and sisters...'

'She stood no nonsense and we all loved her dearly. You shall meet her later on—she has her own rooms in my parents' house. The night nurseries are through there as well as a room for Nanny and a little kitchen. We spent a great deal of time with my mother and father—we all had a very happy childhood.'

They were back in the passage with Matt, breathing heavily with pleasure, at their heels when a gong sounded from below. 'Lunch,' said the professor. 'There's still another floor, but we can look at that later on.'

They talked about nothing much as they ate; the professor steadfastly refused to allow Sophie to ask questions of a personal nature and since she was hungry and the leek soup, bacon fritters and assortment of vegetables were very much to her taste she didn't much mind.

It was like being in a dream, she reflected, pouring coffee for them both; any minute she would wake up and find herself back in the accident room at St Agnes's...

They got into the car presently with Matt crouching in the back, poking his great head between them from time to time and giving great gusty sighs.

'Does he like cats?' asked Sophie.

'I have been told over and over again by well meaning people that he would kill any cat he saw. He takes no notice of them at all; indeed, he is on the best of terms with Tyske's Miep and her kittens, and Miep doesn't care tuppence for him.'

They were on the motorway now, racing towards Leeuwarden, and Sophie stared out of the window, a bundle of nerves.

Without looking at her, the professor began a rambling conversation about Matt which needed no replies and which lasted until he slowed the car to drive through the heart of Leeuwarden. The afternoon was darkening already and the shops were lighted, decked for Christmas, and the pavements were thronged with shoppers, but she didn't have much chance to look around her for Rijk turned away from the main streets and drove through narrow ways lined with tall old houses and then into a brick street beside a canal with a line of great gabled houses facing it. He stopped before one of them.

'Here we are,' he told her.

The man who opened the door to them was elderly, tall and thin, but very upright. He greeted the professor with a dignified, 'A pleasure to see you, Mr Rijk, sir,' and Rijk shook his hand and clapped him on the shoulder.

'How are you, Clerkie? Sophie, this is Clerk, who runs this place for my father and mother—has done for as long as I can remember—taught me to fish and swim and ride a bike—taught us all, in fact.'

Sophie put out a hand and he went on, 'Miss Sophie Blount, my guest for a week. Anyone at home?'

Clerk's calm features broke into a smile. 'Everyone, sir.' He gave Sophie a fatherly look. 'Shall I take Miss Blount's coat? And would she wish to arrange her hair and so forth?'

The professor turned to study her. 'Not a hair out of place and the face looks much as usual. You'll do, Sophie.' He took her arm and crossed the square hall with Clerk's figure slightly ahead to open the door on one side of it.

The room was large, with a high ceiling and enormous windows stretching from ceiling to floor; it was also full of people, children and dogs.

As they went in the loud murmurs of conversation stopped and there was a surge towards them with cries of 'Rijk' and a babble of talk Sophie couldn't understand, but the next minute she found herself face to face with the professor's parents, his arm tucked comfortably under hers.

At first glance Mevrouw van Taak ter Wijsma looked formidable, but that was by reason of her height and well corseted stoutness. A second glance was more reassuring; her blue eyes, on a level with Sophie's, were kind and the smile on her still handsome face was sweet. She was dressed elegantly, her grey hair swept into an old-fashioned coil on top of her head, her twin set and skirt very much in the same style as that of Sophie's mother. It was silly that such a small thing should have put Sophie at her ease.

The professor's father was still a very handsome man with white hair and dark eyes. He kissed Sophie's cheek and welcomed her with a warmth she hadn't expected, before Rijk led her around the room. His five sisters were there, and so were their husbands, their children and a variety of dogs; moreover, his two brothers were there too. She shook hands and smiled and forgot all their names the moment they were said, but that didn't seem to matter in such an atmosphere of friendliness. As for the children, they clung to their uncle, offered small hands and cheeks for a kiss and took her for granted. So did the dogs—two Labradors, a Jack Russell and a small whiskery creature with melting eyes. His name was Friday, she was told, and when she asked why one of the older children said in English, 'That was the day Daddy found him.' They asked, 'We have cats; do you?'

'Well, yes, I have a cat of my own; she's called Mabel.'

'Good, you will bring her here when you marry Uncle Rijk?'

'Well, yes. You speak very good English…'

'We have a nanny. When you and Oom Rijk have babies you will also have a nanny.'

The conversation was getting rather out of hand; she looked round for Rijk and caught his eye and he broke off the conversation with his father and made his way to her. 'Is Timon practising his English? He's Tiele's eldest son—she's the one in the green dress. Three boys so far, but they'd like a daughter… Come and talk to Loewert. He's at Leiden in his last year.'

He was a younger edition of Rijk and brimming over with the wish to be friendly. He obligingly took her round the room once more and told her all the names once again so that by the time they had all settled round the room drinking tea and eating fragile little biscuits she could pick out various members of the family for herself. Rijk's mother, sitting beside her on one of the massive sofas, was carrying on the kind of conversation which didn't need much thought, telling her little snippets of information about the family.

'We are such a large family,' she observed, 'and I am sure that Rijk quite forgot to tell you about us. He is immersed in his work—too much so, I consider.' She smiled at Sophie. 'You will alter that, I hope, my dear.'

Sophie, watching him talking to his brothers at the other end of the room, wondered if she would. It seemed unlikely.

Presently they got up to go. Rijk's parents went away to get their hats and coats, Matt was coaxed away from the garden where he had been romping with the other dogs, and Sophie began a round of goodbyes. She hadn't known about the Dutch kissing three times; by the time she had bidden goodbye to everyone in the room she felt quite giddy. She must remember to ask Rijk about it; he had never kissed her three times. Indeed, his kisses had been few and far between and then brief…

The elders of the party got into the back of the Bentley with Matt, and Sophie found herself sitting by Rijk, and really, she thought a little crossly, I've hardly seen him all afternoon.

He seemed unaware of her coolness, though, talking about his family in a desultory way until they reached his house and once they were there seeing to his parents' comfort, handing them over to Rauke, and then walking her off to the small sitting-room at the back of the house.

'There's half an hour before we need to change,' he told her. 'Come and have a drink and tell me what you think of my family.'

'They are very nice,' said Sophie inadequately. 'I haven't quite sorted them out yet…'

'Time enough to do that,' he said cheerfully. 'Would you like a glass of sherry? We'll meet in the drawing-room just before dinner, but I think you deserve a drink; the family like you.'

'Supposing they hadn't liked me?'

He shrugged huge shoulders. 'That would make no difference as far as I'm concerned.'

He turned away to pour the sherry and she said on impulse, 'Have you ever been in love, Rijk?'

He put the drink down beside her and settled into a chair opposite hers.

'Several times! If you mean the fleeting romances we are all prone to from time to time. But if you are doubtful as to any future entanglements of that nature on my part, I can assure you that I have long outgrown them.'

Once started she persisted. 'But you do believe in people falling in love and—and loving each other?'

'Certainly I do. For those fortunate enough to do both.' He added softly, 'Cold feet, Sophie?'

'No, no.' She blushed a little under his amused gaze. 'I was just being curious; I didn't mean to pry.'

'I'm glad we're good friends enough to be able to ask each other such questions.'

'Yes, well, so am I. I think I'd better go up and change…'

'I must take a quick turn in the garden with Matt. We'll meet again in the drawing-room.'

He got up with her and opened the door and stood watching her as she crossed the hall and started up the staircase. Sophie, aware of that, felt self-conscious, which wasn't like her at all.

She wore the mulberry silk; it suited her well and, studying her reflection in the pier glass, she felt tolerably satisfied with her appearance. She hadn't been quite sure what to wear, but somehow Rijk's mother looked the kind of lady to follow the conventions of her younger days. She was glad that she had decided to wear it when she entered the drawing-room, for Mevrouw van Taak ter Wijsma was in black crêpe, cut with great elegance, and a fitting background for the double row of pearls she was wearing. As for the men, they wore dark grey suits and ties of subdued splendour, so that Sophie felt that she was dressed exactly as she ought to be and heaved a small sigh of relief, noticed with the ghost of a smile by Rijk.

The evening was pleasant; the dinner was superb: mushrooms in garlic, roast duck with an orange sauce, lemon syllabub and a *bombe glacée* to finish.

Getting up from the table, Sophie wondered if the meal was a sample of the week ahead. If so, she would have to take long walks or do exercises in her room each morning.

She didn't have to worry about the exercises; the next morning Rijk took her walking and she was glad of the sensible shoes and a thick woolly under the Jaeger jacket, for the weather was cold and the sky grey with a wind which hinted at snow later on. He took her briskly round the grounds and then down to the village beyond, with Matt prancing along beside them. As they walked he talked about his home and the life he led.

'I am away a good deal,' he told her, 'you know that

already, but I come home whenever I can. Of course, if you wish you can accompany me to England when I go and visit your parents while I am working. You won't be lonely if you stay here; the family will see to that, and besides, you will soon make friends.'

It seemed to her that he was making it clear that he didn't want her with him while he travelled away from home. Reasonable enough, she supposed, it wasn't as though he was head over heels in love with her; theirs was to be a placid, well mannered marriage with no strong feelings, and she supposed that was what she wanted. She had told him that, hadn't she? He had taken her at her word, no doubt content to have found a woman who had the same attitude to marriage as he had.

They walked until lunchtime and had that meal together, for his mother and father had gone to visit neighbouring friends and wouldn't be back until the evening. When they had finished Rijk asked her if she would like to go with him to his study while he looked over the notes on several cases he had been asked to deal with. She was surprised, but settled down in a comfortable leather chair by the window with a pile of magazines, while Matt got under the desk at his master's feet.

The room was pleasantly warm and very quiet and she took care not to speak, even when she glanced out of the window and saw the first snowflakes falling, and presently she had her reward, for the professor closed his case papers and leaned back in his chair. 'How restful you are, Sophie; I'm sure you were longing to tell me that it was snowing...'

'Well, yes, I was, but I know how annoying it is

when you're studying something or writing a report and someone keeps talking in hushed tones or sighing.'

'I can see we're ideally suited. Come and have tea; you deserve a whole pot to yourself.'

His parents came back presently and they dined and spent the rest of the evening sitting in the drawing-room. Mevrouw van Taak ter Wijsma made no bones about questioning Sophie, in the nicest possible way, about her life and home. Sophie answered readily enough; if she were a mother, even if her son were an adult well able to look after his own interests, she felt sure that she would want to know as much as possible about a future daughter-in-law.

Rijk followed her out into the hall when she and his mother went to bed. 'Shall we walk again in the morning?' he asked her. 'I'm going to Leeuwarden after lunch; perhaps you would like to come with me? You can look around the shops while I am at the hospital.'

She agreed readily, and presently, in bed and half asleep, began on a list of presents she would take home with her. She was asleep before it was even half finished.

They walked away from the village in the morning, taking a narrow cart track which wound round the shores of the lake, and Sophie, muffled in her coat and with her head swathed in a cashmere scarf of Rijk's, was glad of them, for the wind was cutting and the snow, long ceased, had frozen on the ground. Looking around her, she had to admit that the scenery was bleak, and yet she liked it. Which, she conceded silently, was a good thing if she were to marry Rijk. She hadn't made up her mind yet, she reminded herself, despite his cool assumption that their marriage was a foregone conclusion.

Even while she thought about it, she knew in her heart of hearts that she would marry him; he would be a good husband, kind and considerate and undemanding, and more than anything else she wanted the security and contentment which he had offered her. Romance, she had decided wistfully, wasn't for her. Her only taste of it had turned sour; far better settle for a comfortable relationship.

He drove her to Leeuwarden in the afternoon, set her down in the centre of the shopping centre, close to the ancient Weigh House, told her that he would wait there for her at four o'clock, and drove himself off to the hospital.

Left to herself, Sophie studied the shop windows and presently made a few purchases. Cigars for her father, a Delft blue vase for her mother, a thick slab of chocolate for Tom and, after a lengthy search, a book on Friesland for George, who was a bookworm, and a pen and pencil set for Paul. She could have bought that in England, but at least it was in a Dutch box and the description was in that language, which made it rather different.

By then it was getting on for four o'clock and she made her way back to the Weigh House and found Rijk waiting. He took her parcels from her, settled her in the car and got in beside her. 'You found shopping easy enough?' he wanted to know.

'Well, yes; once or twice I got a bit muddled, but almost everyone speaks English. Did you have a busy afternoon?'

'An unusual case…' He began to tell her about it and

she listened with intelligence and real interest, so that he observed, 'How delightful it is to discuss my work with someone who knows what I'm talking about and is really interested.'

Which gave Sophie a gentle glow of pleasure.

The next day he put her in the car and took her on a sightseeing tour of Friesland. North first, to Dokkum, where they had coffee at a nice old-fashioned hotel by the canal, and then on to the coast and the Waddenzee, bleak and cold, with a distant view of the islands, looking lonely beyond the dull grey sea.

'Do people live there?' asked Sophie.

'Good heavens, yes. In summer they swarm with holiday-makers. They're very peaceful out of season; there are bird sanctuaries and beautiful beaches. We will go in early spring and you shall see for yourself.'

He drove south again along narrow brick roads built on their dikes, bypassed Leeuwarden, and stopped in Franeker, where they had a lunch of *erwtensoep*, a thick pea soup, rich with pieces of sausage and pork, followed by smoked eel on toast—the kind of food, Rijk assured Sophie, which kept the sometimes very cold winter at bay.

They sat over their coffee until a watery sun decided him that it would be worth going down the coast to Hindeloopen and Staveren before turning for home.

Even on a winter's day, Hindeloopen was charming. They walked along the sea wall before driving on to Staveren, which disappointed her so much that Rijk drove inland to Sloten; the sixteenth-century charm of the tiny town more than made up for the unattractiveness of Staveren.

It was dusk as they arrived back at the house, and the windows glowed with light. The professor got out and opened Sophie's door as Rauke, already on the porch, stood back to allow Matt to hurl himself at his master, and she stood quietly, looking around her.

In the fast-gathering dark the house looked beautiful and a little awe-inspiring. There was already a touch of frost on the lawn before it and the trees surrounding it were rustling and sighing. She wondered how long they had been standing there, guarding the house. After her happy and contented day she felt suddenly uncertain; if it hadn't been for Rauke standing there in the cold waiting for them to go inside she would have unburdened herself to Rijk there and then; as it was she went into the house and allowed Rijk to take her coat before she went to her room to tidy her hair and do things to her face. It glowed with the cold air and her eyes sparkled, but it didn't mirror her feelings. She went down to the sitting-room, where the professor was waiting for her, the tea-tray with its shining silver and delicate china already on the sofa table.

Much though she wanted a cup of tea, she had made up her mind to say what she had to say first. She began at once. 'Rijk…'

He looked up from the letters he was glancing through and studied her face. 'Something is worrying you, Sophie?'

'Yes, how did you know?'

He said quietly, 'We are friends—close friends—are we not, my dear?'

'Yes, oh, yes, we are. I'm a bit worried. You see, I didn't know about all this.' She waved a hand around her at the understated comfort and luxury around them. 'I knew you were a very successful man; I supposed that you would have a nice house in Holland and be—well, comfortably off. But this is different. Are you very rich?'

His firm mouth twitched. 'I'm afraid so. I can only plead that a good deal of my wealth is the result of no doubt ill gotten gains from my merchant ancestors.'

She nodded like a child, glad to have had something explained. 'Yes, I see. You don't think that I am marrying you for your money, Rijk?'

He said gently, 'No, Sophie, I don't think that.'

'Because I'm not. Money's nice to have, isn't it? But it isn't as important as other things. If—if I say I'll marry you it wouldn't make any difference to me if you were on the dole.'

He crossed the room to where she was still standing and took both her hands in his, bent his head, and kissed her. A gentle kiss, as gentle as his voice had been. It reassured her so that she said, 'Well, that's all right, then, isn't it?'

'Perfectly all right. Come and pour the tea and I'll tell you what I have to do tomorrow.'

He was going to Brussels to examine some highly connected man with a suspected brain tumour. 'I shall be away all day. Mother and Father would like you to go with them on a visit to my grandmother—she lives in Heerenveen—for lunch and tea. I hope to be back in time for dinner.'

'You aren't going to drive all that way there and back?' She sounded, did she but know it, like an anxious wife, and he smiled.

'No, I shall fly. I have a light plane I use from time to time.'

'You can fly as well?'

'It saves a great deal of time. Do you drive a car, Sophie?'

'Oh, yes. I take Father round when I'm home; my brothers taught me.'

'Good; we are a little isolated here, but if you have a car you will be able to go where and when you like.' And at her anxious look, he added, 'When I am not at home.'

In bed that night, reviewing her day, she knew that she would marry Rijk. He had, of course, all this time behaved as though she had already agreed to do so, although she was aware that he was prepared to wait for her answer when they got back to England. Her mind made up, there was no point in staying awake; she slept dreamlessly and never heard the plane's engines from a nearby field as Rijk flew off to Brussels.

She was disappointed to find him gone when she went down to breakfast, but, his parents being at the table too, she had no time to brood over that. Bidden to be ready by ten o'clock, she took Matt for a walk in the grounds and joined them in the hall. Rijk's father drove an elderly, beautifully maintained Daimler, and Sophie had expected to be taken at a gentle speed to Heerenveen, but the elderly doctor drove with a speed sometimes alarming on the narrow roads, and since his wife, sitting with Sophie in the back, appeared to find this quite normal, Sophie said nothing, but watched the rolling countryside and made suitable replies to her companions' friendly talk.

Heerenveen was rather nice, she decided as their driver at last slowed down to go through the town and take a narrow road which presently revealed a small lake. Old Mevrouw van Taak ter Wijsma lived in a fair-sized square house close to the water, with a sprinkling of small houses along the road, cared for by several devoted servants. She went out seldom, but kept a sharp eye on her numerous family. She was a tall old lady, very thin, with a high bridged nose and bright blue eyes, dressed in black with a great many gold chains, and she received them in a room overlooking the lake, furnished with old-fashioned heavy furniture, its small tables covered by photos in silver frames, and great cabinets along its walls loaded with beautiful porcelain. She offered a cheek to her son and daughter-in-law and then studied Sophie at some length.

'So you're the girl that Rijk intends to marry. At least you match him with height. Nice-looking too. You'll make him a good wife, no doubt.'

Sophie murmured suitably; there seemed no point in explaining that she hadn't actually said that she would marry Rijk and didn't intend to until he asked her if her mind was made up. She was told to sit by the old lady and spent the next hour making the right replies to that lady's questions.

Lunch was a solemn, long-drawn-out meal and afterwards, their hostess retiring for a brief nap, Sophie was invited to look round the house with Rijk's mother, and by the time they had peered into a great many rather gloomy rooms it was time to join the old lady for milkless tea and very small biscuits.

Presently they drove back to Rijk's home, his father,

doubtless pleased at having been able to leave before it was quite dark, driving with a carefree speed which set Sophie's neat head of hair on end.

Rijk was home and came to help his mother and Sophie out of the car while Matt got in everyone's way. As they went indoors he took Sophie's arm.

'And did you like Granny?' he asked. She nodded. 'She's a darling...'

He paused in the hall so that for a moment they were alone. 'She phoned just now; she says you're a darling too.'

For a moment Sophie thought that he would kiss her, but he didn't; he only smiled.

CHAPTER SIX

THERE WERE ONLY two days left. Sophie went down to breakfast in the morning wondering if Rijk had any plans.

He had: a walk down to the village to meet the dominie and look round the church and then, since it was a clear, cold day, a walk along the lakeside to an outlying farm which he owned. 'And in the afternoon, if you would like, we will drive to Groningen and take a look round—there's a rather splendid church and the university.'

On the way to the village presently he told her that they would go back to his parents' house on the following day, lunch there, and then come back and have an early dinner before driving down to the Hoek to catch the night ferry.

Sophie agreed cheerfully, thankful that she had bought her presents when they had gone to Leeuwarden. 'Do phone your people if you would like to,' went on Rijk. 'We should be back around nine o'clock.'

'Would you like to stay? There's plenty of room—Mother will expect you for lunch, I'm sure.'

'Lunch, by all means, but I've a consultation in the afternoon and I'm operating on the following day and then going to Leeds for a couple of days…'

'But it's almost Christmas…'

'Which I shall have to spend away from home—I did tell you.'

'I forgot. So we can't see each other for a while?'

'No.' He tucked a hand under her elbow. 'May I come and see you on my way home?' He smiled at her. 'Life is one long rush, isn't it?'

'In four days' time? You want to know…'

She paused and he said easily, 'Yes, please, Sophie.'

The dominie was a bearded giant of a man. His wife, fair-haired and blue-eyed, offered coffee and took Sophie to see the youngest of their children, a calmly sleeping baby. 'The other three are at school. You like children?'

'Yes,' said Sophie and blushed when her companion said cheerfully,

'Of course, Rijk will want a family.'

They went round the church when they had had coffee, a severely plain edifice with whitewashed walls and small latticed windows. A number of Rijk's ancestors were buried beneath its flagstoned floor and even more in the small churchyard. His family had lived there for a very long time—centuries.

Presently they said goodbye to the dominie and his wife and took a rough little lane skirting the lake. It was very quiet there and they walked briskly, arm in arm, stopping now and then while he pointed out some thing of interest, telling her about the people and the country round them. Presently they came to the farm, a flat dwelling with a tiled and thatched roof, its huge barn at its back. 'The cows live there throughout the winter,' explained Rijk. 'Come inside with me and meet Wendel and Sierou.'

The farmer was middle-aged and powerfully built and his wife was almost as stoutly built as he was. After the first polite greetings, Rijk murmured an apology and carried on the conversation in Friese. Dutch is bad enough, reflected Sophie, Friese is far worse; but she enjoyed sitting there in the vast kitchen, drinking more coffee and listening to Rijk's quiet voice and the farmer's rumbling replies.

They got up to go presently and walked back the way they had come, and over lunch presently the talk had been of a variety of matters, none of them personal. Rijk's parents had been out too and lunched with them, but they didn't linger over the meal since they were to drive to Groningen.

Rijk cut through to the motorway from Drachten to Groningen, a journey of twenty-five miles or so, which, while quick, missed a good deal of the smaller villages. 'We shall come home through the side-roads,' he promised her.

The city delighted her. The old houses lining the canals were picturesque and the fifteenth-century old St Martinkerk was magnificent. 'A pity the tower is closed for the winter,' observed the professor. 'It is three hundred and fifteen feet high; a splendid climb.'

'I don't like heights,' said Sophie baldly.

The university was a fairly modern building, its thousands of students each wearing a coloured cap to denote his or her faculty, and since the professor knew several of the lecturers there they were allowed to wander around while he patiently answered Sophie's questions.

Presently he took her to a restaurant on the Gedempte Zuiderdiep and, while they drank their coffee, explained the layout of the city to her. 'Of course you can see very little of it in such a short time, but we will come again.'

She let that pass. 'Do you come to the hospitals here as well?'

'From time to time, but of course Leeuwarden is my home territory.'

Since they had finished their coffee he took her to the Prinsenhof Gardens, which even in winter were beautiful.

True to his promise, they drove back along country roads, taking a roundabout route which went through several small villages. It was already dusk but the sky was clear and there were still a few golden rays from the setting sun. The villages looked cosy and there were lighted windows in the farms they passed. There was little traffic, but they were held up from time to time by slow-moving farm carts, drawn by heavy horses. 'I like this,' said Sophie.

'So do I; this is Friesland, how I think of it when I'm away.'

Rauke, without being asked, brought in the tea-tray as soon as Sophie joined Rijk in the drawing-room. It was already five o'clock, well past the normal tea hour, but all the professor said was, 'We will dine later—there is no hurry this evening.' He said something to Rauke, who murmured a reply and went soft-footed from the room.

The tea was hot and quite strong. Sophie, when she had first arrived, had expected Earl Grey or orange pekoe—it was that kind of a house, she had decided—

so it was delightful to find that the tea in the lovely old silver pot was the finest Assam. It hadn't occurred to her that the professor—a perfectionist in all he did—had taken the trouble to find out her preference. There were tiny sandwiches too and fairy cakes and a plate of biscuits which Matt was allowed to enjoy, leaning his furry bulk against his master, delighted to have them home again.

'He will miss you,' observed Sophie, sinking her nice white teeth into a fairy cake.

'Indeed, as I shall miss him. And you, Sophie, will you miss me?'

He was watching her intently and she wished that she knew how to give him a light-hearted answer which promised nothing. After all, he might be joking…

A quick glance at his impassive face made it clear that he wasn't joking; she said simply, 'Yes, I shall. I like being with you, Rijk.'

When he smiled she went on impulsively, 'And there is no need to wait…'

The door opened and his mother came into the room and Rijk got up, to all intents and purposes delighted to see her. Sophie, on the very brink of telling him that she would marry him, wondered if it was a sign of some sort to make her change her mind at the last minute.

As for the professor, there was nothing in his manner to indicate whether he regretted the interruption; his mother sat down, declaring that they had had a cup of tea an hour or more ago. 'I am very fond of your aunt Kinske, but she serves a poor cup of tea; she should speak to her cook.' She turned to Sophie. 'You enjoyed your afternoon, Sophie?'

Sophie said that yes, she had and added that she liked the villages they had driven through.

'Not at all like your own countryside, though,' Rijk's mother commented. 'I shall enjoy looking around me when we come to your wedding.'

Sophie opened her mouth to speak, caught Rijk's eye, and closed it again. He wasn't smiling, but she knew that he was amused. She went rather red and Mevrouw van Taak ter Wijsma, thinking that she was blushing for quite another reason, nodded her head in a satisfied manner.

Really, thought Sophie, they all take it for granted and I haven't even said… She remembered what she had been on the point of saying only a short time ago and made some trivial remark about the English countryside without mentioning a wedding. The professor's lips twitched and his mother thought what a nice girl Sophie was, and so exactly right for her eldest son.

The rest of the day passed pleasantly enough, but Sophie had no opportunity to speak to Rijk alone, even if she had wanted to, and, as she told herself in bed later on, she hadn't wanted to. What a good thing his mother had joined them when she had, although it would have been interesting to see what he would have done or said. He wouldn't do anything, she reflected peevishly, probably shake hands—wasn't that what friends did when they agreed to do something together? She bounced over in bed and thumped the big square pillow, feeling put out and not sure why.

She felt better in the morning; after all, she was doing what she wanted: marrying someone who shared her ideas of married life as well as a mistrust of romantic nonsense, which led only to unhappiness. She went down to breakfast with a cheerful face.

They drove to Leeuwarden later in the morning, to be joined by all five of Rijk's sisters at his parents' house, although, rather to Sophie's relief, the husbands and the children were absent. As were his brothers.

'You will see them all at the wedding,' said Mevrouw van Taak ter Wijsma in a consoling voice. She didn't appear to expect an answer, which was a good thing, for Sophie hadn't been able to think of one.

They sat over lunch; the talk was all of Christmas and the New Year and there was a good deal of sympathy for Rijk, although Tiele said, 'Next year will be different, Rijk. We'll have a marvellous family house party at your place; we can come over for the day and you can put up the rest of us.' She glanced at Sophie, 'You have brothers, haven't you, Sophie? And parents. What a splendid time we'll have…'

Sophie smiled and the professor sat back in his chair, saying nothing and looking wicked. He had put her in a very awkward position, fumed Sophie, and she would make no bones about telling him so.

Her chance came as they drove back to his home. The goodbyes had been protracted and affectionate; she had been thoroughly kissed and warmly hugged and Rijk's father had taken her hands in his and told her that Rijk would make her happy. 'I shouldn't boast of my own children, but I am sure that you will suit each other very well, and that,' he had added deliberately, 'is just as important as loving someone.'

She remembered that now, peeping at Rijk's calm

profile. 'Your family seem to have made up their minds that we are to marry...'

He said easily, 'Yes, indeed. What did you think of Nanny?'

It was a successful red herring. 'Oh, she's an old darling, isn't she? A bit peppery but I can quite see why you have such an affection for her.' She paused, remembering her brief visit to the old lady, sitting cosily in the sitting-room leading from the kitchen, surrounded by dozens of photos of her charges. The room had been most comfortably furnished and Sophie had seen the bedroom leading from it.

'She wanted to be there,' explained Rijk, 'within sound of the kitchen, and of course people are popping in and out all the time so that it never gets lonely. Mother quite often has coffee with her.'

Sophie remembered that she was annoyed with him. 'You could have explained—' she began.

'No need.' He sounded placid. 'If you should decide against marrying me, then that is time enough to explain.'

'Will you be annoyed if I do that?'

'Annoyed?' He considered the question. 'Why? I thought I had made it clear that you were free to make up your mind; you are surely old and wise enough to do that.'

That nettled her. 'How well you put it,' she said peevishly.

He ignored the peevishness. 'Will you mind having your tea on your own? I still have some work to clear and we must dine early. We need to leave here around half-past seven—if we dine at half-past six? Will that suit you?'

'Yes, of course. I've only a few things left to pack.' Her ill humour had vanished; indeed, upon reflection, she wasn't quite sure why she had felt so cross in the first place.

They went on board the ferry with little time to spare, but that, she realised, was what Rijk had intended, taking Matt for a last-minute romp in the dark, cold grounds, bidding Rauke and Tyske a leisurely goodbye, and then racing smoothly through the dark evening, over the Afsluitdijk and down the motorway until they reached the Hoek with just sufficient time to go on board before the ferry sailed.

Sophie, who had watched the clock worriedly for the last fifteen minutes or so, realised that she had been anxious about nothing. Rijk was a man who knew exactly what he was doing, and she had no need to fuss. The thought was reassuring as she curled up in her bunk and went to sleep.

Her mother was waiting for them as they stopped outside her home the next morning. The door was flung wide to allow Monty and Mercury to rush out to greet them, closely followed by the lady of the house. They drank their coffee in a flurry of talk, although the professor said little.

'You must be tired,' said Mrs Blount. 'Are you sure you can't stay?'

'Quite sure, I'm afraid. I must go to St Agnes's this afternoon, but I'll come in four—no, three—days, if I may.'

'You're always welcome.' Mrs Blount gave his

massive shoulder a motherly pat. 'Arthur will be back presently. You can have a nice chat while you unpack, Sophie, and I can get on with lunch.'

So Sophie had little chance to be alone with Rijk, and she wasn't sure if she was glad about that or not; certainly he gave no sign of annoyance at the lack of opportunity to be with her and presently, after lunch, when he took his leave, his placid, 'I'll see you in three days, Sophie,' and the peck she received on her cheek hardly stood for any eagerness on his part to have more of her company.

The car was barely out of sight when her mother asked, 'What have you decided, darling?' She glanced at her beautiful daughter's face. 'Perhaps you still aren't quite sure…'

Sophie sat down on the edge of the kitchen table. 'I'm sure—I think I was sure before we even went to Holland. You see, Mother, he thinks as I do; we both want a sensible, secure marriage. We like each other and we like the same things and we do get on well together. There won't be any violent feelings or quarrels. Rijk has had his share of falling in love and so have I. We shall be very happy together.'

Mrs Blount listened to this speech with an expressionless face. It sounded to her as though her dear daughter was reassuring herself, and all that nonsense about being sensible and secure. That was well enough, but no use at all without love. A good thing that Rijk loved Sophie so much that he was willing to put up with her ideas. Indeed, she suspected that he might even be encouraging them for his own ends, whatever they might be.

She said comfortably, 'Now just sit there and tell me what his home is like.'

'It's beautiful and rather grand, a long way from everywhere, although there's a village ten minutes' walk away. There's a lake close by. Mother, Rijk's a rich man—I didn't know that. Oh, I knew he was comfortably well off—I mean, he's well known internationally for his brain surgery—but I had no idea. There's a butler and a housekeeper and two maids, only he doesn't seem to be rich, because he never mentions money or his possessions. His parents have a large house in Leeuwarden and of course he has his house in London.' She cast a worried glance at her parent. 'Do you suppose it will be all right? I do like him, he's become a dear friend, and I don't care tuppence if he's without a shilling.'

'Money is nice to have, love, and I'm sure it won't make any difference to you—you're too sensible and well brought up—and someone like Rijk who has been born into it and been taught its proper place in life isn't likely to let it interfere with his way of life.' She became all at once brisk. 'I suppose you will marry quite soon? After Christmas? You will need clothes…'

'Yes, but I won't do anything until I see Rijk.'

'Of course not, dear. Now come upstairs. The boys will be home tomorrow and I've still any number of presents to tie up; do come and help me.'

The three days went quickly; there were the preparations to make for Christmas, last-minute shopping, friends calling, and the last Christmas cards to send. Sophie was in the kitchen making mince pies when Rijk arrived. She saw that he was tired and put down her rolling-pin at once and came across the kitchen to meet him.

'You've been working hard?' And then she added, 'It's nice to see you, Rijk.' She put a hand on his sleeve. 'You'll stay for lunch?'

He put a hand over hers. 'No. I must get back to the hospital as quickly as possible; I've an out-patients clinic this afternoon and a consultation. I mustn't miss the evening ferry.'

'At least have a cup of coffee—it's here, on the Aga.'

'That would be nice.' He sat down at the table and ate a mince pie, still warm from the oven. 'You're ready for Christmas?'

'Yes.' She put a mug of coffee before him and went to sit down opposite him. He took another mince pie. 'I've come for my answer, Sophie.'

'I'll marry you, Rijk, and I'll try to be a good wife—I hope I'll be able to cope…'

'Of course you will. I'll get a special licence. You would like to marry here?'

'Yes, please, and would you mind if we had a quiet wedding?'

'I should like that myself. My mother and father and Bellamy for my best man—I was his…'

'When will you be back here?'

'In two weeks' time.' He thought for a moment. 'Any day after the seventeenth of January will be fine.' He smiled suddenly at her. 'The eighteenth or nineteenth?' And when she nodded, 'I'll try to come over before then so that we can see your rector.' He put down his mug. 'I must go…'

'Where have you come from?'

'Leeds.'

'That's miles away; you must be worn out.'

'Not a bit of it.'

He came round the table and put his hands on her shoulders. 'We shall be happy, Sophie.' He bent and kissed her gently. 'And here is a token of our happiness.' He fished a small box from his pocket and opened it. The ring inside was exquisite; sapphires and diamonds in an old-fashioned gold setting. 'My grandmother's ring; she had it from her husband's grandmother.'

He slipped it on her finger and then kissed her hand.

'Were you so sure?' asked Sophie.

'Oh, yes. *Tot ziens*, Sophie.' He had gone as unfussily as he had come, leaving her looking at the ring on her finger and wondering if other girls arranged their weddings in such a businesslike way, and all in the space of a few minutes. Of course neither she nor Rijk were hampered by sentimental ideas about getting married. She heaved a sigh and began cutting rounds of pastry and when her mother came into the kitchen she said soberly, 'He'd driven down from Leeds and he's got a full afternoon's work…'

Her mother, who had seen the professor getting into his car and been the pleased recipient of a warm hug, said cheerfully, 'Yes, dear, but I should imagine that he knows just how much he can do before he needs to rest. He's a very strong man.' She admired the ring and noted with satisfaction that Sophie was still fretting about Rijk.

'When you are married I dare say you will be able to persuade him to work a little less hard, dear. Have you fixed a date for the wedding?'

When Sophie told her she said, 'You might go and see the rector tomorrow before he gets tied up with Christmas. A quiet wedding?'

'Yes. We would both like that. Just you and Father and the boys and Rijk's mother and father and the best man—Mr Bellamy from St Anne's—they've been friends for years.'

'His sisters and brothers?' prompted Mrs Blount.

'I don't know, but I dare say they'll come—they're a close family.'

'How nice. What will you wear?'

They finished the mince pies together, arguing the merits of a winter-white outfit or a pale grey dress and jacket. It was bound to be cold and probably a grey day to boot. 'Directly Christmas is over you must go shopping.' She frowned. 'Of course the sales will be on, but you might find something.'

The boys came home presently, wished her well with brotherly affection, stated their intention of being at her wedding, and demanded to know every detail of her holiday.

'It sounds super,' commented Paul. 'We'll all come and stay and you can be the gracious lady of the house.'

'Why not?' said Sophie placidly. 'There's heaps of room and I dare say there'll be ice-skating if it gets cold enough.'

'You won't want us to visit you as soon as that,' declared Tom. 'You'll need a few weeks to be all soppy with each other.'

Sophie laughed, knowing it was expected of her. She couldn't imagine Rijk being soppy. For that matter, she had no intention of being soppy either.

She went out the next morning and bought a Dutch grammar; she must do her small best to make their marriage a success, and a good start would be to speak at least a few words of Rijk's language. There was very little time to do more than glance through its pages, what with helping around the house and helping to cook the nourishing meals her brothers constantly needed, besides entertaining various friends and acquaintances who popped in for a drink and to admire the ring. It was amazing how quickly the news had spread through the village; it wasn't until she picked up the *Telegraph* and saw the announcement of their engagement that she discovered why.

There had been no message from Rijk and although she hadn't expected one she had hoped that he might find time to phone before he left. He would be back at his home. She corrected herself; he wasn't going home, he was going straight to Schiphol. He would be in Greece now, bringing his skill to bear upon a patient with no thought of Christmas and certainly not of her.

She was mistaken. On Christmas Eve a basket of red roses, magnificent enough for a prima donna, was delivered and the card with it was in his handwriting too. He wished her a happy Christmas and was hers, Rijk.

She placed it in a prominent position in the drawing-room and looked at it every time she went into the room. He had thought of her even though he was so busy. Her lovely face took on an added sparkle and she bore her brothers' teasing remarks about red roses for love with good humour. Of course, that hadn't been Rijk's meaning; red was, after all, the colour for Christmas. It was only much later, going to bed after going to midnight service with her family, that Sophie allowed the thought which had been nagging her to be faced. Surely Rijk could have written to her or telephoned? She had made all kinds of excuses for him, but she found it hard to believe that he couldn't have scribbled a postcard before he got on the plane. The roses had been a lovely surprise, of course, but if he had had time to arrange for those he surely could have phoned her too? She lay awake wondering about it and when, at length, she slept she dreamt of him.

She hadn't been home for Christmas for several years and, despite her uneasy thoughts, she found herself soothed and reassured by the ritual of giving and receiving presents, lighting the tree, going to church again and helping her mother serve up a dinner which never varied from year to year. As she ate her turkey and Christmas pudding she wondered where she would be in a year's time—here with Rijk or in Friesland, sharing Christmas with him and his family.

'Such a pity Rijk isn't here,' observed her mother. 'I wonder what kind of a Christmas he is having?'

THE PROFESSOR WASN'T having Christmas at all; he was undertaking a tricky piece of surgery on his patient's brain and, being a man with plenty of will-power, he hadn't allowed his thoughts to stray from this difficult task. Even when the long and complicated operation was over, he stayed within call, for the next day or two were crucial. On New Year's Eve, flying back to his home, satisfied that his work had been successful, he allowed himself to think of Sophie. He had swept her into a promise of marriage to him, but that, he was only too well aware, was only the beginning.

Rauke was waiting for him at Schiphol with an ecstatic Matt on the back seat, and he drove through the early evening back to his home, to change his clothes, wish his household a happy New Year, and then get back into his car again and drive to his parents' house, where the entire family were celebrating. He was a tired man, but no one looking at him would have seen that; he joined in the final round of drinks before midnight, piled his plate with the delicious food, and on the stroke of midnight toasted the New Year with champagne. The ceremony of kissing everyone, shaking hands and exchanging good wishes over, the professor slipped away to his father's study, and picked up the phone to dial a number.

SOPHIE AND HER family were still sitting round the fire, drinking the last of the port her father had brought up from the cellar and making sleepy plans to go to bed, when the phone rang and, since Sophie was nearest to it, she got up to answer it. Rijk's quiet voice, wishing her a happy New Year, sent a pleasant little thrill through her person; she had hoped that he might phone, but she hadn't been sure about it. She said fervently, 'Oh, Rijk,' and then, 'A happy New Year to you too. Where are you?'

'In Leeuwarden. I got back a few hours ago. I'll be with you the day after tomorrow—I'm not sure when. You'll be at home?'

'Yes, oh, yes.'

'I'll see you then. *Tot ziens*, Sophie.' He rang off and

she felt vague disappointment at the brevity of his call, but it was quickly swamped at the thought of seeing him again. It surprised her that she had missed him so much.

She was in the kitchen washing her mother's best china when Mrs Broom put her head round the door.

'Yer young man's at the door, love.' She beamed at Sophie. 'Ere, give me them plates and wipe yer 'ands, mustn't keep 'im awaiting.'

Sophie thrust a valuable Wedgwood plate at Mrs Broom and dashed out of the kitchen, wiping wet, soapy hands on her pinny as she went. It was a deplorable garment, kept hanging behind the kitchen door and worn by anyone who needed it, regardless of size, but she had forgotten that.

The professor was in the hall talking to her mother, towering over her, immaculate in his cashmere overcoat and tweeds. He looked as though he might have come fresh from his valet's hands, and Sophie slithered to a halt, suddenly conscious of the apron and the fact that she hadn't bothered with her hair but tied it back with a ribbon.

The knowledge that she wasn't looking her best made her say crossly, 'I didn't expect you so soon,' and then, 'It's lovely to see you, Rijk.'

She rubbed her still wet hands on the apron. 'I was just washing the best china…'

The professor's eyes gleamed beneath their lids. 'I like the hair,' he said and bent to kiss her. 'Shall I come and help you with the plates?'

'No, of course not.' She smiled, her good humour restored, feeling comfortable with him just as friends should with each other. 'I'll fetch the coffee—did you come over on the night ferry?'

'Yes. I've a case this afternoon at St Agnes's but I wondered if we might go and see your parson this morning? I'll come back this evening and we'll go out to dinner; there is a good deal to discuss.'

She nodded. 'Yes. Are you going to be in England for a while?'

'I'm afraid not. Two or three days. I've a good deal of work waiting for me and I'd like to get it done before the wedding.'

'Yes, of course.' They went into the sitting-room, where her mother had prudently retired, and presently, over coffee which that lady brought, the conversation turned to the wedding.

'A quiet one?' her mother asked and went on, 'Just a handful of people—we can all come back here for lunch afterwards if you would like that. I dare say you'll want to be off somewhere or other.'

'We shall catch the night ferry to Holland; I can spare only a couple of days.'

'Well, let me know what you arrange between you,' said Mrs Blount comfortably, 'and I'll fit in.' She spoke cheerfully; like all mothers she would have liked to see her beautiful daughter swanning down the aisle in white satin and her own wedding veil, which she had kept so carefully for just such an occasion; it might have comforted her if she had known that Sophie had had a fleeting regret that the white satin and veil weren't for her. Only for a moment, however; a romantic wedding would have been ridiculous in their case. All the same, she would find something suitable for a bride, however modest the wedding…

Her father and Tom came in presently and she slipped away to take great pains with her face and hair and present herself in a quilted jacket and woolly gloves, ready to go to the rectory with Rijk.

They walked there, talking idly about this and that, very much at ease with each other, and when they reached the rectory the professor, while giving the appearance of asking Sophie's opinion about dates and times, had everything arranged exactly as he had planned it. The wedding was to be at eleven o'clock in the morning in two weeks' time by special licence; it was to be a quiet ceremony. As they would be leaving for Holland that same day they were both most grateful to the rector for arranging to marry them at rather short notice.

'Delighted, delighted,' observed the old man, 'and I trust that I may have the happy task of christening your children.'

Sophie smiled, murmured and avoided Rijk's eye, and was a little surprised to hear his agreement, uttered in a grave voice, although she felt he meant it. Of course, she told herself, he didn't want to hurt the rector's feelings. That was the one doubt she had about their marriage; she liked children and she rather thought that Rijk did too, but if they kept to their agreement and lived the life he had envisaged there wouldn't be any. Of course, perhaps later on… In the meantime, she told herself, they would share a very pleasant life together without heartbreak and the pitfalls of falling in love. She walked back with Rijk, quite content with her future.

He left shortly after they got back with the reminder that he would be back in the early evening. As he got into the car he asked her, 'Have you any preference as to where we should go?'

'Must it be a restaurant?' she asked diffidently. 'Would it be a bother to Percy and Mrs Wiffen if we dined at your house?'

She was rewarded by his pleased look. 'No bother at all; they're all agog at the idea of a wedding and I'm sure they're longing to see the bride again.' He kissed her cheek lightly, got into the car, and drove off, leaving her to go into the house and go through her wardrobe for something suitable to wear. The brown velvet skirt and ivory silk blouse with the frilled collar would do nicely…

The evening was a great success; Percy and Mrs Wiffen had presented them with a delicious meal and afterwards they had sat in the drawing-room by the fire, talking. Waking in the night, Sophie had been unable to remember what they had talked about, only the satisfying memory of it. It was only when she woke again just as it was getting light that she knew without any doubt at all that she had fallen in love with Rijk.

CHAPTER SEVEN

SOPHIE GOT UP and dressed, although it was still early; to lie in bed was quite impossible. She dragged on an old raincoat, tied a scarf over her hair, pulled on her wellies, and went quietly out of the house.

Montgomery and Mercury, delighted at the prospect of a walk so early in the day, slid through the back door after her, and she was glad of their company.

It was drizzling with a cold rain and the wind was bitter, but she really hadn't noticed either. 'Now I'm in a pickle, aren't I?' she asked them. 'Must I say that I've changed my mind or shall I go ahead and marry him and then pretend for the rest of my days that I've nothing but friendly feelings towards him?'

Mercury gave a sympathetic yelp and Montgomery huffed deep in his throat.

'The thing is,' went on Sophie, intent on getting things straight in her head, 'is it better never to see him again or marry him and never let him know that I love him?' She added in a shaky little voice, 'He's the one, you see. I know that now; I can't think why I didn't discover it earlier. No one else really matters. He does like me, we get on so well together—like old friends, if you see what I mean—and I don't think I could bear never to see him again...'

She stopped in the middle of the muddy lane and the dogs stopped with her, looking at her with sympathetic eyes. 'I'm going to marry him,' she told them briskly. 'Half a loaf is very much better than no bread.'

She turned for home, her mind made up, and feeling relieved, so that when, over breakfast, her mother broached the subject of buying clothes she agreed that the sooner she did some shopping the better.

'And I wonder how many of Rijk's family are coming to the wedding?' her mother mused. 'Should I invite them?' She didn't wait for an answer. 'I'll write a note to his mother and invite any member of the family who might wish to come.' She began to reckon on her fingers. 'There will be nine of them if they all come, and I haven't counted the husbands…'

'They won't come to the wedding,' said Sophie. 'Just his mother and father and perhaps a brother or sister. He told me that there will be a big family gathering when we get back to Friesland.'

'Then I'll cater for about twenty to be on the safe side. I must see about the wedding-cake this morning. When will you go shopping, love?'

'Tomorrow; I don't need much…'

'No, dear, perhaps not, but one or two good outfits besides your wedding clothes.'

Sophie gave her mother a dreamy look, her head full of Rijk. 'Winter-white if I can find it, a coat and dress, and I'll have to buy a hat.'

Her mother gave her a thoughtful look; if she hadn't known better she would have said that the dear girl was in love, her head in the clouds and her wits addled.

'That would be very nice,' she said in a matter-of-fact voice. 'Will you be seeing Rijk before the wedding?'

'No, he goes back to Holland tomorrow. He wants to clear up as much as possible before we are married.'

SHE WENT UP to London the next morning. Her father drove her into Chipping Ongar and put her on the London train with instructions to spend the cheque he had given her, and if she needed more money she had only to ask for it. There was money in her own bank account too; if she wanted to she could be wildly extravagant. Why not? she reflected. It was her wedding and she wanted Rijk to be proud of her.

She avoided the big stores where the sales were in full swing; there were several boutiques where, even if they had sales, they would have something to suit her tucked away.

By late afternoon she was tired, hungry and triumphant. She also had a charming outfit for the wedding, a winter-white dress and long loose coat to match it in a fine woollen material. Even with a few pounds taken off as a concession to the sales, the price had been horrific, but, as the owner of the boutique had said, it was an outfit which could be worn repeatedly and not lose its chic. There was a hat to go with it too, a confection of velvet and feathers, faintly pink-tipped.

'A wedding outfit?' murmured the saleslady, who had seen Sophie's ring.

'Well, yes—a very quiet wedding…'

'Exactly suitable and very elegant. You have a splendid figure, if I may say so, madam. I expect you have already bought a good deal, but I do have a jersey suit—so suitable for this time of year. It is your size and I would be pleased to make a reduction on its price.'

A jersey suit would be useful, Sophie had reflected, and, since it was a perfect fit and a mixture of blues and greens which suited her dark hair and eyes, she bought that too.

She had snatched a hasty lunch then before going in search of something for the evening. Rijk lived in some style; certainly there would be at least one dance or dinner. This time she found exactly what she wanted—a dress with a full long skirt, the bodice square-necked and with tiny sleeves. It was in almond-pink chiffon and suitable, she hoped, for an eminent surgeon's wife, and since she still had some money in her purse she bought a brown and gold brocade top, high-necked and long-sleeved; it would go well with her brown velvet skirt… Marks and Spencer provided her with new undies and, well pleased with her purchases, she went back home.

It had been a lovely day and beneath the excitement of buying new clothes was the knowledge that she loved Rijk, and that was exciting too, so that when he phoned later that evening she was for the moment bereft of words.

In answer to his quiet 'Sophie?' she said breathlessly, 'Rijk, where are you?'

'At Eernewoude. What have you done with your day?'

'I bought a wedding-dress… Will you be there until you come back here?'

'No, four or five days here and then a quick trip to Brussels to see a patient and then here again until

I leave for England. You may not hear from me for a day or two…'

'That's all right,' said Sophie. She wanted him to phone her every day—twice a day if possible—just to hear his voice, but on no account must he ever know that. 'You don't need to bother; we'll see to everything.'

She wasn't sure, but it sounded as though he had laughed before he said goodbye.

There was plenty to keep her occupied at home; her mother had sent invitations to Rijk's family and was happily immersed in preparations for the wedding breakfast. 'Something simple,' she declared, 'if you have to leave for the ferry.' She paused. 'But doesn't that go at night? Rijk said he would want to leave directly after we have had lunch.'

'Perhaps he wants to call at his London house,' suggested Sophie.

'Probably.' Her mother frowned. 'Smoked salmon and those little cheese puffs, baby sausage rolls and tiny quiches—the kind you can hold in your hand without them going crumbly—and the cake, of course…'

Sophie said, 'Yes, Mother,' in a dreamy voice. As far as she was concerned they could chew cardboard just as long as she and Rijk were safely married. It would take time, she reflected, to get him to fall in love with her. She knew that she was a lovely girl and, while not in the least bit conceited, she knew that it was an asset. Rijk thought of her as a friend; all she had to do was to get him to see her in a different light…as an attractive woman as well as a practical young woman who understood his work and was prepared to take second place to it in his life.

She thought about it a good deal during the next few days. The thing was to make him see her in a new light. She still hadn't planned a course of action by the time he returned, and it was hard to behave as she always had done, to greet him with the friendly pleasure he expected and answer his questions about their wedding in a matter-of-fact voice.

His parents and two of his sisters had travelled over at the same time, driven their own car, and gone straight to his London home; only he had driven on to see her and make sure that everything was in train for the next day.

'Loewert and Iwert are flying over this evening—Bellamy will bring them down in the morning. That makes seven on my side. How many have you?'

They were sitting in the kitchen drinking coffee, and she tried not to look at him too often; just having him there, close to her, was sending her heart thumping at her ribs. She told herself silently not to be silly. 'Well, there's Mother and Father and the boys—that's five—and me, of course, and you... That's fourteen. The rector and his wife will come to lunch—it's a buffet.' She cast him a quick look. 'We weren't sure when you would want to leave.'

'I thought we might have dinner at home, just the two of us, before we go to the ferry.'

She nodded agreement. 'Mother would love everyone to stay for tea and supper; it would be nice if everyone got to know everyone else.' She added, 'I forgot Mr Bellamy...'

'He'll have to go back soon after we leave.'

The professor got up from his chair opposite her and

came and sat on the corner of the table, close to her. 'No doubts?' he asked softly.

She gave him a direct look. 'None at all,' she told him clearly.

He bent and kissed her. 'Nor I. Shall we go for a walk? I'm going back after lunch; I'm sure you want to wash your hair or whatever women do before they get married.'

Sophie laughed. 'Well, as a matter of fact, I do have to do that—however did you know?'

'Remember that I have five sisters.' He pulled her to her feet. 'Get a coat and I'll find your mother.' He glanced at his watch. 'Is lunch at one o'clock? Then we have all of two hours.'

It was a cold morning, but there was a watery sun and they walked briskly.

'Tell me about your trip to Greece,' said Sophie. 'Was the op successful?'

She listened with real interest, understanding what he was talking about and asking sensible questions from time to time, and the professor paused in the middle of a particularly complicated explanation to say, 'What a pleasure it is to be able to talk about my work to someone who understands me. It is said that one shouldn't take one's work home with one, but how satisfactory it will be to come home and mull over my work without fear of boring you.'

'You would never bore me,' said Sophie and went bright pink because she had sounded a bit too fervent. She wasn't looking at him and didn't see his slow smile. She added quickly, 'Don't forget that I've been nursing for a long time.'

'Shall you miss it?' he asked casually. 'Life at Eernewoude is quiet…'

'I shall like that and there will be so much to keep me busy—I must learn to speak Dutch and understand it, and there's Matt and getting to know everyone in the village and your family.'

'We shall entertain too, Sophie. I have many friends and there is a surprisingly brisk social life. And when we are married I suspect it will be even brisker.'

'You will like that?'

'Not very much. I shall rely on you to fend off all but my closest friends.'

'You'll have to give me a list,' said Sophie, 'and I'll do my best.'

The professor went again after lunch, but not before he had given Sophie his wedding gift—diamond and sapphire earrings, the sapphires surrounded by diamonds, hanging from diamond-studded pendants. She put them on, struck dumb with their beauty. 'They're magnificent,' she told him. 'Thank you, Rijk, I'll wear them tomorrow…' She reached up to kiss his cheek. 'I can't give you diamonds and sapphires, can I? Only a wedding-ring…'

'Which I shall wear with pride.'

SOPHIE WAS UP early on her wedding-day; she had slept well, but once awake there was no point in lying in bed—she was too excited. She was happy too and at the same time apprehensive. It would be heaven to be with Rijk each and every day, but supposing, just supposing he found her boring or, worse, fell in love with another woman? A beautiful face wasn't enough; she knew that… She crept down to the kitchen and made herself some tea and sat drinking it by the Aga with the dogs on either side of her. Soothed by the warmth and the ordinary action, she went back upstairs to bath and presently have an early breakfast in her dressing-gown.

Even if she had wanted to brood she had no chance; her brothers saw to that until her mother bustled her back to her room to dress.

'Mother, there's heaps of time,' she protested.

'You must dress and then sit quietly and compose yourself,' said her parent. 'Anyhow, I want everyone out of the way. Mrs Broom will be here with her daughter in a few minutes and I must make sure that everything is ready in the drawing-room.'

So Sophie dressed and went to sit in her window; she could see the church spire above the trees. In less than an hour she would be beneath it, getting married. She wondered what Rijk was doing; supposing he got held up on the way—an accident, roads up for repair, a puncture? She was glad when her mother came in to ask her advice as to the exact angle of her new hat. They studied it together in the looking-glass. 'Very mother-of-the-bride,' said Sophie. 'You do look nice, Mother, dear.'

'Will Rijk's mother look nice too?'

'I'm sure she will—she looks a bit fierce but she isn't. I think you'll like each other.'

The house was quiet once her mother and brothers had gone; she sat in the drawing-room with her father, waiting for the hired limousine to take them to the church. In a few hours she would have left home, she reflected, and took comfort from the thought that Rijk had said that she might come over to England whenever he did and see her family. He was a kind man, she mused, as well as a close friend. And, of course, a husband.

The car came and they got in and were driven the short distance to the church, and, Sophie being Sophie, there was no nonsense about being late—it was striking eleven o'clock as, holding the small, exquisite bouquet Rijk had sent her, and her arm tucked in her father's, she walked down the aisle.

For a quiet wedding the church was remarkably full. The village, delighted to have a dull winter day enlivened by such an event, had turned out in force, crowding the pews behind Sophie's family and Rijk's parents, two of his sisters and his brothers, sitting on the other side of the aisle. But she barely glanced at them; Rijk was there, waiting for her, his massive bulk reassuring even though he didn't turn to look at her. Only when they were standing beside him did he turn and smile into her eyes for a moment before the service began.

She became aware then that there was music and the choir and flowers. She wondered who had arranged that and then made herself listen to the rector's old voice and presently, obediently following his quavering tones, promising to love, honour and obey…

They went out of the church arm in arm and she smiled vaguely from side to side, feeling as though she were in a dream, and at the church door they had to pause for a moment while someone took photos, and then everyone else crowded round them and she was being kissed and everyone was talking at once.

In the Bentley, beside Rijk, she asked, 'Who arranged for the choir and the organ and all those lovely flowers?'

'I did. I wanted you to have a fitting background, Sophie.'

'Thank you, it was all so—so… I don't know the right word, but do you know what I mean?'

'Yes. I think I do. You look very beautiful, my dear.'

'Oh, thank you.' She glanced sideways at him; his grey suit was magnificently cut, his tie a rich silk in a darker shade, a white carnation in his buttonhole; he was the epitome of a well dressed man. 'You look awfully nice yourself.'

He dropped a hand on her knee. 'A well suited couple, are we not?'

The wedding breakfast was a triumph. Mrs Blount glowed with pride. She had had to get caterers in, of course, but a good deal of it she had seen to herself. She beamed around her; Sophie looked marvellous, so did Rijk, and she and his mother had taken to each other immediately. She had found his father a little daunting to start with, but then she had seen the twinkle in his eyes—the same eyes as his son. After all, he was only an older edition of Rijk. His sisters and brothers were friendly too and there was no worry about understanding them; their English was as good as hers. She went and sat down by Rijk's mother and that lady patted her arm. 'This is a delightful occasion—we can be proud of our new son and daughter, can we not? As soon as they are settled in you must all come over and stay with us—we have plenty of room for the boys and even if we hadn't there are so many of us that there is always a room for anyone who cares to come and stay.'

'You're very kind,' said Mrs Blount and added, 'I'm very fond of Rijk—we all are. He—he just sort of fitted in from the moment he came to see us.' The two ladies smiled mistily at each other and Mrs Blount said, 'I think it is time to cut the cake; they want to be off by two o'clock.'

They drove away in a shower of confetti, still in their wedding clothes, for they were to change at the London house.

'Warm enough?' asked Rijk.

'Yes, thank you. Won't your family want to come to the London house this evening?'

'After we have gone—Father has arranged for everyone to dine at Ingatestone...'

'The Heybridge Moat House?'

'That's the one. They can discuss the wedding at their ease; it won't matter how late they are. He's arranged for a car for Loewert and Iwert and he'll drive Mother and the girls back himself. He phoned your father this morning...'

'How very kind and thoughtful of him.' She looked out of the window at the wintry fields. 'What time do we have to leave London?'

'About eight o'clock; we'll dine first.' He smiled down at her. 'I enjoyed our wedding, did you?'

She realised with some surprise that she had. She had expected it to be a kind of dream in which she wouldn't feel quite real, but it had been real enough and she had felt happy... 'Yes, I did. I've heard people say that they couldn't remember their wedding clearly, but I can remember every word.'

She didn't say any more; the wish to tell him that she loved him was so strong that she had to clench her teeth, and presently he asked, 'Tired? We'll soon be home.'

She hurried to tell him that she wasn't in the least tired, that it was excitement. 'So much has happened today—it was so nice having your people here, and our mothers took to each other at once, didn't they?'

She embarked on a rather pointless conversation about the wedding and felt relief when they reached the outskirts of London and he was forced to slow down and give his whole attention to the traffic.

Percy opened the door with a flourish as the professor stopped before his house. 'Heartiest congrats, guv, and you, madam. All the best and lots of little 'uns. This is an 'appy day and no mistake.'

'Why, thank you, Percy.' The professor sounded at his most placid and Sophie, doing her best to follow his example, shook Percy's hand and thanked him.

'Well, now. There's champagne in the drawing-room and Mrs Wiffen 'as bust her stays over yer dinner.' Percy beamed at them as he took Sophie's coat.

'If I may say so, madam, you look smashing. I'll fetch in the luggage in half a mo'—you'll want to change before you leave.'

He urged them into the drawing-room, softly lighted and decked with enough flowers to stock a florist's shop. 'Me and Mrs Wiffen thought as 'ow it'd be nice ter 'ave a few flowers,' explained Percy, and something in his voice sent Sophie across the room to take his hand in hers.

'Percy, how kind of you both, and the room looks beautiful. It's such a lovely surprise; how I wish we could take them all with us to Holland.'

'Well, there is that… P'raps yer could take a small bunch wiv yer?'

'I most certainly shall. I've never seen such a wonderful display. Thank you and Mrs Wiffen; you couldn't have pleased us more, could they, Rijk?'

The professor, thus addressed, made haste to add his appreciation to Sophie's, and Percy, looking pleased with himself, went away, back to the kitchen to tell Mrs Wiffen that the newly wed pair looked a treat and no mistake. 'A bit of all right is the missus and that's for sure,' he pronounced.

Sophie sat by the fire in the steel grate and drank the champagne which Rijk had poured for her. Rijk sat down and with a word of excuse became immersed in a pile of letters beside his chair.

'It looks as though I shall have to come back here in about six weeks' time.' He glanced at her, smiling. 'You might come too if you wish to see your parents. I shall have to go to Denmark too very shortly, just to operate; I dare say you will find plenty to do at home…'

She saw that she wasn't to be allowed to interfere with his work in any way. She agreed serenely and drank her champagne.

Mrs Wiffen had excelled herself: crab mousse, surrounded by a sauce of her own invention, followed by grilled Dover sole with tiny potatoes and braised celery in a cheese sauce and rounded off by a confection of fresh pineapple and meringue. They drank their coffee at the table and Sophie said, diffidently, 'Would you mind if I went to the kitchen and thanked Mrs Wiffen? She has gone to a great deal of trouble…'

Rijk got up as she did. 'I'll come with you.'

Mrs Wiffen, treated to a sight of the bride's outfit, was almost tearful. 'I'm sure we so wish you happiness, madam, and you, sir. I 'opes you'll be back soon to sample some more of my cooking.'

'I look forward to that,' said Sophie. 'The professor often comes here and I shall come with him.'

She went upstairs presently to a charming bedroom, its satinwood furniture gleaming in the soft pink glow of the shaded lamps, the bedspread and curtains in quilted pastel chintz. Someone had unpacked her case and her travelling clothes were lying ready. She got out of her wedding outfit, folded it carefully in tissue paper, and packed it. There was really no point in taking it with her, but to leave it behind was unthinkable...

Presently, dressed for the journey, she went downstairs again in the jersey suit and her winter coat. It was a cold night and it might be even colder in Holland; she had prudently stuffed a scarf and thick gloves in her pockets.

Rijk, in tweeds and his cashmere overcoat, was waiting for her in the hall, talking to Mrs Wiffen and Percy.

'Oh, have I kept you waiting?' Sophie hurried forward to be reassured by Rijk's placid,

'Not at all, my dear! You are most punctual and we have plenty of time.'

She made her goodbyes, taking the little bouquet of flowers which Percy offered her. 'I'll put them in water the moment we arrive,' she told him, 'to remind me of your beautiful decorations for us this evening.'

'Be seein' you,' said Percy cheerfully, and he and Mrs Wiffen waved from the door as Rijk drove away.

IT HAD BEEN cold in London; it seemed to Sophie as they drove away from the Hoek the next morning very early that it was a great deal colder in Holland. The Bentley was warm, though, and they stopped presently for coffee at a small café by the motorway.

Sophie bit into a *kaas broodje*. 'How long a holiday have you got?' she asked.

'I've several patients to see in two days' time, then I shall be in Amsterdam for a few days; after that I shall be home for some time…'

He spoke casually, but his eyes were on her face.

Sophie summoned an interested smile. 'Oh, yes, you must have a marvellous secretary keeping tabs on your appointments.' She reflected that it was only what she had expected after all. He was no lovesick bridegroom and she must take care not to dwindle into a lovesick bride. If she hadn't fallen in love with him she would have been quite content with his answer.

They drove on presently, going north along the east side of the Ijsselmeer, skirting Utrecht and then on to Meppel and Drachten. The short day was drawing to its close as they turned in between the gates of his home. They had stopped a few miles before Zwolle and had their lunch at a small restaurant tucked away from the main road. They had had the typical Dutch lunch—*koffietafel*—omelette, a basket of rolls and bread, cheese and cold meats and as much coffee as they could drink. The restaurant was fairly full and pleasantly warm and Sophie left it reluctantly to go back outside into the grey day, but once she was in the car beside Rijk her spirits rose again. They were starting this, their married life, together and she had every intention of making a success of it—and that was the least of it; surely, with a little encouragement on her part, he might, in time, fall in love with her…

They received a warm welcome, with Matt racing out of the house to lean against them, and Rauke, Tyske and the two maids were waiting in the porch despite the cold.

There was tea waiting for them, and Sophie, bidden to hurry down from her room as quickly as possible, did so to find Rijk sitting in his great wing-chair by the fire, sorting through a pile of letters. He got up as she went in and put the letters down, and she said at once, 'Do read your post; there may be something important,' and sat down beside the tea-tray and poured the tea, feeling unreasonably hurt when he did so. It was, after all, only yesterday that they had married.

She drank her tea and ate the little cakes Tyske had made and tried to look as relaxed as Rijk, sitting there going through his correspondence as though they had been married for years… Presently she went back to her lovely room to find that her things had been unpacked and put away in the wall closet and the tallboy drawers. There was nothing for her to do but bathe and change into the brown velvet skirt and one of the silk tops to go with it. That done, she went and sat by the window and looked out on to the dark grounds around the house, the darkness pierced by the light streaming from its many windows. She could hear Matt barking and presently saw him dashing across the lawns below, followed by Rijk, who looked up and, when he saw her, waved.

She went downstairs then and found him waiting for her. 'I dare say you're tired,' he observed kindly. 'I usually dine at eight o'clock when I'm here, but I asked Rauke to serve us earlier this evening. Come and sit down and have a drink first. Is your room quite comfortable? If there is anything that you need you have only to ask.'

She had the strange feeling that she was a guest in his house as she assured him that she had everything that she could possibly want, glad of Matt's attentions as she sat down and then took the glass offered to her. Presently, she felt better; Rijk was completely at ease, much as though they had been married for years and sitting there chatting over drinks was something they had done forever…

However matter-of-fact Rijk was over their homecoming, Rauke and Tyske had seen to it that it should be marked in an appropriate manner. The dining-table, decked with white damask, gleamed with silver and crystal, and the arrangement of flowers at its centre was decidedly bridal: white roses and freesias, pale pink tulips and lilies of the valley and blue hyacinths; they smelled delicious. The professor, who had conferred with Rauke over this, their first dinner as a married couple in their own home, watched Sophie's face and was content at the look of surprised delight upon it.

The dinner itself was delicious: watercress soup, lobster thermidor with a potato salad and dishes of vegetables followed by a lemon sorbet and a spectacular *bombe glacée*. They ate unhurriedly and Sophie found her initial vague disappointment melting under her husband's undemanding conversation, and presently, when they went back to the drawing-room to have their coffee by the fire, she said, 'What a nice homecoming, and how beautifully Rauke and Tyske look after you.'

'They will look after you just as well, Sophie. In a few days, when you feel at your ease here, Tyske will take you round the house—she is most anxious to inspect the household linen and the kitchen cupboards with you. Rauke will translate for you, but I'm sure that within a short time you'll be able to manage on your own. I dare say you would like some Dutch lessons? I'll see to that for you. Tomorrow we will go and see those of the family who were not at the wedding, and if you like to come to Leeuwarden with me on the following day…? I'll show you where the hospital is and you had better meet the head porter so that if you should need me they can arrange for you to see me at once.'

She agreed quietly; life was going to be strange for a time, but she would learn quickly. She suspected that he expected her to have her own interests when he was away, and she would have to be careful not to infringe upon his life but just to be there when he wanted her company. That would all be altered, she told herself, but it might take time. He had got what he wanted, the kind of wife and marriage he wanted—it was up to her to change his mind for him.

She glanced across at him, loving very much every line of his face, longing to shout her feelings out loud; instead, after a suitable time had elapsed, she wished him a friendly goodnight and took herself off to bed. He had opened the door for her and kissed the top of her head as she passed him, an action she treasured as she lay in bed, considering the future.

They were to have lunch with his three sisters who

hadn't been at the wedding. Siska, the eldest of them, welcomed them to her house and Sophie found all three of them there. They hugged Rijk and kissed her with warmth and wanted to know everything there was to tell about the wedding. 'We would have loved to have come,' said Siska, 'but you knew about the measles, didn't you? When Mother and Father are back and the rest of us as well, we shall have a family party. There are many uncles and aunts and cousins all wishing to meet you.'

Sophie, having assured her sisters-in-law that she had had the measles, was taken to visit her spotty little nephews and nieces. Later, going back home with Rijk, she said, 'What a nice family you have, Rijk; I do like them.'

'They like you too. You will see a good deal of them, you know.'

Breakfast was to be early in the morning since Rijk was due at the hospital by nine o'clock. Sophie, well wrapped against the chilly morning, drove with him to Leeuwarden, was shown where the hospital was, told at what time to be there in the afternoon, given a roll of notes, and told to go and enjoy herself, which, rather to her surprise, she did. There was plenty to see and she spent a long time choosing wool. Knitting was something she had never had much time for; but now there was the chance to get expert at it. She bought canvas and tapestry wools too and several paperbacks as well as a notebook and a useful book entitled *A guide to Dutch for the tourist*. Even a smattering of that language would be useful.

Rijk went to Amsterdam the following day, leaving while it was still dark, and, since he wouldn't be home again until early evening, Sophie filled the hours by inspecting cupboards of linen—enough to last forever, she considered—and more vast cupboards in the kitchen and the pantry, filled with china and glass, and then, lastly, she was shown the safe where the family silver was kept. By the time Rijk got home she was beginning to feel that she was a married woman with a home to run.

The next day she went to the kitchen and sat down at the table there with Tyske while Rauke translated his wife's detailed account of just how the house was run. She enjoyed that; it was a lived-in room and something on the massive Aga smelled delicious. There was a cat and kittens too in a basket before the stove and Matt sitting beside her, watching her lovingly with his yellow eyes.

Rijk was tired when he got home, but not too tired to tell her of his day, and she made a good listener, sitting there with her knitting, asking all the right questions in a quiet voice. Halfway through an account of a patient's treatment he paused to say, 'Did I ever tell you what a restful girl you are, Sophie? I enjoy coming home and finding you here, knowing that I can talk to you and that you will listen intelligently and we are good friends enough for you to tell me when I begin to bore you.'

'Oh, I'll do that,' she assured him, making her voice briskly friendly, 'but it's not likely.'

'I must arrange for you to meet some of my friends so that they may be your friends too, and you must come to the hospital…' He smiled suddenly. 'No one expects us to be very social for a week or two.'

She summoned a smile in return. She hoped it looked like an understanding smile between friends.

Rijk finished at Amsterdam and, although he went to Leeuwarden or Groningen each day, she saw more of him. They walked together in the early mornings with Matt and, although he spent most of the evening in his study, at least he was in the house. Sophie began to feel cautiously happy.

It was several days after he had come back from Amsterdam that she decided to go to Leeuwarden. Rauke was taking the Land Rover in to fetch groceries and she went with him, assuring him that she would go to the hospital and return home with the professor. She spent the early afternoon searching for the extra wools and needles she would need for her tapestry and then made her way to the hospital, nicely in time to meet Rijk.

She was opposite the hospital forecourt, waiting for a lull in the traffic, when she saw him coming out of the entrance. He wasn't alone; a tall, slender woman was beside him, laughing up at him, and he was holding her arm as they walked towards the Bentley. Sophie shut her eyes and then opened them again; they hadn't deceived her. The pair of them were in the car and Rijk swiftly drove it out of the forecourt; moreover, he was going in the opposite direction from his home…

CHAPTER EIGHT

SOPHIE WATCHED THE tail-lights of the Bentley disappear, oblivious of the impatient people jostling her as they hurried past her. Who was the woman Rijk was with and where were they going? It was plain that they knew each other. Rijk had been laughing… Sophie ground her splendid teeth and looked around for a policeman.

Yes, he told her, holding up the traffic while he explained where the bus depot was, there would certainly be a bus to Grouw, but she would need to hurry. She thanked him nicely from a white face and hurried through the streets and found the bus, already full, on the point of leaving. Once on it, jammed between two old men with baskets of eels and smelling strongly of fish, she pondered what she would do when she got to Grouw. Eernewoude was still some miles further at the end of a secondary road which meandered round the lake. She would have to hire a taxi… One of the old men spoke to her and she dredged up her few words of Dutch—'*Ik ben Engels*'—and gave him a smile, and he broke into instant speech. Not even Dutch, she thought despairingly, but Friese, which sounded even more unintelligible than Dutch. There was a stirring in the bus, for he had a loud voice, and someone said, 'English—Professor van Taak ter Wijsma's wife, yes?'

'Yes,' said Sophie, feeling awkward.

'On a bus?' said the same voice. 'You have no car? You are alone?' The owner of the voice sounded quite shocked. 'The professor is not allowing that?'

Of course, in this sparsely populated part of Friesland, he would be known, at least by name. She said clearly, 'I was to go home with him, but I have missed him in Leeuwarden. He will fetch me in Grouw.

'That's not likely,' she murmured to herself, listening to the satisfied chat around her.

The bus stopped frequently, presumably to suit the wishes of the passengers getting on and off in the dark night. There were few villages, for the bus was travelling along a country lane, away from the main road, but there would be farms. Indeed, when she bent to peer out of a window she could see a light here and there away from the road. It looked lonely country and she wished that she was at home, sitting by the fire, working away at her tapestry. The two old men were still on either side of her, talking across her as though she weren't there, and she allowed her thoughts to wander. Where was Rijk? she wondered. And if she asked him when she got home would he tell her?

The bus rattled to a halt in Grouw and she got out last of all, her ears ringing with the chorus of '*Dag*' from her companions on the journey. Now to find a taxi... She turned round to get her bearings and found Rijk right behind her.

Surprise took her breath, but only for a moment. She said in a rush, 'I went into Leeuwarden with Rauke and I meant to meet you at the hospital, but they said you'd already left, so I caught a bus...'

He had a hand on her arm. 'I left early. I'm sorry you had this long, cold ride.' He was walking her across to the Bentley.

'I enjoyed it. Everyone talked and I didn't understand any of it. How did you know that I would be on the bus?'

'Rauke had expected you to be with me. You're a sensible girl; I knew you would get yourself back, and this was the last bus to Grouw. I got back into the car and drove over.'

'I was going to get a taxi.'

The car was blissfully warm and Matt's breath was hot on the back of her neck. Seated comfortably, she was waiting for him to tell her why he had left with that girl, but it was evident that he wasn't going to, even though she stayed silent so that he had the chance to do so. Instead he observed casually that the following week there was to be a reception at the hospital in their honour. 'And Mother phoned today; they are back and there is to be a family dinner within the next week or so. You will enjoy that, will you not, Sophie? Perhaps life is a little dull for you here.'

'Dull? Certainly not. The days aren't long enough—not that I do anything useful, but I'm always busy.'

'I'm glad you are happy here. I hear that cold weather is expected, with snow, which means that we shall be able to skate.'

'I can't…'

He stopped the car in front of the house and turned to look at her. 'I'll teach you; it's splendid exercise—the children have days off from school and they light up the canals.'

She forced herself to answer with a show of enthusiasm, hoping against hope that he would explain. He didn't, however. They reached home and he got out and helped her from the car and over the icy steps to the door. He nodded to Rauke as they went inside but made no move to take off his coat.

'I've a meeting in Leeuwarden this evening; shall you mind dining alone? I shall probably be back late.'

She minded very much but she wasn't going to say so. 'What about your dinner?'

'Oh, we have sandwiches and coffee and Rauke will leave something for me in the kitchen. Don't wait up, my dear.' He dropped a casual kiss on her cheek. 'I'll see you in the morning.'

He took Matt with him so that she had no company as she dined and afterwards, sitting by the fire, savagely poking her needle in and out of her tapestry work.

She went to bed early because he had made it clear that he didn't expect to see her when he got home, and she lay awake until she heard the car whisper to a halt below her window and presently his quiet footsteps in the house.

'I've made a mess of things,' muttered Sophie, weeping into her pillow.

In the morning at the breakfast-table she was bright and brisk, making a brief reference to his meeting without waiting for an answer. He asked her then what she was going to do with her day, and she told him that she intended to explore the attics, take Matt for a walk, and be home in time for Loewert, who had phoned to say that he would call.

'I dare say he'll stay for dinner,' she observed, and Rijk looked surprised.

'By all means; I should be home in good time this evening.'

'How nice,' said Sophie sweetly. She met his thoughtful look with a smile. 'Do you suppose it will snow today?'

'Very likely. Don't go near the lake; it's beginning to freeze over, but it won't be safe for several days.' He got up from the table and offered her a handful of envelopes. 'Invitations—will you look through them? And we'll decide what to do about them.'

'Yes, of course.' She gave him an overbright smile. 'Don't do too much.'

Loewert arrived just before lunch. 'I'm playing truant,' he told her happily. 'I've exams at the end of the week and I thought a day away from my books might help.'

'What exams are they?' She led him into the drawing-room and they sat down before the fire with the coffee-tray between them.

'Ear, nose and throat and gynae.'

She passed him his cup and watched him spoon sugar with a lavish hand.

'You think you'll pass?'

He grinned and she thought with a little leap of her heart that Rijk must have looked like that when he was younger. 'I hope I will. With old Rijk as an example, what else can I do? He's the one with the brains, of course, though he'd give me a good thump if he heard me saying that.'

He looked at Sophie, quite serious for a moment. 'He's a splendid fellow, you know—but of course you do; you're married to him.' He passed his cup for more coffee and took another biscuit. 'We were beginning to think that he would never find himself a wife, and then you turned up, an answer to our prayers—a beautiful angel and a darling…'

'You'll turn my head,' said Sophie and laughed gently, 'but that's kind; thank you for the compliment.'

'You get enough of those from Rijk,' said Loewert and grinned again so that she blushed a little, remembering the things he had said to her before they married; nothing romantic, of course, but nice all the same. It was a pity that he hadn't found it necessary to repeat any of them now that they were married. It was as though they had slipped at once into a comfortable state of middle-aged marriage, and that within weeks…

She listened to Loewert's cheerful talk and wondered what she should do about it. She supposed that if she hadn't fallen in love with Rijk she would have been quite content to let their relationship dwindle into the state he seemed to want: pleasant companionship, a hostess for his table and complete lack of interest in his life. She loved him, though, which made it an entirely different matter. So something had to be done to remedy the matter, and she would do it…

'You do look fierce,' said Loewert. 'Have you got a headache?'

'No, no. I was trying to remember if Matt had his breakfast before he went with Rijk. So sorry; I was listening… You were telling me about the blonde nurse in Out-patients. Is she very pretty?'

The description of this blue-eyed paragon took some time. 'But of course I'm not serious,' he told her firmly. 'Time enough for all that when I've qualified and got established. I mean, look at old Rijk; plenty of girlfriends, mind you, but he never lost sight of the fact that he intended to be on top of the ladder before he settled down for good.' He sighed. 'If I'm half as good as he is when I'm as old, I'll be very satisfied.'

'Rijk isn't old,' protested Sophie.

'No, no, I know that—he's twelve years older than I am and eight years older than Iwert, who's doing quite well for himself. I suppose Rijk's the goal we are both aiming for.' He beamed at her confidingly. 'He's made a name for himself.'

'I'm sure you'll succeed. Are you going to specialise?'

He plunged into a rose-coloured version of his future. 'Though I'll never be as good at it as Rijk.' He smiled rather shyly. 'But I hope I meet someone as beautiful as you and marry her.'

'Why, thank you, Loewert—she'll be a lucky girl.' She got to her feet. 'Shall we have a short walk before lunch? Rijk says it will snow…'

They took the lane down to the lake and stood looking at its grey, cold water. 'It's certainly going to snow,' said Loewert. 'Look at those clouds.'

They were massing on the horizon, a nasty grey with a yellowish tinge sweeping towards them, driven by a mean wind.

They didn't stay out long but went back to the house and had lunch together on the best of terms.

They were playing draughts on the discarded tea-tray beside Sophie's chair when Rijk got home. She looked up and smiled as he came into the room, and he bent to kiss her cheek before greeting his brother.

'I've had a wonderful day,' said Loewert. 'I had no idea that a sister-in-law could be such fun. I hope I'll be invited again…'

'Any time you like,' said Rijk. 'Stay to dinner?'

'I promised Mother that I'd go home. I'd better go now or she may think I've forgotten.'

Sophie got up too and he kissed her with obvious pleasure. 'Next time I'll stay for dinner if you'll have me,' he told her.

'I've enjoyed our day together; pass your exams and we'll have a celebration dinner.'

Rijk went out of the room with him and she sat down again and picked up her knitting, presenting a picture of serene domesticity to Rijk when he came back to the room.

He said quietly, 'I'm glad you enjoyed your day; Loewert is great fun. Did you have time to look through the invitations?'

'Yes, I did, and there is a note from your mother asking us to go to dinner next week.'

'The entire family will be there—aunts and uncles and cousins, and, of course, Grandmother. Which reminds me—I've opened an account for you at my bank; maybe you will want to buy clothes.' He gave her a cheque-book and she turned it over slowly and then looked inside. It was very like her own cheque-book, save for the sum of money written on its first stub.

'Your quarterly allowance,' said Rijk, watching her. 'If you need more money you have only to ask.'

'That's a fortune.' She raised troubled eyes to his.

'You will need every cent of it; it won't do for you to be seen too often in the same dress. You dress charmingly, Sophie, but I can't have my friends saying that I don't give you enough pin money.' He smiled at her. 'Do you want to shop in London or den Haag? I'll make some time to go with you.'

'No, no, there are some lovely shops in Leeuwarden. I'll have a good look round. I have brought one or two dresses with me, but perhaps they aren't grand enough.'

He crossed the room and took her hands in his. 'They don't have to be grand, my dear, but there will be tea-parties and coffee-parties and several dinner parties we cannot refuse. You don't like dressing up?'

'I've never had much chance to do that.' She smiled up into his face. 'But I think I shall enjoy it as long as it's not too often.'

'I'll promise you that. I'm not very social myself, only, now that I have a wife, friends and acquaintances are going to invite us.'

Rauke came in then to take away the tray, and Matt, who had been having his supper in the kitchen, came with him, delighted to see Sophie again, rolling his yellow eyes at the prospect of his evening walk.

'I'll come with you,' said Sophie and, wrapped in an elderly loden cloak kept in the hall closet, went out into the dark evening. The cold hit her like a blow, and Rijk took her arm.

'I said that it would snow,' he said with satisfaction as the first feathery flakes fell.

They walked fast down towards the lake and back again while Matt, impervious to the cold in his thick coat, dashed to and fro, barking. He had a deep, very loud bark.

They went back indoors presently to eat their dinner and discuss which of the invitations they should accept. Afterwards, back in the drawing-room, leafing through them once again, Sophie asked, 'Who is Irena van Moeren? She's written a little note at the bottom, but I don't know what it means.'

'Irena? A very old friend; we must certainly accept.' He stretched out a hand for the card. 'She writes at the bottom, "You must come for old times' sake".' He glanced at the date. 'I must make a point of being free—you'll like her.'

Sophie murmured a gentle reply; she would hate her. Old times' sake, indeed… And what if she turned out to be the woman she had seen Rijk with?

She sat, the picture of tranquillity, stitching away at her tapestry, not looking at him. If she had done so she would have been surprised to see the look on his face as he watched her.

It was snowing hard when she got up the next morning, and there was already a thick layer covering the lawn and shrubs. She went down to breakfast presently and was met in the hall by Rauke.

His 'Good morning' was grave and fatherly. 'The professor left early, *mevrouw*; he was called to an urgent case at four o'clock this morning.'

'He is operating this morning too; the list starts at nine o'clock. I do hope he gets some breakfast…'

'I'm sure that he will be looked after, *mevrouw*. I'll bring the coffee; you must have your breakfast.'

As he set the pot before her Sophie asked, 'Rauke, you speak such good English—have you been there?'

'No, *mevrouw*. I was with the professor's father during the occupation—underground, of course; we had a good deal to do with escaped prisoners and Secret Service personnel.'

She put out an impulsive hand. 'Oh, Rauke, I'm proud to know you.'

He took her hand gravely. 'Thank you, *mevrouw*. Would you care for a boiled egg?'

She was finishing breakfast with Matt in loving attendance when Rijk telephoned.

'Good morning, Sophie; you slept well?'

'Me? Slept? Oh, yes, thank you.' Ungrammatical and incoherent; she must do better. 'Are you tired? Was the op a success?'

'Yes, I think so; the next forty-eight hours will determine that.'

'Have you had breakfast?'

'Oh, yes.' She fancied that he was laughing. 'I'm going to scrub in a few minutes. If you go out, be careful, wear wellies—there are several pairs in the outer kitchen—and do take Matt with you.'

'Well, yes, I will. Will you be home in time for tea?' She did her best to make her voice sound brisk and friendly.

'Doubtful; I'll let you know later.' He rang off and she put the receiver down slowly. It was ridiculous to want to cry about nothing. She gave a sniff and blew her beautiful nose and went along to the kitchen to start the difficult but interesting business of deciding what to eat for the rest of the day.

It started to snow while she was out with Matt and she was glad of the wellies, for it was freezing now and the ground was icy. She walked down to the lake and took the track running beside it, which would lead her eventually to the village. The water, grey and sullen, reflected heavy cloud which covered the skies, and here and there there were great patches of ice forming.

'A winter's day and no mistake,' said Sophie to Matt, 'and I rather like it; it's like being in a Bruegel painting.'

In the village she bought stamps and a bar of chocolate in the small, crowded shop, exchanging greetings in her awkward Dutch, wishing she knew more words and making do with smiles and nods. The shop's owner was an old woman dressed severely in black, her hair dragged back in a severe bun, bright blue eyes almost hidden in her wrinkled face. She chattered away, not minding that Sophie understood one word in twenty, but she was friendly and when other customers came into the shop they all had a few words to say. Sophie went on her way feeling as though she belonged, munching chocolate. Matt munched too, keeping close to her as they took the narrow road to the house.

Rijk phoned late in the afternoon. It was snowing hard now and Rauke had drawn the heavy curtains across the windows, shutting out the dark early evening. Sophie, conning her Dutch phrase book, snatched the phone from its cradle. 'Rijk, when will you be home?'

He sounded placid. 'Very late, I'm afraid. I may have to operate again shortly. I'll get something to eat here. Don't wait up. What have you done with your day?'

'Well, I went for a long walk with Matt by the lake and then to the village and this afternoon I wrote letters and knitted.'

How dull it sounded; she was fast turning into an idle woman, and he would get bored with her. She said urgently, 'I should like to start Dutch lessons…'

'I'll see about it—I know the very person to teach you. What are you knitting?'

He sounded so kind that she felt the tears pricking her eyelids.

'A sweater for you,' she mumbled.

'That's the best thing I've heard all day,' he observed and with a brief '*Tot ziens*' rang off.

He was already sitting at the table when she went down to breakfast the next morning. His 'Good morning' was cheerful as he stood up and pulled out the chair opposite his.

Sophie sat down and poured her coffee. 'Were you very late?' she asked. She had waited until she had heard his footsteps soon after eleven o'clock, but she wasn't going to say so.

'Later than I had intended; the snow is piling up in the country roads, although the main roads are clear for the moment.'

'Oh—is it going to snow still?'

'Yes, and the temperature has dropped; we shall be skating by the end of the week.' He passed his cup for more coffee. 'Don't attempt to go on the lake, Sophie. The ice looks solid enough, but it isn't safe yet.'

'Will you be home for dinner this evening?' She added quickly, 'I only want to know so that Tyske can plan her cooking.'

'I should be home around six o'clock, so tell Tyske to go ahead. You should receive a phone call some time this afternoon from Mevrouw Smit, who will give you lessons in Dutch.'

'Oh, good, thank you, Rijk. Will she come here or shall I go to her?'

'You can arrange that between you. There will be a car for you in a few days, although I suggest that you wait for the weather to improve before you drive yourself; the roads are very bad at the moment.'

He dropped a hand on her shoulder as he went, but he didn't kiss her. Sophie gave Matt the rest of her toast and went along to the kitchen. To keep busy was important. She would answer their invitations during the morning and take Matt for a walk after lunch. There was the family dinner party to think about too…

The snow stopped during the morning and after lunch she wrapped herself in her top coat, tugged a woolly cap over her head, put on the thick gloves she had prudently bought in Leeuwarden, and began to walk briskly towards the village with Matt. It was slippery underfoot and very cold but the air was exhilarating and when she reached the village the few shops had their lights on and those people she saw called a greeting to her. There were lights on in the one hotel too; she supposed that if there was a good deal of skating, they would have plenty of custom. It was a sports centre, even if it was a small one.

Matt expected chocolate; she bought a bar and, since it was still reasonably light, decided to walk back along the track by the lake.

The water had become ice overnight; it looked solid enough but she remembered what Rijk had said. Once it was pronounced safe she supposed the whole lake would be crowded with skaters; he had told her that she would find it easy to skate, but she felt doubtful about that. The lake looked cold and vast and very lonely in the gathering gloom.

The track curved away from the water for a short distance and then turned back to the lake, and now she could see the lights from the house; in a few minutes she would go through the little wooden gate which led to the grounds. There would be tea waiting and perhaps a phone call from Rijk…

High-pitched shrieks brought her to an abrupt halt; there were children ahead of her, standing dangerously near the edge of the lake and screaming; they sounded excited until one of them darted on to the ice and started to run.

Sophie ran too; she had reached them when the ice cracked and the small figure disappeared. The children were silent now, dumb with shock, and she turned to the nearest. 'Help!' she shouted, and then, gathering her sparse vocabulary together, added urgently in Dutch, 'Go and get help! Quick!'

The child, a small boy of six or seven, gave her a frightened look and ran off and the others followed him as she took off her coat and boots and started across the lake; it gave at once under her weight, and Matt, slithering and slipping beside her, sent up great splashes of icy water. The child was standing now, the water up to his chest, shrieking his head off and not moving, and when she reached him he stopped his screams, his small face bluish with cold and his teeth rattling. She put an arm, heavy with freezing water, around him. 'Come on.' She tried to smile from a face rigid with cold. 'We can get back easily.'

He didn't move, however, and she realised that in a few minutes she would be in like case; the numbness was already creeping into her legs and in a very short time she wouldn't be able to use them.

Matt had kept close to her, uncertain but willing, and now she said, 'Fetch the master, Matt. Hurry—the master.'

He didn't like to leave her, but he went, plunging through the broken ice and racing away, jumping the gate and tearing up to the house. She watched him go, and then, fighting the bitter cold, she took a deep breath and started to scream for help. It was a quiet evening and surely someone would hear her.

Rijk had just stopped in front of his door when Matt reached him and he said sharply, 'You're soaked—you've been in the lake.' He put out a hand, but Matt shook it off, barking furiously and then turning and running back round the house, to appear a moment later, still barking, dancing impatiently round Rijk, then running off again.

The professor was a fit man despite his vast size; he ran as fast as Matt, vaulted the gate, and came to a halt by the lake in time to hear Sophie's shouts. Matt was already in the water; Rijk tossed off his coat and waded in after him. The water was already freezing over…

It wasn't far but it was hard going, for the ground was a slithering mud. When he reached her he put an arm round her. 'All right, my darling, we'll be out of here in no time…'

'Legs,' said Sophie through chattering teeth.

'I know. I'm going to put an arm round you both. Hold on to the child; it's only a few yards.'

They were halfway there when the first of the men arrived with torches and ropes. They waded into the water and, while one of them took the boy in his arms, the other one took Sophie's arm and between them he and Rijk half carried Sophie in to the bank.

The professor said something to the men, picked Sophie up and started towards the house, the man and the child with him, Matt panting beside him, while the second man ran ahead.

The door leading to the kitchen was open, light streaming from it and Rauke waiting there. The professor spoke to him and he went away to return within minutes with an armful of blankets. Moments later the child was being undressed by Tyske and one of the men and rolled into a blanket and Sophie, her sodden person swathed in yet more blankets, was laid carefully in one of the old-fashioned basket chairs by the Aga.

Rijk hadn't spoken; he went over to the child and Tyske took his place, taking off Sophie's stockings and rubbing her feet and legs with a towel. She talked soothingly as she did so and Sophie bit her lip, trying not to cry as life began to return to them.

She turned her head to see where the boy was and asked, '*De kind*? Is OK?' Tyske nodded and smiled and went on rubbing.

The kitchen seemed full of people; the boy's mother had been fetched and the child was sitting up now, drinking warm milk, still shaking and crying. The professor had been telephoning from a corner of the kitchen and the boy was sitting on his father's knee now, still crying.

Sophie looked up at Rijk as he came over to her. 'He's all right?'

'He's fine. I'm sending him to the cottage hospital

at Grouw for the night—he can have a check-up there. His father can borrow the Land Rover.'

He smiled at her. 'I'm going to carry you up to your room and Tyske will help you have a warm bath and get to bed. One of the maids is getting you a warm drink.' His eyes searched her face. 'You'll feel better after a good night's sleep.'

'But you—you're cold and wet too.'

He stooped and dropped a kiss on to her wet head. 'All in good time.'

'Matt's all right?'

'Rauke's giving him a good rub down and a warm meal. He can come and see you presently.'

He scooped her up then and carried her upstairs, with Tyske trotting in front to open the door and throw a blanket over the bed.

'I'll be back,' he told her and went away.

Half an hour later she was in bed, blissfully warm once more, her newly washed hair tied back, sipping warm milk which Tyske brought her before she bustled round the room collecting discarded clothes and tidying up.

When Rijk knocked on the door Matt came in with him, coming to lean against the bed and stare at her, his tongue hanging out with pleasure.

'You splendid brave fellow,' said Sophie and rubbed his rough head in the way he liked best, glad of something to do, because she felt shy of Rijk, who had come to sit on the bed.

He took her hand, but only to feel her pulse, his manner impersonal but friendly. 'Feeling better?' he asked.

'I'm fine really. I feel a fraud lying here in bed.' She

sat up straighter. 'Thank you, Rijk, for saving us—you were so quick. We really couldn't move, you know.'

He was still holding her hand. 'Cold, wasn't it?' He smiled at her.

'Very. You've changed? You're all right? And the boy?'

'Gone to Grouw to the hospital there for the night. His mother and father asked me to tell you that they would be indebted to you for the rest of their lives.'

'I was so frightened…'

'Which makes you doubly brave.' He laid her hand on the coverlet. 'You'll eat your supper in bed and then go to sleep.' He got up, towering over her. 'I'll look in later just to make sure that you are asleep.'

'You don't have to go anywhere? You'll be here?'

'I'll be here.' He went quietly, with Matt crowding at his heels.

Anneke, one of the housemaids, brought her supper presently: soup, creamed chicken, potatoes whipped to an unbelievable lightness and a *crème brûlée* to finish off. She ate the lot with a splendid appetite and drank the glass of hock accompanying it and when Anneke came for the tray told her in awkward Dutch that she wanted nothing more.

The house was very quiet and the room pleasantly warm; the curtains drawn across the windows shut out the cold dark outside. Sophie closed her eyes and slept. Rijk, coming to see how she fared around midnight, stood for several minutes, looking down at her. She lay curled up in bed, her hands pillowing her cheek, her lovely mouth slightly open, so that there was no mistaking the faintest of snores. He bent and dropped a kiss on her head and then went away.

She was young and strong and healthy; she got up the next morning feeling none the worse for her ducking. She was halfway down the staircase on her way to breakfast when Rijk's voice stopped her. His study door was half open and he was on the phone and, hearing her own name, she stopped and listened.

He was speaking Dutch, but she understood a word here and there, enough to know that he was saying something about the accident at the lake. It was when he said, laughing, 'Oh, Irena,' that she stiffened. He had a rather slow, clear voice and she could pick out more words now. Something about this evening and dinner… He stopped speaking and she nipped smartly upstairs again, and then, as he came from his study and crossed the hall, she started down again. He looked up and saw her and they went into breakfast together.

'You're feeling perfectly fit?' he wanted to know. 'It might be a good idea if you stayed indoors today. I've a busy day ahead of me and, alas, I shan't be home for dinner, so have something and go to bed early.'

'Very well. Surely you aren't operating this evening?' She was pleased at her casual tone.

'No.' He stared at her across the table. 'An evening engagement with an old patient that I prefer not to put off. I can, of course, do so if you want me at home, but since you are looking quite yourself and it is a matter of some importance I should like to go.'

'No, no, of course you don't have to come home. I've so much to keep me occupied; the days are never long enough. Besides, Tiele is coming to tea.'

She gave him a dazzling smile. ‘It would be silly of me to ask you to drive carefully, wouldn’t it?’

He got up, ready to leave. ‘Very silly, but rather nice too.’ He touched her lightly as he went. ‘Don’t wait up,’ he said casually as he went through the door.

CHAPTER NINE

SOPHIE SAT AT the table after Rijk had gone, feeding Matt pieces of toast while she thought. It had been wrong of her to eavesdrop, she knew that, but if she hadn't she wouldn't have known, would she? She wasn't sure what she did know, but it seemed likely that Rijk was still seeing someone—a woman—whom he had known and perhaps loved or been in love with before he met her and decided that she would fill the empty space he had allocated for a suitable wife. 'The heartless brute,' said Sophie in a stony little voice and, since she loved him with all her heart, not meaning a word of it.

She had told Rijk that she would stay indoors, but Matt had to go out; she put on the woolly cap and the loden cloak, stuck her feet into wellies, and took him for a brisk run in the grounds. The sky was still grey and the wind bitter, but the snow had stopped. When she got back to the house Rauke told her that tomorrow everyone would be skating.

Tiele came after lunch, bringing with her another young woman, a friend with whom she had been lunching and who had professed a keen desire to meet Rijk's bride. She was older than Tiele, tall and fair and with cold blue eyes, quite beautifully dressed. Sophie didn't like her and knew that she wasn't liked either, but on the surface at least they appeared good friends, and Tiele—kind, warm-hearted Tiele—noticed nothing, and there was plenty to talk about—the children, the family dinner party, only two days away now, and finally Elisabeth Willenstra's engagement.

'I shall have a big wedding,' she told Sophie, 'for we have so many friends, Wim and I. You and Rijk must come, of course—it will be in two months' time. Such a pity that I shall be away for your party, but we're sure to meet again—Rijk has so many friends.' She gave Sophie a sharp glance. 'I expect you have met Irena—Irena van Moeren—by now? One of his oldest friends.'

Sophie busied herself with the teapot. 'We haven't met yet; there has hardly been time. We had an invitation—'

'I'm sure Rijk will have found time.'

There was so much spite in Elisabeth's voice that Tiele looked up. 'If he has, it must have been by chance,' she said, 'and I'm sure Sophie knows about her, anyway, don't you, Sophie?'

'Oh, yes, of course,' said Sophie. It was surprising how easily the lie tripped off her tongue. It was in a good cause, she decided, for Elisabeth looked disappointed.

Alone again, she allowed herself half an hour's worry about the tiresome Irena. Elisabeth had been trying to needle her; all the same, this Irena van Moeren was someone to reckon with. Sophie decided that she would feel much better if she met the woman…

Rijk was late home, which was a good thing, for Sophie was in a bad temper and ripe for a quarrel.

The same bad temper prevented her from going to

Leeuwarden to look for a dress for the family party. She would wear the pink she had bought in London. What did it matter what she wore? she reflected pettishly, wallowing in a gloomy self-pity; no one would notice. And of course by no one she meant Rijk.

She had tried hard to forget Elisabeth Willenstra's sly remarks. All the same, she hadn't been very successful; Irena van Moeren was beginning to loom very large on her horizon, and she wished with all her heart that she didn't need to go to the family gathering.

There was to be a family dinner first before the guests arrived, and Rijk had come home early and spent half a hour with her in the drawing-room before they'd parted to dress, and now she was on the point of going downstairs.

The pink dress had lifted her spirits; it was pretty without being too girlish and flattered her splendid person. She had done her hair in its usual complicated coil, hooked in the diamond earrings, and fastened the pearl necklace; now she took a last look at her reflection in the pier-glass in her room and, catching up the mohair wrap to keep her warm on their journey, she went downstairs.

Rijk was in the drawing-room, standing by the open French window while Matt pranced around in the snow. Sophie, coming quietly into the room, thought that he was the handsomest man she had ever set eyes on; certainly a dinner-jacket, superbly cut, set off his massive proportions to the very best advantage.

He turned round at the soft sound of her skirt's rustle and studied her at his leisure. 'You look beautiful,' he said quietly.

She thanked him just as quietly; she had very little conceit, but she knew that she was looking her best. If only her best would match up to Irena van Moeren…

Matt came bounding in to stand obediently and have his great paws wiped clean before going to his basket, and Rijk said, 'If you are ready, I think we had better be on our way.'

He was perfectly at ease as they drove to Leeuwarden, telling her about his day's work, asking her what she had been doing, promising that since he was free on the following day he would take her on to the lake and give her her first skating lesson. She answered suitably in a voice so unlike her open manner that he asked her if she was nervous.

'You don't need to be,' he assured her. 'The family may be overpowering but they love you and, as for the guests, I'll be there to hold your hand.'

She said, 'You have so many friends, haven't you? I shan't remember any names, and will they all speak English?'

'Oh, yes. Although I expect Grandmother will make a point of addressing you in Dutch—she can be very contrary—although I have it from Mother that she approves of you, largely because you look as a woman should look.'

'You mean my clothes?'

'No, Sophie, your person. Your curves are generous and in the right places; she considers that a woman should look like one, not like a beanpole.' He glanced sideways at her in the dimness of the car. 'And I do agree with her, I certainly do.'

Her face flamed and she was glad that he couldn't

see that. Her 'Thank you' was uttered in a prim voice which made him smile.

The whole family were waiting for them as they entered the drawing-room, and she was glad that she had worn the pink dress; she felt comfortable in it and it matched the other dresses there in elegance. Rijk had taken her hand, going from one person to another after they had greeted his parents, reminding her of names. Aunts and uncles, cousins and the older nieces and nephews, there seemed to be no end to them, but presently, after they had drunk their champagne and spoken to everyone, she found herself at the dinner-table, sitting on the right of her father-in-law, and thankfully Loewert was on her other side. Rijk was at the other end of the table, sitting beside his mother, and the meal was conducted in a formal manner since it was, as her host assured her, a most important occasion in the family.

Dinner was lengthy and delicious and, between father and son, Sophie began to enjoy herself. By the time they rose and made their way back to the drawing-room she felt quite at ease, and when Rijk joined her and slipped an arm round her waist she smiled up at him, momentarily forgetful of her worries, only to have them all crowding back into her head as the guests began to arrive and her foreboding was realised.

Irena van Moeren was one of the first to arrive and she was indeed the woman Sophie had seen with Rijk; moreover, she was a strikingly handsome one, not young any more, but beautifully turned out in a black gown of utter simplicity.

That she knew everyone there was obvious and when she reached Rijk and Sophie she lifted her face for his kiss in a way which made it plain that she had done it many times before. She kissed Sophie too, and held her hand, telling her how delighted she was to meet her. 'We must become friends,' she said, and sounded as though she really meant it.

If Rijk was in love with her, reflected Sophie, agreeing with false enthusiasm, then she couldn't blame him; Irena was charming and obviously kind and warm-hearted. If Sophie hadn't hated her so thoroughly, she would have liked her. There was no sign of her husband and she must either be married or a widow, for she wore a ring. Perhaps, thought Sophie, allowing her thoughts to wander, Rijk had been unable to marry her when her husband was alive, and, now that he was dead, he was married himself.

She became aware that Irena was saying something to her. 'Rijk has asked me to spend an afternoon with you both, skating on the lake.'

'I don't skate,' said Sophie bleakly. She would have to stand and watch the two of them executing complicated figures together…

'You'll learn in no time, Rijk on one side of you and me on the other.'

Rijk hadn't spoken; she summoned up an enthusiasm she didn't feel and said heartily, 'Oh, that sounds wonderful. Do come.' She glanced at Rijk. 'I'm not sure when you're free, but if you could bring Irena for lunch one day soon?'

He didn't remind her that he had already told her that he was free on the following day. 'Tomorrow? I'll fetch you, Irena; we'll have an early lunch so that we can get the best of the afternoon.'

'Oh, yes,' Sophie added, 'and stay for dinner; I shall look forward to it.'

They were joined by several other guests then and it wasn't until the end of the evening that Sophie spoke to Irena again. She had come over to say goodbye and Sophie said gaily, 'Don't forget tomorrow—I do look forward to it.'

They were the last to leave; the family had stayed for a little while after the last of the guests had gone, mulling over the evening and then going home, until only Rijk's brothers and parents were left.

'It was a perfectly lovely evening,' declared Sophie, kissing and being kissed. 'Thank you very much. I—I feel one of the family now and I hope you will let me be that.'

Mevrouw van Taak ter Wijsma embraced her with warmth. 'You dear child, you have been one of us since the moment we saw you. I look forward to a delightful future with my new daughter. You are so exactly right for Rijk.'

Sophie smiled; of course she was right for Rijk, but did he think so too? Was she to be second best in his life? He would be good to her and care for her as his wife, but would he always be eating his heart out for Irena?

If he were, he showed no signs of it as they drove back home. It was a clear night with a bright moon, turning the snow-clad countryside to a fairytale beauty; he talked about their evening and the various people who had been there, apparently not noticing her silence. Only when they got home did he remark that it had been an exciting evening for her and that she must be tired. 'Go to bed, my dear,' he told her, 'and get some sleep. You have no need to get up for breakfast—I'll fetch Irena about midday and I'm sure that Tyske will cope with lunch.'

A remark which brought her out of her silence. 'It was a lovely evening and I am a little tired, but I don't want to stay in bed in the morning. Since you aren't going to the hospital in the morning perhaps we might have breakfast a little later, though?'

'Of course; tell Rauke before you go to bed. Would you like coffee or tea now?'

She shook her head, wished him goodnight, had a word with Rauke, and went to her room. She undressed slowly and got into bed and lay awake long after the house was quiet. The thought of the hours she must spend in Irena's company made her feel quite sick. She slept at last, to dream that Irena had come to the house, accompanied by piles of luggage, and that she herself was transported, in the way of dreams, on to an icy waste and told to skate back to England. It took her all of half an hour, using all her common sense, to face the grey light of early morning.

She got up thankfully and dressed carefully, wishing that she had gone to Leeuwarden as Rijk had suggested and bought some new clothes. She got into corduroy trousers and a heavy sweater and was rewarded by Rijk's genial, 'Ah, all ready to skate, I see.' He had given her face, pinched by worry and lack of sleep, a quick look. 'It should be excellent on the lake; there's not much wind. I've been down to have a look and there's plenty of hard, smooth ice, just right for you.' He added kindly, 'Of course, if you don't feel like it, you have no need to skate today—there will be ice for some time, I should think.'

She took a reviving sip of coffee. The idea of allowing him and Irena to spend half the day on the lake was sufficient to make her doubly keen to skate; jealousy was a great incentive, she had just discovered, although she despised herself for giving way to it. She said airily, 'Oh, but I'm longing to learn—I must be the only person living in Friesland who can't skate.'

He laughed then and began to talk about other things and presently went away to his study to emerge in time to take Matt for a walk before he went to fetch Irena.

Sophie, making sure that lunch was going to be ready by the time they returned, wondered how she was going to get through the day.

Standing at the window, she watched the car stop before the house and Irena and Rijk get out. Irena was laughing, obviously happy, and looking eye-catching in a scarlet anorak and stretch leggings, a scarf, tied with careless elegance, over her blonde hair.

Sophie went into the hall to meet them, the very picture of a smiling and delighted hostess, hurrying her guest away to take off her jacket and tidy herself, keeping up a flow of chat in a manner so unlike her that Rijk, getting drinks for them all, turned away to hide a smile, at the same time puzzled as to her manner…

With Matt in delighted attendance, they went down to the lake in the early afternoon and Rijk fastened skates on to Sophie's boots. They were broad and, she was assured, just right for a learner. He and Irena put on a quite different skate, specially used in Freisland and very fast.

Once on the ice Sophie did her best, held firmly on either side, sliding and slipping, until Rijk said, 'You're doing splendidly; lean forward a little and don't think about your feet. Irena is going to let go of you in a moment, but you won't fall; I have you safe.'

She didn't fall; the sight of Irena, skimming away with casual grace, inspired her to keep on her feet and presently she said, 'I believe I could go alone; may I try?'

She struck out bravely, letting out small screams of delight as she went forward. 'Look, look,' she called to Rijk. 'I'm skating; I can—'

The next moment she was tottering, waving her arms wildly in an effort to keep her balance as Rijk put a bracing arm around her and stood her upright again.

'That was splendid,' he observed, but Sophie, floundering around trying to regain her balance, could see Irena gliding gracefully back with an effortless ease which did nothing to improve Sophie's self-confidence.

'Sophie—but how splendid, you were skating alone. Never mind that you lost your balance; in a few days you will be good. Rijk, I will stay with Sophie while you take a turn around the lake.'

Of course Rijk had every right to go off on his own, but did he need to go so willingly, with nothing but a nod and a smile for her? She watched him race away, his hands clasped behind his back, moving effortlessly.

'He's very good,' said Irena. 'He has taken part in our *Elfstedentocht* several times, and twice he has won. It is a great test for a skater, for they must skate on the canals and waterways between eleven towns in Friesland.'

'I suppose he was taught when he was a little boy.'

'Yes, we all skate almost as soon as we can walk; we all learned together, but he was always the best of us.' She put a firm arm under Sophie's elbow. 'Now let us continue… Strike out with your right foot, so. Good, now do it with your left foot, and again, faster… You know about Rijk and us…?'

She spoke very quietly and when Sophie shot her a glance she looked sad.

'Yes,' said Sophie; she looked to where Rijk was tearing back across the ice.

'Good, then we do not need to speak of it; it is for me very sad.' She became brisk once more. 'Now if you will go alone, and if you fall I shall pick you up.'

If only she could go somewhere quiet and have a good cry, thought Sophie despairingly, but she was quite unable to deal with her wretched skates, and anyway, what would be the use? How much easier it would be if she could hate Irena, even dislike her a little, but she liked her; she could quite see why Rijk loved her. She plunged forward, not caring if she fell and broke a leg or an arm, and to her great surprise she kept on her feet for several yards until she was neatly fielded by Rijk, back again.

'You're an excellent pupil,' she was told, 'but that's enough for today; let us go home and have tea.'

'Wouldn't you and Irena like to skate together? I don't mind a bit; if you would take off my skates I'll go on ahead and make sure tea is ready.'

He gave her a quick look, his eyes thoughtful. 'We've had enough, haven't we, Irena? We'll have tea and then I'll take you back.'

'I thought Irena was staying for dinner?' Anyone

would think, reflected Sophie, that I am enjoying this conversation.

'I did tell Rijk; I'm so sorry that I didn't tell you too—' Irena looked quite crestfallen '—but I have an appointment this evening and it is important that I should be there. Forgive me, Sophie.'

'Well, of course; you must come another time. We'll have tea round the fire…'

Which they did, with Matt crouching beside his master, accepting any morsel which might come his way, and the talk was all of skating and how well Sophie had done, and presently Irena said that she really must go.

Sophie, the hospitable hostess even though it was killing her, murmured regret and the wish that they might meet again soon, and waved them away from the porch, Matt beside her, puzzled as to why he wasn't going too. Sophie was puzzled as well; after all, Rijk was only driving into Leeuwarden and back again.

The pair of them went back to the fireside, Matt to snooze and she to sit and worry. It had been a horrendous day; she had been hopelessly outclassed on the ice and Irena's calm acceptance of the situation had left her uncertain and unhappy. She was deeply hurt too that Rijk hadn't talked to her about it. After all, it could happen to anyone, and she was fair enough to realise that to have been in love, perhaps for years, with each other with no hope of marrying and then to find the way clear, only for Rijk to have married someone else in the meantime, must be a terrible thing to happen. Was Irena's husband dead, she wondered, or were they divorced? When Rijk came home she would ask him; after all, they were the best of friends and should be able to discuss the problem without rancour.

She gave a great sigh and Matt opened his eyes and grunted worriedly. 'I think my heart is broken,' said Sophie. 'It would be so simple if only I didn't love him.'

Matt got up and laid his great head on her lap and presently, when she went upstairs to change her dress, even went with her. He wasn't allowed in the bedrooms, but she sensed that he was disobeying out of kindness. She put on one of her prettiest dresses, took pains with her face and hair, and went downstairs to wait for Rijk.

Only he didn't come. It was only a few minutes to dinner when the phone rang.

'Sophie.' Rijk's voice sounded urgently in her ear. 'I shall be delayed. Don't wait dinner and don't wait up.'

'Yes,' said Sophie and hung up. It had been an inadequate answer; she might have said, 'I quite understand,' or even, 'Very well.'

She dined alone with Rauke serving her and taking away the almost uneaten plates of food with a worried air. She saw the look and said hastily, 'I'm not hungry, Rauke; it must be all that skating. If the professor isn't back by eleven o'clock will you lock up, please, and leave the door for him and something in the kitchen? He may be cold and hungry. He didn't say when he would be home, but it sounded urgent.'

She added that last bit to make it sound convincing, even though in her mind's eye she could see Rijk and Irena spending the evening together. With a mythical headache as an excuse, she went to bed early.

She didn't sleep; it was almost two o'clock when she

heard Rijk's quiet tread on the stairs. Only then did she fall into a troubled sleep.

He was already at the table when she went down to breakfast in the morning.

'Don't get up,' she told him sharply. 'I dare say you're tired after your short night.' Then, because she was beside herself with lack of sleep and unhappiness and worry, she allowed her tongue to say things she had never meant to utter.

'I'm only surprised that you bothered to come home, but of course you weren't to know that I know all about it.'

She stopped then, otherwise she might have burst into tears, and poured herself a cup of coffee with a shaking hand. After a heartening sip, she added, 'You might have told me.'

The professor sat back in his chair, watching her. He was bone-weary, after operating for hours, but his voice was placid enough as he asked, 'And why should I not come home, Sophie? I live here.'

Sophie mauled the slice of toast on her plate. 'Bah.' Her voice shook. 'I've just told you, I know about you and Irena…'

The professor didn't move. 'And?' he asked in an encouraging voice.

'Well, are we supposed to go on like this for the rest of our lives? Elisabeth Willenstra said—'

'Ah—Elisabeth.' His voice was quiet, but his blue eyes were hard.

'Well, that you and Irena were old friends… She didn't say anything in so many words, but I can take a hint. Besides—' she gulped back tears and went on steadily '—that evening I came back by bus—I had gone to the hospital to go home with you. It was as I was waiting to cross the street opposite the entrance that I saw you both coming out together. She looked so happy and you were smiling at her and holding her arm and… yesterday Irena asked if I knew about you… Those were her words—"You know about Rijk and us?"—and of course I said yes.' She could hear her voice getting louder and shrill, but she couldn't stop now. 'And you stayed out almost all night and she was coming to dinner but then she said she had to go back and you went with her.'

The professor still hadn't moved. 'You believe that I would do this to you?'

Something in his calm voice made her mumble, 'You can't help falling in love, can you? I mean, when you do it matters more than anything else, doesn't it?'

'Indeed it does. I see no point in continuing this conversation at the moment. I shall be late home; don't wait up.'

He was at the door when she asked in a small voice, 'Are you very angry, Rijk?'

He turned to look at her. He wasn't just tired, he was white with anger, his eyes blazing.

'Dangerously so, Sophie,' he said and went away, closing the door softly behind him.

She wished with all her heart that she had held her tongue.

She took Matt for a walk presently, in the cold stillness of the icy morning, and she was able to think clearly. She would have to apologise, of course, and ask to be forgiven, although it was she who should be doing the forgiving, and she would insist on a sensible discussion. They had always been good friends, able to talk easily and communicate with each other. It was a great pity that she had fallen in love with him; it was a complication she hadn't envisaged.

She went back home and made a pretence of eating the lunch Rauke had ready for her and then wandered around the house, unable to settle to anything. She was in the small sitting-room, looking unseeingly out of the window, when Rauke announced Irena.

Sophie pinned a smile on her face and turned to welcome her guest. Rijk would have seen her, of course, and she had come to explain…

Irena came in with an outstretched hand. 'Sophie, I am on my way back to Leeuwarden and I thought I would come and see you. You don't mind?'

Sophie took the hand. 'Of course not. I expect you've seen Rijk?'

Irena looked puzzled. 'Rijk?' She frowned. 'No.' She looked suddenly anxious. 'He has telephoned here? He would like to speak to me urgently?' She had gone quite white. 'Jerre—he is not so well… I must telephone… He was improving; what can have happened?'

She sounded distraught and Sophie said, 'Who is Jerre?'

'My husband—you knew? You said that you did. He had a brain tumour and Rijk saved his life, but we told no one because Jerre is director of a big business concern and if it were known that he was so very ill it would have caused much panic and shareholders would have lost money…but I must telephone.'

'It's all right, Irena, I'm sure your husband is all

right. It's just that I thought that you might have seen Rijk. It's just that I didn't know about your husband.'

Irena was no fool. 'Oh, my poor dear, you thought Rijk and I… He is Jerre's best friend; we all grew up together. Why should you think that of us?'

'Someone called Elisabeth…'

'That woman… She pretends to be everyone's friend, but she is spiteful; she likes to make trouble. Nothing of what she said to you is true; you must believe me.'

'I do, only I've quarrelled with Rijk, and, you see, I'm in love with him and he doesn't know that. I can't explain…'

'No, no,' said Irena soothingly, 'a waste of time. Get your coat and hat and come to Leeuwarden with me. He will be at the hospital; you must find him there and explain to him. He is angry, yes? He has a nasty temper, but he controls it. Tell him you love him.'

Sophie shook her head. 'I can't do that; if I do I shall have to leave him…'

'You must do what you think is best, but I do beg you, get your coat.'

Irena dropped her off outside the hospital, kissed her warmly, and waited in the car until she saw Sophie through the doors.

The porter was in his little box. Seeing Sophie, he shook his head. 'The professor is not here, *mevrouw*.' His English was surprisingly good. 'He is gone.'

'But his car is outside.'

'He holds his clinic five minutes away from here; he walks.'

'Will you tell me where the clinic is?'

The directions were complicated and she wasn't sure if she had them right, but she had wasted enough time already. She thanked him and he said, 'The clinic lasts until five o'clock; you should hurry, *mevrouw*.'

She hurried, trying to remember his directions, but after five minutes' walking she knew that she had gone wrong; the street she was in was narrow, lined with old houses and run-down shops, and it didn't appear to have a name. A matronly woman was coming towards her and Sophie stopped her, gathered together the best of her Dutch, and asked the way. Precious moments were lost while she repeated everything under the woman's beady eyes.

'*Engelse*?' she wanted to know, and, when Sophie nodded, broke into a flood of talk, not a word of which Sophie understood. She was wasting time. When the woman paused for breath, Sophie thanked her politely and hurried on. There was a crossroads ahead, not a main street, but it might lead somewhere where she could ask again. She was in a quite nasty temper by now; she was lost and unhappy and she was never going to find Rijk, and that was more important than anything else in the world. She shot round a corner head first into a broad expanse of cashmere overcoat.

'What a delightful surprise,' said Rijk, wrapping both arms around her.

'So there you are,' said Sophie in a very cross voice. 'I've been looking for you.' And she burst into tears.

Rijk stood patiently, rock-solid, while she sniffed and wept and muttered into his huge shoulder. Presently he took a very large white handkerchief from a pocket, still holding her close with his other arm, and mopped her face gently.

'Have a good blow and stop crying and tell me why you were looking for me.'

'I didn't mean a word of it,' said Sophie wildly. 'I've been mean and jealous and silly and I'm so ashamed and I can't skate and you only want us to be friends—' she gave a great sniff '—but I can't because I've fallen in love with you and I'll have to go away; I really can't go on like this.'

'My darling wife, I have been waiting patiently to hear you say that.' He smiled in the darkness. 'Ever since the moment I first saw you standing on the pavement outside St Agnes's and fell in love with you.'

'Then why didn't you say so?'

'My dear love, you weren't even sure if you liked me.'

She thought this over. 'But you do love me? You were so angry this morning that I didn't know what to do, but Irena came to see me and told me about Jerre and I came to say that I was sorry.'

'What a delightfully brave wife I have. Have you any idea where you are?'

'No, the porter told me where to go, but I couldn't understand him.'

He gave a rumble of laughter. 'However, you found me.' He bent his head and kissed her soundly. 'I shall always take care of you, my darling love.'

He did kiss her again, and an old man, shuffling past, shouted something and laughed.

'What did he say?' asked Sophie.

Rijk said gravely, 'Translated into polite English, he begged me to kiss and hug you.'

Sophie lifted her face to his. 'Well, hadn't you better take his advice?'

* * * * *

The Moon for Lavinia

CHAPTER ONE

IT WAS QUIET now that the day's lists were over; the operating theatre, gleaming with near-sterile cleanliness and no longer lighted by its great shadowless lamp, looked a very different place from the hive of ordered activity it had been since early morning, for now the surgeons and anaesthetists had gone, as well as Theatre Sister and most of her staff; indeed, the department held but one occupant, a nurse sitting on a stool in front of one of the trolleys, sorting instruments with swift precision.

She was a small, neat person, a little plump, and with a face which was neither plain nor pretty, although when she laughed her hazel eyes widened and twinkled and her too large mouth curved charmingly. It was a pity that she laughed all too seldom, and now, deep in thought as she worked, she looked rather on the plain side and sad with it. She finished her task, tidied everything away neatly and began a final inspection of the theatre before she went off duty. It was a Sunday evening, and for some reason one staff nurse was considered sufficient to be on duty after six o'clock; presumably on the principle that it being a Sunday, people would be less prone to require emergency surgery, and for once this had been proved right; the evening hours, spent in doing the necessary chores had been too quiet, so that Lavinia Hawkins had had time to think, which was a pity, for she had nothing pleasant to think about.

She went along to take off her gown, threw it into the laundry bin, and then sat down again, this time on the only chair the changing room possessed. The June sun, still warm and bright, streamed in through the window, and she could hear, very faintly, the subdued hum of the London evening traffic, most of it returning from an outing to the sea. It would have been a perfect day for them, thought Lavinia without envy, although she wasn't very happy herself; it was a good thing that she was going to Aunt Gwyneth's in two days' time and would have the chance to talk to Peta, her young sister—perhaps they would be able to plan something. Quite forgetful of the time, she took Peta's letter from her pocket and read it once more.

Peta was dreadfully unhappy; when their mother had died, more than a year ago now, and Aunt Gwyneth had offered her a home, Lavinia had been grateful for her help. There was no money, the annuity her mother had lived upon died with her; her father had died a number of years earlier, and although she herself had been self-supporting and had even been able to help out with Peta's school fees, her sister's education had been at a stage when to make changes in it would have been nothing short of criminal. For one thing, Peta was clever and working for her O levels, and for another, Lavinia was only too well aware that a sound education for her sister was essential if she was to be self-supporting too, so that when her mother died Lavinia accepted her aunt's offer with an eager gratitude which she had since come to regret.

It hadn't worked out at all. Aunt Gwyneth was a widow and comfortably off, living in a large house on the outskirts of Cuckfield which was run by a highly efficient housekeeper, leaving her free to indulge her passion for bridge and committee meetings. Lavinia had honestly thought that she would be glad to have Peta to live with her; she had no children of her own and Peta was a darling, pretty and sweet-tempered and anxious to please. It was after she had been at Cuckfield for several months that Lavinia began to sense that something was wrong, but it had taken her a long time to persuade Peta to tell her what was amiss and when, at last, she had got her to talk about it it was to discover that it wasn't just the natural unhappiness she felt at the loss of her mother—life wasn't fun, she confided to Lavinia; her aunt had discovered that having a teenager in the house had its drawbacks. True, Peta was at school all day, but at the week-ends and during the holidays she was made to feel a nuisance, and whenever she suggested that she might spend a few days with Lavinia, there were always good reasons why she shouldn't…

Lavinia, her arm round her sister's slim shoulders, had frowned. 'Darling, you should have told me,' she had said. 'I could have spoken to Aunt Gwyneth,' but even as she uttered the words she had known that it wasn't going to be as easy as all that. Peta was due to take her O levels in a week or two's time, and the plan had been for her to stay on at school and try for her A levels in a couple of years. Even if Lavinia had had a flat of her own, which she hadn't, it would still be difficult, for there would still be the question of where Peta should go to school and how would she ever afford the fees? 'Look,' she had advised, 'could you hang on for another year or two, love—just until you've got those A levels? I'm to have Sister Drew's job when she retires, and that's less than a year now; I'll save every penny I can and find a flat.'

And Peta had agreed. That had been barely a week ago, and now here was her letter, begging Lavinia to take her away from Aunt Gwyneth, promising incoherently to stay until the exam results were out, if only she would take her away… Lavinia folded the letter up once more and put it in her pocket. She had a headache from worrying about what was to be done, for whatever it was, it would have to be done quickly, and at the moment she had no ideas at all. She went down to supper, turning over in her mind a variety of ideas, none of which, unfortunately, stood up to close scrutiny.

Most of her friends were already in the canteen, queueing for baked beans on toast and cups of tea. They shared a table, making the beans last as long as possible while they discussed the day's work. It was as they lingered over the last dregs of their tea that Shirley Thompson from Women's Surgical declared herself to be completely fed up with that ward, its Sister, the patients, and indeed the whole hospital. 'I'm sick of Jerrold's,' she declared. 'I'm going to look for another job. I've got the *Nursing Mirror* in my room, let's go and make a pot of tea and find me a new job.'

No one quite believed her; for one thing, she was

going steady with one of the house surgeons; and for another, she made this same announcement every few months, but it was too soon for bed and there wasn't much else to do; they trooped from the canteen and across to the Nurses' Home, where they crowded into the Sisters' lift, strictly forbidden, but no one was likely to see them on a Sunday evening, anyway, and besides, everyone did it and hoped not to be caught, and once on the top floor they disposed themselves around Shirley's room, ready to drink more tea and give her their not very serious advice.

They were debating, in a lighthearted manner, the advantages of nursing an octogenarian recovering from a fractured femur in Belgravia, as opposed to a post as school nurse in a boarding establishment in Cumberland, when the *Nursing Mirror* came into Lavinia's hands. She glanced through it idly and turning a page had her eye instantly caught by a large advertisement headed simply 'Amsterdam'. She read it carelessly, and then, struck by a blindingly super idea, very carefully.

Registered nurses wanted, said the advertisement, with theatre experience and at a salary which was quite fabulous. Knowledge of Dutch was unnecessary; lessons could be arranged, and provided the applicant proved suitable and wished to remain for a period of not less than six months, outside accommodation would be found for her. Lavinia, never very good at her sums, got out her pen and did some basic arithmetic on the underside of her uniform skirt. Supposing, just supposing that the job was all it said it was, if she could get somewhere to live, Peta could live with her, for they could manage on that salary if they were careful. Of course, the plan was completely crazy; Peta's education would come to a halt, but then, Lavinia feared, it would do that if Peta stayed at Cuckfield; her sister's vehemence was clear enough in her letter, it would be awful if she were to run away… Lavinia shuddered just thinking about it—and wouldn't it be better to have her sister under her eye and once she had settled down, devise some plan whereby she might finish her education? She calculated quickly; Peta was only a week or two under sixteen when she could leave school quite legitimately, so there would be no trouble there, and although she knew nothing about education in Holland there would surely be some way of completing her studies.

When the gathering broke up, she begged the journal from Shirley and before she went to bed that night, applied for the job.

She went down to Cuckfield two days later and found Peta alone in the house, waiting for her, and when she saw her sister's face any doubts which she had been secretly harbouring about a plan which common sense told her was a little short of hare-brained were put at rest. Peta was dreadfully unhappy and Lavinia, ten years her senior, felt a motherly urge to set things right as quickly as possible.

Aunt Gwyneth was out and would be back for lunch, and, the housekeeper told Lavinia, Mrs Turner was looking forward to a nice chat before her niece went back that evening.

Lavinia sighed. The nice chats were really nothing but questions and answers—her aunt asked the questions; rather rude ones usually, and she answered them with a polite vagueness which invariably annoyed her elderly relation, for her aunt, while professing a fondness for Peta, had never liked her. Even as a small girl she had refused to be browbeaten by her father's elder sister and her hectoring manner had left her quite unimpressed; it had never worried her father either, who had brushed it aside like a troublesome swarm of flies, but her mother, a gentle creature like Peta, had often wilted under her sister-in-law's tongue. Lavinia, made of sterner stuff, had refused to be intimidated, and Aunt Gwyneth, annoyed at this, took her petty revenge by never inviting her to stay at her home, either for her holidays or her free days. She was too clever to do this openly, of course, but somehow, when holidays came round, the bedrooms were being decorated, or her aunt was going away herself or felt too poorly to have visitors, and as for her days off, invariably at teatime Lavinia would be asked which train she intended to catch and some reference would be made as to her eagerness to get back to Jerrold's, in order, presumably, to plunge into a hectic round of gaiety with every doctor in the place.

This veiled assumption of her popularity with the men was something which amused Lavinia very much; her aunt knew well enough that she had no men friends; she got on very well with the doctors and students she worked with, but none of them had shown her any decided preference and she doubted if they ever would; she had no looks to speak of and a quiet manner which, while encouraging young men to confide in her, did nothing to catch their fancy.

They were sitting together in the sitting room having their morning coffee when Peta burst out: 'Lavinia, I can't stay here—I simply can't! Aunt Gwyneth keeps telling me how good she's been to me—and you, though I can't think how—she makes me feel like a—a pauper. I know we haven't any money, but she is our aunt and our only relation, and do you know what she said? That in a year or two, when I've finished school and am earning my living, you'll have to leave your job in hospital and be her companion, because she'll need someone by then and it's only natural that you should be the one because she's given me a home.' She added unhappily: 'Lavinia, what are we going to do?'

Lavinia refilled their coffee cups. 'I'll tell you, darling.'

She outlined her plan simply, making light of its obvious drawbacks, glad that Peta hadn't spotted them in her excitement. 'So you see, Peta, everything will be super, only you must promise to stay here and take your O levels and say nothing about our plan to anyone. I haven't heard from these people yet, but I think I've got a good chance of getting a job. I'll have to give a month's notice at Jerrold's—give me a couple of weeks to find my way about, and I'll come for you. Could you stick it for just a little longer?'

Peta nodded. 'Darling Lavinia, of course I can. You're sure we can live on what you'll earn in Amsterdam? I could get a job…'

'Yes, love, I know, but I think we'll be able to manage. I'd rather you went on with your studies—perhaps if you could learn Dutch, enough to help you get a job later on? UNO and all that,' she added vaguely, and looked at the clock. 'Aunt Gwyneth will be here very soon, let's talk about something else so that we're just as usual when she comes. Tell me about school.'

Their aunt found them poring over school books, arguing cheerfully about applied physics although Lavinia knew almost nothing about the subject. She got up to greet her aunt and received a chilly peck on her cheek while the lady studied her. 'You must be twenty-six,' she observed. 'Such a pity you have no looks, Lavinia. How fortunate that you took up nursing as a career, although waiting until you were twenty-two seems to me to have been a needless waste of time—you could have been a ward Sister by now.'

Lavinia thought of several answers to this unfortunate remark, but none of them were very polite; they went in to lunch in a little flurry of polite and meaningless remarks.

Lunch was excellent; Aunt Gwyneth enjoyed her comforts and made sure that she had them, although she pointed out during dessert that her nieces were lucky girls indeed to enjoy the benefits of her generosity. Lavinia, still peevish about her aunt's remark about her lack of looks, felt an urge to throw her trifle across the table at her. No wonder poor little Peta was fed up; anything would be better than putting up with the succession of snide remarks which tripped off her relation's tongue. For once she answered with relief when she was asked at what time she was returning to hospital.

'I daresay you have plans for the evening,' said Aunt Gwyneth, 'and I'm not so selfish as to delay you in any way. After tea, you say? That is admirable, for I have a small bridge party this evening, and Peta has a great deal of studying to do in preparation for her exams.' Her two listeners expected her to add a rider to the effect that if it hadn't been for her, there would have been no possibility of exams, but she contented herself with a smug smile.

So Lavinia went back after tea, not liking to leave Peta, but seeing no alternative, but at least she was heartened to see how much more cheerful her sister was. They parted under their aunt's eye, so that all Lavinia could say was: 'See you next week, Peta—if I may come down, Aunt?' she added politely, and received a gracious nod of assent.

There was a letter for her on Monday morning, asking her to go for an interview, either that afternoon or on the following morning, and as luck would have it she had been given a split duty because Sister wanted the evening, and the morning's list was too heavy for them both to be off duty at the same time. She changed into a plain coffee-coloured linen dress, coiled her long hair with care, made up her face, and caught a bus; only as she was going through the open door of the hotel where the interviews were to be held did she pause to think what she was doing, and by then it was too late. There were a dozen or more girls waiting, some of them younger than she, and most of them prettier; there was a possibility of her not getting a job after all; she hadn't expected quite so many applicants.

She was brooding over this when her turn came, and she found herself on the other side of the door, invited to sit down by a middle-aged lady sitting at a table, and stared at by the two people on either side of her. A man, a large comfortable-looking man in his fifties, and another woman, young this time—not much older than herself and very fair with a wholesome out-of-doors look about her.

The lady in the middle opened the interview with a pleasant: 'Miss Hawkins? We are pleased that you could come and see us. My name is Platsma—Mevrouw Platsma, and this is Juffrouw Smid and also Professor van Leek, who is the Medical Director of our hospital in Amsterdam. Miss Smid is the Sister-in-Charge of the theatre unit.' She paused to smile. 'What are your qualifications, Miss Hawkins?'

Lavinia gave them without trying to make more of them than they were.

'And your reasons for wishing to work with us?'

She told them the truth, fined down to the facts and without enlarging upon Aunt Gwyneth. 'I think I could live on the salary you offer and have my sister to live with me, something we both would like very much—I can't do that here because I can't afford a flat—I live in at Jerrold's. I should like to live in Amsterdam too; I've never been out of England.'

'You like your work?'

'Very much.'

'You are accustomed to scrub?'

'Yes. There are four theatres in our unit, I work in

General Surgery and take most of the cases when Sister is off duty.'

'You have no objection to us referring to your superiors at the hospital?'

'No, none at all. If I should be considered for the job, I should have to give a month's notice.'

They all three smiled at her and Mevrouw Platsma said: 'Thank you, Miss Hawkins, we will let you know at the earliest opportunity.'

She went back to Jerrold's feeling uncertain; her qualifications were good, she would be given excellent references she felt sure, but then so might the other girls who had been there. She told herself sensibly to forget about it, something easily done, as it turned out, for there was an emergency perforation that evening, followed by a ruptured appendix. She went off duty too tired to do more than eat a sketchy supper, have a bath, and go to bed.

There was a letter by the first post in the morning. She had got the job. She did an excited little jig in the scrubbing-up room, begged permission to go to the office at once, and presented herself, rather breathless still, before the Principal Nursing Officer's desk.

Miss Mint heard her out, expressed regret that she should want to leave, but added in the same breath that it was a splendid thing to broaden one's mind when young and that should Lavinia wish to return to Jerrold's at some future date, she could be sure of a post—if there was one vacant—at any time. She finished this encouraging speech by observing that probably she had some holidays due to her, in which case she should be able to leave sooner.

Lavinia becamed at her. 'Oh, Miss Mint, I have—a week. I knew you would understand about me wanting to go somewhere where I could have Peta with me…I only hope I'll make a success of it.'

Miss Mint smiled. 'I can think of no reason why you shouldn't,' she said encouragingly. 'Come and see me before you go, Staff Nurse. I shall of course supply references when they are required.'

Lavinia went through the rest of the day in a daze, doing her work with her usual efficiency while she thought about her new job. She spent a good deal of her lunch hour writing to accept the post, and only restrained herself by a great effort from writing to Peta too, but there was always the danger that their aunt would read the letter, and telephoning would be just as chancy; she should have thought of that sooner and arranged for her sister to telephone her on her way home from school. Now the news would have to wait until she paid her weekly visit on Saturday.

The days flashed by; she received particulars of her job, how she was to travel, and the day on which she was expected, as well as the gratifying news that her references were entirely satisfactory. She had a few pounds saved; the temptation to spend some of them on new clothes was very strong, so on her morning off she went along to Oxford Street.

It was a splendid day and the gay summer clothes in the shop windows exactly matched her mood; discarding all sensible ideas about practical rainwear, hard-wearing shoes and colours which wouldn't show the dirt, she plunged recklessly, returning to the Nurses' Home laden with parcels; new sandals—pretty pink ones to match the pink cotton dress and jacket she hadn't been able to resist, a pale green linen skirt with a darling little linen blouse to go with it, and as well as these, a long cardigan which happily matched them both. There was a dress too, pale green silk jersey, and as a sop to her conscience, a raincoat, coffee-coloured and lightweight. She laid everything out on her bed and admired them and tried not to think of all the money she had spent, cheering herself with the thought that she still had something tucked away and enough besides to get her through the first month in Amsterdam before she would be paid. And when Peta joined her, she would buy her some pretty dresses too; Aunt Gwyneth's ideas ran to the serviceable and dull for her niece; the two of them would scour Amsterdam for the sort of clothes girls of Peta's age liked to wear.

Her sister was waiting for her when she got to Cuckfield on Saturday morning and so was their aunt. There was no chance to talk at all until after lunch, and then only for a few minutes while Aunt Gwyneth was telephoning. 'It's OK,' said Lavinia softly. 'I've got the job—I'm going two weeks today. I'll tell Aunt when I come next week, but only that I'm going—nothing about you yet—and don't say anything, love, whatever you do.' She smiled at Peta. 'Try not to look so happy, darling. Tell me about your exams—do you think you did well?'

She didn't stay as long as usual; her aunt had a bridge

date directly after tea and was anxious for her to be gone, and a tentative suggestion that she might take Peta out for the evening was met with a number of perfectly feasible reasons why she shouldn't. That was the trouble with Aunt Gwyneth, thought Lavinia crossly, she never flatly refused anything, which made it very hard to argue with her. She wondered, as she went back to London, how her aunt would take the news of her new job.

She thought about it several times during the ensuing week, but theatre was busy and there really wasn't much time to worry about anything else. Saturday, when it came, was another cloudless day. Lavinia, in a rather old cotton dress because she was starting on the business of packing her things, felt cheerful as she walked the short distance from the station to her aunt's house. And her aunt seemed in a good mood too, so that without giving herself time to get nervous, Lavinia broke her news.

It was received with surprising calm. 'Let us hope,' said her aunt ponderously, 'that this new venture will improve your status sufficiently for you to obtain a more senior post later on—it is the greatest pity that you did not take up nursing immediately you left school, for you must be a good deal older than the average staff nurse.'

Lavinia let this pass. It was partly true in any case, though it need not have been mentioned in such unkind terms. Everyone knew quite well why she had stayed at home when she had left school; her mother was alone and Peta was still a small girl, and over and above that, her mother hadn't been strong. She said now, schooling her voice to politeness: 'I don't know about that, Aunt, but the change will be nice and the pay's good.'

'As long as you don't squander it,' replied Aunt Gwyneth tartly. 'But it is a good opportunity for you to see something of the world, I suppose; the time will come when I shall need a companion, as you well know. Peta will be far too young and lively for me, and I shall expect you, Lavinia, to give up your nursing and look after me. It is the least you can do for me after the sacrifices I have made for you both.'

Lavinia forbore from commenting that she had had nothing done for her at all; even holidays and days off had been denied her, and though she was a fair-minded girl, the worthy stockings, edifying books and writing paper she had received so regularly at Christmas and birthdays could hardly be classed as sacrifices. And her aunt could quite well afford to pay for a companion; someone she could bully if she wanted to and who would be able to answer back without the chain of family ties to hold her back. She sighed with deep contentment, thinking of her new job, and her aunt mistaking her reason for sighing, remarked that she was, and always had been, an ungrateful girl.

Lavinia wasn't going to see Peta again before she left England, although she had arranged to telephone her at a friend's house before she went. She spent the week in making final arrangements, aided, and hindered too, by her many friends. They had a party for her on her last night, with one bottle of sherry between a dozen or more of them, a great many pots of tea and a miscellany of food. There was a great deal of laughing and talking too, and when someone suggested that Lavinia should find herself a husband while she was in Holland, a chorus of voices elaborated the idea. 'Someone rich—good-looking—both—with an enormous house so that they could all come and stay…' The party broke up in peals of laughter. Lavinia was very popular, but no one really believed that she was likely to find herself such a delightful future, and she believed it least of all.

She left the next morning, after a guarded telephone talk with Peta and a noisy send-off from her friends at Jerrold's. She was to go by plane, and the novelty of that was sufficient to keep her interested until the flat coast of Holland appeared beneath them and drove home the fact that she had finally left her safe, rather dull life behind, and for one she didn't know much about. They began to circle Schiphol airport, and she sat rigid. Supposing that after all, no one spoke English? Dutch, someone had told her, was a fearful language until you got the hang of it. Supposing that there had been some mistake and when she arrived no one expected her? Supposing the theatre technique was different, even though they had said it wasn't…? She followed the other passengers from the plane, went through Customs and boarded the bus waiting to take her to Amsterdam.

The drive was just long enough to give her time to pull herself together and even laugh a little at her silly ideas. It was a bit late to get cold feet now, anyway, and she had the sudden hopeful feeling that she was going to like her new job very much. She looked about her eagerly as the bus churned its way through the morning traffic in the narrow streets and at the terminal she did as she had been instructed: showed the hospital's address to a hovering taxi-driver, and when he had loaded her luggage into his cab, got in beside it. The new life had begun.

CHAPTER TWO

THE HOSPITAL WAS on the fringe of the city's centre; a large, old-fashioned building, patched here and there with modern additions which its three-hundred-year-old core had easily absorbed. It was tucked away behind the busy main streets, with narrow alleys, lined with tiny, slightly shabby houses, round three sides of it. On the fourth side there was a great covered gateway, left over from a bygone age, which was still wide enough to accommodate the comings and goings of ambulances and other motor traffic.

Lavinia paused to look about her as she got out of the taxi. The driver got out too and set her luggage on the pavement, said something she couldn't understand, and then humped it up the steps of the hospital and left it in the vast porch. Only when he had done this did he tell her how much she needed to pay him. As she painstakingly sorted out the *guldens* he asked: 'You are nurse?' and when she nodded, refused the tip she offered him. London taxi drivers seldom took tips from a nurse either, sometimes they wouldn't even accept a fare—perhaps it was a worldwide custom. She thanked him when he wished her good luck and waited until his broad friendly back had disappeared inside his cab before going through the big glass doors, feeling as though she had lost a friend.

But she need not have felt nervous; no sooner had she peered cautiously through the porter's lodge window than he was there, asking her what she wanted, and when he discovered that she was the expected English nurse, he summoned another porter, gave him incomprehensible instructions, said, just as the taxi driver had said: 'Good luck,' and waved her into line behind her guide. She turned back at the last moment, remembering her luggage, and was reassured by his cheerful: 'Baggage is OK.'

The porter was tall and thin and walked fast; Lavinia, almost trotting to keep up with him, had scant time in which to look around her. She had an impression of dark walls, a tiled floor and endless doors on either side of the passages they were traversing so rapidly. Presently they merged into a wider one which in its turn ended at a splendid archway opening on to a vestibule, full of doors. The porter knocked on one of these, opened it and stood on one side of it for her to enter.

The room was small, and seemed smaller because of the woman standing by the window, for she was very large—in her forties, perhaps, with a straight back, a billowing bosom and a long, strong-featured face. Her eyes were pale blue and her hair, drawn back severely from her face, was iron grey. When she smiled, Lavinia thought she was one of the nicest persons she had ever seen.

'Miss Hawkins?' Her voice was as nice as her smile. 'We are glad to welcome you to St Jorus and we hope that you will be happy here.' She nodded towards a small hard chair. 'Will you sit, please?'

Lavinia sat, listening carefully while the Directrice outlined her duties, mentioned off-duty, touched lightly on uniforms, salary and the advisability of taking Dutch lessons and went on: 'You will find that the medical staff speak English and also some of the nurses too—the domestic staff, they will not, but there will be someone to help you for a little while. You will soon pick up a few necessary words, I feel sure.'

She smiled confidently at Lavinia, who smiled back, not feeling confident at all. Certainly she would make a point of starting lessons as soon as possible; she hadn't heard more than a few sentences of Dutch so far, but they had sounded like gibberish.

'You wish to live out, I understand,' went on the Directrice, 'and that will be possible within a week or so, but first you must be quite certain that you want to remain with us, although we should not stand in your way if before then you should decide to return to England.'

'I was thinking of staying for a year,' ventured Lavinia, 'but I'd rather not decide until I've been here a few days, but I do want to make a home for my young sister.'

Her companion looked curious but forbore from pressing for further information, instead she rang the bell on her desk and when a young woman in nurse's uniform but without a cap answered it, she said kindly:

'This is Juffrouw Fiske, my secretary. She will take you over to the Nurses' Home and show you your room. You would like to unpack, and perhaps it would be as well if you went on duty directly after the midday meal. Theatre B, major surgery. There is a short list this afternoon and you will have a chance to find your feet.'

Lavinia thanked her and set off with Juffrouw Fiske through more passages and across a couple of small courtyards, enclosed by high grey walls until they finally came to a door set in one of them—the back door, she was told, to the Home. It gave directly on to a short passage with a door at its end opening on to a wide hall in which was a flight of stairs which they climbed.

'There is a lift,' explained her companion, 'but you are on the first floor, therefore there is no need.'

She opened a door only a few yards from the head of the stairs and invited Lavinia to go in. It was a pleasant room, tolerably large and very well furnished, and what was more, her luggage was there as well as a pile of uniforms on the bed.

'We hope that everything fits,' said Juffrouw Fiske. 'You are small, are you not?' She smiled widely. 'We are quite often big girls. Someone will come and take you to your dinner at twelve o'clock, Miss Hawkins, and I hope that you will be happy with us.'

Nice people, decided Lavinia, busily unpacking. She had already decided that she was going to like the new job—she would like it even better when she had a home of her own and Peta with her. Of course, she still had to meet the people she was to work with, but if they were half as nice as those she had met already, she felt she need have no fears about getting on with them.

The uniform fitted very well. She perched the stiff

little cap on top of her tidy topknot and sat down to wait for whoever was to fetch her.

It was a big, well-built girl, with ash blonde hair and a merry face. She shook hands with enthusiasm and said: 'Neeltje Haagsma.'

For a moment Lavinia wondered if she was being asked how she did in Dutch, but the girl put her right at once. 'My name—we shake hands and say our names when we meet—that is simple, is it not?'

Lavinia nodded. 'Lavinia Hawkins. Do I call you *juffrouw*?'

Neeltje pealed with laughter. 'No, no—you will call me Neeltje and I will call you Lavinia, only you must call the Hoofd Zuster, Zuster Smid.'

'And the doctors?' They were making for the stairs.

'Doctor—easy, is it not? and *chirurgen*—surgeon, is it not?—you will call them Mister this or Mister that.'

Not so foreign after all, Lavinia concluded happily, and then was forced to change her mind when they entered an enormous room, packed with nurses sitting at large tables eating their dinner and all talking at the tops of their voices in Dutch.

But it wasn't too bad after all. Neeltje sat her down, introduced her rapidly and left her to shake hands all round, while she went to get their meal; meat balls, a variety of vegetables and a great many potatoes. Lavinia, who was hungry, ate the lot, followed it with a bowl of custard, and then, over coffee, did her best to answer the questions being put to her. It was an agreeable surprise to find that most of her companions spoke such good English and were so friendly.

'Are there any other English nurses here?' she wanted to know.

Neeltje shook her head. 'You are the first—there are to be more, but not for some weeks. And now we must go to our work.'

The hospital might be old, but the theatre block was magnificently modern. Lavinia, whisked along by her friendly companion, peered about her and wished that she could tell Peta all about it; she would have to write a letter as soon as possible. But soon, caught up in the familiar routine, she had no time to think about anything or anyone other than her work. It was, as the Directrice had told her, a short list, and the technique was almost exactly the same as it had been in her own hospital, although now and again she was reminded that it wasn't quite the same—the murmur of voices, speaking a strange language, even though everyone there addressed her in English.

Before the list had started, Zuster Smid had introduced her to the surgeon who was taking the list, his registrar and his houseman, as well as the three nurses who were on duty. She had forgotten their names, which was awkward, but at least she knew what she was doing around theatre. Zuster Smid had watched her closely for quite a while and then had relaxed. Lavinia, while not much to look at, was competent at her job; it would take more than working in strange surroundings to make her less than that.

The afternoon came to an end, the theatre was readied once more for the morning's work or any emergency which might be sent up during the night, and shepherded by the other girls, she went down to her supper and after that she was swept along to Neeltje's room with half a dozen other girls, to drink coffee and gossip—she might have been back at Jerrold's. She stifled a sudden pang of homesickness, telling herself that she was tired—as indeed she was, for no sooner had she put her head on her pillow than she was asleep.

It was on her third day, at the end of a busy morning's list, that she was asked to go up to the next floor with a specimen for section. The Path. Lab. usually sent an assistant down to collect these, but this morning, for some reason, there was no one to send and Lavinia, not scrubbed, and nearest to take the receiver with the offending object to be investigated, slid out of the theatre with it, divested herself of her gown and over-shoes and made her way swiftly up the stairs outside the theatre unit.

The Path. Lab. was large—owing, she had been told, to the fact that Professor ter Bavinck, who was the head of it, was justly famed for his brilliant work. Other, smaller hospitals sent a constant stream of work and he was frequently invited to other countries in order to give his learned opinion on some pathological problem. Neeltje had related this in a reverent voice tinged with awe, and Lavinia had concluded that the professor was an object of veneration in the hospital; possibly he had a white beard.

She pushed open the heavy glass doors in front of her and found herself in a vast room, brightly lighted and full of equipment which she knew of, but never quite understood. There were a number of men sitting at their benches, far too busy to take any notice of her, so she walked past them to the end of the room where there was a door with the professor's name on it; presumably this was where one went. But when she knocked, no one answered, so she turned her back on it and looked round the room.

One man drew her attention at once, and he was sitting with his back to her, looking through a microscope. It was the breadth of his shoulders which had caught her eye, and his pale as flax hair, heavily silvered. She wondered who he might be, but now wasn't the time to indulge her interest.

She addressed the room in general in a quite loud voice. 'Professor ter Bavinck? I've been sent from Theatre B with a specimen.'

The shoulders which had caught her eye gave an impatient shrug; without turning round a deep voice told her: 'Put it down here, beside me, please, and then go away.'

Lavinia's charming bosom swelled with indignation. What a way to talk, and who did he think he was, anyway? She advanced to his desk and laid the kidney dish silently at his elbow. 'There you are, sir,' she said with a decided snap, 'and why on earth should you imagine I should want to stay?'

He lifted his head then to stare at her, and she found herself staring back at a remarkably handsome face; a high-bridged nose dominated it and the mouth beneath it was very firm, while the blue eyes studying her so intently were heavy-lidded and heavily browed. She was quite unprepared for his friendly smile and for the great size of him as he pushed back his chair and stood up, towering over her five feet four inches.

'Ah, the English nurse—Miss Hawkins, is it not? In fact, I am sure,' his smile was still friendly, 'no nurse in the hospital would speak to me like that.'

Lavinia went a splendid pink and sought for something suitable to say to this. After a moment's thought she decided that it was best to say nothing at all, so she closed her mouth firmly and met his eyes squarely. Perhaps she had been rude, but after all, he had asked for it. Her uneasy thoughts were interrupted by his voice, quite brisk now. 'This specimen—a snap check, I presume—Mevrouw Vliet, the query mastectomy, isn't it?'

'Yes, sir.'

'I'll telephone down.' He nodded at her in a kindly, uncle-ish way, said: 'Run along,' and turned away, the kidney dish on his hand. She heard him giving what she supposed to be instructions to one of his assistants as she went through the door.

She found herself thinking about him while they all waited for his report; the surgeon, his sterile gloved hands clasped before him, the rest of them ready to do exactly what he wanted when he said so. The message came very quickly. Lavinia wondered what the professor had thought when his sharp eyes had detected the cancer cells in the specimen, but possibly Mevrouw Vliet, lying unconscious on the table and happily unaware of what was happening, was just another case to him. He might not know—nor care—if she were young, old, pretty or plain, married or unmarried, and yet he had looked as though he might—given the right circumstances—be rather super.

It was much later, at supper time, that Neeltje wanted to know what she had thought of him.

'Well,' said Lavinia cautiously, 'I hardly spoke to him—he just took the kidney dish and told me to go away.'

'And that was all?'

'He did remark that I was the English nurse. He's… he's rather large, isn't he?'

'From Friesland,' explained Neeltje, who was from Friesland herself. 'We are a big people. He is of course old.'

Lavinia paused in the conveyance of soup to her mouth. 'Old?' she frowned. 'I didn't think he looked old.'

'He is past forty,' said a small brown-haired girl from across the table. 'Also he has been married; his daughter is fourteen.'

There were a dozen questions on Lavinia's tongue, but it wasn't really her business. All the same, she did want to know what had happened to his wife. The brown-haired girl must have read her thoughts, for she went on: 'His wife died ten years ago, more than that perhaps, she was, how do you say? not a good wife. She was not liked, but the professor, now he is much liked, although he talks to no one, that is to say, he talks but he tells nothing, you understand? Perhaps he is unhappy, but he would not allow anyone to see that and never has he spoken of his wife.' She shrugged. 'Perhaps he loved her, who knows? His daughter is very nice, her name is Sibendina.'

'That's pretty,' said Lavinia, still thinking about the professor. 'Is that a Friesian name?'

'Yes, although it is unusual.' Neeltje swallowed the last of her coffee. 'Let us go to the sitting-room and watch the *televisie*.'

Lavinia met the professor two days later. She had been to her first Dutch lesson in her off duty, arranged for her by someone on the administrative staff and whom probably she would never meet but who had nonetheless given her careful instruction as to her ten-minute walk to reach her teacher's flat. This lady turned out to be a retired schoolmistress with stern features and a command of the English language which quite deflated Lavinia. However, at the end of an hour, Juffrouw de Waal was kind enough to say that her pupil, provided she applied herself to her work, should prove to be a satisfactory pupil, worthy of her teaching powers.

Lavinia wandered back in the warmth of the summer afternoon, and with time on her hands, turned off the main street she had been instructed to follow, to stroll down a narrow alley lined with charming little houses. It opened on to a square, lined with trees and old, thin houses leaning against each other for support. They were three or four stories high, with a variety of roofs, and here and there they had been crowded out by much larger double-fronted town mansions, with steps leading up to their imposing doors. She inspected them all, liking their unassuming façades and trying to guess what they would be like on the other side of their sober fronts. Probably quite splendid and magnificently furnished; the curtains, from what she could see from the pavement, were lavishly draped and of brocade or velvet. She had completed her walk around three sides of the square when she was addressed from behind.

'I hardly expected to find you here, Miss Hawkins—not lost, I hope?'

She turned round to confront Professor ter Bavinck. 'No—at least…' She paused to look around her; she wasn't exactly lost, but now she had no idea which lane she had come from. 'I've been for an English lesson,' she explained defensively, 'and I had some time to spare, and it looked so delightful…' She gave another quick look around her. 'I only have to walk along that little lane,' she assured him.

He laughed gently. 'No, not that one—the people who live in this square have their garages there and it's a cul-de-sac. I'm going to the hospital, you had better come along with me.'

'Oh, no—that is, it's quite all right.' She had answered very fast, anxious not to be a nuisance and at the same time aware that this large quiet man had a strange effect upon her.

'You don't like me, Miss Hawkins?'

She gave him a shocked look, and it was on the tip of her tongue to assure him that she was quite sure, if she allowed herself to think about it, that she liked him very much, but all she said was: 'I don't know you, Professor, do I? But I've no reason not to like you. I only said that because you might not want my company.'

'Don't beg the question; we both have our work to do

there this afternoon, and that is surely a good enough reason to bear each other company.' He didn't wait to hear her answer. 'We go this way.'

He started to walk back the way she had come, past the tall houses squeezed even narrower and taller by the great house in their centre—it took up at least half of that side of the square, and moreover there was a handsome Bentley convertible standing before its door.

Lavinia slowed down to look at it. 'A Bentley!' she exclaimed, rather superfluously. 'I thought everybody who could afford to do so drove Mercedes on the continent. I wonder whose it is—it must take a good deal of cunning to get through that lane I walked down.'

'This one's wider,' her companion remarked carelessly, and turned into a short, quite broad street leading away from the square. It ran into another main street she didn't recognize, crowded with traffic, but beyond advising her to keep her eyes and ears open the professor had no conversation. True, when they had to cross the street, he took her arm and saw her safely to the other side, but with very much the tolerant air of someone giving a helping hand to an old lady or a small child. It was quite a relief when he plunged down a narrow passage between high brick walls which ended unexpectedly at the very gates of the hospital.

'Don't try and come that way by yourself,' he cautioned her, lifted a hand in salute and strode away across the forecourt. Lavinia went to her room to change, feeling somehow disappointed, although she wasn't sure why. Perhaps, she told herself, it was because she had been wearing a rather plain dress; adequate enough for

Juffrouw de Waal, but lacking in eye-catching qualities. Not that it would have mattered; the professor hadn't bothered to look at her once—and why should he? Rather plain girls were just as likely two a penny in Holland as they were in England. She screwed her hair into a shining bun, jammed her cap on top of it, and went on duty, pretending to herself that she didn't care in the least whether she saw him again or not.

She saw him just one hour later. There had been an emergency appendix just after she had got back to theatre, and she had been sent back to the ward with the patient. She and one of the ward nurses were tucking the patient into her bed, when she glanced up and saw him, sitting on a nearby bed, listening attentively to its occupant. The ward nurse leaned across the bed. 'Professor ter Bavinck,' she breathed, 'so good a man and so kind—he visits…' she frowned, seeking words. 'Mevrouw Vliet, the mastectomy—you were at the operation and you know what was discovered? When that is so, he visits the patient and explains and listens and helps if he can.' She paused to smile. 'My English—it is not so bad, I hope?'

'It's jolly good. I wish I knew even a few words of Dutch.' Lavinia meant that; it would be nice to understand what the professor was saying—not that she was likely to get much chance of that.

She handed over the patient's notes, and without looking at the professor, went back to theatre. Zuster Smid had gone off duty, taking most of her staff with her, there were only Neeltje and herself working until nine o'clock. She had been sorting instruments while her companion saw to the theatre linen, when the door opened and Professor ter Bavinck walked in. He walked over to say something to Neeltje before he came across the theatre to Lavinia.

'Off at nine o'clock?' he asked.

'Yes, sir.'

His mouth twitched faintly. 'Could you stop calling me sir? Just long enough for me to invite you out to supper.'

'Me? Supper?' Her eyes were round with surprise. 'Oh, but I…'

'Scared of being chatted up? Forget it, dear girl; think of me as a Dutch uncle anxious to make you feel at home in Amsterdam.'

She found herself smiling. 'I don't know what a Dutch uncle is.'

'I'm vague about it myself, but it sounds respectable enough to establish a respectable relationship, don't you agree?'

A warning, perhaps? Letting her know in the nicest way that he was merely taking pity on a stranger who might be feeling lonely?

'Somewhere quiet,' he went on, just as if she had already said that she would go with him, 'where we can get a quick snack—I'll be at the front entrance.'

'I haven't said that I'll go yet,' she reminded him coldly, and wished that she hadn't said it, for the look he bent on her was surprised and baffled too, so that she rushed on: 'I didn't mean that—of course I'll come, I'd like to.'

He didn't smile although his eyes twinkled reassuringly. 'We don't need to be anything but honest with each other,' a remark which left her, in her turn, surprised and baffled. He had gone while she was still thinking it over, and any vague and foolish ideas which it might have nurtured were at once dispelled by Neeltje's, 'You go to supper with the Prof. Did I not tell you how good and kind a man he is? He helps always the lame dog…'

Just for a moment the shine went out of the evening, but Lavinia was blessed with a sense of humour; she giggled and said cheerfully: 'Well, let's hope I get a good supper, because I'm hungry.'

She changed rapidly, not quite sure what she should wear or how much time she had in which to put it on. It was a warm evening and still light; still damp from a shower, she looked over her sketchy wardrobe and decided that the pink cotton with its jacket would look right wherever they went. As she did her face and hair she tried to remember if there were any snack bars or cafés close to the hospital, but with the exception of Jan's Eethuisje just across the road and much frequented by the hospital staff who had had to miss a meal for some reason or other, she could think of none. She thrust her feet into the pink sandals, checked her handbag's contents and made her way to the entrance.

The professor was there; it wasn't until she saw him, leaning against the wall, his hands in his pockets, that she realized that she hadn't been quite sure that he would be. He came across the hall to meet her and she noticed that his clothes were good; elegant and beautifully cut if a little conservative—but then he wasn't a very young man.

He said hullo in a casual way and opened the door for her and they went out to the forecourt together. It was fairly empty, but even if it hadn't been, any cars which might have been there would have been cast into the shade by the car outside the door.

'Oh, it's the Bentley!' cried Lavinia as her companion ushered her into its luxury.

'You like it? I need a large car, you see.' He got in beside her. 'One of the problems of being large.'

She sat back, sniffing the faint scent of leather, enjoying the drive, however short, in such a fabulous car. And the drive was short; the professor slid in and out of the traffic while she was still trying to discover which way they were going, and pulled up after only a few minutes, parking the car on the cobbles at the side of the narrow canal beside an even narrower street, and inviting her to get out. It seemed that their snack was to be taken at what appeared to be an expensive restaurant, its name displayed so discreetly that it could have passed for a town house in a row of similar houses. Lavinia allowed herself to be shepherded inside to a quiet luxury which took her breath and sitting at a table which had obviously been reserved for them, thanked heaven silently that the pink, while not anything out of the ordinary, at least passed muster.

It was equally obvious within a very few moments that the professor's notion of a quick snack wasn't hers. She ran her eyes over the large menu card, looking in vain for hamburgers or baked beans on toast, although she doubted if such an establishment served such homely dishes.

'Smoked eel?' invited her companion. 'I think you must try that, and then perhaps coq au vin to follow?' He dismissed the waiter and turned to confer with the wine waiter, asking as he did so: 'Sherry for you? Do you prefer it sweet?'

She guessed quite rightly that it wasn't likely to be the same sort of sherry they drank at hospital parties. 'Well…' she smiled at him, 'I don't know much about it—would you choose?'

The sherry, when it came, was faintly dry and as soft as velvet. Lavinia took a cautious second sip, aware, that she hadn't had much to eat for some time, aware, too, that conversationally she wasn't giving very good value. Her host was sitting back in his chair, completely at his ease, his eyes on her face, so that she found it difficult to think of something to talk about. She was on the point of falling back on the weather when he said: 'Tell me about yourself—why did you take this job? Did not your family dislike the idea of you coming here? There are surely jobs enough in England for someone as efficient as you.' He saw the look on her face and added: 'Dear me, I did put that badly, didn't I? It just shows you that a lack of female society makes a man very clumsy with his words.'

She took another sip of sherry. 'I haven't a family—at least, only a sister. She's fifteen, almost sixteen, and lives with an aunt. She hasn't been happy with her and when I saw this job advertised I thought I'd try for it—I shall be able to live out, you see, and Peta will be able to come here and live with me. I couldn't do that in England—not in London at any rate, because flats there are very expensive and nurses don't earn an awful lot.'

She finished the sherry. It had loosened her tongue; she hadn't told anyone her plans, and here she was pouring out her heart to a stranger—almost a stranger, then, though he had never seemed to be that, rather someone whom she had known for a very long time.

'You are prepared to take that responsibility? You should marry.' There was the faintest question in his voice.

'Well, that would be awfully convenient, but no one's asked me, and anyway I can't imagine anyone wanting to make a home for Peta as well as me.'

She couldn't see his eyes very well; the heavy lids almost covered them, probably he was half asleep with boredom. 'I think you may be wrong there,' he said quietly, and then: 'And what do you think of our hospital?'

It was easy after that; he led her from one topic to the next while they ate the smoked eel and then the chicken, washed down with the wine which had been the subject of such serious discussion with the wine waiter. Lavinia had no idea what it was, but it tasted delicious, as did the chocolate mousse which followed the chicken. She ate and drank with the simple pleasure of someone who doesn't go out very often, and when she had finished it, she said shyly: 'That was quite super; I don't go out a great deal—hardly ever, in fact. I thought you meant it when you said a quick snack.'

He laughed gently. 'It's quite some time since I took a girl out to supper. I haven't enjoyed myself so much for a long while.' He added deliberately: 'We must do it again.'

'Yes, well…that would be…' She found herself short of both breath and words. 'I expect I should be getting back.'

He lifted a finger to the hovering waiter. 'Of course—a heavy day tomorrow, isn't it?'

He spoke very little on their way back to the hospital, and Lavinia, trying to remember it all later, couldn't be sure of what she had replied. He wished her good night at the hospital entrance and got back into his car and drove off without looking back. He was nice, she admitted to herself as she went to her room; the kind of man she felt at ease with—he would be a wonderful friend; perhaps, later on, he might be. She went to sleep thinking about him.

There was the usual chatter at breakfast and several of her table companions asked her if she had had a good supper. Evidently someone had told them. Neeltje probably; she was a positive fount of information about everything and everyone. She informed everyone now: 'The Prof's going to a conference in Vienna; he won't be here for a few days, for I heard him telling Doctor van Teyl about it. We shall have that grumpy old van Vorst snapping our heads off if we have to go to the Path. Lab.' She smiled at Lavinia. 'And he is not likely to ask you to go out with him.'

Everyone laughed and Lavinia laughed too, although in fact she felt quite gloomy. Somehow she had imagined that she would see Professor ter Bavinck again that morning, and the knowledge that she wouldn't seemed to have taken a good deal of the sparkle out of the day.

She settled down during the next few days into her new way of life, writing to Peta every day or so, studying her Dutch lessons hard so that she might wring a reluctant word of praise from Juffrouw de Waal, and when she was on duty, working very hard indeed. She had scrubbed for several cases by now and had managed very well, refusing to allow herself to be distracted or worried by the steady flow of Dutch conversation which went on between the surgeons as they worked, and after all, the instruments were the same, the technique was almost the same, even if they were called by different names. She coped with whatever came her way with her usual unhurried calm.

Only that calm was a little shattered one morning. They were doing a gastro-entreostomy, when the surgeon cast doubts on his findings and sent someone to telephone the Path. Lab. A minute or two later Professor ter Bavinck came in, exchanged a few words with his colleagues, collected the offending piece of tissue which was the cause of the doubt, cast a lightning look at Lavinia, standing behind her trolleys, and went away again.

So he was back. She counted a fresh batch of swabs, feeling the tide of pleasure the sight of him had engendered inside her. The day had suddenly become splendid and full of exciting possibilities. She only just stopped herself in time from bursting into song.

CHAPTER THREE

BUT THE DAY wasn't splendid at all; she was in theatre for hours as it turned out, with an emergency; some poor soul who had fallen from a fourth floor balcony. The surgeons laboured over her for patient hours and no one thought of going to dinner, although two or three of the nurses managed to get a cup of coffee. But Lavinia, being scrubbed and taking the morning's list, went stoically on until at length, about three o'clock in the afternoon, she had a few minutes in which to bolt a sandwich and drink some coffee, and because the morning's list had been held up it ended hours late; in consequence the afternoon list was late too, and even though she didn't have to scrub, she was still on duty. When she finally got off duty it was well past seven o'clock. There was no reason why she should look for the professor on her way to supper; he was unlikely to be lurking on the stairs or round a corner of any of the maze of passages, so her disappointment at not meeting him was quite absurd. She ate her supper, pleaded tiredness after her long day, and retired to the fastness of her room.

A good night's sleep worked wonders. She felt quite light-hearted as she dressed the next morning; she would be off at four o'clock and the lists weren't heavy; perhaps she would see Professor ter Bavinck and he would suggest another quick snack... She bounced down to breakfast, not stopping to examine her happiness, only knowing that it was another day and there was the chance of something super happening.

Nothing happened at all. Work, of course—there was always plenty of that; it was a busy hospital and the surgeons who worked there were known for their skill. The morning wore on into the afternoon until it was time for her to go off duty. Neeltje was off too—they were going out with some of the other nurses; a trip round the city's canals was a must for every visitor to Amsterdam and they would take her that very evening. She got ready for the outing, determined to enjoy herself. She had been silly and made too much of the professor's kindness—it was because she went out so seldom with a man that she had attached so much importance to seeing him again. Heaven forbid that she should appear over-eager, indeed, if he were to ask her out again she would take care to have an excuse ready, she told herself stoutly. She stared at her reflection in the looking glass—he wasn't likely to ask her again, anyway. He was in the hospital each day, she had heard someone say so, and there had been plenty of opportunities...

She left her room and took the short cut to the hospital entrance where she was to meet the others. The last few yards of it gave her an excellent view of the forecourt so that she couldn't fail to see the professor standing in it, talking earnestly to a young woman. It was too far off to see if she was pretty, but even at that distance Lavinia could see that she was beautifully dressed. She slowed her steps the better to look and then stopped altogether as he took the girl's arm and walked away with her, across the tarmac to where his motorcar was standing. She didn't move until they had both got into it and it had disappeared through the gates, and when she did she walked very briskly, with her determined little chin rather higher than usual and two bright spots of colour on her cheeks.

When they all got back a couple of hours later, the professor was standing in the entrance, talking to two of the consultants, and all three men wished the girls *Goeden avond.* Lavinia, joining in the polite chorus of replies, took care not to look at him.

She wakened the next morning to remember that it was her day off. The fine weather still held and she had a formidable list of museums to visit. She was up and out soon after nine o'clock, clad in a cool cotton dress and sandals on her bare feet and just enough money in her handbag to pay for her lunch.

She went first to the Bijenkorf, however, that mecca of the Amsterdam shopper, and spent an hour browsing round its departments, wishing she had the money to buy the pretty things on display, cheering herself with the thought that before very long, she might be able to do so. But it was already ten o'clock and the museums had been open half an hour already, so she started to walk across the Dam Square, with its palace on one side and the stark war memorial facing it on the other, down Kalverstraat, not stopping to look in the tempting shop windows, and into Leidsestraat. It was here that she noticed that the blue sky had dimmed to grey, it was going to rain—but the museum was only a few minutes' brisk walk away now, she could actually see the imposing frontage of her goal. The first few drops began to fall seconds later, however, and then without warning, turned into a downpour. Lavinia began to run, feeling the rain soaking her thin dress.

The Bentley pulled into the curb a little ahead of her, so that by the time she was level with it the professor was on the pavement, standing in the rain too. He didn't speak at all, merely plucked her neatly from the pavement, bustled her round the elegant bonnet of the car, and popped her into the front seat. When he got in beside her, all he said was: 'You're very wet,' as he drove on.

Lavinia got her breath. 'I was going to the museum,' she began. 'It's only just across the road,' she added helpfully, in case he wanted an excuse to drop her off somewhere quickly.

'Unmistakable, isn't it?' he observed dryly, and drove past it to join the stream of traffic going back into the city's heart.

Her voice came out small. 'Are you taking me back to St Jorus?'

'Good lord, no—on your day off? We're going to get you dry, you can't possibly drip all over the Rijksmuseum.'

He was threading the big car up and down narrow streets which held very little traffic, and she had no idea where she was; she didn't really care, it was nice just to sit there without question. But presently she recognized her surroundings—this was the square she had visited that afternoon, and she made haste to tell him so. 'I remember the houses,' she told him, 'they've got such plain faces, but I'm sure they must be beautiful inside. If you want to set me down here, I know my way—I expect you're going to the hospital.'

'No, I'm not.' He circled the square and on its third side stopped before the large house in the middle of the row of tall, narrower ones, and when she gave him a questioning look, said blandly: 'I live here. My housekeeper will dry that dress of yours for you—and anything else that's wet.' He spoke with friendly casualness. 'We can have our coffee while she's doing it.'

'Very kind,' she said, breathless, 'but your work—I've delayed you already.'

He leaned across her and opened the door before getting out of the car. 'I have an occasional day off myself.' He came round the car and stood by the door while she got out too, and then led her across the narrow cobbled street to his front door.

She had no idea that a house could be so beautiful; true, she had seen pictures of such places in magazines, and she was aware that there were such places, but looking at them in a magazine and actually standing in the real thing were two quite different things. She breathed an ecstatic sigh as she gazed around her; this was better than anything pictured—a large, light hall with an Anatolian carpet in rich reds and blues almost covering its black and white marble floor, with a staircase rising from its end wall, richly carved, its oak treads uncarpeted and a chandelier of vast proportions hanging from a ceiling so high that she had to stretch her neck to see it properly.

'You don't live here?' she wanted to know of her companion, and he gave a short laugh. 'Oh, but I do—have done all my life. Come along, we'll find Mevrouw Pette.'

He urged her across the floor to a door at the back of the hall, beside the staircase and opened it for her, shouting down the short flight of stairs on the other side as they began to descend them. At the bottom there was a narrow door, so low that he was forced to bow his head to go through. It gave on to a surprisingly large and cheerful room, obviously the kitchen, decided Lavinia, trying not to look too curiously at everything around her. Nice and old-fashioned, but with all the modern gadgets any woman could wish for. There were cheerful yellow curtains at the windows, which looked out on to a narrow strip of garden at the back of the house, and the furniture was solid; an enormous wooden dresser against one wall, a scrubbed table, equally enormous, in the centre of the brick floor and tall Windsor chairs on either side of the Aga cooker. There were cheerful rugs too, and rows of copper pots and pans on the walls. It was all very cosy and one hardly noticed the fridge, the rotisserie and the up-to-date electric oven tucked away so discreetly. Out of sight, she felt sure, there would be a washing-up machine and a deep-freeze and anything else which would make life easier. The professor must have a very good job indeed to be able to live so splendidly—and there were no fewer than three persons working in the kitchen, too. The elderly woman coming to meet them would be the housekeeper and as well as her there was a young girl cleaning vegetables at the sink, while another girl stood at the table clearing away some cooking utensils.

The professor spoke to them as he went in and they looked up and smiled and then went on with what they were doing while he talked to Mevrouw Pette at some length. She was a thin woman, of middle height, with a sharp nose and a rosy complexion, her hair, still a nice brown, drawn back severely from her face. But she had a kind smile; she smiled at Lavinia now and beckoned to her, and encouraged by the professor's: 'Yes, go along, Lavinia—Mevrouw Pette will take your dress and lend you a dressing gown and bring you down again for coffee,' Lavinia followed.

So she went back up the little stair once more and across the hall to the much grander staircase and mounted it in Mevrouw Pette's wake, to be ushered into a dear little room, all chintz and dark oak, where she took off her dress and put on the dressing gown the housekeeper produced. It was blue satin, quilted and expensive; she wondered whose it was—surely not Mevrouw Pette's? It fitted tolerably well, though she was just a little plump for it. She smoothed back her damp hair, frowned at herself in the great mirror over the oak dower chest against one wall, and was escorted downstairs once more, this time to a room on the right of the hall—a very handsome room, although having seen a little of the house, she wasn't surprised at that. All the same, she had to admit that its rich comfort, allied with beautiful furniture and hangings of a deep sapphire blue, was quite breathtaking.

The professor was standing with his back to the door looking out of a window, but when he turned round she plunged at once into talk, feeling shy. 'You're very kind, and I am sorry to give you so much trouble.'

He waved her to an outsize chair which swallowed her in its vast comfort and sat down himself opposite her. 'I'm a selfish man,' he observed blandly. 'If I hadn't wished to trouble myself, I shouldn't have done so.' He crossed one long leg over the other, very much at his ease. 'You didn't look at me yesterday evening,' he observed. 'You were annoyed, I think—I hope…and that pleased me, because it meant that you were a little interested in me.'

He smiled at her look of outrage. 'No, don't be cross—did I not say that we could be nothing but honest with each other, as friends should be? I have been back for three days and I had made up my mind not to see you for a little while, and then yesterday I changed my mind, but I met an old friend who needed advice, so I was hindered from asking you to come out with me.'

She had no idea why he was telling her all this, but she had to match his frankness. 'I saw her with you.'

He smiled again. 'Ah, so you were hoping that I would come?'

The conversation was getting out of hand; she said with dignity and a sad lack of truth: 'I didn't hope anything of the sort, Professor,' and was saved from further fibbing by Mevrouw Pette's entrance with the coffee tray, but once the coffee was poured, her relief was short-lived.

'You probably think that I am a conceited middle-aged man who should know better,' said the professor suavely.

She nibbled at a spicy biscuit before she replied. 'No. You're not middle-aged or conceited. And I did hope you'd ask me out again, though I can't think why, me being me. If I were a raving beauty I don't suppose I'd be in the least surprised…'

He laughed then, suddenly years younger. 'Is your young sister like you?' he wanted to know.

'To look at? No; she's pretty, but we like the same things and we get on well together—but then she's easy to get on with.'

'And you are not?'

'I don't know. My aunt says I'm not, but then she doesn't like me, but she has given Peta a home for a year now and sent her to school…'

'But not loved her?'

'No.'

He passed his cup for more coffee. 'You think your sister will like Amsterdam?'

'I'm sure she will. She takes her O levels this week and then she'll leave school—just as soon as I can get somewhere to live here she can come. I thought she could have Dutch lessons…'

'And you plan to stay here for the foreseeable future?'

Lavinia nodded cheerfully, happy to be talking to him. 'I like it, living here. I feel quite at home and I earn so much more, you see, and if I stay here for a year or two I could save some money, enough to go back to England if Peta wanted to, and start her on whatever she decides to do.'

'No plans for yourself?'

She said a little stiffly: 'I'm quite happy, Professor.'

His thick eyebrows arched. 'Yes? I ask too many questions, don't I?' He got up and went to open the french window and a small hairy dog, all tail and large paws, came romping in, followed by an Irish setter, walking with dignity. 'You don't object to dogs?' asked the professor. 'Dong and Pobble like to be with me as much as possible when I'm home.'

Lavinia was on her knees making friends. 'Nonsense Songs!' she cried happily. 'Which one's Dong?'

'The setter. My daughter named them—most people look at me as though I'm mad when I mention their names, but then the Nonsense Songs aren't read very widely.'

'No—my father used to read them to me when I was a little girl.' She got to her feet. 'I'm sure my dress must be dry by now—you've been very kind, but I'm wasting your morning; I'll go and find your housekeeper if I may.'

For answer he tugged the beautifully embroidered bell-pull beside his chair, and when Mevrouw Pette came said something or other which caused her to smile and nod and beckon to Lavinia, who got up obediently and followed her out of the room.

Her dress was dry once more and moreover pressed by an expert hand. She did her face and hair, laid the dressing gown lovingly on the thick silk bed quilt, and went downstairs. The professor was in the hall, and she stifled a pang of disappointment that he appeared so anxious to speed her on her way, even as she achieved a bright, friendly smile and hurried to the door. He opened it as she reached his side and she thrust out a hand, searching frantically for something suitable to say by way of farewell. But there was no need to say anything; he took her hand, but instead of shaking it, he gripped it firmly, whistled piercingly to the dogs, and went out of the door with her. At the car she halted. 'Thank you,' she tried again, in what she hoped was a final sort of voice. 'There's really no need…I know where I am.' She glanced up at the sky, the greyness had changed back to blue once more. 'I shall enjoy walking.'

'Fiddle,' declared her companion, and opened the car door. 'I'm going to show you the Rijksmuseum, and we'll have to take the car because these two like to sit in the back and guard it when I'm not there.'

He opened the other door as he spoke and the two astute animals rushed past him and took up position with a determination which brooked no interference on Lavinia's part; she got in too, at a loss for words.

Her companion didn't appear to notice her silence but drove off with the air of a well-contented man, and only when they were almost at the museum did he remark: 'Everyone comes to see the Nachwacht, of course—it's a wonderful painting, but there are several which I like much better. I'd like to show them to you.' He paused and added gently: 'And if you say how kind just once more, I shall wring your neck!'

Lavinia jumped and gave him a startled look; he wasn't behaving like a professor at all, nor, for that matter, like a man who would never see forty again. 'I can't think why you should speak to me like that,' she reproved him austerely, and was reduced to silence by his: 'Am I cutting the corners too fine for you? It seemed to me that since we liked each other on sight, it would be a little silly to go through all the preliminaries, but if you would prefer that, I'll call you Miss Hawkins for a week or two, erase from my mind the sight of you in Sibendina's dressing gown, and drop you off at the next bus stop.'

She had cried: 'Oh, don't do that,' before she could stop herself, and went on a little wildly: 'You see, I'm not used to—to...well, I don't get asked out much and so none of this seems quite real—more like a dream.'

'But dreams are true while they last—your Tennyson said so, what's more doesn't he go on to say: "And do we not live in dreams?" So no more nonsense, Lavinia.'

He swept the car into the great forecourt of the museum, gave the dogs a quiet command and opened her door. He took her arm as they went in together and it seemed the most natural thing in the world that he should do so. She smiled up at him as they paused before the first picture.

There was no hurry. They strolled from one room to the next, to come finally to the enormous Nachtwacht and sit before it for a little while, picking out the figures which peopled the vast canvas, until the professor said: 'Now come and see my favourites.' Two small portraits, an old man and an old woman, wrinkled and blue-eyed and dignified, and so alive that Lavinia felt that she could have held a conversation with them.

'Nice, aren't they?' observed her companion. 'Come and look at the Lelys.'

She liked these even better; she went from one exquisitely painted portrait to the next and back again. 'Look at those pearls,' she begged him. 'They look absolutely real…'

'Well, most likely they were,' he pointed out reasonably. 'Do you like pearls?'

'Me? Yes, of course I do, though I'm not sure that I've ever seen any real ones. The Queen has some, but I don't suppose there are many women who possess any.'

He smiled and she wondered why he looked amused. 'Probably not. Will you have lunch with me, Lavinia?'

She hesitated. 'How k…' She caught the gleam in his eye then and chuckled delightfully. 'I've never fancied having my neck wrung in public, so I'll say yes, thank you.'

'Wise girl.' He tucked an arm in hers and began to walk to the exit, then stopped to look at her. 'How old are you?' he wanted to know.

She breathed an indignant: 'Well…' then told him: 'Twenty-six,' adding with an engaging twinkle: 'How rude of you to ask!'

'But you didn't mind telling me. I'm getting on for forty-one.'

'Yes, I know.' And at his sharp glance of inquiry: 'One of the nurses told me—not gossiping.'

He said very evenly: 'And you were also told that I am a widower, and that I have a daughter.'

'Oh, yes. You see, they all like you very much—they're a bit scared of you too, I think, but they like it that way—you're a bit larger than life, you know.'

He didn't answer at once, in fact he didn't speak at all during their short drive back to the house, only as he drew up before his door he said in a quiet voice: 'I don't care for flattery, Lavinia.'

Her pleasant face went slowly pink; a quite unaccountable rage shook her. She said on a heaving breath: 'You think that's what I'm doing? Toadying to you? Just because you're smashing to look at and a professor and—and took me out to supper…and so now I'm angling for another meal, am I?'

She choked on temper while she made furious efforts to get the car door open. Without success at first and when she did manage it, his hand came down on hers and held it fast. His voice was still quiet, but now it held warmth. 'I don't know why I said that, Lavinia, unless it was because I wanted to hear you say that I was wrong—and you have. No, leave the door alone. I'm sorry—will you forgive me?' And when she didn't answer: 'Lavinia?'

She said stiffly: 'Very well,' and forgot to be stiff. 'Oh, of course I will; I fly off the handle myself sometimes—only you sounded horrid.'

'I am quite often horrid—ask my daughter.' His hand was still on hers, but now he took it away and opened the door for her, and when she looked at him he smiled and said: 'Mevrouw Pette has promised us one of her special lunches, shall we go in?'

She smiled back; it was all right, they were back

where they had been; a pleasant, easy-going friendship which made her forget that she wasn't a raving beauty, and allowed her to be her own uncomplicated self.

'Super, I'm famished, though I keep meaning not to eat, you know—only I get hungry.'

He was letting the dogs out and turned round to ask: 'Not eating? A self-imposed penance?'

'No—I'm trying to get really slim.'

Dong and Pobble were prancing round her and she bent to rub their ears and then jumped at his sudden roar. 'You just go on eating,' he said forcefully. 'I like to be able to tell the front of a woman from her back, these skeletal types teetering round on four-inch soles don't appeal to me.'

She laughed. 'It would take months of dieting to get me to that state, but I promise you I'll eat a good lunch, just to please you.'

They went into the house then, the dogs racing ahead once they were inside so that they could sit as near the professor as possible, while Lavinia went upstairs to do things to her face and hair, and when she came down again they had drinks, talking companionably, before going into lunch, laid in what the professor called the little sitting-room, which turned out to be almost as large as the room they had just come from.

'The dining-room is so vast that we feel lost in it,' he explained, and then as a door banged: 'Ah, here is Sibendina.'

Lavinia had only just noticed that there were places laid for three on the table and she wasn't sure if she was pleased or not; she was curious to meet the professor's daughter, but on the other hand she had been looking forward to being alone with him. She turned to look over her shoulder as the girl came into the room, at the same time advising herself not to become too interested in the professor and his family; he had befriended her out of kindness and she must remember that.

Sibendina was like her father, tall and big and fair, with his blue eyes but fortunately with someone else's nose, for his, while exactly right on his own handsome face, would have looked quite overpowering on her pretty one. She came across the room at a run, embraced her father with pleasure and then looked at Lavinia, and when he had introduced them with easy good manners, she shook hands, exclaiming: 'I've heard about you—may I call you Lavinia? I've been looking forward to meeting you.'

She sat down opposite her father and grinned engagingly. 'Now I can practise my English,' she declared.

'Why not, Sibby? Although Lavinia might like to practise her Dutch—she's already having lessons.'

'And hours of homework,' said Lavinia, 'which I feel compelled to do, otherwise Juffrouw de Waal makes me feel utterly worthless.'

They all laughed as Mevrouw Pette brought in lunch, and presently the talk was of everything under the sun, with Sibendina asking a great many questions about England and Peta's school. 'She isn't much older than I am,' she observed, 'but she sounds very clever—what is she going to study next?'

'Well, I don't really know; if she comes here to live with me I thought she might have Dutch lessons, then if she's passed her eight O levels, she might be able to take a secretarial course—the Common Market,' Lavinia finished a little vaguely.

'Not nursing?' the professor wanted to know.

Lavinia shook her head. 'Peta's too gentle—she can't stand people being angry or bad-tempered, and there's quite a bit of that when you start training.'

Sibendina was peeling a peach. 'She sounds nice, I should like very much to meet her. When does she come?'

'I don't know if the hospital will keep me yet—if it's OK I'll find somewhere to live and then go and fetch her.'

'And this aunt she lives with—will she not mind?'

Lavinia smiled at the girl. 'I think perhaps she will mind very much—I'm rather dreading it, but I promised Peta.'

'But if you did not go what would your sister do?'

'I think she might run away,' said Lavinia soberly. 'You see, she's not very happy.'

Sibendina looked at the professor, sitting quietly and saying almost nothing. 'Papa, you must do something.' She looked at the Friesian wall clock. 'I have to go; I shall be late for class—you will excuse me, please.' She went round the table and kissed her father. 'Papa,' she said persuasively, 'you will do something, please. I like Lavinia very much and I think that I shall like Peta too.'

He spoke to her but he looked at Lavinia. 'Well, that's a good thing,' he observed blandly, 'for I'm going to ask Lavinia to marry me—not at once, I shall have to wait for her to get used to the idea.'

Lavinia felt the colour leave her face and then come rushing back into it. She hardly heard Sibendina's crow of delighted laughter as she ran out of the room, calling something in Dutch as she went. She was looking at the professor who, in his turn, was watching her closely. 'Don't look like that,' he said in a matter-of-fact voice. 'I shan't do anything earth-shattering like dropping on one knee and begging for your hand; just let the idea filter through, and we'll bring the matter up again in a few days. In the meantime what about a brisk walk to the Dam Palace? It's open for inspection and worth a visit.'

She spoke in a voice which was almost a whisper. 'Yes, that would be very nice—I've always wanted to see inside a palace. Is it far?'

'No, but we'll go the long way round; the nicest part of Amsterdam is tucked away behind the main streets.'

She could see that he had meant what he had said; he wasn't going to do anything earth-shattering. With an effort she forced herself back on to the friendly footing they had been on before he had made his amazing remark, and even discussed with some degree of intelligence the architecture of the old houses they passed, and once they had reached the palace, her interest in it and its contents became almost feverish in her efforts to forget what he had said.

They had tea at Dikker and Thijs and then walked slowly down Kalverstraat while she looked in the shop windows; a pleasant, normal occupation which soothed her jumping nerves, as did her companion's gentle flow of nothings, none of which needed much in the way of replies on her part. They turned away from the shops at last and the professor led her through the narrow streets without telling her where they were going, so that when they rounded a corner and there was the hospital a stone's throw away, Lavinia almost choked with disappointment. He was going to say good-bye; he had decided to deliver her back safely after a pleasant day, foisted on him by the accident of the rain. He had been joking, she told herself savagely—he and Sibendina, and she had actually been taken in. She swallowed the great unmanageable lump in her throat and said politely: 'Well, good-bye—it's been lovely…'

His surprise was genuine. 'What on earth are you talking about? I've only brought you back so that you can change your dress—we're going out to dinner.'

She didn't stop the flood of delight which must have shown in her face. 'Oh, are we? I didn't know.'

He shepherded her across the street and in through the hospital gates. 'I'll be here at seven o'clock, Lavinia—and don't try and do any deep thinking—just make yourself pretty and be ready for me.'

Her, 'Yes, all right,' was very meek.

CHAPTER FOUR

LAVINIA HADN'T BROUGHT many clothes with her; she hadn't much of a wardrobe anyway. She searched through her cupboard now and came to the conclusion that it would have to be the green silk jersey, with its tucked bodice gathered into a wide band which emphasized her small waist and its full sleeves, deeply cuffed; it wasn't exactly spectacular, but it would pass muster. All the same, as she put it on, she wished fervently that it had been a Gina Franati model; something quite super to match the professor's faultlessly tailored clothes.

Anxious not to be late, she hurried down to the entrance to find him already there, deep in conversation with one of the doctors, and at the sight of his elegance she regretted, once again, the paucity of her wardrobe. But there was no point in brooding over that now. She hitched her coat over one arm and when he turned and saw her, went to meet him, and the pleased look he gave her quite compensated her for having to wear the green jersey. It was flattering too, the way he took her arm and included her in the conversation he was having for a few minutes. She liked him for that; his manners were beautiful, even if he did startle her sometimes with the things he said.

As they got into the Bentley he said: 'I thought we

might drive over to den Haag, it's only thirty miles or so. We'll go on the motorway; it's dull, I'm afraid, but I've booked a table for eight o'clock.'

She had expected to feel a little awkward with him, but she didn't. They talked about all manner of things, but not about themselves; she still wasn't sure if he had been joking with Sibendina, and there was no way of finding out, only by asking him, and that she would never do. She would have to wait and see; in the meantime she was going to enjoy herself.

And she did. They dined at the Saur restaurant in the heart of den Haag—upstairs, in a formal, almost Edwardian room, and the food was delicious. She wanted the evening to go on for ever; she knew by now that she liked the professor very much, although she wasn't going to admit to any deeper feelings, not until she knew the truth about his astonishing remark about marrying her. She didn't know much about falling in love, but she suspected that this was what was happening to her, but presumably it was something one could check or even smother before it became too strong.

They walked about the town after they had dined, and the professor pointed out the Ridderzaal, the Mauritshuis museum, some of the more interesting statues, an ancient prison gate and the old City Hall, and then strolled goodnaturedly beside her while she took a brief peep at the tempting displays in the shop windows.

On the way back to Amsterdam, tearing along the motorway, they didn't talk a great deal and then only of trifling things, but as they neared the hospital the professor said: 'I have to work tomorrow—a pity, I should have enjoyed taking you for a run in the car. We could have had a swim.'

Lavinia made a mental note to buy a swimsuit first thing in the morning. 'I've a whole lot of museums to see,' she told him brightly.

'Yes? May I pick you up tomorrow evening? Seven o'clock?'

She watched his large capable hands on the wheel and felt her heart tumbling around inside her. 'I'd like that very much,' she said in a sedate voice.

At the hospital entrance he got out to open her door and walk with her across the forecourt to the farther side where a covered way led to the nurses' home. His good night was pleasant and formal.

Lavinia went to bed, her head filled with a muddle of thoughts; the pleasant and the not so pleasant jostling each other for a place until she fell into an uneasy sleep.

She was pottering along the corridor to make herself some tea the next morning when she met Neeltje and several other nurses going down to breakfast. They were almost late, but that didn't prevent them from stopping to greet her and then break into a babble of questions. It was Neeltje who said in her own peculiar brand of English: 'We hear all—Becke Groeneveld sees you with Professor ter Bavinck as you return—that is for the second time that you go out with him. We are all most curious and excited.'

The ring of cheerful faces around her wore pleased smiles, rather as though their owners had engineered her outing amongst themselves. She was touched by their interest and their complete lack of envy; the least she could do was to tell them about her day—well, at least parts of it. 'Well, you see,' she began, 'I got caught in the rain and the professor happened to be passing in his car, so he took me to his house and his housekeeper dried my dress.'

Her listeners regarded her with motherly expressions. 'Well?' they chorused.

'We went to the Rijksmuseum after lunch—oh, and I met his daughter, she's a sweet girl.' The memory of the professor's conversation with Sibendina was suddenly vivid in her mind and she went rather pink. 'I—we, that is, went to dinner in the Hague.'

'You and the Prof?'

She nodded.

'And you go again?' asked Neeltje.

'Well, as a matter of fact, yes.'

'We are glad,' declared Neeltje, 'we have pleasure in this, you understand. But now we must hurry or we do not eat.'

They cried their *tot ziens* and tumbled down the stairs, laughing and talking, and Lavinia made her tea and got dressed slowly, trying not to think about the professor. But it wasn't easy, and later in the morning, even in the most interesting museums, his face kept getting between her and the exhibits she examined so carefully. She had her coffee and then, satisfied with her morning's sightseeing, went to the Bijenkorf and had a snack lunch, then went to look in the shop windows again, making a mental and ever-lengthening list of things she would buy when she had some money. And always at the back of her mind was the professor. By five o'clock she decided that she might well return to the hospital and get ready for her evening, and it was only with the greatest difficulty that she stopped herself from tearing back as though she had a train to catch. She told herself to stop behaving like a fool and forced her feet to a slow pace, so that she was in a fine state of nervous tension by the time she reached the hospital. She went at once to the home and looked at the letter board; there might be a letter from Peta. There was. There was another one, too, in a scrawled handwriting which she knew at once was the professor's. She tore it open and read the one line written on the back of a Path. Lab. form. It stated simply: 'Sorry, can't make it this evening,' and was signed M. ter B. She folded it carefully and put it back in its envelope, then took it out again and re-read it with the air of someone who hoped for a miracle, but there it was, in black and white.

She went slowly to her room, put the note in her handbag and kicked off her sandals. Her disappointment was engulfing her in great waves, but she refused to give way to it; she sat down and opened Peta's letter and started to read it. It was lengthy and unhappy too; Aunt Gwyneth, it seemed, was taking every opportunity to remind Peta that she depended entirely upon her charity and had made veiled hints as to what might happen should Peta fail to get her O levels. Ungrateful girls who didn't work hard enough for exams could not be expected to live in the lap of luxury for ever; there were jobs for them, simple jobs which required no advanced education costing a great deal of money, her aunt had said—a great girl of sixteen would do very well as a companion to some elderly lady…

Lavinia, noting the carefully wiped away tear stains, longed for just half an hour with her sister, but although that wasn't possible, a letter was. She sat down and wrote it, then and there, filling it full of heartening ideas, painting a cheerful picture of the life they would lead together, and that was not so far off now. She went out to post it and then went to supper, where she parried her new friends' anxious questions as cheerfully as she could. It was when Neeltje joined them that she discovered where the professor had gone: Utrecht, to some urgent consultation or other. The news cheered her a little. It wasn't until that moment that she admitted to herself that she had been imagining him spending the evening with some fascinating and exquisitely dressed beauty.

Theatre was busy the following day and Lavinia scrubbed for the afternoon list. They were half way through a splenectomy when the professor came in; he was in theatre kit, and after a nod in the general direction of those scattered around, took his place by the surgeon who was operating. He stayed for five minutes or so, peering down at the work being done while he and his colleague muttered together. Finally, he took the offending organ away with him. Lavinia had the impression that he hadn't seen her.

She felt even more certain of this by the time she went off duty at five o'clock, for she had seen him with her own eyes, leaving the forecourt; she had glanced idly out of an upstairs window and then stayed to watch him drive the Bentley out of the gates—out of sight.

Some of the nurses had asked her to go to the cinema with them, but she had pleaded letters to write, aware that if the professor should ask her to go out with him the letters would get short shrift, but now it looked as though that was the way she was going to spend her evening. She showered and changed into slacks and a cotton blouse and made herself some coffee, having no wish for her supper, and then started on her writing; it wasn't very successful, probably because her mind wasn't on it; she gave up after the second letter and went down to the post, thinking, as she went through the hospital, that she would ask to see the Directrice in the morning about living out; perhaps if her future plans were settled she might feel more settled herself. She was turning away from the post box in the front hall when she came face to face with the professor. Her first reaction was sheer delight at seeing him, the second one of annoyance because she must surely look a fright, consequently her 'Good evening, Professor,' was distant, but he ignored that.

'I was on my way over to see you,' he said cheerfully. 'I thought we might spend the evening together.'

A medley of strong feelings left her speechless. Presently she managed: 'I hadn't planned to go out this evening.'

His answer infuriated her. 'Well, I didn't expect you would have—just in case I came…' He gave her an interested look. 'Are you sulking?'

'I have no reason to sulk.'

'Oh? I thought you might because I had to cancel our date yesterday.' He grinned. 'I did think of mentioning it in theatre this afternoon, but I didn't think you would like that.'

She drew a deep breath. 'Professor…' she began, and was cut short by his bland: 'My dear girl, how is our relationship going to progress if you insist on calling me professor at every other breath? My name's Radmer.'

'Oh, is it? I've never heard it before.'

'Naturally not; it's a Friesian name, and you're English.' He smiled with great charm. 'Shall we go?'

'Like this? I'm not dressed for going out.'

He studied her deliberately. 'You're decently covered,' he observed at length. 'I like your hair hanging down your back. If it will make you happier, we're only going home for dinner—just two friends sharing a meal,' he added matter-of-factly.

'Well, all right.' She gave in with a composure which quite concealed her indignation. No girl, however inadequately dressed, likes to be told that she's decently covered—not in that casual, don't care voice. She got into the Bentley with an hauteur which brought a little smile to her companion's mouth, although he said nothing. But he did set himself out to entertain her over dinner, and his apologies for breaking their date the previous evening were all that any girl could wish for; her good nature reasserted itself and she felt happier than she had felt all day. His undemanding small talk, allied to the smoked salmon, duckling with orange sauce, and fresh fruit salad with its accompanying whipped cream and served on exquisite china, all combined to act on her stretched nerves like balm. She found herself telling him about Peta's letter and what she intended doing about it.

He listened gravely, watching her across the table. When she had finished he observed: 'I see—well, Lavinia, I said that you should have time, did I not, but now I think that we must settle the matter here and now.' He smiled at her with faint mockery. 'Any maidenly ideas you may have been cherishing about being courted, wooed and won must go by the board.'

She sat up very straight in her chair. 'You're not serious?'

'Indeed I am. If you have finished, shall we go to the sitting-room for coffee? Sibby is out with friends and we shall be undisturbed.'

Coffee seemed a good idea, if only to clear her head and dispel the somewhat reckless mood the excellent wine they had had engendered.

She poured it from a charming little silver coffee pot into delicate Sèvres china and wished that her companion wouldn't stare quite so hard at her; she concluded that it was because he was waiting for her to say something, so she asked composedly: 'Would you mind explaining?'

'It's very simple, Lavinia. I have no wife, and a daughter who badly needs female company—to designate you as stepmother would be absurd, but a kind of elder sister? And there is Peta, just a little older than Sibby and an ideal companion for her...'

'They might hate each other.'

He shook his head. 'No, Sibby is likely to take to her on sight; remember that she already likes you very much. And then there is me; I need someone to entertain for me, buy Sibby's clothes, run my home, and I hope, be my companion.' He was silent for a moment. 'I am sometimes lonely, Lavinia.'

He got up and came and stood in front of her and pulled her to her feet, and put his hands on her shoulders. 'There is no question of falling in love, my dear. I think I may never do that again—once bitten, twice shy—as you say in English. Ours would be a marriage of friends, you understand, no more than that. But I promise you that I will take care of you and Peta, just as I shall take care of Sibby.'

Lavinia swallowed. 'Why me?' she asked in a small voice.

He smiled a little. 'You're sensible, your feet are firmly planted on the ground and you haven't been too happy, have you? You will never be tempted to reach for the moon, my dear.'

She was speechless once more. So that was what he thought of her—a rather dreary spinster type with no ambition to set the world on fire. How wrong he was, and yet in a way, how right. If she chose to refuse his strange offer, the future didn't hold very much for her, she knew that. Several more years of getting Peta on to her own feet and then, when her sister married, as she most certainly would, she herself would be left to a bachelor girl's existence. But to marry this man who was so certain that his idea was a good one? She was old-fashioned enough—and perhaps sentimental enough too—to believe in falling in love and marrying for that reason.

'Would it be honest—I mean, marrying you? I've very little to offer. Sibendina might grow to dislike me, you know, and I'm not much good at entertaining or running a large house.'

'If I tell you that I'm quite sure that it will be a success, will you consider it?'

It was a crazy conversation; she said so and he laughed in genuine amusement. 'Will you think about it, Lavinia?'

'Well—yes.' Even as she said it, she marvelled at herself; her usually sensible head was filled with a mass of nonsense which, once she was alone, she would have to reduce to proper proportions. Indeed, it had suddenly become an urgent matter to get away from this large man who so disquieted her, and think coolly about everything, without his eyes watching her face as though he could read every thought. She said abruptly: 'Would you mind very much if I went back now? I have to think.'

He made no attempt to dissuade her; in no time at all she found herself running up the Home stairs, his brief, friendly good night echoing in her ears.

Being alone didn't help at all, she found herself wishing that he was there so that she might ask his advice, which, on the face of it, was just too absurd. Not only that, her thoughts didn't make sense. Probably she was too tired to think clearly, she would go to bed and sleep, and in the morning she would be able to come to a rational decision.

Amazingly, she slept almost as soon as her head touched the pillow, to waken in time to hear the carillons from Amsterdam's many churches ringing out three o'clock. She buried her head in the pillow, willing herself to go to sleep again. There was a busy day ahead of her in theatre, and in another three hours or so she would have to get up. But her mind, nicely refreshed, refused to do her bidding. 'Radmer,' she said aloud to the dark room. 'It's a strange name, but it suits him.' She turned over in bed and thumped her pillows; somehow it helped to talk to herself about him. 'I wish I knew more about his wife. Perhaps he loved her very much, even if no one else seems to have liked her.'

What was it he had said? Once bitten, twice shy. Anyway, he had made it very plain that he wasn't marrying her because he loved her, only because he liked her.

Lavinia gave up the idea of sleep, and sat up in bed, hugging her knees. She didn't know him at all, really, and it was preposterous that after such a short acquaintance, he should wish to marry her. Primarily for his own convenience, of course, he had made no bones about that; someone to look after Sibby and order his household and entertain for him, he had said; just as though she had no feelings in the matter. She was suddenly indignant and just as suddenly sleepy. When she woke, the sun was up and she could hear the maid coming along the passage, knocking on the doors.

By the time she had dressed she had made up her mind not to marry him, although this decision depressed her dreadfully, and that very day she would see the Directrice and arrange about living out; that would make an end of the matter. She sat silently through breakfast so that Neeltje wanted to know if she felt ill. She made some remark about seeing too many museums all at once and everyone laughed as they dispersed to their various wards, and Neeltje, who had taken her remark seriously, took her arm, and began to warn her of the dangers of too much sightseeing all at once. They were close to the theatre unit doors when they were flung wide with a good deal of force and Professor ter Bavinck came through them. He was in theatre kit again, his mask dangling under his unshaven chin. He looked tired, cross and even with these drawbacks, very handsome.

Lavinia, watching him coming towards them, was aware of a peculiar sensation, rather as though she had been filled with bubbles and wasn't on firm ground any more, and at the same time she knew exactly what she was going to do. She gently disengaged her arm from Neeltje and walked briskly forward to meet the professor. She wasted no time over good mornings or hullos; she planted her small person before his large one so that he was forced to stop, staring at her with tired eyes. She said, not caring if Neeltje heard or not: 'I was very silly last night. Of course I'll marry you.'

She didn't wait for his reply but slid through the theatre doors with a bewildered Neeltje hard on her heels. 'Whatever did you say?' asked her friend. 'I didn't hear.'

'I said I would,' Lavinia told her, hardly aware of what she was saying, her mind completely taken up with the sudden wonder of finding herself in love. She would have liked to have gone somewhere quiet to think about it, instead she found herself laying up for the first case.

It wasn't until she was having her coffee, the first case dealt with, the second laid up for and Sister scrubbing, that she had a few minutes in which to think. The delightful, excited elation was still there, although it was marred just a little by the realization that the professor neither expected nor wished her to love him—it really was enough to put any girl off, she thought with a touch of peevishness, but now that she had discovered that she loved him, to marry him would be perfectly all right, or so it seemed to her.

Her feverish thoughts were interrupted by the two nurses having coffee with her. 'There was a patient in the night,' one of them told her, 'a girl with stab wounds, and a laparotomy must be done, you understand. The surgeon is not happy when he looks inside—there is a question of CA—so he calls for Professor ter Bavinck at three o'clock in the morning and they are here for a long time and he finds that it is CA. Is it not sad?'

'Very,' agreed Lavinia. So that was why he had looked so tired… The other nurse spoke. 'And it is not nice for the Prof, for he goes to Brussels this morning—I heard Zuster Smid say so.'

'Oh,' said Lavinia; disappointment was like a physical pain. She added nonchalantly: 'How long for?'

The nurse shrugged. 'Two-three days, perhaps longer, I do not know. There is a seminar… You wish more coffee?'

'No, thanks.' Lavinia felt exactly like a pricked balloon, and it was entirely her own fault for being so stupidly impetuous. As though the professor had been in a hurry to know her answer; he had thought of it as a sensible arrangement between friends with no need to get excited about it. She shuddered with shame at her childish behaviour; quite likely he had been appalled at it. She went back to theatre with the other two girls, and presently, at Zuster Smid's command, scrubbed to take a minor case. It kept her well occupied until dinner time, and because there was a heavy afternoon list, she stayed behind with Neeltje to get the theatre ready. They had just finished when the professor walked in. He was freshly shaven now, his face wore the look of a man who had had a sound night's sleep, he wore a black and white dogtooth checked suit, cut to perfection, and he looked superbly elegant.

He said something softly to Neeltje as he crossed the floor and she smiled widely as she went into the anaesthetic room—which left Lavinia alone behind her draped trolley, thankful that she was masked and gowned and capped so that almost nothing of her showed. He came to a halt a few yards from her so that there was no chance of him sullying the spotlessness around her.

'That was just what I needed,' he declared, and when she looked bewildered: 'This morning. I stayed up half the night wondering if I had been too precipitate—hurrying you along relentlessly, not giving you time to think. I was no nearer a conclusion when I was called in for that poor girl.'

'Oh,' said Lavinia, 'and I've been worrying all the morning, thinking that you might have found me very silly.' And when he smiled and shook his head: 'I thought you were going to Brussels—one of the nurses told me.'

'I'm on my way, I shall be gone two days. When I come back we'll tell Sibby and the rest of them. When are your days off?'

She told him and he nodded. 'Good. I'll take you to see my mother and father.'

This was something she hadn't known about, and the look she gave him was so apprehensive that he burst out laughing. 'Regretting your decision, Lavinia?'

'No, of course not, it's just that I don't know anything about you…'

'We'll have plenty of time to talk, my dear. I must go. *Tot ziens*!'

She was left staring at the gently swinging door. He had been very businesslike; she doubted if many girls had their marriage plans laid before them with such cool efficiency. Come to think of it, he hadn't shown any gratifying signs of satisfaction concerning his—their future. But then why should he? It was, after all, a sensible arrangement between friends.

She was going off duty on the evening before her days off when the hall porter on duty called to her as she crossed the hall. His English was as sparse as her Dutch, but she was able to make out that she was to be at the hospital entrance by nine o'clock the next morning. She thanked him with the impeccable accent Juffrouw de Waal insisted upon, and sped to her room. There was a lot to do; her hair would have to be washed, and since she had nothing else suitable, it would have to be the pink again and that would need pressing. She set about these tasks, daydreaming a little, wondering if Radmer would be glad to see her.

The fine weather held, the morning sun was shining gloriously as she dressed, ate a hurried breakfast and went down to the hospital entrance. The professor was waiting, in slacks and a thin sweater this time. His greeting was cheerful enough although quite lacking in any sentiment.

'Hullo,' he said. 'We'll go back to the house, shall we—we have to talk, you and I.' He got into the car beside her and turned to smile at her. 'We can do that better sitting comfortably and undisturbed. Sibby will be home for lunch. I thought, if you agree, that we might tell her today; she should be the first to know—she and your sister.'

He was a man for getting to the point without any small talk to lead up to it, she perceived. 'Yes, of course I agree,' she told him with composure, 'but I don't think I'd better tell Peta—she might get so excited that she would tell Aunt Gwyneth, and that wouldn't do at all.'

'Well, we'll have to think about that. I should like you to meet my mother and father today, and as soon as I can get away I'll take you up to Friesland.'

'Friesland? But that's in the north, isn't it? Have you family there?'

'No—a house, left to me by my grandfather. I should like you to see it. I have a sister, by the way, married and living in Bergen-op-Zoom.'

They had reached the house and went inside. The gentle gloom of the hall was cool after the bright sunshine outside; its beauty struck her afresh as they crossed it and entered the sitting-room. Here the doors were open on to the small garden and the room was alight with sunshine and they went to sit by one of the open windows as Mevrouw Pette followed them in with the coffee tray. It wasn't until she had gone and Lavinia had poured the coffee that the professor spoke, and very much to the point.

'It takes a week or two to arrange a marriage in Holland,' he explained, 'so I think we might get started with the formalities today, then we can marry at the first opportunity—there is no point in waiting, is there?' He glanced briefly at her. 'The sooner the better, then we can go over to England and fetch Peta together; that might make things easier for you both.'

She tried to keep her voice as casual as his, just as though getting married was an everyday occurrence in her life. 'That's awfully kind of you—I'm sure it would. Do—do I have to do anything about our wedding?'

'Not today—you will need your passport later. Church, I take it?'

'Yes, please.'

'We shall have to be married by civil law first, otherwise we shan't be legally man and wife. Shall we keep it as quiet as possible?'

It cost her an effort to agree to this cheerfully. Was he ashamed of her, or did he suppose they would be the subject of gossip? Perhaps she wasn't good enough for his friends—in that case why was he marrying her? There must surely be girls more suitable amongst his acquaintances.

His voice jolted her gently back to her surroundings.

'None of the reasons you are so feverishly examining are the right ones. When I married Helga we had an enormous wedding, hundreds of guests, a reception, wedding bells, presents by the score, but it was only a wedding, not a marriage. Do you understand? This time it will be just us two, marrying each other for sound and sensible reasons, and no phoney promises of love.' His voice was bitter.

He must have been very unhappy for him to sound like that after all those years. She managed a tranquil: 'I understand perfectly. That's what I should like too, and if you don't want to talk about your—your first wife, you don't have to. I daresay if we were marrying for all the usual reasons, I might feel differently about that, but as you say, this is a sensible arrangement between friends. I shall do my very best to help Sibby in every way, you can depend on that, and I'll learn to run your home as you wish it to be run. I'm not much good at parties, but I expect I'll learn. You're quite sure it's what you want? Peta will be an extra mouth to feed, you know, and I should very much like her to have another year at least of schooling—would you mind paying for that?'

He looked amused. 'Not in the least. I should tell you that I'm a wealthy man—money doesn't have to come into it.' He gave her a thoughtful look. 'And you, my dear—you are content? Perhaps it is an odd state of affairs for a girl—to marry and yet not be a wife; I'm being selfish.'

She answered him steadily. 'No, not really, for I am getting a great deal out of it, too. I—I have no prospects; no one has ever asked me to marry him, and if I didn't marry you, I should be hard put to it to get Peta educated. I'm not much of a catch,' she added frankly. 'I hope Sibendina will like the idea.'

He said on a laugh: 'She was the first one to suggest it, if you remember.' He got up, and the dogs, lying at his feet, got up too. 'Shall we go to the Town Hall and get the preliminaries over?' he asked.

She didn't understand all of what was said when they got there, but it really didn't matter. She stood watching the professor talking to the rather pompous man who asked so many questions, and wished with all her heart that he could love her, even just a little, even though she felt sure that she had enough love for both of them. Of one thing she was sure already; he thought of her as a friend, to be trusted and talked to and confided in, that at least was something. And if he had decided to marry her for Sibby's sake, it was surely better that he should marry her, who loved him so much, rather than some other girl who didn't.

He turned to speak to her and she smiled at him. He had said that she would never be tempted to reach for the moon, but wasn't that exactly what she had done?

CHAPTER FIVE

THEY GOT BACK to the house with just enough time to have a drink before lunch and the return of Sibendina from school, and Lavinia, although outwardly calm, was glad of the sherry to stop the quaking going on inside her. Her companion, she noticed, was sitting back in his chair looking the picture of ease while he drank his gin, just as though the prospect of getting married in a couple of weeks' time had no worries for him at all. She envied him his cool while she kept up a rather feverish chat about nothing in particular, until he interrupted her with a gentle: 'Don't worry, Lavinia—Sibby will be delighted.'

She did her best to believe him while she wished secretly that he might have felt a little more sympathy for her nerves. After all, not every girl found herself in the kind of situation she was in at the moment. And he could have shown some warmth in his feelings towards her…she corrected the thought hastily, for it had made him seem heartless and cold, and he was neither, only most dreadfully businesslike and matter-of-fact about the whole thing. But then she had herself to blame for that. Perhaps she appeared as businesslike to him as he did to her, even though she loved him, but of course he didn't know that, and never would. She moved restlessly and caught his eye and managed a smile as the door opened and Sibendina came in.

There had been no need to be nervous after all; Sibby paused in the doorway, looking from one to the other of them, then swooped on her father while a flow of excited words poured from her lips. She had turned and engulfed Lavinia, still chattering madly, before the professor said on a shout of laughter: 'And here is poor Lavinia worrying herself sick in case you don't approve!'

His daughter gave Lavinia a quick kiss and a bearlike hug. 'That is absurd—I am so pleased I do not know what I must say.'

'But how did you know?' asked Lavinia.

'But I see your face, of course—and Papa, sitting there looking just as he looks when his work has gone well and he does not need to worry any more.' She sat down on the sofa between their chairs. 'When will you marry? Shall I be a bridesmaid? And Peta, of course—What shall we wear?'

Her father answered her. 'We shall marry just as soon as it can be arranged—it will be very quiet, *liefje*, I think Lavinia doesn't want bridesmaids.' He smiled at Lavinia, who smiled back. Of course she wanted bridesmaids and white silk and a veil and flowers—all girls did, but since he had made it clear that he didn't, she would have to forget all that. She said now: 'I really would like a small wedding, but it would be lovely if you and Peta could have pretty dresses.'

Sibby became enrapt. 'Blue,' she murmured, 'long, you understand, with little sleeves and large floppy hats for us both. Peta and I will go shopping together.'

She beamed at Lavinia. 'It is very good to have a step-mother; Papa is a dear, but he is a man—now I shall be able to talk about all the things girls talk about.' She sighed blissfully. 'We shall be most happy. When do we go to fetch Peta?'

'That will have to wait until a day or so before the wedding,' interpolated the professor, 'and Lavinia and I will go—you won't mind that, will you, Sibby? You can make sure that everything is ready for our return.'

His daughter eyed him rebelliously and then giggled. 'Of course, I am stupid—people who are to be married do not like to have companions, do they, so I will not mind at all. I will buy flowers and make the house beautiful and order splendid meals.' She was struck with a sudden idea. 'I will also invite guests—a great many.'

'Oh, no, you don't,' said her father firmly. 'Your grandmother will do that; I daresay there will be a big party at her house.'

'She does not know about you and Lavinia, Papa?'

'Not yet. We're going to see her and Grandfather when we've had lunch.' He heaved himself out of his chair. 'Shall we go and have it now?'

He took an arm of each of them and they all went into the dining-room where they had a hilarious meal, largely due to Sibendina's high spirits.

The drive to Noordwijk was short, a bare twenty-five miles, a distance which the Bentley swallowed in well-bred, silent speed. Lavinia was surprised to see that the town appeared to be little more than a row of rather grand hotels facing the sea, but presently they turned away a little and drove through the small town and took a tree-lined road leading away from its centre. Large villas lined it at intervals and she supposed that Radmer's parents lived in one of them, but he didn't stop, leaving them behind to cross the heath, slowing down to drive over a sandy lane which presently led through open gates into the well laid out grounds of a low solidly built house facing the sea. He stopped before its open front door and giving Lavinia no time to get nervous, whisked her out of the car and into the house, and still holding her arm, walked her across the wide hall and through a pair of doors at the back. The room they entered ran across the width of the house so that it had a great many windows overlooking a delightful garden. There were doors too, flung open on to a verandah, its striped awning casting a pleasant shade on to the chairs scattered along its length. The professor wasted no time on the room, but strode rapidly across it and through to the verandah, to stop by the two people sitting there.

Lavinia had no difficulty in recognizing them; the professor's father might be white-haired and a little gaunt, but in his younger days he must have had his son's good looks—even now he was quite something. And his mother, although she was sitting, was a big, tall woman, considerably younger than her husband, with quite ordinary features redeemed by a pair of sparkling blue eyes, as heavy-lidded as her son's. She looked up now and smiled with pleased surprise, and her 'Radmer!' was full of delight as she said something in Dutch in a soft, girlish voice. He bent to kiss her, still with a hand tucked firmly in Lavinia's arm, shook his father by the hand and spoke in English.

'I want you to meet Lavinia—Lavinia Hawkins. She came from England to work at St Jorus a short while ago.' He paused and they greeted her kindly, speaking English as effortlessly as their own tongue, then embarked on small talk with a total lack of curiosity as to who she was and why she was there. Perhaps presently they would ask questions, but now they sat her down between them, plied her with iced lemonade and discussed the summer weather, the garden, and the delights of living close to the sea. Lavinia had pretty manners. She took her share of the conversation while she wondered why Radmer hadn't dropped at least a hint about their approaching marriage. Surely he wasn't going to keep his parents in the dark about it? She couldn't believe it of him, and her sigh of relief when he at last spoke was loud enough for him to hear and glance at her with a smile of understanding.

There had been a pause in the conversation and old Mijnheer ter Bavinck had suggested that his son might like to accompany him to his study, so that they might discuss some interesting article or other. Radmer got to his feet, pulled Lavinia gently to hers too and turned to face his parents.

'My dears,' he said quietly, 'I think you will have guessed that Lavinia is someone special; we hope to be married within a very short time.'

There was no doubt of their pleasure. There were congratulations and kisses and handshakes, and Mevrouw ter Bavinck picked up a handbell in order to summon a rather staid, middle-aged woman and give her some low-voiced instructions, at the same time telling her the news. She turned to Lavinia as the woman went to wring Radmer's hand and then did the same for Lavinia. 'This is Berthe,' she explained. 'She has been with us since Radmer was a very small boy, so of course she must hear the news too. Joop, her husband, who also works for us, is going to bring up a bottle of champagne.'

She beamed down at Lavinia and touched her lightly on the arm. 'We will allow the men to go away and discuss their dull business; you and I will talk—for now that you are to be our daughter, I may ask you questions, may I not?'

'Of course, Mevrouw ter Bavinck.' Lavinia warmed to the older woman's charm. 'I hope I haven't been too much of a surprise. It—it happened rather suddenly, I'm still surprised myself.'

They were sitting opposite each other now, and her hostess gave her a thoughtful look. 'It has been my dearest wish that Radmer should marry again. Has he told you about Helga—his first wife?'

'Not a great deal, and I told him that if he didn't want to talk to me about her, I wouldn't mind. Should I know?'

Mevrouw ter Bavinck looked doubtful. 'I think you should, but that is something which you will decide between you. But there is one thing, my dear, and you must forgive an old woman's impertinence in asking such a question, but it is important to me—after Helga. Do you love Radmer?'

Lavinia met the blue gaze squarely. 'With all my heart.'

Her companion sighed contentedly. 'That is good—and you will need all that love, Lavinia; he has been a solitary man for more than ten years, he is not young, and he has lived for his work— Now he will live for you, of course, but perhaps he may not realize that just yet.'

Her future mother-in-law was a wise woman who perhaps saw more than she was expected to see. Lavinia said gently: 'He loves Sibendina.'

'Very much, and she, thank God, is wholly his daughter.' The blue eyes twinkled. 'You will be a very young mother for her, but just what she needs. And now tell me, my dear, have you family of your own?'

Lavinia told her about Peta and her parents and Aunt Gwyneth; she found it easy to do this because her listener had the gift of listening as well as putting others at their ease; by the time the two men, followed by the champagne, returned, the two ladies were firm friends, and as Radmer sat himself down close to Lavinia, his mother remarked: 'You are both right for each other, Radmer—I believe you will be very happy. Is the wedding to be a quiet one?'

They drank their champagne and talked in a pleasant desultory way about the marriage, and presently they went into the sitting-room and had tea and small crisp biscuits, and this time Lavinia found herself sitting with Radmer's father, answering his questions, warmed by his kindness.

They got up to go shortly after, with a promise to come again very soon, so that the details of the wedding might be finalized, and when they were once more in the Bentley, driving slowly this time, the professor asked:

'Well, Lavinia, do you think you will like my parents?'

She felt a little tired after the day's excitement, but content too. The answer she gave him must have satisfied him, for he said: 'Good girl, they like you too—I knew they would.'

Which, she supposed with faint bitterness, was, from him, a compliment.

They went out to dine later, but not before he had taken her to a small room at the back of the hall she hadn't previously been into, and opened a drawer in a charming medallion cabinet set against one of its silk-hung walls. The box he took from it was small and leather-covered and when he opened it she saw that it held a ring; a diamond cluster in a cup setting, the gold heavily engraved. He put the box down and came towards her with the ring in the palm of his hand and they looked at it together for a few moments. 'It has been in my mother's family for years,' he said at length. 'I should like you to have it. It hasn't been worn for a long time, for Helga refused to wear it, she considered it old-fashioned.'

Lavinia held up a small, capable hand. It was a pity that Helga had to be dragged into it, but she supposed she was being given the ring for appearances' sake, and anyway, he would have no idea that she was already fiercely jealous of his first wife—indeed, if he found that out, he might cry off, appalled at the very idea of her feeling anything at all but a comfortable, uncomplicated friendship for him. She thanked him nicely, admired the ring, remarked upon its excellent fit, and when he bent and kissed her cheek, received the salute with what she hoped was a warm but not too warm manner. Apparently it was satisfactory, for Radmer took her arm as they went back into the hall, and remarked with some satisfaction that he had no doubt that they would be excellent friends. He even halted half-way to the staircase to say: 'You see, if no emotions are involved, my dear, the success of our marriage is assured; we shall have no bouts of jealousy or imagined feelings of neglect, and no wish to interfere with each other's lives.' He smiled down at her and kissed her for a second time, still on her cheek. 'You do understand that I am deeply engrossed in my work?' he wanted to know.

She said that yes, she quite understood that, and wondered for the first time, deep in her heart, if she would be able to endure living with him in such a manner, but it was a little late to think of that now, and at least she would make him happier than a girl who didn't love him. The thought consoled her as she went upstairs to tidy herself for their evening out.

Time telescoped itself after that evening; some days she didn't see Radmer at all, some days she spent an hour or so at his house or snatched a brief meal with him somewhere, and several times they drove to see his parents.

She had found that, without bothering her with details, he had smoothed the way for her to leave the hospital. All the tiresome formalities had been taken care of, and when she received her salary he had told her to spend it on herself as he had arranged for her to have an allowance which would be paid into the bank on their wedding day. And he had been of the greatest help in writing to Peta, who, they had decided, wasn't to be told anything until they actually arrived at Aunt Gwyneth's house. Lavinia had composed a careful letter, full of optimism about the future, and had told Peta that if she didn't write again for a little while it was because she was going to be busy. She read it out to Radmer on one of their rare evenings together and looked at him anxiously when she had done so. 'Does it sound all right?' she wanted to know. 'And are you sure we're doing the right thing?'

He had reassured her with a patience which soothed her edginess, and when Sibendina had joined them later, he had taken care to keep the conversation light and cheerful, so that she had gone back to hospital and slept like a contented child.

She was still working, of course. Radmer had asked her if she wished to leave St Jorus and she had no doubt that if she had said yes, he would have arranged it for her without fuss or bother, just as he had arranged everything else, but she had chosen to stay on until a few days before they were to marry, going on duty each day, an object of excited attention from her new friends in the hospital.

It was a few days before she was due to leave that Radmer had driven her up to Friesland. They had left very early in the morning, before breakfast, and done the eighty odd miles in under two hours, to eat that meal upon their arrival. Lavinia had been a little overawed at the sight of the large square house set in its small estate to the north of Leeuwwarden. The grounds around it were beautifully laid out with banks of flowers screened by a variety of shrubs and trees, and a freshly raked gravel drive leading from the great iron gateway at the roadside.

The housekeeper had come to welcome them—Juffrouw Hengsma, a tall, homely woman who said little but smiled her pleasure at seeing them before serving the breakfast they didn't hurry over. Lavinia sat listening to Radmer's history of the house and then spent the remainder of the morning going over it with him, lingering over its treasures of silver and glass and porcelain, and admiring the splendid hangings at the windows and the well-polished furniture. But it was a very comfortable house too, for all its age and size. There were easy chairs and sofas and pretty table lamps scattered around the rooms, thick carpets on the floors, and even though each apartment had an enormous chandelier hanging from the centre of its high ceiling, there was an abundance of wall lighting so that even on the gloomiest day, the rooms would glow with soft light.

'You like it?' asked Radmer, and smiled warmly at her when she declared that she had never seen anything as beautiful. 'Except for your house in Amsterdam,' she added. 'I love it.'

'So do I. We come up here quite often, though. Come and see the garden.'

It was a happy day for her, at any rate, and she thought Radmer had been happy too; she had wanted to be reassured about that quite badly and it had been a good test, spending the whole day together like that, with nothing much to do and only each other to depend upon for company. Looking back, she was as sure as she could be that he had enjoyed being with her—they had found a great deal to talk about and they had discovered similar tastes and ideas. She had gone to bed that night full of hope.

She left the hospital two days later, early in the morning, so that they could catch a Hovercraft at Calais and be at Cuckfield by the afternoon, and although it wasn't yet eight o'clock, she had a tremendous send-off when Radmer came to collect her with the Bentley. He had laughed and waved good-naturedly at the small crowd of nurses, then glanced sideways at her. 'That's a new outfit,' he remarked. 'I like it.'

The sun, already shining, seemed to shine a little brighter; it was a good beginning to a day of which Lavinia felt a little uncertain. 'I'm glad,' she said happily. 'I went to Metz and Metz yesterday and bought some clothes...'

'A wedding dress?' he asked lightly.

'Well, yes.' It had been more expensive than she had expected, but the simplicity of the rich cream crêpe had seemed just right, and she had bought a hat too, covered in cream silk roses. She only hoped that it wouldn't seem too bridal for his taste. She looked down at the blue and white coat dress she was wearing, satisfied for once that she was in the forefront of fashion. She had bought blue sandals too and a leather handbag, and now she had very little money left.

It occurred to her at that moment that Radmer had

said nothing at all about a honeymoon; perhaps the Dutch didn't have them, possibly he felt it would be a waste of time. Honeymoons were for people in love, although surely two friends could go on holiday together, and if anyone else wanted to call it a honeymoon, they were at liberty to do so.

They were already out of Amsterdam and as though he had read her thoughts, he asked: 'Would you mind very much if we go straight home after the wedding? I'm up to my ears in work and there's a lecture…'

Her pride wouldn't allow him to finish, to seek more excuses. 'Of course I don't mind—I'll have Peta and Sibby and that lovely house to explore and I shall go shopping.'

He nodded and they didn't talk about themselves or the wedding again. It was much later, when they were leaving Dover behind them, that she asked: 'I expect you know where Cuckfield is? It's not far.'

'I've driven through it, I believe.' He took the Bentley neatly past a great juggernaut and started down the hill towards Folkestone.

'You know England?'

He smiled. 'I was at Cambridge.'

'Oh, were you?' She added with faint bewilderment: 'I don't know anything about you.'

He laughed. 'It will all come out in good time. Shall we stop for an early lunch? I'm going along the coast road, we could have a meal at the Mermaid in Rye.'

It was during that meal that she asked: 'Which church are we being married at? I did ask you, but if you remember you had to go somewhere or other in a hurry before you could tell me.'

He looked rueful. 'What you mean is, I forgot all about it. I'm sorry—I'm not proving very informative, am I? You wanted somewhere quiet, didn't you, so I've arranged it at the English church in the Begijnsteeg—I hope you'll like that.'

Her face showed that she did. 'An English service? How nice, now I can wear my ring on my left hand…'

He laughed again, very softly. 'If it makes you feel more securely married, why not? I thought we might go straight there after we've had the civil wedding. Mama is giving a small reception for us afterwards at Noordwijk and the two girls are going to stay there for a couple of days. We can be back home again in the early evening.' She could almost hear relief in his voice at the thought of getting it all over and done with as speedily as possible. It surprised her when he leaned across the table and took her hand in his. 'Have you ever thought how appropriately you are named, my dear?'

She shook her head, conscious of his hand, wishing very much to clasp it with her own.

'Lavinia was the second wife of Aeneas.'

'Oh—Greek mythology.' She furrowed her forehead in thought. 'But my name isn't appropriate at all—I've just remembered, wasn't there someone called Thompson who quoted something about the lovely young Lavinia, and I'm not lovely; I remember my father telling me about it and laughing…'

He said very gently: 'Kind laughter, I'm sure, and

there are a great many variations on that word, you know—amiable, sweet, angelic…'

If he had loved her—been in love with her, he wouldn't have needed to say that; she winced at the pain his words had given her and smiled back at him. 'I hope you don't suppose me to be angelic? I can be as cross as two sticks sometimes.'

'I know. The first time you spoke to me you were just that. It intrigued me even before I turned round to look at you. I knew you would be different from other girls.'

Her voice was unconsciously wistful. 'I'm just the same inside,' but she smiled widely as she spoke, just to let him see that she wasn't taking their conversation seriously.

They drove on presently and the nearer they got to Cuckfield, the more nervous Lavinia became, twisting her lovely ring round and round her finger, opening and shutting her handbag for no reason at all, and Radmer, who had shown no sign of nerves, smiled a little to himself, ignoring her small fidgets until on the outskirts of the little town he slowed the car and stopped in a layby, and when she looked at him inquiringly, said mildly: 'Look, Lavinia, I know how you feel, but will you stop worrying and leave it all to me?'

She nodded wordlessly. He would, without doubt, sail through the awkward situation without any outward sign of ill-humour, whatever Aunt Gwyneth said to him. Indeed, he looked capable of moving a mountain if he had a mind to; he also looked very handsome and impeccably turned out. He was wearing the dogtooth check again with a silk shirt and a tie of sombre magnificence. She had no doubt that he would get his own way without difficulty, whatever obstacle was put in his path.

And she was right. Aunt Gwyneth was at home, having just finished lunch, and was taken completely by surprise. They listened to her blustering efforts to prevent Peta going with them until Radmer settled the matter with a suave confidence which left her shaken.

'There can be no objection,' he pointed out firmly. 'You are not Peta's guardian, and now that Lavinia and I are to be married and can offer her a good home, I can see no reason for your objection. You have yourself just said that she has cost you a great deal and forced you to make sacrifices. I imagine that you have no plans for Peta's future?'

Aunt Gwyneth eyed him angrily. Her plans, such as they were, would have been torn to shreds by this quiet, dreadfully self-possessed man. She made an exasperated sound and turned her spite on Lavinia, sitting as quiet as a mouse, feeling sick. 'Well, it didn't take you long to find yourself a husband, did it?' she demanded. 'And now I suppose all my kindness and money will have been wasted on the pair of you.'

'I can't remember you spending any money on me, Aunt,' Lavinia said with spirit, 'and Peta's school fees can't have been all that much—Father said you had more money than you knew what to do with.' She added bitterly: 'And I can't remember you being kind.'

'Then we can take the matter as settled,' the professor interrupted quietly. 'You will be glad to be rid of your burden, Mrs Turner, and if you have incurred expense beyond your means, I shall be glad to reimburse you.'

Aunt Gwyneth sniffed angrily. 'Indeed I shall…' she began, and got no further as the door opened and Peta came into the room. 'There's a gorgeous Bentley outside—Lavinia!' She flung herself into her sister's arms. 'Lavinia, you said you'd come and I knew you would—oh, dear, I'm going to howl. You will take me with you…?'

Lavinia gave her sister a hug and turned her round. 'Yes, darling—we have just been talking to Aunt Gwyneth—and this is Radmer, we're going to be married in two days' time and you're coming to live with us.'

Peta crossed the room and gazed into his imperturbable face. 'Of course, the Bentley. However did Lavinia find you? You're super!'

He took her hand and said gravely: 'Hullo, Peta, and thank you. Lavinia didn't find me, I found her.'

She was still staring at him. 'What shall I call you?'

'Won't Radmer do? I've a daughter, you know, she's fourteen, and she calls your sister Lavinia, so that makes it right, doesn't it?'

She nodded and smiled then. 'I like you,' she told him shyly. 'Can we go now?'

He looked over her head and smiled faintly, but it was to Mrs Turner, sitting ignored, to whom he spoke. 'Perhaps if Lavinia might pack Peta's things? We don't wish to take up too much of your time.' He spoke with the utmost politeness, quite sure that he would have his way. Apparently Aunt Gwyneth thought so too, for she said angrily: 'Lavinia can do what she likes; she's always an ungrateful, sullen girl. I'm surprised you're going to marry her—she's plain enough, and I can't think what you can see in her.'

The politeness was still there, tinged with arrogance now. 'Probably not, Mrs Turner, but I must remind you that you are speaking of my future wife.' He looked at Lavinia and smiled, warmly this time. 'Perhaps if Peta goes with you?' he suggested. 'She need only bring the things she treasures—we'll buy anything she needs.'

It took ten minutes. Peta had few possessions and a small wardrobe, the two girls packed a case, talking in excited snatches, and went back to the drawing-room where they found their aunt angrily firing questions at Radmer, who was answering them with a patience and ease of manner which Lavinia couldn't help but admire. He got up as they entered the room, took the case from her, stood silently while they wished their aunt good-bye and then offered his own farewells, but all Aunt Gwyneth said was: 'Don't come running back to me, either of you—you would have had a secure home here, Lavinia, as my companion, but if you're fool enough to marry a foreigner…'

Lavinia rounded on her. 'Aunt Gwyneth, don't you dare speak of Radmer in that fashion! He's a good, kind man and we shall be very happy.'

She went through the door Radmer was holding open for her, her cheeks fiery, her head high, and allowed him to settle her in the car without looking at him. Only when he got in beside her did she whisper: 'Oh, I'm so ashamed—she had no right…'

His hand covered hers for a brief moment. 'Thank

you, dear girl,' then he took it away and turned to look at Peta, bouncing with impatience on the back seat. 'We're going to spend the night in London. I thought we might go to a theatre this evening, and if we don't stop on the way for tea I think there might just be time for you girls to do some shopping.'

It was Peta who answered him. 'I say, you are super. What sort of shopping?'

'Well, a dress for this evening, perhaps. How about Harrods?'

Peta made a small ecstatic sound and Lavinia murmured: 'But we shan't have time. I thought we were going to spend the night at Dover—I haven't anything with me, only night things.'

'Then you must have a new dress too.'

'Oh, Lavinia, yes!' Peta had leaned forward to poke her pretty face between them. 'Oh, isn't this marvellous? I simply can't believe it! And now tell me about the wedding and where you live and your daughter's name, and am I to go to school…?'

He laughed. 'Lavinia, I leave it to you. See how much you can get into the next half hour.'

Almost everything; enough to satisfy Peta and make her sigh happily. By the time they reached Knightsbridge and Harrods, she was starry-eyed.

It was surprising how much shopping could be done in a short space of time when one didn't need to look too closely at the price tags, and there was someone waiting with a cheque book to pay. They had begun by looking at the less expensive dresses; it was Radmer who had got up from the chair he had taken in the middle of the salon, caught Lavinia by the hand, and pointed out several models which had taken his fancy. She had tried them on, not daring to ask their price, and when she had been unable to decide which of them she preferred—the apricot silk jersey or the grass green patterned crêpe, he had told her to have them both. She went and stood close to him, so that no one should hear, and murmured: 'Radmer, they're frightfully expensive…'

His blue eyes twinkled kindly. 'But you look nice in them,' he pointed out, 'so please do as I ask,' and when she thanked him shyly he only smiled again and then said briskly: 'Now where is Peta—for heaven's sake don't let her buy black with frills.'

But Peta, though young, had as good a taste as Lavinia. She had picked out a cotton voile dress in a soft blue, a Laura Ashley model, and came hurrying to display it. 'Only I don't know how much it is,' she said in a loud whisper, 'and I don't like to ask.'

Radmer settled himself in his chair. 'Try it on,' he suggested. 'I'm sure it's well within my pocket.'

She looked sweet in it, and when he suggested that they might as well buy shoes while they were there, Lavinia gave in, but only because Peta would have been disappointed if she had refused. They were going through the shop when he whispered in her ear: 'It's quite proper, you know, a man may give his future wife anything he chooses. You mustn't forget that we are to be married in two days' time.'

As though she could forget! She smiled and thanked him and turned to admire the sandals Peta had set her heart on.

She had no idea where they were to stay the night. It was Peta who recognized the hotel. 'Claridges!' she breathed. 'I say, how absolutely super. Are you a millionaire, Radmer?'

He chuckled. 'Not quite. Out you get.'

They had a belated tea before they went to their rooms. Lavinia gasped when she saw the luxury of her room, with its bathroom, and Peta's room on the other side. She changed, constantly interrupted by visits from her excited sister, who was full of questions, when Radmer came across from his room on the other side of the corridor to take them down to dinner—a merry meal, but how could it be otherwise, with Peta chattering so happily? They were enjoying their sorbets when she leaned across the table to say: 'Radmer, what a lucky man you are—you've got everything you want, and now you've got Lavinia too, you must be wildly happy.'

Lavinia found herself listening anxiously for his reply. 'Isn't it apparent?' he asked lightly. Which was a most unsatisfactory answer.

They went to a musical show, an unsophisticated entertainment which Lavinia suspected must have bored Radmer for most of the time, but it was entirely suitable for Peta's youthful ears and eyes, and she thanked him warmly when they got back to the hotel, and when she had gone to bed, Lavinia thanked him once more for taking Peta under his wing. 'It's like a dream,' she told him, 'and everything has happened so quickly, it doesn't seem quite real.'

He touched her cheek with a gentle finger. 'It's real, my dear.' He spoke so softly that she exclaimed: 'Oh,

Radmer, are you sorry that…? Do you want to change your mind…? It would be all right, truly it would. I can't think why you chose me in the first place.'

He took her hands in his, there in the empty corridor outside her room. 'Don't be a goose! I'm not sorry and I don't want to change my mind, although, like you, I'm not quite sure why I chose you.'

He bent to kiss her and wished her good night and she slipped into her room, glad that Peta was already asleep. It was silly to cry about nothing, and that was what she was doing. She told herself that over and over again before she at last fell asleep.

CHAPTER SIX

LAVINIA WAS CURLED up in a corner of one of the great sofas in the drawing-room of the Amsterdam house, leafing through a pile of magazines, and opposite her, sitting in his great wing chair, was Radmer, reading his post. They had been married that morning, and as she stole a quick glance at him, the wry thought that anyone coming into the room might have mistaken them for an old married couple crossed her mind. She dismissed it at once as being unworthy. No one could have been kinder than Radmer during the last two days, and at least he liked her, she thought bleakly. He had considered her every wish and his generosity had been never-ending. She turned a page and bent her head, pretending to read while she reflected on the past forty-eight hours or so. She was bound to admit that everything had gone splendidly. They had arrived back with Peta to find Sibby waiting for them, and the liking between the two girls had been instantaneous and genuine; she had felt almost sick with relief, and Radmer, who had been watching her, had flung an arm around her shoulders and observed easily: 'Exactly as I anticipated; they're just right for each other—give them six months and they'll be as close as sisters.'

Lavinia had been grateful for his quick understanding, but when she had tried to thank him he had stopped her with a careless word and gone on to talk about something quite trivial. And that night, after the hilarious dinner they had shared with the girls, he had taken her to spend the night with an aunt of his—a nice old lady living on the other side of Amsterdam in a massive house furnished in the heavy style of Biedermeier. She had been surprised at being whisked off in that fashion; quite under the impression that she would stay in Radmer's house. It was only after he had left her with Mevrouw Fokkema that that lady had remarked in her slow, careful English: 'It is correct that you stay here until your marriage, my dear—we are an old-fashioned family, but we all know, and dear Radmer too, what is due to a ter Bavinck bride.'

Lavinia, somewhat taken aback, had smiled and agreed, and wished that her betrothed had taken leave of her with a little more warmth; his casual: 'See you tomorrow, Lavinia,' had sounded positively brotherly.

But the next day had been all right. He had fetched her after breakfast and although he had been at the hospital most of the day, she and the two girls had gone shopping together and come home laden with parcels and talking excitedly about the wedding; at least Peta and Sibby had; Lavinia had been wholly occupied in overcoming a severe attack of cold feet… She thought that she had concealed her apprehension rather well, but that evening, when the girls had gone to Sibby's room to try on their new dresses and she had found herself alone with Radmer, he had asked quietly: 'Wanting to cry off, Lavinia?'

She had put down the letters she had been reading, and because she was an honest girl, had given him a straight look and said at once: 'No, not that—I think I'm a little scared of all this…' She waved an arm at the splendid room they were in. 'I'm afraid I shall let you down, Radmer.'

'Never!' He was emphatic about it. 'And it isn't as though I have quantities of friends, you know—I've friends enough, but most of them are sober doctors and their wives, and I don't entertain much.' For a moment he looked bleak. 'Helga entertained a great deal—she liked that kind of life; the house always full of people—and such people!' He blinked and smiled. 'Mind you, we shall have to do our best for Sibby and Peta in a year or two, but I think you like a quiet life, too, don't you?'

She imagined herself as he must think of her—a home body, content to slip into middle-age, running his house with perfection and never getting between him and his work. The hot resentment had been bitter in her mouth even while she knew that she had no right to feel resentful.

Her rather unhappy musings were interrupted by his quiet: 'You haven't turned a page in five minutes, Lavinia,' so that she made haste to throw him a warm smile and a cheerful: 'I was thinking about today; trying to remember your family—it was all so exciting.' She thought she had convinced him, for he smiled a little and commented: 'The kind of wedding I like,' before he picked up the next letter and became absorbed in it.

Lavinia put down her magazine, picked up her letters again, and re-read them before casting them down once more and choosing another magazine. She must remember to turn the pages this time, while she let her thoughts wander. If I were a raving beauty, she pondered sadly, we wouldn't be here; he wouldn't be reading his letters—we'd be out dancing, or going for a trip round the world, or buying me lashings of diamonds and clothes, just because he loved me. She jumped when he spoke with sudden urgency: 'Good lord, I quite forgot!' and went out of the room, to return almost at once with a jeweller's velvet case in his hand. 'A wedding present,' he explained, and opened it to take out a pearl necklace and stoop to clasp it round her neck. She put a surprised hand up to feel its silky smoothness and then looked up at him. His face was very close; she kissed him on a hard cheek and said in a wondering voice: 'Oh, Radmer, for me? Thank you—they're beautiful!' She managed a smile. 'Now I feel like the Queen…and you've given me so much!'

She was thinking of the new cheque book in her handbag and the abundance of flowers in her beautiful bedroom, the accounts he had opened for her at several of the fashionable shops, and last but not least, the gold wedding ring he had put on her finger that morning.

He stood up, said to surprise her: 'You're a very nice girl, Lavinia,' and went to sit down again and pick up the *Haagsche Post*, which left her with nothing to do but sit and think once more.

Their wedding had been a happier and gayer affair than she had anticipated; she hadn't expected quite as many people, but then she hadn't known that Radmer had such a large family or so many old friends. She had dressed at his aunt's house and he had come to fetch her with his offering of flowers—roses and orchids and orange blossom in creamy shades to match her gown—and they had driven together, first to the civil wedding and then to the little church in the peaceful Beguinehof, where they had been married again, this time by the English chaplain. It wasn't until they had stood together in the old church that she had felt really married.

They had driven to Noordwijk after that, to the reception Radmer's mother had arranged for them, and where she had met aunts and uncles and cousins and watched Peta and Sibby flitting amongst the guests, having the time of their lives. At least the two girls were blissfully happy. Sibby had hugged and kissed her and declared that she looked super and would make a marvellous mother, and Peta had kissed her and whispered: 'Oh, Lavinia, I'm so happy! Who could have dreamt that this would happen—aren't you crazy with joy?'

Lavinia assured her that she was, and it was true—she was; life wasn't going to be quite the wonder-world it might have been, but at least she could do her best to be a good wife. She turned a page, mindful of his watchful eye. If this was what he wanted then she would do her best to give it to him; peace and quiet at home and a self-effacing companionship. It sounded dull, but it wouldn't be; they got on well together, she knew that for certain; the drive back from Noordwijk had been relaxed and pleasant, even amusing. Dinner had been fun too, with champagne and Lobster Thermidor and an elaborate dessert in her honour.

She turned another unread page and glanced at the

clock—a magnificent enamel and ormolu example of French art. It was barely ten o'clock, but probably Radmer was longing to go to his study and work on the pile of papers which never seemed to diminish on his desk. Lavinia said good night without fuss, thanked him again for the pearls, and walked to the door.

He reached it before she did, to open it for her, and then, just as she was passing through, caught her by the shoulder. 'I enjoyed my wedding,' he told her soberly, 'and I hope you did too. Anyone else but you would have felt hard done by, coming back on your wedding day to sit like a mouse, pretending to read…' His eyes searched her face. 'I've not been fair to you, Lavinia.'

'Of course you have.' She was glad to hear her voice so matter-of-fact. 'You explained exactly how it would be when you asked me to marry you.' She drew a sharp breath. 'It's what I want too,' she told him steadily.

He bent and kissed her. 'You understand, don't you? You're the only girl I felt I wanted for a wife without getting involved—I've known that since the moment we met. I've built a good life, Lavinia, and a busy one, my work is important to me, you know that, and now we will share that life, but only up to a point, you know that too, don't you?'

'Oh, yes. I don't know much about it, but I can guess that losing your—your first wife made you so unhappy that you've shut the door on that side of your life—there—the loving part. I'll not open that door, Radmer.' She smiled and asked lightly: 'May I have breakfast with you? I'm used to getting up early—besides, I've an English lesson tomorrow morning with Juffrouw de Waal—she was annoyed because I've missed several just lately.' She nodded brightly at him, crossed the hall and started up the stairs. At the top she turned to lift a hand. The smile she had pinned on her face was still there, and he was too far away to see the tears in her eyes.

She didn't sleep much, but she was up early to bathe her puffy eyelids and rub the colour back into her cheeks, and when she went downstairs she looked just as usual; a little pale perhaps, but that was all. She was wearing the blue and white dress and sandals on her bare feet, and when Radmer saw her as he came in from the garden with the dogs, he wished her a cheerful good morning and said how nice she looked. 'It's going to be a hot day,' he remarked, 'and you look delightfully cool.' They walked together to the small room at the back of the house where they were to have breakfast, his arm flung round her shoulders. 'I've a busy day,' he told her as they sat down. 'Don't expect me back for lunch, but with luck I'll be home about four o'clock, and if you feel like it, we might go out for dinner.'

She poured their coffee carefully. 'That would be delightful—but can you spare the time?'

He looked up from the letters he was examining, his eyes narrowed, but she had been innocent of the sarcasm he had suspected. He said blandly: 'My dear, you had the shabbiest treatment yesterday evening, and we aren't going away for a holiday; the least I can do is to take you out and about—besides, I should like very much to do that. We'll go to the Amstel and dine on the terrace overlooking the canal—you'll enjoy that, and tomorrow evening I've booked a table at the Hooge Vuursche Hotel. It's near Baarn—we might dance as well as dine there.'

Her eyes sparkled. 'It sounds fun. Are they very smart places?'

He took his cup from her. 'Yes, I suppose so. Why not go out after your session with Juffrouw de Waal and buy a couple of pretty dresses? I like you in pink.' He picked up the first of his letters. 'You looked pretty in that cream silk dress, too.'

She said thank you in a contained little voice; a triumph, albeit a small one—he had noticed what she was wearing and liked it. 'I'll go along to the Leidsestraat, there's a boutique—oh, and Kraus en Vogelzang in Kalverstraat…' She saw that he wasn't listening any more, but frowning over a sheaf of typewritten pages. Someone had placed a *Daily Telegraph* by her place. She poured herself some fresh coffee and began on its headlines.

Juffrouw de Waal received her sternly, only relaxing sufficiently to congratulate her on her marriage, observe that the professor was a fine man and deserved a good wife, and point out that now Lavinia was that wife, it behoved her to learn Dutch in the quickest possible time.

'And not only conversation, Mevrouw ter Bavinck,' she pointed out soberly. 'It is necessary that you read, and understand what you read, so that you may take part in talk of a serious nature—politics, for instance, as well as the day-to-day events in our country—the world too. You must also learn about our prices and the keeping of accounts as well as how to order household requirements. I suggest that you read a small portion of a daily newspaper to me, which you will translate and discuss in Dutch, and I hope that you will use every opportunity to speak our language.'

Thus admonished, Lavinia applied herself to her lesson with more enthusiasm than ever before; how pleased Radmer would be when she could discuss the meals with Mevrouw Pette without the aid of dictionary or sign language; lift the receiver off the hook and order the groceries in Dutch; ask him—in his own language, how his day had gone… Fired with this praiseworthy desire, she accepted a great deal of homework from her teacher, promised that she would see her in two days' time, and made her way to the Leidsestraat.

It was exciting to examine the elegant clothes in the shop windows and know that she could buy any of them if she wished. Finally, she found just what she was looking for in a boutique; a pink organza dress with a brief tucked bodice, a deep square neckline, and elbow sleeves, very full and caught into satin bands which matched the narrow band below the bodice. The skirt was wide, the darker pink roses of the pattern rambling over it. It was a beautiful dress and very expensive, but she bought it; she bought a peach-coloured chiffon which caught her eyes, too—after all, Radmer had told her to get two dresses and she couldn't wear the same dress twice running. She shopped for matching slippers and a white velvet shoulder wrap which would go nicely with both dresses, and then, very happy with her purchases, went back to the house in the square.

She had her lunch, held a long telephone conversation with Peta and Sibby, took the dogs for a walk and then settled down to wait for Radmer. It had gone four o'clock when he telephoned; he would be late—something had turned up, but would she go ahead and dress? He would be home as soon after six o'clock as he could.

But it was almost two hours until then; she took the delighted dogs for another walk, made herself work at her Dutch lesson, and then at last permitted herself to go to her room and dress. She took a long time about it, trying not to look at the little gilt clock ticking away the minutes so slowly, until finally, complete to the last dab of powder on her ordinary little nose, she went downstairs.

She was half-way down the staircase when Radmer came in, flung his case into the nearest chair and paused to look at her. 'Oh, very nice,' he said, 'very nice indeed. I can see that coming home is going to be a real pleasure now that I have a wife. I like the dress.' He was crossing the hall to meet her as he spoke and took her hands and held her arms wide while he studied her person. She stood quietly, her heart capering around beneath her ribs, making it difficult for her to breathe calmly; all the same she managed a very creditable, 'I'm glad you like it,' and then lost her breath altogether when he suddenly pulled her close and kissed her; not a gentle kiss at all, but fierce and hard.

'I like you too,' he told her, and then: 'I'll be fifteen minutes—pour me a drink while I'm changing, will you? Whisky.'

Lavinia waited for him in the sitting-room, the whisky ready, and with nothing better to do but wonder why he had kissed her in that fashion, it augured well for their evening—it might even augur well for their future. The memory of the look on his face when he had come home stirred her pulse, and the tiny flame of hope which flickered so faintly, and which she had promised herself she would keep alive at all costs, glowed more strongly, so that when she heard his step in the hall, she turned a smiling face to the door.

He had changed into a dinner jacket and he looked good in it—she saw that with her first glance. The second showed her that whatever feeling had prompted him to kiss her in that fashion had been cast off with his other clothes, without him uttering a word she could see that. So she said hullo with a lightness she didn't feel and added: 'I've poured your drink—it's over there, on the drum table,' and as he went to fetch it: 'Have you had a busy day?'

He went and sat down. 'Yes, there was a heavy list in both theatres—and Mevrouw van Vliet—you remember her?' He began to tell her about the case. 'We did another frozen section, you know—I'm afraid there's nothing much to be done. We had several positives today, too.'

'I'm sorry,' said Lavinia, and meant it. 'It clouds the day, doesn't it?'

He gave her an appreciative glance. 'Yes—but I shouldn't bring my work home with me, I'm afraid it's rather a temptation to talk about it with you—you see I never could…and with Sibby, it's been out of the question, of course.' He smiled a little. 'What have you been doing with yourself? And did the girls telephone?'

She related the peaceful happenings of her own day and passed on the messages Sibby and Peta had sent him, adding: 'They're having a lovely time. Peta says she's never been so happy before in her life, and that's true, you know—when she was a little girl, there was never much money and besides that, Mother wasn't very strong…!'

'And you, Lavinia—were you happy?'

She considered his question. 'For most of the time, I think; at least until Father died.' She got up and straightened a few cushions, wishful to change the conversation. 'I went to the kitchen today,' she told him, 'and Mevrouw Pette and I had a long talk—I had my dictionary, and we got on quite well.'

She succeeded in making him laugh. 'I should have enjoyed the conversation. How is the Dutch coming along?'

'I know a great many words,' she told him hopefully, 'and a few sentences.'

He put down his glass. 'When you know a few more, we will give a dinner party.' He grinned at her look of horror. 'Don't worry, we'll invite only those who speak English—all the same, you must try and speak Dutch as often as possible.'

She promised him that she would as they walked to the door together and she had the satisfaction of seeing that he was not on his guard with her. The kiss had been a reaction after a bad day, she decided, and he had been afraid that she would take advantage of it, despite what she had told him. She got into the car beside him, determined to be a pleasant, undemanding companion for the rest of the evening.

It was perfect weather and warm. They had a table in the window, where they could watch the barges chugging steadily up and down the canal, and they talked of a great many things while they ate. Radmer, once more his usual friendly, faintly impersonal self, took pains to please her. She had looked at the vast menu in some perplexity until he had suggested that she might like him to choose for her: hors d'oeuvres, Poulet Poule mon Coeur and syllabub, and when he asked her what she would like to drink, she left that to him too and drank the chilled Amontillado and then the white Burgundy with enjoyment, pronouncing the latter to be very pleasant, an innocent remark which caused her husband's mobile mouth to twitch very slightly; the bottle of Corton Charlemagne which he had ordered had been treated with due reverence by the wine waiter, being a wine to be taken seriously, but he only agreed with her and refilled her glass, remarking at the same time that wine was an interesting subject for anyone who cared to learn about it.

Lavinia took a sip and eyed him thoughtfully. 'I expect this is a very good one, isn't it? I don't know one from the other, but I'll have to learn, won't I?' She frowned. 'Would Mevrouw Pette…?'

A smile tugged at the corner of his mouth. 'Well, I daresay she's an authority on cooking sherry and so forth—I'm by no means that myself, but I daresay I could put you on the right track—remind me to do so when we have a quiet evening together.'

They sat over their meal, and as the evening darkened slowly, Lavinia, sitting in the soft glow of the pink-shaded table lamp, her ordinary face brought to life by excitement and the wine, became positively pretty.

'Do you come here often, Radmer?' she asked.

'Occasionally, with friends. I don't—didn't go out a great deal. It must be months since I was here.'

She poured their coffee. 'But the head waiter knew you.'

He chuckled. 'That's his job. Shall we bring the girls here one evening? When is Peta's birthday?'

She told him, smiling with pleasure. 'She'd love it—she hasn't had much fun…' She looked away quickly because of the expression on his face; she didn't quite know what it was, but it might have been pity—it disappeared so quickly that afterwards she told herself that she had imagined it.

They drove back in a companionable silence and when they reached the house she wished him good night at once and went upstairs to bed; probably he had had enough of her company for one evening; she would have to give him time to get used to having her around. He made no effort to detain her and when she had thanked him he had replied that he had enjoyed himself too and looked forward to the following evening.

She knew better than to be chatty at breakfast; she poured his coffee, replied quietly to his query as to whether she had slept well, and sat down to her own meal and the *Daily Telegraph*. Her good-bye was cheerful as he got up to leave her, and she added a: 'And I hope it's a better day for you all,' for good measure as he left the room. She was heartily ashamed of the forlorn tears which dripped down on to her uneaten toast. She wiped them away fiercely, telling herself that she was becoming a regular cry-baby, and then took the dogs for a walk in the park before telephoning Peta and Sibby, who were coming home again on the following day. The pair of them sounded very pleased with life, taking it in turns to talk so that there was very little need for her to say more than a word or two. She put the receiver down at length and went along to find Mevrouw Pette, who had suggested that she might like to go through the linen cupboard with her.

Radmer came home earlier than she had expected him to. She was on her knees in the middle of the sitting-room carpet, the dogs sprawled on either side of her, learning Dutch verbs, when he walked in. The dogs rushed to greet him and she would have got to her feet if he hadn't said at once: 'No, don't move—I'll join you. What on earth are you doing?'

He glanced through the dry-as-dust grammar and shut the book. 'My poor dear,' he observed. 'I had quite forgotten how difficult our language is. Is Juffrouw de Waal a tyrant?'

She giggled. 'Well, yes, a bit. She gave me quite a lecture yesterday, though it was a useful one too…she told me that it was even more necessary that I should master Dutch quickly now that I was married to you. I have to read the papers each day, and translate what I read, so that I can discuss politics with you.'

He shouted with laughter. 'My dear girl, I almost never talk politics, and I should find it boring if you did. I'd rather come home to a wife in a pink dress who listens sympathetically to my grumbles about work and makes sensible comments afterwards.'

She sat back on her heels. 'Did you have a good day?'

He had stretched out beside her, lying full length with his hands behind his head, looking up at her. 'Yes, it was a good day. Have we had tea?'

'No, not yet. I'll ask for it right away. Do you want it here or in your study?'

His eyes were closed, but he opened them to stare at her. When he spoke it was so softly that she almost didn't hear him. 'I like your company, Lavinia—it grows on me—don't ever doubt that; even when I'm irritable or tired or worried—you have the gift of serenity.' He closed his eyes again and added: 'I'm hungry; somehow or other I missed lunch.'

It would have been very satisfying to have asked him what he had meant, instead she whisked down to the kitchen, made herself understood by the co-operative Mevrouw Pette and hurried back to assure Radmer that a sustaining tea was on the way. It gave her deep satisfaction presently, to watch him make short work of the sandwiches, anchovy toast and wholesome homemade cake Bep brought in a few minutes later, and when he had finished and closed his eyes in a nap, she sat, as still as a mouse, until he opened them again, wide awake at once, to look at the clock and suggest that they should change. 'I've booked a table for half past seven,' he told her, 'it's only half an hour's drive, but I thought it would be nice to sit over our drinks.'

The peach chiffon looked stunning; she did her face

with care, brushed her hair until it shone and went downstairs to find him already waiting and any last lingering qualms she might have entertained about the extravagance of purchasing two dresses and expensive ones at that, at the same time, were successfully extinguished by his surprised admiration. 'Very nice,' he commented. 'I liked the pink, but this one is charming.'

'Well, it is a kind of pink,' she told him seriously. 'I didn't really need it, but it looked so pretty and fitted so well…'

He studied her carefully. 'Very well.' He took the wrap from her and put it round her shoulders. 'Remind me to buy you a fur wrap.'

She turned round slowly to face him. 'I wouldn't dream of doing that,' she assured him earnestly. 'Wives don't remind their husbands to buy them things like furs,' and then she giggled when he took his handkerchief out of his pocket to tie a knot in a corner of it. 'Don't be absurd!'

'Ah, but you don't understand, Lavinia. I'm a little out of touch when it comes to remembering what husbands do and don't do—it's been a long time.'

And what, in heaven's name, was a second wife's answer to a remark like that? She decided to ignore it and said instead: 'Shall we go? I'm looking forward to seeing this hotel. I told Sibby that we were going there and she said it was super.'

Sibby had been right; it was a splendid place, a castle once, but now a famous hotel standing in its own grounds, and as the evening was, for once, windless and warm still, they strolled about the terraces and then sat down by one of the fountains for their drinks, and presently, seated at a table by the window so that they had a splendid view of that same fountain, they dined off kipper paté, entrecote sauté Cussy, and crêpes soufflés aux pêches, and as the steak had been cooked with port wine, and the soufflé was flavoured with kirsch and they, in their turn, had been washed down with the excellent claret Radmer had chosen, Lavinia began to enjoy herself, and when he suggested that they might dance, she got up with all the will in the world, determined not to miss anything of her treat. She danced delightfully, and Radmer, after the first few seconds, realized it. He was a good dancer himself—they went on and on, not talking much, sitting down for a drink from time to time and then, by common consent, taking to the floor again. She had been surprised to find that he was as good at the modern dances as the more conservative waltz and foxtrot, and at the end of one particularly energetic session he had said almost apologetically: 'Sibby taught me; I find them rather peculiar, but they're fun sometimes—you're very good yourself.'

'But I prefer waltzing,' said Lavinia, as indeed she did; she could have danced all night and the evening was going so fast—probably once the girls were back home, he wouldn't ask her out again; not just the two of them. Their outings would more than likely be family ones from now on.

They danced a last, dreamy waltz and she went to fetch her wrap. As they got into the car she said: 'That was wonderful, Radmer, thank you for a lovely evening.'

'We'll do it again,' he promised her as he manoeuvred the car on to the road, and Lavinia stifled disappointment because he hadn't said that he had enjoyed it too. She smoothed the soft stuff of her gown, and sat quietly, thinking about the evening, until he broke into her reverie. 'It's a splendid night,' he observed casually. 'We'll go back down the country roads, shall we? There'll be no traffic—we can miss Hilversum completely and work our way round the Loosdrechtsche Plassen, go through Loenen and back on to the motorway below Amstelveen—almost as quick, and far nicer.'

She agreed happily. She wasn't in the least tired, on the contrary, the dancing had left her glowing and wide awake. They talked with idle contentment about nothing in particular as Radmer drove across the golf course, under the motorway and on to the narrow roads which bordered the lakes. They were already two-thirds of the way to Loenen; indeed, Lavinia could make out a few lights, still well ahead of them across the water when, looking idly around her at the quiet, moonlit countryside, she exclaimed suddenly: 'Radmer—that light, over there, on the right…'

'I've seen it, dear girl—a fire, unless I'm mistaken. There's a lane somewhere—here it is.' He swept the big car into a rough, unmade road, a mere cart track. 'This will take us somewhere close, I fancy.'

The fire could be seen more plainly now; a dull glow brightening and fading, almost dimmed by the brilliant moonlight. And it was further away than Lavinia had thought—it must be an isolated farmhouse set well back from the road, in the rough heath bordering the lakes. She fancied she could smell smoke now and hear the faint crackling of fire in the quiet of the night, and presently they had their first real view of the house. A farmhouse, right enough, standing amongst trees and rough grass; the lane they were driving along ended in its yard. Radmer came to a halt well away from the farm buildings, said 'Stay here,' and got out, to disappear quickly through a side door which he had had no compunction in breaking down with a great shoulder. Lavinia could hear him calling and someone answering faintly. She heard other sounds too, now—horses, snorting in fright, and cows bellowing; they would be in the great barn at the back of the house. The fire wasn't visible from where she sat, only a faint flickering at the windows; it might not be too bad at the moment, but by the time Radmer had roused the family, it might be too late to save the animals. She got out of the car and looked about her; she could see no one. She put her handbag and wrap carefully on the car seat, shut the door, and ran towards the barn.

CHAPTER SEVEN

IT WAS EASY enough to find the door in its vast side; the moonlight showed Lavinia that—it crept in after her, too, showing her the enormous lofty place, with cow stalls down each side of a wide cobbled path, two horses, giants to her shrinking eyes, stamping and snorting in the partitioned-off stables at the further end. There were a medley of farm carts in another corner, and bales of hay… She wasted no more time in looking, but shaking with fright, went to unbar the great doors opening on to the yard and the fields beyond, and then, uttering loud, encouraging cries, more for her own benefit than those of the beasts, went to untie the horses, relieved to find that despite their fear, they had no intention of kicking her to pieces, merely snorting violently as they backed out of their stable and trotted ponderously out into the yard. She wasn't too keen on cows, either, but she went from one spotless stall to the next, taking down the bars and trusting to their readiness to respond to her pleas that they should bestir themselves. And they did, to her great relief; they hurried, as well as cows will hurry, jostling each other in their common wish to get away from the smell of smoke.

She saw them on their way and then made a cautious round of the vast place to make sure that there was nothing left alive in it. A bull, she thought despairingly—if there's a bull I'll not dare go near it, but there was no bull, only a cow dog, growling at her from his fenced-off pen in a dark corner. Lavinia remembered now that she had heard him barking when she had been seeing to the horses. She went to him at once and started to untie the rope attached to his collar, talking hearteningly the while, so anxious to set him free that she hardly noticed his curled lip. 'Good dog,' she encouraged him as she let him go, still happily unaware of his fierceness, 'run along and look after those cows.' And he rolled a yellow eye at her and went.

The smell of smoke was strong now and wisps of it were oozing through the end wall of the barn. When Lavinia found another small door, obviously leading to the house, and went through it, she was instantly enveloped in a thick smoke which set her coughing and made her eyes smart and water, but there was no going back; she wasn't sure where she was, but Radmer must be somewhere close by and he might be needing help. The thought sent her blundering ahead, out of the worst of the smoke into a comparatively clear space which she took to be a lobby between the kitchen and the front of the house. She could see the fire now and hear it as well; and although the stairs were still intact she saw flames licking the stair head above. There seemed to be no one downstairs. Lavinia started to climb, just as Radmer came carefully down, a child in his arms.

'I told you to stay in the car,' he said calmly, 'but since you're here, will you take this infant? Not injured, just terrified.'

She received the small, shaking form. 'Who else is there?'

'The mother—had a baby yesterday—I'll have to carry them down. The man of the house got up to see what was the matter and was overcome by smoke. I dragged him on to the doorstep.' He grinned at her and went back upstairs.

The farmer was lying outside his front door, recovering slowly, not really aware of her, all the same she told him in a bracing tone as she stepped carefully over him, 'Don't worry, you'll be all right. I'll be back in a minute.'

Lavinia put the child in the back of the car and closed the door on its frightened bawling; she would have liked to have stayed to comfort it, but she had to go back into the house again. Radmer couldn't manage the mother and baby all at once and the fire might get fiercer.

There had been more smoke than flames, but now, looking up the narrow stairs, she could see that the landing was well alight and filled with a thick smoke. She ran through to the kitchen, snatched up a tea towel, wrung it out with furious speed under the sink tap and swathed it round her nose and mouth and then ran upstairs, where she was far more frightened by Radmer's furious look than the fire. 'Get out of here!' he told her furiously. 'You little fool, do you want to be killed?'

'No!' She had to shout because of the tea towel. 'But now I am here, I'll take the baby.'

She snatched the small scrap from the bed and raced downstairs and out to the car, saying 'Excuse me,' politely to the farmer as she stepped over him once more.

The baby was whimpering; she laid it on the car's floor, begged the toddler not to cry and went back to the man. He was feeling better, although his colour was bad. '*Mijn vrouw—die kinderen*,' he muttered urgently, and tried to get up. Lavinia didn't know the word for safe, so she smiled, nodded reassuringly and said OK, a useful phrase which she had found of the greatest help since she had arrived in Holland. But he had lapsed into semi-consciousness again and could offer no help as she began to heave him to one side—and only just in time, for a moment later Radmer came through the door with the woman in his arms. Lavinia got to the car ahead of him, flung open the door, whisked up the baby and toddler and hugged them to her while he deposited his burden on the back seat, then handed them over to be tucked in with their mother.

Radmer spoke in a reassuring voice, shut the door again and said briefly:

'See if you can get the man to come round a bit while I get the animals out of the barn.'

'I have.'

He looked at her in astonishment. 'All of them? Cows—horses?'

She nodded. 'And a dog. There's nothing left there, I looked to see.'

He said on a laugh: 'You brave girl—were you frightened?'

'Terrified. The man…?' As he turned away: 'Is there anywhere I can go for help?'

He paused. 'I imagine someone will have seen the fire by now even in this remote area; thank heaven it took its time before it got a hold. If I could get the man on his feet we might save quite a lot of furniture, but we can't put the fire out, I'm afraid.' He gave her a thoughtful look.

'Lavinia, can you drive?'

'Yes. I took lessons and passed my test—ages ago—I haven't driven more than a couple of times since.'

'Think you can handle the Bentley? I'll reverse her for you—take her back to the road and stop at the nearest house.' He saw the look on her face and went on: 'I know you're scared to do it, my dear, but the woman needs to go to hospital as soon as possible.' He smiled suddenly. 'Do you suppose you could make yourself understood?'

'I'll do my best.'

'Good girl—now let's get the car turned.' He left her for a moment and went to bend over the farmer; when he came back he said: 'I think he'll be all right—I'll get to work on him when you've gone.'

She waited while he turned the Bentley and then got into the driver's seat. He had left the engine running, she only had to drive away… She turned a white face to his as he put his head through the open window.

'Off with you,' he said cheerfully, and kissed her.

She went very slowly at first; the car seemed huge, and although she hadn't forgotten how to drive, she was decidedly slow. But there was nothing to hinder her and the moon was still bright, lighting up the countryside around her. She gained the main road, turned clumsily into it and put her foot down gingerly on the accelerator; there must be something within a mile or so, and at the worst, Loenen was only a short drive away.

The road wound along, close to the water and there were no houses at all, but presently, as she slowed down to take a bend in the road, she saw a massive pair of gates opened on to a drive. The house might be close by; it was worth trying anyway. She edged the Bentley between the posts and sent the car up the tree-shadowed drive, to slither to a halt before a sizeable house, shrouded in darkness. She got out, murmuring reassuringly to the occupants of the back seat, and then turned back to look at the clock on the dashboard. Two o'clock in the morning—whatever would the occupants say? She rang the bell, not waiting to give herself an answer.

The elderly man who came to the door after what seemed a very long time, stood and stared at her in astonishment; as well he might, she conceded. Callers in grubby evening dress didn't usually ring door bells at that hour of night. She wished him good evening, and not wanting to get involved in a conversation she surely wouldn't understand, asked urgently: 'Telephone?' She added helpfully: '*Politie*,' and waved towards the car.

The man gave her a sharp look and spoke at some length until she interrupted him with another urgent 'Telephone?' but he still hesitated, and she was marshalling her Dutch to try again when there were steps behind him and a voice demanded: '*Wat is er aan de hand*?'

'Oh, if only someone could speak English,' cried Lavinia, very much frustrated, and found herself looking over the man's shoulder at a woman's face that smiled at her and asked: 'What is it that you want? You are in trouble?'

'Yes,' said Lavinia, and drew a relieved breath before explaining briefly what had happened. 'And my husband says that the woman must be got to hospital as soon as possible,' she finished. 'Could an ambulance be called?'

The woman smiled again. 'Of course, but first we bring the mother and children in here. Does your husband know where you are?'

Lavinia shook her head. 'No, he told me to go to the first house I saw.'

Her questioner turned to the elderly man and spoke quietly and he went away; Lavinia could hear his voice somewhere inside, presumably telephoning. 'And now the children…' The lady held out a hand, obviously meaning it to be shaken. 'Mevrouw van der Platte.'

It seemed funny to stop for introductions at such a time, but Lavinia shook the hand and murmured: 'Mevrouw ter Bavinck.'

Her hostess's smile broadened. 'The wife of Radmer? We know him slightly.' She nodded her head in a satisfied fashion, pulled her dressing gown more closely round herself and followed Lavinia to the car, and in a moment the elderly man joined them.

Between them they bore the woman and children indoors, into a large hall, comfortably furnished, where the three unfortunates were made comfortable on a large sofa and the elderly man was dispatched to warm some milk.

'My husband is away from home,' explained Mevrouw van der Platte. 'Henk is our houseman, he lives here with his wife, who is the cook, but I think there is no reason to call her. Can I do anything to help you, Mevrouw ter Bavinck?'

Lavinia was bending over her patient, who looked ill and very pale. The toddler was asleep now, and the baby tucked up with his mother.

'I don't think so, thank you. I don't think they have burns, but the smoke was very bad. Will the ambulance and fire engine take long?'

As if in answer to her question she heard the sing-song wail coming towards them along the road, followed by a second. 'Fire engine, police,' said Mevrouw van de Platte unnecessarily, and handed her a glass of warm milk. 'You will want this for your patient. When you have done, there is coffee for you.'

She watched while Lavinia gave the woman the milk. 'Tell me, you saw the fire?'

'We were coming home from Baarn—Radmer thought it would be pleasant to drive through the country roads.'

'And he is there now? At the fire?'

'Yes. If he could get the farmer on to his feet, he thought they might be able to save some of the furniture.'

'The animals?'

'I let them out of the barn—I do hope they won't stray. The dog was with them.'

The companion eyed her with respect. 'You are a sensible girl—your husband must be proud of you.'

Lavinia wiped her patient's mouth and said nothing to that, only: 'I hope he knows where to find me.'

'He will. Henk told the police where you were and they will tell your husband. The ambulance should be here very soon now.'

Radmer got there first, though. Lavinia heard his voice when Mevrouw van der Platte went to answer the door bell. He came in quickly and went at once to her and took her hands. 'You're all right?' he wanted to know, wasting no time in greeting her.

Her heart had given a joyful skip at the sight of him although she answered him calmly enough. 'Yes, thanks—I'm fine, but will you take a look at Mum? I've given her some milk, but she doesn't look too good.'

They were bending over the woman when their hostess came back with a tray of coffee. Radmer straightened himself as she set the tray down. 'She needs treatment—there's an ambulance on the way?'

'Yes—are the babies to go with her?'

'Yes. The father went straight to hospital in one of the police cars—he's all right, but he'll need a check-up. They'll keep him there until they've had a look at this dear soul and the children.'

'Do you want me to go with them?' Lavinia was sipping coffee and looking quite deplorable, with her pretty dress covered in soot and bits of straw and a great tear in its skirt. Her hair had tumbled down too, giving her the look of a lost waif.

Radmer shook his head. 'There'll be a nurse with the ambulance, once we've seen them safely on their way, I'll take you home.'

She smoothed back a wisp of hair in an absent-minded fashion. 'You're coming home too?'

'I shall go over to the hospital when I've seen you indoors.'

Lavinia put her cup down. 'I'd like to come with you—that's if you don't mind. Just to be sure she's all right—and the babies.'

He raised his eyebrows. 'My dear girl, it's getting on for three o'clock in the morning.' He smiled at her kindly. 'Besides, what could you do? And I'll probably be there some time.'

She stooped to pick up the toddler who had wakened suddenly and burst into outraged tears. 'Yes, of course,' she answered in a colourless voice, 'how silly of me not to think of that.' She began wandering about the hall, the moppet against her shoulder, murmuring to it, not looking at Radmer at all.

The ambulance came almost immediately after that and she went and stood out of the way, in a corner with Mevrouw van de Platte, watching the mother and her children being expertly removed by two ambulance men and a pretty nurse, with Radmer quietly in charge of the whole undertaking, and presently, when he had bidden their kind hostess good-bye, she added her own thanks to his, wished the older lady good-bye in her turn, and went out to the car with him.

'You must be tired,' Radmer observed as they went down the drive and into the road. 'Did you find the car difficult to handle?'

'Yes,' said Lavinia baldly, 'I did. At least, it wasn't

the car, it was me—I've only ever driven an Austin 1100, and that was years ago.'

He grunted noncommittally and didn't speak again for quite some time, and then it was to make some remark about Peta and Sibby's return; it was very obvious that he didn't want to talk about the fire; which was a pity, for she longed, like a little girl, to be praised for her help. She swallowed tears and stared resolutely out of the window at the dark streets of Amstelveen. They would soon be home.

At the house he got out with her, opened the massive front door and followed her in, and when she said in a surprised voice: 'Oh, I thought you were going to the hospital,' he said with the faintest hint of impatience: 'I can hardly go like this—I'll change.'

Lavinia looked him over carefully. His clothes, at first glance, appeared to be ruined; filthy with stains of heaven knew what and grimy with soot and smoke, and there was a jagged tear in one trouser leg. She asked suddenly: 'You're not hurt?'

'Not in the least. We look a pretty pair, don't we?' He smiled briefly. 'Go to bed, Lavinia.'

She went towards the staircase, her bedraggled wrap trailing from one arm. At their foot she turned to encounter his hard stare. 'Good night, my dear, you were splendid.'

She didn't answer; she wanted to be hugged and fussed over and told she was the most wonderful and bravest girl in the world. She summoned up a smile and went slowly up the stairs, dragging her feet, sliding her hand along the polished balustrade. She was almost at the top when he spoke again, so quietly that she almost didn't hear him. His voice sounded as though the words had been dragged out of him. 'These last few hours have been the worst I have ever known—and I've only just realized it.'

She supposed him to be talking about the fire and the efforts he had made to rescue the farmer and his family; he must be tired… She said in a motherly little voice, meant to soothe: 'Yes—I was scared too, and I wasn't even in danger…'

Radmer had started towards the staircase, now he stopped to laugh so that Lavinia looked at him in bewilderment. She was on the point of asking him what was so funny when Mevrouw Pette, swathed in a dressing-gown and with her hair severely plaited, appeared on the landing above and leaned over the head of the stairs to stare down at them both, burst into speech and bear down upon Lavinia, whom she swept under a motherly wing and led towards her room, exchanging a rapid fire of question and answer with the professor as she did so.

Lavinia was tired and dispirited; it was pleasant to be fussed over, to have a bath run for her, to have her ruined gown removed with sympathetic tuts, and after a quick bath, to be tucked up in her vast bed like a small child. She drank the hot milk Mevrouw Pette insisted upon and went to sleep at once despite the kaleidoscope of events, nicely muddled with her tiredness, going on inside her head.

She woke to find Bep standing by her bed with a tray in her hands, and when she looked at the little bedside clock she saw to her astonishment that it was almost ten o'clock. She sat up, struggling to assemble her Dutch, and came out with: 'Late—I must get up.'

Bep smiled and shook her head, put the tray on Lavinia's lap and indicated the folded note propped against the coffee pot. It was a scrawl from Radmer, telling her simply that he would go straight from the hospital after he had finished his work there, to fetch Sibby and Peta; she could expect them all home for dinner, he hoped she would enjoy a quiet day, he was hers, R.

Lavinia had been looking forward to the drive to Noordwijk, for she had quickly gathered that Radmer had no intention of allowing her to infringe upon his work, and somehow he seemed to have very little leisure. It was obvious to her now that their two evenings out together had been in the nature of a sop to her acceptance without fuss of his plans for their wedding, and yet she had thought on the previous evening, while they had been dancing, that he was enjoying her company.

Wishful thinking, she told herself, drank the rest of her coffee, fed the toast to the birds on the balcony so that Mevrouw Pette would think that she had made a good breakfast, and got up. She would have to do something to take her mind off her problems, just for a little while. She didn't know how to handle the situation and panicking about it wouldn't help. One thing was certain; the quicker she got herself used to the manner of living Radmer expected of her, the better; she would have to learn to fill her days for herself and never take the sharing of his leisure for granted. She had the two girls, of course, and naturally there would be evenings out with his friends and family and some entertaining at home as well, when they would be together, but any vague hope which she had cherished that they might sometimes slip off together just for the sheer pleasure of each other's company could be scotched.

She dressed rapidly, snatched up her handbag and her lesson books, and after a short conversation with Mevrouw Pette, left the house. Her Dutch lesson would take care of the next hour and after that, she told herself, with a touch of defiance, she would go shopping.

Juffrouw de Waal was sharp with her; not only did she not know her lessons, she was decidedly distraite. She was sent on her way at the end of the hour, with a stern recommendation to apply herself to her Dutch verbs, and by way of penance, write a short essay on any subject she wished—in Dutch, of course. She agreed meekly to her teacher's views on her shortcomings, rather to that lady's surprise, and went out into the sunny streets. Five minutes' walk brought her to the shops and here she slowed her pace until her eye was caught by the sight of an extremely exclusive hair dressing salon. She went inside on an impulse and luckily for her the exquisite damsel at the reception desk felt sure that someone could be found to attend to her immediately and when she was asked to give her name, the damsel murmured: 'Oh, Mevrouw ter Bavinck,' rather as though she had introduced herself as the Queen of the Netherlands, and before she knew where she was, she had been whisked away to be attended by the proprietor himself, Monsieur Henri, who talked a great deal about the ter Bavinck family in a tone of reverence which greatly astonished her.

She emerged an hour later, considerably poorer, with her hair transformed from its usual simple style to an artless coiffure which looked simple but wasn't. Such a transformation deserved a new outfit; she spent a delightful half hour in La Bonneterie, emerging presently with a splendid collection of boxes and parcels, so that she was forced to get a taxi back to the house. Besides, she was very late for lunch, for it was long past one o'clock and she had told Mevrouw Pette that she would be back well before half past twelve.

The taxi driver was so kind as to carry her packages up to the door; Lavinia gathered them up in both arms, opened it with some difficulty and went inside.

Radmer was standing at his open study door, and at the expression on his face she faltered a little on her way across the hall. He looked tired; he looked furiously angry as well. She made for one of the marble-topped console tables in order to shed her purchases and he came to meet her, taking them from her and laying them down carefully, and when she stole another look at him, he didn't look angry at all, only tired.

He said blandly: 'I had expected you to be still in bed, sleeping off last night's exertions.' He smiled faintly. 'Have you had lunch?'

She flushed. 'No. I—I was shopping and I didn't notice the time.' They entered the dining-room together and Bep, by some well-managed miracle, was already there, waiting to serve the soup. 'I didn't expect you to come home,' she went on coldly. 'From your note…'

He stared at her across the table. After a pause he

said merely: 'I hope you had a good morning's shopping?'

She took a good drink of wine and felt it warm her cold inside. 'Yes, thank you. I spent a great deal of money.'

He was still staring at her and there was a gleam of amusement in his eyes now, although she didn't see it. Surely he would say something about her hair? It had looked quite different at the hairdressers, but all he said was: 'I'm sure you will have spent it to advantage. I'm sorry that pretty dress was ruined.'

'Oh, it's not ruined,' she told him earnestly. 'I'll have it cleaned and I can mend the tear quite easily. I'll send your dinner jacket to the cleaners too and see if they'll repair that tear in the leg...'

He answered her seriously although the gleam was decidedly more pronounced. 'Oh, I don't think I should bother about that—I've more than one suit, I believe, and why not buy another dress instead of—er—patching up the torn one?' He leaned over to re-fill her glass. 'If you need any more money, just say so.'

Was he annoyed because she had spent so much that morning? She went rather pink and said gruffly: 'I've a great deal of money left, thank you.'

He nodded rather vaguely and she asked him how the farmer and his wife were, and then, desperate for a nice neutral subject, enlarged on the weather. It was almost a relief when he said that he would have to be getting back to the hospital.

'I'll bring the girls back in good time,' he told her, and was gone before she had time to frame a careful request to go with him. Left alone, she reflected that perhaps it was a good thing that she had had no chance to say anything, for if he had wanted her to go with him, surely he would have said so. She wandered out of the dining-room and upstairs to her room, where her shopping had been laid out for her. It should have been great fun trying on the pretty things she had bought, but it wasn't; if Radmer was indifferent enough not to notice that her waist-length hair, instead of being pinned in a neat topknot, had been swathed round her head and the strands twisted and crossed high in front and pinned by a handsome tortoiseshell comb, he certainly wouldn't notice what clothes she wore. She took a close look at her reflection now and wondered if she would ever be able to dress her hair herself—probably not, but at least she would leave it as it was until Sibendina and Peta came home to admire it; she would wear one of her new dresses too. She decided on a silver grey silk jersey smock with an important colour and very full sleeves caught into deep cuffs. It was floor-length and she considered that it was exactly the sort of garment a stepmother might be expected to wear. Studying it in the mirror, she came to the erroneous conclusion that it added dignity to her appearance and made her look much older. In fact, it did nothing of the sort—indeed, she looked younger if anything, and positively pretty.

She got back into a cotton dress finally and took the dogs out into the park. The lovely summer day had become a little overcast and as she turned for home with Dong and Pobble at her heels, she could see black clouds massing over the rooftops. There was going to be a storm, and she hated them; it wouldn't be quite so bad if she were back home with Mevrouw Pette and Bep in the kitchen. She put the dogs on their leads and hurried. They gained the porch, very out of breath as the first slow drops of rain fell.

Lavinia had her solitary tea sitting with her back to the enormous windows, and tried not to flinch at each flash of lightning, and the dogs, quite as cowardly as she, pressed themselves close to her. But presently the storm blew over, leaving a downpour of rain, and she got out her lesson books and applied herself to her homework until it was time to go and change her dress. She took a long time over this; even so, there was still plenty of time before Radmer and the girls would arrive. She filled it in by inspecting the table in the dining-room. While she was there Mevrouw Pette came in, and together they admired the stiffly starched linen, the polished silver and sparkling glass. Between them they had concocted a festive menu too, and Lavinia, glad to have something to do, accompanied the housekeeper back to the kitchen to sample the delicacies prepared in honour of the girls' homecoming.

It was pleasant in the kitchen, warm and fragrant with the smell of cooking, and the copper pans on the wall glowed cosily and it was nice when its occupants complimented her upon her appearance, even Ton, who came in each day to help, a good hard-working girl but hardly talkative, managed to tell her that she looked pretty. Lavinia went back upstairs sparkling with their praise, and the sparkle was still there a few minutes later when the front door was flung open and hurrying feet across the hall heralded the family's return. The girls came in together, calling 'Lavinia!' at the tops of their voices, to stop and stare at her waiting for them in the centre of the drawing-room. 'Gosh, you look absolutely gorgeous!' cried Peta. 'You've done something to your hair, and look at that wizard dress…'

'Why, you're pretty,' declared Sibby with the candour of youth. 'You always are,' she added hastily, 'but you know what I mean.'

The pair of them fell upon her, hugging and kissing her in a fashion to warm her heart although she cried laughingly: 'Oh, darlings, do take care of my hair!'

They let her go then, still holding her hands, turning and twisting her from side to side, admiring every aspect of her person, talking and giggling until Sibby cried: 'Papa, doesn't Lavinia look absolutely super? No wonder you wanted to marry her—and don't you just love the way her hair is done?'

Lavinia hadn't known that he was in the room. She said too quickly: 'Dinner's all ready—hadn't you two better go upstairs and wash your hands?' She smiled rather blindly at them and then turned round to face him. 'I do hope you had a pleasant drive and that your parents are well,' she observed cheerfully; she sounded like a hostess, anxious to please, and the two girls exchanged puzzled glances as they went from the room.

He poured their drinks with a brief: 'Yes, thanks,' but when he brought her glass over, he remarked ruefully: 'I should have said something about the hair, shouldn't I? I'm sorry, I did notice it, you know. I told you that I had become clumsy with women, didn't I? Please forgive me. And your dress is very pretty.'

Lavinia thanked him quietly and took a heartening sip of her sherry; she felt that she needed it. Perhaps when the girls had gone to bed, she should have a talk with him; try and get back on to the old friendly footing which somehow they had lost. On the other hand, he was probably tired and the awkwardness she felt between them was due to that. She finished her sherry and asked for another, and when he handed it to her he said with a twinkle: 'Dutchman's courage, Lavinia?'

Of course he thought that she was nervous because the girls had come back; quite likely he imagined that she had dressed up and had her hair done with the same reason in mind. She smiled at him and lied cheerfully: 'Yes, I think I need it—I'm nervous, isn't it silly? though I'll get over it. It's lovely to have them here, isn't it?'

Radmer's voice was bland. 'Delightful,' he agreed, and added lightly: 'And such a weight off my shoulders, I shall be able to catch up on my reading without feeling guilty of leaving Sibendina alone.' He put down his glass. 'How do you like the idea of Peta having Dutch lessons with Juffrouw de Waal? Not with you, of course, and I thought it might be a good idea if she had lessons in Dutch history and geography, and as soon as she has a smattering of Dutch, she could go to Sibby's school—I'm sure they will take her. Do you suppose she would like that?'

Lavinia lifted a grateful face to him. 'Oh, Radmer, how kind you are—I'm sure she'll love it. Have you asked her?'

He looked surprised. 'Well, no—I hadn't spoken to you about it, my dear.'

She wished most fervently that she was his dear. 'Is there anything I can do to save your time?' she asked, and when he shook his head, she repeated: 'You've been more than kind,' and then before she could stop herself because the sherry was doing its work: 'Why didn't you want me to go with you to Noordwijk?'

He was standing close to her, watching her. Now he frowned. 'I'm not sure,' he told her. 'I...' Whatever he had been about to say was cut short by the entry of the two girls and they all went in to dinner.

The meal was a gay one, with a great deal of laughing and talking, and if Lavinia was a little quieter than the others, no one seemed to notice. They made plans later, sitting in the drawing-room while Lavinia poured the coffee, and Peta immediately professed the greatest satisfaction with the plan for her to have lessons with Juffrouw de Waal; she was to join Sibby's tennis club too, and go swimming whenever she wished, and when Radmer disclosed his plans for sending her to Sibby's school just as soon as she had mastered a little Dutch, she was in transports of delight.

'And now what about going to bed?' he wanted to know, cutting her thanks short. 'Sibby has to go to school in the morning and I suggest that you go with Lavinia, Peta, and meet Juffrouw de Waal.'

They said good night, embracing Lavinia first and then going to kiss Radmer. It was Peta who observed bracingly: 'You mustn't be shy about kissing Lavinia, you know, while we're here—we shan't mind at all.'

She continued reflectively: 'You didn't when we came home this evening.'

It was Sibendina who unconsciously saved the situation by remarking: 'Well, they're only just married, you know, I expect they like to be alone. Don't you, Papa?'

'Oh, decidedly,' agreed the professor mildly. 'And now bed, my dears.'

They went, giggling and talking still, up the stairs, and when their voices could no longer be heard, Lavinia got up too. 'Well, I think I'll go to bed as well,' she told him. 'I daresay you want the house quiet so that you can read in peace.'

'Good lord, did I say that?' he asked her, and when she laughed, 'You're a very nice girl, Lavinia.' He walked to the door with her and opened it, but when she made to pass him, he put out a sudden hand and caught her by the shoulder.

'We're quite alone,' he said lightly. 'We'd better do as Sibby suggested.'

He bent to kiss her, a brief salute on one cheek, and then to her utter surprise, a quite rough kiss on her mouth. He let her go at once and she flew away, up the staircase and into her room before she really knew what she was doing. Undressing, she told herself that she had behaved in the stupidest fashion; like a silly schoolgirl. She should have made a graceful little joke about it, instead of tearing off in that way. He must think her a complete fool. She got into bed, determined that it wouldn't happen again; she would be careful to keep such incidents as lighthearted as possible, if ever they should occur again. She closed her eyes resolutely upon this resolve, although her last thought before she slept was that being kissed in that fashion was decidedly interesting, even if he had intended it as a joke.

CHAPTER EIGHT

IT WAS A simple matter to slip into the well-ordered way of living which Radmer's household enjoyed. Lavinia, aided by the kindly Mevrouw Pette, took upon herself those household tasks which the housekeeper considered were suitable for the lady of the house, although in actual fact they took up very little of her time, but she worked for hours over her Dutch lessons and she was always home when the girls got back at lunchtime, and never failed to be sitting by the tea tray when they came home in the afternoon. Of Radmer she saw very little. True, they breakfasted together, but then so did the girls, and conversation, such as it was, was general. He was always the first to leave the table, and perhaps because of what Peta had said, he never neglected to come round the table and bend to kiss her cheek, and if Sibby and Peta were with her when he got back in the evenings, he repeated this, while she, for her part, greeted him with a welcoming smile and a few wifely inquiries as to how his day had gone. Very rarely he came home for lunch, although he never went out in the evenings, retiring after a decent interval to his study, so that before very long Lavinia was forced to the conclusion that he was avoiding her as often as he could.

On one or two occasions they had dined out with

friends and they all paid regular visits to Noordwijk, but the opportunity to talk to him, even get to know him better, was non-existent. And yet, on the rare occasions when they were together, he appeared to take pleasure in her being with him, and from every other aspect she supposed that their marriage was a success, for Sibby was deeply fond of her already and even though she regarded her more as an elder sister than a stepmother, she confided in her to an extent which proved how much in need she had been for an older and wiser head with which to share her youthful problems.

Peta was happy too. Lavinia had never seen her so carefree and content, treating Radmer like a big brother and yet quite obviously regarding him as the head of the household to be obeyed, as well as the one to go to when in trouble.

The house had taken on a new air, too. It had always been beautifully managed by Mevrouw Pette, but now Lavinia was slowly setting her own mark upon it; arranging great bowls of flowers in every room, bearing home baskets of plants from the flower market and bedding them in great masses of colour in the small garden. She had taken over the conservatory too, buying new lounge chairs and a hammock seat which was the delight of the girls, and attending with loving care to a vine she had planted there. She did these things gradually and by the end of a month she had made a niche for herself, so that, while not absolutely essential to the life of the house, she certainly contributed to its well-being. Her Dutch was making strides too, and now that Peta was having many more lessons than she herself was, it was an incentive to work even harder at her books. And as for Radmer, he seemed content enough and at weekends at least, quite prepared to take them out and about, but there had been no more tête-à-tête dinners, and as the days slipped by, Lavinia resigned herself to the fact that there probably never would be again.

They were to go to Friesland for a short holiday in August; the professor had a yacht which he kept at Sneek and they would go sailing for a good deal of the time, as well as touring Friesland. Lavinia, collecting a suitable wardrobe with the help of Sibby, who knew all about life on board a boat, hoped that she would quickly pick up all the salient points about sailing. She had mentioned, rather diffidently, that she didn't know one end of a boat from the other, but Radmer had only laughed and told her that she would soon learn.

They set off one Saturday, in a brilliant morning which promised to become hot later in the day, and drove straight to the ter Bavinck estate, where Juffrouw Hengsma was waiting for them, and this time Lavinia was able to address her in Dutch, which pleased her mightily and made Radmer laugh.

'You are making progress, Lavinia,' he observed. 'Now you must learn the Friesian language, because Juffrouw Hengsma prefers to speak that.' He had spoken to her in Dutch too, to her secret delight, and she answered him haltingly in that tongue, feeling that sharing his language was a small link between them.

They had coffee together before they went to their rooms to unpack and then meet again to wander round the house and grounds. Radmer ran a small stable and naturally enough they spent a good deal of time there, and when he offered to teach Peta to ride, she flung her arms round his neck. 'You really are a darling!' she declared. 'I do hope there'll be someone like you for me when I grow up.'

He laughed gently at her and tweaked her ear. 'I'll make a point of finding just the right one,' he assured her. 'Sibby has already told me whom she intends marrying, so I'll only have you to worry about.'

He flung an arm round Sibby's shoulders. 'Sibby has made a very wise choice, too,' he added, and she grinned widely.

'I don't mind Lavinia and Peta knowing,' she told him, and tucked an arm into Lavinia's. 'He's a student at St Jorus, but I've known him for years, ever since I was a baby. Peta, who do you want to marry?'

'I've just said—someone like Radmer, and we'll have dozens of babies and they'll grow up very clever and be doctors…' She looked at Lavinia. 'Are you going to have some babies, Lavinia?'

Lavinia felt her cheeks redden, although she said airily enough: 'There's certainly heaps of room for them, isn't there? And wouldn't this be a gorgeous place for their holidays? Did you like coming here when you were a little girl, Sibby?'

She only half listened to Sibby's reply. She was dreaming, just for a few delightful moments, of a carload of little boys, blue-eyed and flaxen-haired like their father, and a sprinkling of little girls, much prettier than their mother, tumbling around, laughing and shouting.

She blinked the dream away and asked Radmer when he intended to go sailing.

The marvellous weather held. They spent long, lazy days swimming in the pool in one corner of the grounds, playing tennis on the court behind the house, or just sitting and doing nothing. Lavinia felt herself unwinding slowly so that she was able to think of the future, if not through rose-coloured spectacles, at least with a degree of optimism.

'I shall get fat,' she worried out loud as they lounged on the terrace after breakfast. 'I don't do anything…'

Radmer looked up from his newspaper and allowed his gaze to sweep over her. 'Never fat—curvaceous is the word, I believe. It suits you—besides, you're hardly idle; you swim and play tennis, and now you're not frightened any more on Juno, we shall have you galloping in all directions before we go back to Amsterdam.' He stood up slowly. 'I've some telephoning to do, then we'll drive over to Sneek and take a look at the yacht.'

She watched him go, her heart in her eyes, and in turn she was watched by Peta and Sibby. When he had rounded the corner of the house Sibby spoke: 'You are happy, aren't you, Lavinia?' She sounded anxious, so that Lavinia said at once and warmly: 'Oh, my dear—yes. Why do you ask?'

It was Peta who joined in. 'We've noticed—you never kiss each other or—or hold hands, do you? Oh, I know Radmer pecks your cheek twice a day—I don't mean that—I mean…' she hesitated. 'Well, we expected you'd be… You act like good friends.'

'We are good friends, my dears,' said Lavinia

steadily. 'There are lots of ways of loving people, you know, and perhaps you forget that your papa—Radmer—is a busy man. He comes home tired. Besides, his work is more important to him than anything else.' She looked across at Sibendina and smiled. 'That doesn't mean you, Sibby.'

And because the girls looked so unhappy still, she went on gaily: 'How about getting ready?' She looked down at her nicely tanned person. 'Ought I to wear slacks?'

They decided that she should and they all went upstairs, laughing together, so that Lavinia was quite reassured that Sibby's little outburst had been quite forgotten.

She was the last down, and she hadn't known that they would all be waiting for her in the hall. She had put on the pale blue denim slacks and an Indian cotton shirt which matched them exactly, and her hair she had brushed back, plaited into a waist-long rope and tied with a blue ribbon. She looked, she had considered, exactly right for a day's sailing.

It was therefore a little disconcerting to hear Sibby's cry of: 'Oh, smashing, Lavinia, and very sexy too—isn't she, Peta?'

'Oh, rather,' echoed Peta. 'Hey, Radmer, what do you think…?'

But Lavinia interrupted her, studying herself worriedly. 'But I thought it was exactly right…'

Radmer had been bending over the straps of the picnic basket, but he had straightened up to watch Lavinia come down the stairs. His blue eyes, very bright under their heavy lids, met hers. 'It's exactly right,' he told her, and his placid voice set her doubts at rest at once, so that, quite happy again, she skipped down the last stair or two, declaring that she must just have a word with Juffrouw Hengsma before they went. She was pleased that Radmer found her appearance quite normal, although a small, sneaking wish that he could have found her sexy too persisted at the back of her mind. She dispelled it sternly; of course he wouldn't, and come to think of it, she wasn't.

She felt that she had further proof of this when they got into the car, for Radmer suggested in the nicest possible way that Sibby might like to sit in front with him, which meant that Lavinia shared the back seat with Peta and the dogs. She listened to Sibby's happy chatter, and told herself it was foolish of her to feel hurt; Sibby had as much right to sit beside Radmer as she had—besides, it had seemed to her just lately that he had become somehow remote, retreating behind a friendly front which while pleasant enough, kept her at arms' length. Was he regretting their marriage already, and if he were, what had she done or not done to make him feel that way?

She made up her mind to discover what it was. Perhaps she had been spending too much? There had been clothes, more than she needed, she thought guiltily, and although Radmer invariably complimented her when she appeared in something new, he might be annoyed at her extravagance, and then there had been clothes for the girls, the new furniture for the conservatory, the flowers she delighted in buying, her lessons, Peta's lessons… He had told her not to worry about money, but she had no idea how much of it he had. She had better ask him at the first opportunity and have a sensible talk at the same time before the constraint between them had built itself up into an insurmountable barrier.

Having come to this decision, she sensibly decided to forget about it for the time being, and applied herself to the pleasant task of answering the girls' excited babble. An opportunity would present itself sooner or later, she felt sure.

Sooner, as it turned out. They had boarded the *Mimi* at Sneek, and Lavinia had been quite overcome by the size and comfort of her. Sibby had taken her and Peta on a tour of inspection while Radmer got the yacht ready to sail, and she had admired the cabins and the galley and all the mod cons which she had never expected to find. It was all simply lovely. She went back on deck and told him so, a little breathless with the excitement of it all, that the *Mimi* was the most marvellous boat she had ever thought to see, and he had thanked her gravely. 'And later on,' he had added, 'when we've had lunch, the girls can sunbathe and I'll give you your first lesson in sailing her.'

They had set sail then, using the *Mimi*'s engine to travel down the canal which took them to Sneekemeer, and once there, they had bowled along before a stiff breeze until the girls clamoured for their lunch, when they tied up to a small, broken-down jetty on the further bank of the lake and eaten their sandwiches and fruit. The younger members of the party had packed up afterwards while Lavinia was shown how to sail the yacht out into the lake again. She managed rather well; almost stammering with pleased surprise at herself, she cried: 'I did it—isn't it a marvellous feeling? May I carry on for a while?' She looked around her; there were plenty of other boats about, but none very near. 'I shan't bump into anything, shall I?'

Radmer was lounging beside her, apparently content to let her take the yacht where she wished. 'Not at the moment. Set a course for that clump of trees at the end of the lake; there's a canal close by which leads to a charming stretch of water.'

Peta and Sibby had stretched themselves out in the bows, lying on their stomachs, half asleep. There was only the gentle splash of water around them and the faint sounds from the shore mingling in with the bird cries. Very peaceful, thought Lavinia, and closed her eyes to enjoy it all better. But only for a second; she felt Radmer's hand clamp down on hers and his voice, half laughing, said: 'Hey, you can't sail a boat with your eyes shut!' His blue eyes surveyed hers. 'Would you like to sunbathe too?'

She was very conscious of his hand, still holding hers fast. 'No—no, I'd like to talk, if you don't mind.'

He was lighting his pipe, but he paused to look at her. 'Of course we can talk, dear girl. What about?'

She met his gaze bravely. 'You and me—us. It's a little awkward and I daresay I'll get a bit muddled, only if we don't talk about it now it'll only get worse.' She paused, but he said nothing, looking at her now with the faintest of smiles. 'You see, we were friends, weren't we? I mean before we married, and afterwards too, and I thought it was going to be all right—we both knew what it was going to be like, didn't we? Only it's not turning out…I thought we were getting on rather well; I tried to keep out of your way as much as I could—I still do, for you did tell me that your work was more important to you than anything else and I—I can understand that, and I can understand you not wanting to talk about your wife—you must have loved her very much, even if…so it's natural for you to…' She came to a stop, finding it much harder to explain than she had imagined it would be. 'I told you it would be muddled,' she said crabbily.

He had taken his hand away. Now he put it back again in an absent-minded manner, but he said nothing, so that after a moment she felt forced to go on. 'I wondered if I'd been spending too much money…' and stopped at his laugh.

'Lavinia, did I not tell you not to worry about money? You could buy a dozen dresses at a time if you had a mind to do so. I think you have been very careful in your spending—and there is not the least need of that.'

She looked ahead of her. 'Are you very rich?' she asked.

'Very. You see, I have money of my own—I inherited it from my grandparents—a great deal of money, Lavinia, and besides that, I make a good living at my work.'

'Oh, well, it isn't that, is it?' She smiled at him with relief. 'That's one thing settled. So it must be your wife…'

He gave her a long searching look from under his heavy lids. 'Are you not my wife, my dear?'

She frowned at him. 'Yes, of course I am, but you know very well what I mean.' She rushed on, anxious to say what she intended as quickly as possible. 'You see, now we're married, perhaps you feel that I'm trying…that is, I do want you to understand that I'll never come between you and her.' Her voice became rather high and very earnest. 'I wouldn't want to anyway.'

'Shall we be quite blunt?' His voice was bland. 'What you are trying to say, in carefully muffled-up ladylike phrases, is that you have no wish to—er—form a deeper relationship with me and that any fears I had on that score may be safely put at rest and we can be friends again. Is that not the gist of the matter? Well, Lavinia,' he spoke with deliberation, 'let me set your mind at rest; you could never come between me and Helga.'

Lavinia heard these words with a sinking heart. She had said what she had wanted to say, true enough, but his answer, which should have satisfied her, had only served to make her wish to burst into tears. But she did know where she stood now—any faint hopes she might have been cherishing that he might fall in love with her could be killed off once and for all. She let out a long sigh, quite unconscious of doing so, and slamming a mental lid down on the conversation exclaimed: 'Oh, look, we're almost at the end of the lake. Shall I hand over to you now?'

She was looking away from him as she spoke, studying the scenery with eyes which really saw none of it, so that she failed to see the expression on her companion's face.

Peta came to take her place soon afterwards and she

went and lay down close to Sibendina, letting the sun warm her, although she felt that the coldness inside her would never go away again.

They had another few days of sailing before they returned to Amsterdam, and although Radmer treated her with an easy-going friendliness and consideration, Lavinia couldn't help but notice that he avoided being alone with her, so although she was sorry to leave the lovely old house and the simple pleasures of their holiday, she was relieved to be involved once more in the routine of their Amsterdam home. Sibendina was still on holiday, and although Peta went each day to Juffrouw de Waal, she was free for a good deal of the day. The three of them went out a good deal together, exploring the city, and in the evenings Radmer, putting aside his work for the time being, took them to the Concertgebouw, the Stadsschouwburg for the opera, and on a tour of the city's canals after dark. He was an excellent escort, she discovered, for he knew the city well and took pains to tell her as much about it as possible. They went to den Haag too, to dine out and visit the Koninklijke Schouwburg. The season was over, but although the ballet was finished, there were plays—in Dutch, which Radmer pointed out were very good for Lavinia and Peta.

They went to Delft, to watch the military tattoo. Lavinia had never been out so much in her life before, nor, for that matter, had she been able to indulge her taste in clothes to such an extent. She should have been very happy, and she tried hard to present a bright face to the world while she saw Radmer becoming increasingly remote—if only he wasn't so nice, she thought desperately, if only there was a good reason to have a quarrel—it might clear the air. But he remained kind, good-natured, and despite his preoccupation with his work, careful that she should want for nothing. All the same, they were almost never alone, and on the two occasions when the two girls had gone to bed, leaving them sitting together in the drawing-room, Radmer had excused himself within a very few minutes on the grounds of work to be done, and after that second time Lavinia had taken care to follow the girls upstairs, to sit lonely in her room with her unhappy thoughts.

It was a morning shortly after this, as she faced him across the breakfast table before the girls got down, that he said casually: 'I've ordered a Mini for you, Lavinia. I thought you might like a car of your own—you've proved yourself a good driver, so I don't need to worry on that score, but I'm afraid you will have to wait several weeks for it to be delivered.'

She had picked up the coffee pot, but now she set it down again. 'For me?' she asked. 'A car for me? How very kind of you, Radmer—thank you very much—how absolutely super! I'll have to get a licence, won't I?' She smiled with delight. 'I'll be able to visit your mother…'

He was buttering toast and didn't look at her. 'You get on well with her?'

'Oh, yes, we're already the best of friends. She calls here quite often, you know—when she comes to Amsterdam to shop. She's going to take me to Bergen-op-Zoom one day soon, to visit your sister.'

He frowned. 'Something I should have done already.'

She had picked up the coffee pot once more. 'Why should you? You're at St Jorus all day and almost every day,' she answered quietly. She smiled at him as she spoke and was astonished at the expression on his face—Rage? Exasperation? She wondered which; she had always supposed him to be an even-tempered man, but now suddenly she wasn't sure. The look had gone so quickly, though, that she was left wondering if she had imagined it, and his face was as bland as his voice. 'That is so, my dear—you don't object?'

She buttered a roll. 'You said once that I was a sensible girl and that my feet were planted firmly on the ground. They still are, Radmer.'

Their eyes met and he made an impatient gesture. 'Did I really say that?' he wanted to know, and added inexplicably: 'But in another world.'

An odd remark which she would have challenged if the girls hadn't come in at that moment.

It was Sibendina who remarked, after they had exchanged good mornings: 'You look awfully pleased with yourself, Lavinia. Has Papa given you a diamond coronet?'

'Oh, much nicer than that,' said Lavinia, stifling an ungrateful wish that his gift had indeed been some extravagant trifle to adorn her commonplace person. 'A car—a Mini.'

The two of them chorused their pleasure and Sibby wanted to know when she would have one too.

'When you're eighteen, *liefje*,' her father declared firmly. 'And Peta too, of course.'

This statement was met with cries of delight and a

sudden surging of the pair of them from their places at table, to hug him. He bore their onslaught with fortitude, looking at Lavinia over their heads with a faintly mocking smile which caused her to pinken deeply; the difference between the girls' rapturous thanks and her own staid gratitude was only too well marked. Should she have leapt to her feet and rushed round the table and hugged him too? She wondered what he would have done if she had. She busied herself with the coffee cups and didn't look at him again, not until she raised startled eyes to his, when, Peta and Sibby once more settled in their chairs, he remarked: 'I've ordered another car too, though we shall have to wait a long time for it. It's the new Rolls-Royce—the Camargue.'

The girls burst into excited chatter, but he took no notice of them, looking down the table at Lavinia, her mouth a little open with surprise. 'You'll like that, Lavinia?'

'Like it?' she managed. 'It'll be out of this world! But won't it be too big?'

'Not a bit of it—just right for holidays with the four of us—besides, I take up a lot of room. You'll look nice sitting in a Rolls, my dear.' He got up from the table. 'I shall be late home this evening; I have to go to Utrecht to give a lecture. I'll leave there about six o'clock, I expect, and get here half an hour later.' He kissed Sibby good-bye and then Peta, and last of all Lavinia, a brief peck on her cheek. 'Unless, of course,' he added smoothly, 'I meet any old friends who want me to spend the evening with them.'

'Old friends?' Sibby giggled. 'Lady friends, Papa?'

'That's telling,' he grinned at her, and a moment later the front door closed behind him.

Lavinia had a busy day before her; her usual lesson with Juffrouw de Waal, some shopping to do for Sibby, who was going back to school the next day, and some books to buy for Peta's lessons. Besides, her mother-in-law was coming to have coffee with her and in the afternoon she had promised to go to the hospital to Zuster Smid's tea party, given in honour of Neeltje's birthday. She bustled around, seeing the girls off for a walk with the dogs, arranging lunch with Mevrouw Pette and arranging the flowers she had bought from the nice old man who came past the door each week with his barrow. She was running downstairs after tidying herself at the conclusion of these housewifely exertions, when Mevrouw ter Bavinck was admitted, and the two ladies went at once to the sitting-room, gossiping happily about nothing in particular, pleased to be in each other's company.

It was after they had been seated for ten minutes or so and the first cups of coffee had been drunk that Mevrouw ter Bavinck inquired: 'Well, Lavinia, how do you like being married to Radmer?'

Lavinia cast her companion a startled glance, wondering why on earth she should ask such a question. 'Very much,' she said at length.

'And has he told you about Helga?'

'No—I don't think he intends to.'

Her companion blinked at her. 'No? And do you not wish to know?'

'Very much, but I wouldn't dream of asking him.'

The older woman put her cup and saucer down on the table beside her. 'Radmer has led a solitary life for a good many years now, and it is all a long time ago—all the same, I find it strange that he hasn't explained…'

Lavinia stirred uncomfortably. 'Perhaps he can't bear to talk about her—he must have loved her very much.' She didn't look up. 'Oh, I know—at least I heard at the hospital that she was—was rather frivolous…'

She was cut short abruptly. 'Loved her?' questioned her mother-in-law. 'My dear child, after the first few months he had no feeling for her at all. She was quite unfitted to be his—any man's wife, but because she was expecting Sibby by then, he looked after her and to the outside world at least, they were happily married. Perhaps Radmer thought that when the baby was born, they might be able to patch things up again, but it was actually worse. She had not wanted Sibby in the first place, and once she was born she was left to a nurse and Helga went back to her own way of living, and although Radmer no longer loved her, he had Sibby to consider. When Helga was killed—and I will leave him to tell you about the accident—he told me that he would never allow himself to love a woman again, and at the time he meant it. Then you came along, my dear, and everything was changed.'

She beamed at Lavinia, who smiled back with an effort. As far as she could see, nothing was changed. Radmer lived in a world of his own making, content with it, too, not needing her or her love, only a sensible young woman who would mother his daughter and order his household. She said now: 'That is very sad. What does Sibby think of it?'

'It was explained to her that her mother died in an accident when she was visiting a friend, and as she cannot remember her at all, it has never mattered to her very much. She loves her father very much, you will have seen that for yourself, and he has done his best to be father and mother to her, although I believe that you will make her an excellent mother, Lavinia—she loves you already, you know. The dear child goes back to school tomorrow, does she not?'

They talked of other things after that, and presently the elder lady went off to do her shopping and Lavinia was left to do her own small chores while she mulled over what her mother-in-law had told her. She would have to get used to the idea of Radmer not loving Helga, although that fact made it clearer than ever why he had chosen to marry herself. He must have felt quite safe in marrying her, knowing that he had not a spark of love for her. The idea of falling in love with her must have been so remote to him that it would have been laughable.

She did her shopping in a sour state of mind and for the first time found Sibby's and Peta's chatter at lunch almost more than she could bear, but they went off arm-in-arm to play tennis at last, and Lavinia was able to indulge her desire to be alone and think. It was only a pity that after a few fruitless minutes she discovered that her rather woolly thoughts were of no value to her at all, and she had no idea as to how she could charm Radmer into loving her. She gave up and took the dogs out.

Six o'clock came and went and there was no sign of Radmer, an hour later the three of them sat down to dinner, and Lavinia did her best to check the girls' uneasiness. She was uneasy herself, but perhaps not for the same reasons as they; she remembered only too clearly what he had said about spending the evening with old friends, and he hadn't really denied it when Sibby had teased him about going out with a lady friend. Perhaps he had already arranged to meet her. He talked cheerfully to her two companions while her imagination ran riot, providing her with an image of some strikingly beautiful girl, superbly dressed and loaded with charm—the type men fell for…

The evening passed emptily and at nine o'clock the girls, at her suggestion, went to bed.

'I'll stay up,' she told them bracingly. 'Probably your papa has met old friends after all, Sibby.'

'Then why didn't he telephone?' demanded his daughter.

'Oh, darling, probably there wasn't a telephone handy.' It was a silly remark; Radmer, if he had wanted to telephone, would have found the means of doing so. But it contented Sibby, who gave her an affectionate kiss and went off to bed with Peta.

The bracket clock had chimed eleven o'clock in its small silvery voice when Lavinia went down to the kitchen. Bep had already gone to bed, Mevrouw Pette was sitting at the table, knitting. He looked up as Lavinia went in and said: 'The professor is late, Mevrouw.'

Lavinia answered in her careful, slow Dutch. 'Yes, I'll stay up, Mevrouw Pette, you go to bed. Perhaps you would leave some coffee ready?' She said good night and went back upstairs into the quiet room, where she sat down on one of the enormous sofas, a dog on either side of her. The house was still now, and the square outside was silent. She sat doing nothing, not thinking, watching the hands of the clock creep round its face. It was almost two o'clock when she fell asleep, still sitting bolt upright, the dogs' heads on her lap.

She wakened from an uneasy nap to hear the gentle click of the front door lock. Radmer was home. Lavinia's eyes flew to the clock's face; its delicately wrought hands stood at twenty minutes to three in the morning. She had been sitting there for simply hours. Rage and relief and love churned together inside her as she got off the sofa and erupted into one vast surge of feelings which manifested themselves in a cross, wifely voice. 'Where have you been?' she demanded in a loud whisper as she sped across the hall, quite forgetting that she had been weeping and that her face was puffy and stained with tears.

Radmer had given her a penetrating look as she spoke, not missing the tears or the sharp anxious voice on her white, tired face. If she had been nearer to him and the light had been brighter, she might have seen the sudden gleam in his eyes, very much at variance with his calm face.

He said now, as meekly as any husband would: 'I got held up, dear girl.'

Lavinia was so angry that she didn't wait for him to continue. 'You've been spending the evening with your old friends, I suppose,' she declared in a waspish whisper, 'not that I can blame you; you married me because I was sensible, not because I was good company…' She drew a deep breath and went on, anxious only to have her say, and not bothering about the consequences. 'Was she good fun, or shouldn't I ask that?' She paused, gave a snort of sheer temper and went on: 'I'm being vulgar, aren't I? and I'm quite enjoying it! Just to say what I…' She stopped, choked a little and went on in a quite different voice: 'I beg your pardon, Radmer, you look very tired, though I don't suppose that matters to you if you enjoyed yourself.' She wanted to giggle and cry at the same time, and it cost her quite an effort to say quietly: 'There's coffee in the kitchen, shall I fetch you some?'

He shook his head. 'No, thank you. Go to bed, Lavinia.' He spoke quietly and she knew that he was angry. She turned on her heel without another word and went upstairs to her room.

CHAPTER NINE

LAVINIA WAS LATE for breakfast, for after tossing and turning until the sky was light, she had fallen into a heavy sleep and wakened only when she had heard Sibby and Peta laughing and talking their way downstairs.

Radmer was reading his newspaper when she entered the dining-room, but he got up, wishing her good morning as he did so, pulled the bell-rope for more coffee, and sat himself down again. The girls greeted her with rather more animation, and then seeing her swollen eyelids and peaky face, demanded to know if she was feeling well. 'Not that I am surprised that you look as you do,' explained Sibby, 'for you must have been greatly upset when Papa came home and told you about the accident.'

'Accident? What accident?' Lavinia looked at them in turn, their faces expressing nothing but concern and astonishment. Radmer, invisible behind his paper, had apparently not been listening.

'But, Lavinia, you must have seen Papa when he came home…?'

'I dozed off in the drawing-room, I hadn't gone to bed. Radmer?'

The newspaper was lowered and his blue eyes, very

calm, met hers. His bland: 'Yes, my dear?' was all that a wife could have wished for, but she almost snapped at him: 'You didn't tell me what happened? Were you hurt?'

'You were tired, Lavinia.' He smiled kindly. 'You shouldn't have stayed up for me, my dear.'

She wished irritably that he would stop calling her his dear when she wasn't anything of the sort. 'Yes—well, now I'd like to know.'

Before he could reply, Sibendina and Peta chorused together: 'There was a pile-up on the Utrecht motorway—it was on the news this morning, we heard it while we were dressing—and Papa stopped to help.'

'What a pair of gossips you are,' Radmer interpolated mildly. 'Suppose you go and get ready to go to school?'

They went, grumbling a little. Lavinia heard them going upstairs to their rooms, and when she could no longer hear their voices, she asked crossly: 'And why didn't you tell me? You let me say all those things about—about…you could have stopped me…'

'And then you wouldn't have said them,' he pointed out reasonably, 'only thought them to yourself. At least you have been honest.'

'I wasn't—I'm not.' Her voice, despite her best efforts to remain calm, had become a good deal higher. 'Anyone would suppose that you had done it deliberately so that I should say all the…' She stopped, because he wasn't looking at her, but over her shoulder, towards the door, and when she turned her head to look, there were the two girls, standing silently, watching them. She wondered if they had been there long.

But Radmer was smiling at them and he spoke easily, just as though they had been enjoying a pleasant conversation. 'I'll give you a lift,' he told them, 'and drop you off at the end of the street; Peta can walk round to Juffrouw de Waal from there.'

He wished Lavinia a cheerful '*Tot ziens*' and a few minutes later she heard the three of them leave the house, the two girls chattering happily. Probably, she told herself uneasily, they hadn't heard anything—Radmer would have seen them the moment they reached the door.

He came home at teatime—a great pity, for Lavinia, with the whole day in which to indulge in self-pity, was spoiling for a quarrel, but as he brought the girls with him, there was nothing she could do but turn a cool cheek to his equally cool kiss, inquire as to his day, and then join in the schoolgirl high spirits of Peta and Sibendina, both of whom had a great deal to say for themselves. They looked at her curiously once or twice, for in her efforts to be bright and gay, she only succeeded in talking much too much and laughing a great deal too often.

Nobody mentioned the traffic pile-up of the previous evening. Lavinia, who had struggled with little success to read about it in the newspapers, had actually started out to enlist Juffrouw de Waal's help in the matter, but on the point of doing so, she remembered that this was one of the days when Peta would be there with the teacher until teatime. And what would the pair of them think if she were to burst in, demanding to know about something which any husband, in normal circumstances, would have told his wife the moment he opened his own front door?

Presently the girls went away to do their homework together in the small sitting-room on the first floor, and as Radmer got up in his turn and started for the door, she said humbly: 'I did try to read the papers, and I was going to get Juffrouw de Waal to help me, but Peta was there—and your parents were away from home. There is no one else I can ask about last night, so please will you…? I'm sorry about last night.'

He came back at once and sat down opposite her. 'One is apt to forget that your Dutch is fragmental,' he observed in a faintly amused voice. 'There was a multiple crash—a tanker jack-knifed and caught a car as it was passing on the fast lane. The cars behind couldn't stop in time—there were thirty or so cars damaged, I believe.'

She asked impatiently: 'But you? What about you?'

He gave her a quick, hooded glance. 'There was a fair amount of first aid to be done,' he observed mildly.

'Couldn't you have telephoned?'

He smiled faintly at some private joke. 'No. There was a great deal to do.' And before she could speak again, he was on his way to the door again. 'And now I really must get those notes written up.'

Lavinia dressed defiantly and rather grandly for dinner that evening. Mijnheer de Wit and his wife were coming, and another surgeon whom she had met briefly at their wedding, and she had taken the precaution of inviting Sibby's student friend as well as a young cousin of Radmer's, still in his first year at Leiden medical school.

She was downstairs long before anyone else, wandering restlessly from room to room in her pink-patterned organza dress, the pearls clasped round her throat, her hair carefully coiled. She was giving the dining table a quite unnecessary inspection when Radmer looked in.

'Very nice,' he commented, and she wondered if he was referring to the table, the beautiful room, or her own person. She played safe. 'White linen always looks perfect,' she assured him earnestly, 'and I thought the pink roses would be just right with the silver and glass.'

He left the door and strolled across the room to where she was standing. He was in a dinner jacket and looked somehow taller and broader than ever. A few inches from her he stopped, half smiling. 'I must admit,' he said suavely, 'that considering your low—your very low opinion of me as a husband, you have excelled yourself in the management of our home, and since I am now quite beyond the pale, I might, if I may mix my metaphors, as well be hanged for a sheep as a lamb.'

She felt herself held fast and pulled close by one great arm, while his other hand lifted her chin. He kissed her fiercely, and when she opened her mouth to speak, he kissed her again, but this time gently, still holding her tightly.

'You know,' he told her, 'I've been wanting to do that, and now that I have I feel much better.'

'Oh,' said Lavinia in a very small voice. 'Why?'

His smile mocked her. 'For all the wrong reasons, my dear.'

She hadn't known what he was going to say, but she had hoped for something else without realizing it, so that sudden tears pricked her eyelids and filled her throat. His arms had slackened a little. She tore herself away from him and rushed to the door, to collide with Peta and Sibby, on the point of coming in. Lavinia caught a glimpse of their surprised faces as she ran up the staircase.

She mustn't cry, she told herself in her bedroom. She dabbed her eyes, powdered her nose and drank some water, and then, with her chin well up, went downstairs again, where she joined the others in the sitting-room, making light conversation as though her life depended upon it, and not once looking at Radmer, or for that matter, speaking to him.

The evening should have been a failure, she had felt convinced that it would be, but it was nothing of the sort; dinner was superb, the talk lighthearted and never flagging, and the party, adjourning to the drawing-room afterwards, broke up only after its members had expressed themselves enchanted with their evening. Lavinia, standing on the top step outside the front door, waving good-byes, felt no enchantment, however. The evening for her had been endless; all she had wanted to do was to have gone somewhere quiet and had a good cry.

The girls went to bed almost at once, and pausing only to make sure that the dining-room had been set to rights, and plump up a few cushions in the drawing-room, Lavinia made haste to follow them, bidding Radmer a subdued good night as she went, not waiting to see if he had anything else to say to her but his own quiet good night.

She managed to avoid Radmer during the next few days, coming down to breakfast a little earlier than anyone else, so that she excused herself almost as soon as he got to the table, on the plea of having to see Mevrouw Pette about something or other, and if he came home for tea, there were the girls to act as an unconscious barrier between them, and as for the evenings, if he didn't go to his study, she engrossed herself in letter writing or grocery lists so that she wasn't called upon to take more than a desultory part in the conversation around her. She felt rather pleased with herself on the whole; she had remained pleasant and friendly, she considered, just as she always had been. Certainly there had been one or two small lapses; she preferred not to remember them. But she didn't know how pale she had become, causing her to look positively plain as well as sad, nor did she know how false her gaiety was and how stiff she was with Radmer.

It was a week after the dinner party when she came home from her Dutch lesson at lunch time to find a worried Mevrouw Pette, and because there was no one there to help them understand each other, it took her a few minutes to get the gist of what the housekeeper was saying.

'The girls,' said Mevrouw Pette, anxiously. 'They came home not half an hour ago, *mevrouw*, and they went to Sibendina's room and talked, and then they asked me for coffee, and when I asked if they couldn't wait until you came home at lunch time they said no, they had to go out. I gave them their coffee, *mevrouw*—I hope I did right?—and a little later, I came into the hall to fetch the tray and they were going out of the house, and they each had a case with them. They didn't see me, but I heard Sibendina talking about the train and the Zuidplein and the metro.' She broke off and cast a worried look at Lavinia. 'There is a shopping centre at the Zuidplein, *mevrouw*, but that is in Rotterdam—there is also a metro there.'

Lavinia had gone rather white. She hadn't followed Mevrouw Pette's speech easily and for the moment she was totally bewildered. 'Are you sure?' she asked. 'I mean, there are masses of shops in Amsterdam, why should they go there? I'll look in their rooms, perhaps they've left a note—they must have left something. Will you look downstairs?'

There were no notes, but some clothes had gone; night clothes, toilet things, undies. Lavinia raced downstairs again and telephoned the school. It had been one of the mornings when Peta went with Sibby to join her class. Neither of them would normally come home until lunch time. While she waited to be connected she remembered unhappily that Peta had asked her only the previous evening if she were happy, and when she had assured her that she was, her sister had said forcefully: 'Well, Sibby and I don't think you are—and Radmer isn't either.' She had run away to her room then, and Lavinia had thought it wiser to say nothing more about it. Now she wished that she had.

The authoritative voice which answered her query about the girls assured her that there had been no reason why they had left school early—indeed, no one, it seemed, had been aware of their absence. The voice, speaking very concise English, wanted to know if they were ill.

'No,' said Lavinia. 'I'll telephone you later, if I may.'

She went to her room then, found her handbag, stuffed some money into it, and without bothering to see if she were tidy enough to go out, went to find Mevrouw Pette. 'I'll go after them,' she explained to that good lady. 'I'll go to Rotterdam just in case they went there. Will you get a taxi for me? Perhaps they haven't gone there...'

'I heard them,' said Mevrouw Pette. 'Shall I tell the Professor?'

Lavinia shook her head. 'I'm not quite sure where he is, and he's got that very important post-mortem today. Besides, the girls may be back long before he comes home. If they are, don't let them go out again, Mevrouw Pette, and if I don't find them, I'll telephone you later.' She added hopefully: 'It's just a joke, I expect—how did they look? Did you see them laughing?'

Mevrouw Pette shook her head. 'They were very earnest.' She frowned. 'And you, *mevrouw*, you have had no lunch—I will fetch you some coffee.'

But Lavinia shook her head; she had wasted quite enough time already and she had no idea how frequently the trains ran to Rotterdam or how long they took over the forty-five-mile journey, and even when she got there, she still had to find Zuidplein.

She sat in the taxi, fretting, and when she reached the Central Station wasted a few precious minutes finding the ticket office and the right platform. She arrived on it to see the tail end of a Rotterdam-bound train disappearing from sight.

The trains ran frequently, though; she watched the outskirts of Amsterdam slide away and reviewed the situation, but somehow, because she was tired and frightened about the girls, her brain refused to function. She stared out of the window, seeing nothing of the view from it, her head quite empty.

At Rotterdam station she wandered around for a short time, trying out her Dutch without much success, until a kindly ticket collector pointed out the way to the metro and told her to get on it and stay there until it stopped at the end of its run—that would be Zuidplein, he explained carefully.

It was easy after that. She left the metro thankfully, but dismayed that it was more than two hours since she had left home, and for all she knew, she reminded herself, she had come on a wild goose chase.

She followed everyone else hurrying off the platform and disappearing through various exits, and after several false starts, went down a flight of stairs and pushed open the heavy doors at the bottom, to find herself in a vast hall, brightly lighted and noisy with the hum of a great many people all talking at once. It was lined with shops of every sort and size, and Lavinia started to walk towards the centre, appalled at the prospect of trying to find anyone in such a crowded place.

She turned her back on the big stores of Vroom and Dreesman, which took up the whole of one end of the enormous place, and began to revolve slowly, getting her bearings. She was two thirds of the way round when she saw Radmer standing a little way off, watching her.

She didn't know how her joy at seeing him there showed on her worried face. She ran towards him without a moment's hesitation, bumping into the shoppers milling around her as she went, and when she reached him, she clutched at his jacket rather in the manner of someone half drowned hanging on to a providential tree trunk.

'Radmer!' she babbled. 'How did you know? How did you get here so quickly? They're here somewhere; Mevrouw Pette heard them talking—I don't know why they had to come so far…I got on the first train I could—they couldn't have got here much before I did… well,' she paused and added worriedly: 'It must be hours by now. Radmer…' She stopped to gulp back all the terrifying thoughts she longed to voice.

He had her hands in his, nice and firm and secure, and although he looked grave, he smiled a little at her. 'How fortunate that I should have gone home early—I wanted to talk to you. Mevrouw Pette told me what had happened and I drove down; I had just got there when I saw you. And don't worry, Lavinia, it shouldn't be too difficult to find them if they're here.' His voice was comfortably matter-of-fact as he tucked an arm in hers and went on calmly: 'I think our best plan will be to walk right round this place, not too fast, just in the hope of meeting them. If we have no luck, we'll think of what is to be done.'

It took them almost an hour, for there were lanes of shops leading from the centre hall, and these led in turn to other lanes. There was even a market, packed with shoppers, and any number of snack bars and cafés. At any other time, with nothing on her mind, Lavinia would have found it all rather fun and enjoyed exploring the shops; now, looking in all directions at once, she hardly saw them.

Back where they had started from, Radmer said easily: 'Now, supposing we go round once more, but this time we'll look in every shop.' He smiled down at her. 'We can ask in all the most likely ones if anyone has seen them—you must tell me what they were wearing. Are you tired, Lavinia?'

She was, but she shook her head. She had hardly spoken as they had walked round, but now she said in a polite little voice: 'No, not in the least, thank you. Where shall we start?'

He took her arm again. 'What about Hema?' he asked. 'Isn't that the sort of shop they would enjoy looking round?' He started across the shopping centre, skirting the small, circular boutiques, chic confectioners and knick-knack shops which occupied its hub. They were almost across it when she felt his fingers tighten on her arm. 'There they are!' his voice was quiet, but she could hear the relief in it. 'Over there, in that teashop.'

It was another circular structure, glass and wood, with a tiny terrace built around it, its interior brilliantly lighted. Lavinia could see Sibby and Peta, their two heads close together over a table in the window, deep in conversation. Even at that distance she saw that although they were in earnest conversation, they didn't look dejected.

Radmer was walking her briskly towards the tea-shop. At its door he said calmly: 'Go and join them, my dear, I'll bring you a cup of tea.' His eyes met hers briefly and he smiled as she made her way through the crowded little place and sat down opposite Sibby. She was quite unprepared for her: 'Oh, good—we've been praying ever so hard that you'd come,' and Peta chimed in with: 'Did Radmer come after you, Lavinia?'

She nodded, not daring to speak, for if she had done so, she would have burst into tears and spoilt her image of stepmother and elder sister for ever. Fortunately Radmer joined them then, sitting down beside Sibby and facing her.

'I'm glad we found you,' he observed in a cheerful voice, and Sibendina said at once: 'So are we, Papa. We were just wondering what we should do next—we counted on you coming after us; at least, we guessed Lavinia would, and if you came after her…it was a gamble.'

'Why did you run away, my dears?' His voice was placid with no hint of anger.

Peta answered him. 'It seemed a good idea. We didn't do it on the spur of the moment, you know; we talked about it for days. We had a reason, didn't we, Sibby?' She paused, but he made no effort to prompt her, instead he put milk and sugar in Lavinia's cup and put it into her hands.

'Drink up, dear girl,' he urged her, and she drank obediently, swallowing her tears with the tea, still not daring to trust her voice.

'It isn't our business,' began Peta awkwardly, and

looked at Radmer to see if he was going to agree with her, but all he did was to smile faintly, so that she felt encouraged to go on. 'Sibby and I—we thought that if we did something really drastic, like almost drowning, or being knocked down by a car or running away, you would both have to help each other and it would make you fond of each other, because you love Sibby and Lavinia loves me, and that would make you understand each other and share the same feelings…' She looked at him anxiously. 'Perhaps that's not very clear?'

'On the contrary, I get your point very clearly.' He had stretched out a hand and taken Lavinia's small clenched fist in his, but he hadn't looked at her.

'We decided we'd run away,' said Sibby, taking up the tale, 'because we both swim too well to drown easily, and to walk in front of a car—just like that—' she waved an expressive hand, 'we found that we were unable to do that—besides, we might have been killed instead of just a little wounded and then our idea would have been wasted. So we ran away, and if you had not come after us we would have known that you did not love each other.' She beamed at them both. 'I explain badly, but you must agree that it was a good idea.'

Lavinia found her voice then, a little gruff but quite steady. 'But, my dears, supposing we hadn't found you in this crowd of people? Whatever would I do without you both?'

Sibby said softly: 'It would have been OK. You have Papa, you belong…'

Lavinia clenched her hands tightly so that the knuckles showed white. For a few moments she forgot where she was, she forgot, too, her well-ordered upbringing which had taught her so painstakingly never to display her feelings in public and always to speak in a well-modulated voice. She said loudly and rather fast: 'You're wrong, I don't belong. It's your papa who belongs—to his work and your mother—or her memory. He—he…' She stopped, appalled at her words, to look at their faces, Sibby and Peta expectant and inquiring, Radmer, daring to lounge in his chair like that and actually smiling… She glared at him, muttering, snatched up her handbag, pushed her stool violently away and made for the kiosk's second door. She had no idea where she was going and she really didn't care. She hurried blindly ahead, quite unaware that Radmer was right behind her.

The two girls watched their progress with interest until Sibby said: 'It has worked, Peta, I do believe it has! In a few minutes they will have what you call a showdown, although I cannot think that this is a very good place.' She looked around her. 'There is no romance here.' She shrugged her shoulders and grinned at Peta. 'They will be back, but not yet—we have time for one of those delicious ices—the one with the nuts and chocolate.'

They went arm-in-arm to the counter to give their order.

Lavinia walked very fast through the throng of shoppers, colliding with one or other of them continuously and apologizing carefully in English each time she did it. She wanted to lose herself as quickly as possible, although common sense was already asking the nagging question where she should go and what would she do when she got there. And what would happen to the girls? Of Radmer she refused to think. She shut her eyes for an instant on the memory of his smile and bumped into a stout matron with a shopping basket. She was close to Vroom and Dreesman now, so she plunged into the mass of people thronging its open shop front, and allowed herself to be pushed and shoved from one counter to the other, getting lightning glimpses of watches, gloves, tights and costume jewellery. She managed to stop here, and stood staring at the bead necklaces and bangles and diamanté brooches until the salesgirl looked at her inquiringly, so that she felt she should walk on, into a corner this time where there was a circular stand with a display of scarves on it. For the moment there was no one there, so she stood forlornly, staring at the bright silky things, her mind quite empty.

'Darling,' said the professor very quietly in her ear, and clamped a hand on to her shoulder. Lavinia cried 'Oh!' so loudly that a smartly dressed woman who had paused to finger the scarves gave her a sharp look and moved away.

'I don't think that this is the ideal spot for a man to tell his wife that he loves her…'

She choked on a sob and then said woodenly, addressing the merchandise before her: 'But you don't…'

She was swivelled round in gentle hands and held fast, so that all she could see was a portion of waistcoat and the glimpse of a white silk shirt. She muttered into it: 'You told me, you know you told me—that I could never come between you and Helga.'

A finger tilted her chin so that she was forced to look into his face, and the expression on it made her catch her breath. 'Oh, yes, I said that, and it was true, you know—for how could you come between me and someone who is no longer there—has not been there for very many years? Helga means nothing to me, my darling—nor did she for the greater part of our life together. One day I'll tell you about that, but not now. We have other, more important things to talk of.'

She stared up into his calm, assured face. 'But when we married—no, before that, when you asked me to marry you—you told me that you didn't love me. You said you wanted a friendly relationship, you said…'

He kissed her to a halt. 'Quite right. What a fool a man can be, for even then the idea of not marrying you was quite insupportable, even though I pretended to myself that I was going to marry you for a number of very sensible reasons. And my darling, you were so very careful to let me know as often as possible that you wanted it that way, too. But that night at the farm, when I saw you standing at the bottom of the stairs, waiting for me in the smoke, I had to admit to myself that I loved you too much to go on as we had intended—either I would have to tell you that or keep out of your way.'

'You made me drive the Bentley,' she reminded him, following her own train of thought, 'and I was terrified, and when you came to that house you were quite beastly.'

He pulled her closer so that a young woman with a pushchair could pass them. 'My darling, I wanted to wring your neck and take you in my arms and tell you how wonderful you were and how you were driving me slowly mad.'

She said idiotically: 'I bought those dresses and had my hair done…'

'And I wanted to tell you that you were the most beautiful girl in the world, but I was afraid to in case I frightened you away.' He bent to kiss her. 'I never thought to love like this,' he told her. 'Nothing means anything any more if you aren't with me.' He paused and smiled at a massive woman in Zeeuwse costume who was edging past them. 'The other night, when I came home late and I knew that you loved me…'

'I never said a word!'

'You said a great many words. You were very cross, my darling.'

'I was angry because I was frightened.'

'I know.' He kissed her again, not minding in the least that a small boy and two girls had stopped to watch them.

Lavinia caught their fascinated eyes and went pink. 'Don't think I don't like being kissed, Radmer darling, but isn't it rather public?'

He looked around him. 'You are probably right, my love. Let us go back to Sibby and Peta, who are probably congratulating each other and making themselves sick on ice-cream.'

'Well, they did what they set out to do; I mean, running away like that, it did make us come together.'

They began to walk, not hurrying in the least, back to the teashop.

'Why do you suppose I came home early?' asked Radmer.

'I don't know—tell me.'

'Because I couldn't go on any longer as we were. I was going to ask you if you could forgive me for being so blind, and start all over again.'

She stopped to smile at him. 'Oh, yes, please, Radmer,' and she looked away quickly from his eyes. 'Oh, look, there are the girls, watching.'

They both waved, and Radmer said: 'I once said that you were a girl who would never reach for the moon, dearest Lavinia, but you will have no need to do that, for I intend to give it to you—I'll throw in the sun and the stars for good measure.'

'How nice,' said Lavinia, 'but I'd just as soon have you, my darling.'

* * * * *

Here's a sneak peek at DARING TO TRUST THE BOSS
by Susan Meier

SOMEHOW THEY'D ENDED up standing face-to-face again. Under the luxurious blanket of stars, next to the twinkling blue water, the only sound the slight hum of the filter for the pool.

He reached out and cupped the side of her face.

"You are a brave, funny woman, Miss Prentiss."

Though she knew it was dangerous to get too personal with him, especially since his nearness already had her heart thrumming and her knees weak, she was only human. And even if it was a teeny tiny inconsequential thing, she didn't want to give up the one innocent pleasure she was allowed to get from him.

She caught his gaze. "Olivia."

"Excuse me?"

"I like it when you call me Olivia."

He took a step closer. "Really?"

She shrugged, trying to make light of her request. "Everybody calls me Vivi. Sometimes it makes me feel six again. Being called Olivia makes me feel like an adult."

"Or a woman."

The way he said *woman* sent heat rushing through her. Once again, he'd seen right through her ploy and might even realize she was attracted to him—

Oh, who was she kidding? He *knew* she was attracted to him.

HREXP0114

But even as yearning nudged her to be bold, reality intruded. The guy she finally, finally wanted to trust was rich, sophisticated, so far out of her league she was lucky to be working for him. She knew better than to get romantically involved with someone like him.

She stepped back. “I wouldn’t go that far.”

He caught her hand and tugged her to him. “I would.”

He kissed her so quickly that her knees nearly buckled and her brain reeled. She could have panicked. Could have told him to go slow because she hadn’t done this in a while, or even stop because this was wrong. But nobody, no kiss, had ever made her feel the warm, wonderful, scary sensations saturating her entire being right now. Not just her body, but her soul.

His lips moved over hers smoothly, expertly, shooting fire and ice down her spine. Her breath froze in her chest. Then he opened his mouth over hers and her lips automatically parted.

The fire and ice shooting down her spine exploded in her middle, reminding her of where this would go if she didn’t stop him. Now. She was so far out of Tucker’s league, it was foolish to even consider kissing him.

She jerked away, stepped back. His glistening green eyes had narrowed with confusion. He didn’t understand why she’d stopped him.

Longing warred with truth. If he could pretend their stations in life didn’t matter, she could pretend. Couldn’t she?

The Greek's Tiny Miracle
Rebecca Winters

Could happily ever after be in the cards, after all?

Navy SEAL captain Nikos Vassalos is a shell of the man he once was. Tortured by PTSD, he isolates himself on his luxurious yacht. But his bitter solitude is interrupted—by a heavily pregnant woman who tells him he's about to be a dad!

Putting her own deep-rooted fears of rejection aside, Stephanie Marsh is determined that her baby will know its father. Only, this cold, suspicious Nikos is not the man she once fell for. Will the tiny miracle growing inside her help them find the happy ending they *both* deserve—together?

Available next month from Harlequin Romance, wherever books and ebooks are sold.